MARRYING THE MISTRESS

MARRYING THE MISTRESS

JOANNA TROLLOPE

BLOOMSBURY

First published 2000

Copyright © 2000 by Joanna Trollope

The moral right of the author
has been asserted

Bloomsbury Publishing Plc, 38 Soho Square,
London W1V 5DF

A CIP catalogue record for this book is
available from the British Library

ISBN 0 7475 4727 0

10 9 8 7 6 5 4 3 2 1

Typeset by Hewer Text Ltd, Edinburgh
Printed by Clays Ltd, St Ives plc

CHAPTER ONE

'It would be advisable,' the court official said to the security guard, 'just to keep the laddie up here for half an hour.'

They both looked along the courtroom waiting area at the defendant. He was smoking rapidly. He was also head and shoulders taller than the little group of women clustered round him, like hens preening a cockerel, clucking and soothing and flattering.

The security guard rattled the bunch of keys chained to his belt.

'Trouble downstairs then?'

'Not exactly trouble,' the court official said, 'but there's a few of the girl's friends and family waiting. Just waiting. Like they do.'

The security guard sighed.

'Wish he hadn't got bail. Wish I could just take him back inside. At least I'd know where he was then.'

The court official glanced again at the defendant. Good-looking chap, in a flashy, come-and-get-it-girls way. But not reliable-looking; not reliable, at least, where his step-daughter had been concerned.

'He won't skip.'

'I'd still rather have him behind bars.'

A young woman went past, a briskly-walking, black-clad young woman with reddish-brown hair tied back behind her head with a black ribbon. She was carrying a square black attaché case and she had a black coat over her arm. She nodded to the court official as she passed.

'Night,' she said.

The security guard watched her go. He'd been watching her all day in court, Miss Merrion Palmer, counsel for the prosecution, and admiring the way the tail of her wig sat so precisely above the tail of her natural hair.

'Nice legs,' he said.

The court official blew out a little breath and heaved at the slipping shoulders of his black gown.

'Oh,' he said, 'nice all right.'

He glanced along the waiting area to right and left, then said, *sotto voce*, 'Know our judge?'

'Come on,' the security guard said, 'I'm here half the month, aren't I? Course I know the judge.'

The court official leaned closer.

'What's just gone past,' he said, his eyes fixed on the glazed door at the end of the waiting area that led to the judges' corridor, 'is not just an advocate, any old lady advocate. What's gone past is His Honour's totty.'

Back in his room the other side of the glazed door, Judge Guy Stockdale took off his wig and hung it on its wooden stand. Both wig and stand had belonged to his father, as had the pocket watch in his waistcoat pocket which he carried every day out of a superstitious apprehension that he might make a public fool of himself if he didn't, and the silver pencil with which he made his meticulous notes up there, alone, on the Bench.

He then took off his robe – purple, claret and black silk – and hung it on the plastic hanger from a nationwide dry-cleaning chain that seemed to have replaced the heavy, curved wooden one he had brought in especially for the purpose. Then he removed his black coat and put it over the back of a grey vinyl armchair and sat in the chair, leaning his head in his hands and putting the heels of his hands into his eye sockets.

'Would you like me to take off my wig?' he'd asked the girl-child witness over the courtroom's video link at ten-thirty that morning. 'Would it be easier for you?'

She'd stared back at him, a clever little foxy face framed in a fake-fur coat collar.

'I don't mind,' she'd said. She hadn't seemed daunted. She hadn't seemed daunted by anything, all that day, except, occasionally, by the miserable intensity of remembering what she had felt, what had happened to her. 'You suit yourself.'

Oddly, he had rather wanted to take his wig off. He didn't usually. Usually, he was so conscious of being an upholder of an office and a representative of justice, rather than Guy Stockdale aged sixty-two, height six foot one, shoe size ten, no need yet – impressively – for spectacles or false teeth, that he was happy to have his wig and gown remove him from the particular to the impersonal. But today had been different. Today had been different because he had come, without particularly intending to, to a point when he had to implement a choice; he couldn't go on just looking at it and thinking about it and laying it carefully to one side to act upon some other day when the light was clear and courage was high. This knowledge had made him look at the girl on the video link not just as an abused child – there were thirteen charges against her stepfather, six of indecent assault, five of unlawful sexual intercourse, two of rape – but as something of a fellow traveller in a world where things you wanted and needed began to conflict badly with the things you already, acceptably, had.

There was a light knock and the door opened. Penny Moss, a young clerk who had come to work at Stanborough Crown Court as a school-leaver, came in with a

3

file. Guy took his hands away from his face and blinked at her. She took no notice of having found the Resident Judge with his head in his hands. She took no notice, ever, of anything except the immediate matter she had in hand at any given moment. She put the file down on the desk.

'It's Mr Weaverbrook of the animal sanctuary, Judge.'

Guy looked at the file. Mr Weaverbrook ran a so-called animal sanctuary as inadequate cover for dealing in stolen farm machinery and horse-boxes. When required to come to court, he pleaded acute anxiety levels. His wife usually came instead and sat shaking in her seat, worn out with the effort of trying to divide her loyalty between Mr Weaverbrook and the need for law-abiding conduct. Guy felt pity and admiration for Mrs Weaverbrook.

'Do you want the case reserved to you, Judge?'

'Yes, Penny, I do.'

'And Mrs Mitchell and the order concerning her children?'

Guy shut his eyes again. Mrs Mitchell was a nymphomaniac with sado-masochistic tendencies whose three children, by three different fathers, were being removed, with difficulty, from her nominal care.

'That, too, Penny. I'd like an earlier date for that case.'

'Judge –'

'Penny,' Guy said, 'I'm not delaying. I have the future of an eight year old to consider.'

Penny opened her mouth. She was going to say, as she always said when asked to do something she didn't want to do, 'Martin won't like it.' Martin was the court manager.

Guy stood up.

'Good-night, Penny. And thank you.'

She picked up Mr Weaverbrook's file. He noticed that she wore, on her wedding finger, a band made of two little gold hands clasping one another. It looked vaguely Celtic.

'Night, Judge,' she said.

Outside, in the early spring dark, the narrow court car-park was bathed in a weird orange glow from the street lights beyond its wall. The buildings that ringed the court were as modern and uncompromising as the court itself, mixtures of blood-red brick and concrete, with a lot of glass set into brushed metal frames. They managed to look, without exception, profoundly inhuman, with elements even of menace, such as the great steel doors that slid shut across the court entrance at night. Guy was all for the impressive in architecture, and especially in architecture pertaining in any way to the rule of law, but not for threat, not for anything that suggested pitilessness, inclemency.

His car was one of only three left. The other two belonged to the two regular district judges who, like him, were inclined to work on until six most evenings, even though the courts rose at four-thirty.

'I work,' he said often, and meaning it, 'with lovely people.'

He opened one of the car's rear doors and put his work bag on the back seat. Then he climbed into the driving seat and turned the engine on. Then he turned it off again, and sat looking at the neat little red lights on the dashboard, bright, precise little lights who knew what their business was and how to do it.

I do not, Guy thought, want to go home. He took his hands off the steering wheel and put them on his knees. I do not want to go home and confront the fact that I have finally decided and must now implement that decision. What I hate, he told himself, closing his eyes, is the inevitable infliction of pain. Whatever I do, I'll cause that, to myself as well as to everyone else. In fact I am already, have been for years. It's just that they haven't all known.

Merrion had looked at him – when she did infrequently look at him – very directly that day. She had never appeared in court before him until today, and he had thought, and said, that she never should. But she had accepted this case, had indeed never considered doing otherwise, and when it became plain that they two would be in public together professionally and for the first time, she'd said he wasn't to make anything of it.

'It's no big deal,' she said. 'A three-day trial and I won't even be staying in Stanborough. You know my feelings about Stanborough.'

He did. He knew her feelings about most things. It was one of the elements of her character that charmed him most, her directness, her candour, her capacity (and courage) to see and describe things as they were, and not as they might have been or as she wished they were.

'You're married,' she'd said. 'You've been married for over thirty years. You've got two sons and you've got grandchildren. I'm young enough to be your daughter. I'm not married. I'm mad about you. *Mad*. We have a big, big problem and it's going to get bigger. No question.'

She'd been twenty-four when they met. That was almost seven years ago. He'd been taking an evening train up to London to have dinner with his son, Simon, one of those attempt-at-bonding dinners that Simon's mother, Laura, was so keen on.

'Do go. Oh do. How will you ever cross all these gulfs between you if you won't even try to *talk*?'

There was a girl in his train compartment reading a book which was convulsing her with laughter. She was helpless, crying with it, holding the book up to her face every so often so that she could shake privately behind it. He could see that it was a battered old paperback of Lawrence Durrell's *Esprit de Corps*. He could also see that she had wonderful hair and long legs encased in narrow blue jeans. She wasn't in the least pretty, in any conventional sense, but once he had started looking at her, he found he didn't much want to look anywhere else. So he stopped trying. He watched her steadily, smilingly, until she put the book upside down on her knees and said, still laughing, 'I can't *help* it.'

He bought her a drink at Paddington Station. She'd been to see her mother in South Wales and was on her way back to London and work. She was pupil in a set of barrister's chambers specialising in family law. She had a lot of theories – which he admired – about the need for more women at the Bar, especially in family law.

'People want it. The public does. They feel safer with us in this particular area.'

He didn't tell her he was a judge. He didn't tell her anything much except his name, and roughly where he lived and why he was in London. Then he took her telephone number, put her in a taxi, and went to meet Simon. He ordered a bottle of champagne.

'What's this for?' Simon demanded. 'What are we celebrating?'

Guy raised his glass.

'It's purely medicinal.'

Almost seven years ago. Seven years of what the newspapers would call his double life – home with Laura and the house and the garden and the dogs and the familiarity, and away, with Merrion. Sometimes away was in London, sometimes in hotels, sometimes abroad when he went to conferences, once – when they were desperate – it was a ten-minute meeting in the buffet on Reading Station.

'I'm your mistress,' she said.

'No,' he said, flinching a little, 'no, not that. My love –'

'Nope,' she said, 'sorry. Mistress it is. We sleep together, you pay for some things for me, I keep myself exclusively for you. That's what they do, mistresses.'

Guy lifted his right hand and turned the ignition key again. He'd heard that word again today in court.

'Did your stepfather,' the defending counsel asked the girl witness, 'ever refer to you as his mistress?'

'No,' she said. She licked her lips. 'He said, "We're lovers, we are." That's what he said. And then –' She paused.

'And then what, Carly?'

'He'd say, "You're better than your mum." '

'Better? In what way were you better?'

'At sex,' the girl said clearly.

Guy reversed his car out of its parking space, and drove slowly out into the one-way system of central Stanborough. There were few people about, but the roads were busy, streams of cars with their headlights on passing beneath the orange sodium lights.

He'd glanced very briefly at the jury when the girl said that. They'd started the day, as most fresh juries did, looking reasonably alert and capable and then, as the time wore on, and the alleged facts of the case were spelled out in the baldest language imaginable they had shrunk in their seats, their gazes fixing, their minds struggling to take in precisely what they were hearing.

'He liked it in the mornings before I went to school,' the girl said. 'When I had my uniform on. In the living room.'

'In the *living* room?'

'Yes. With the door open.'

'With the door *open*? While your mother and sister slept upstairs and the foot of the staircase was immediately opposite to the living-room door, he liked to have that door *open*?'

'Oh yes,' she said, 'he liked the idea that Mum might catch us. That's why he liked it in the bathroom and the kitchen.'

A picture was emerging, a picture of an apparently commonplace three-bedroomed terraced house on an estate on the edge of Stanborough in which a family lived, an equally apparently commonplace modern family of a woman and a man and the woman's two child daughters by a previous husband, where nothing was in fact what it seemed.

'He never touched Heather,' the girl said. She sounded almost proud. 'She's younger than me, but he never touched her.'

'Why,' the defending counsel demanded, 'did you let him touch you?'

She looked sulky, almost angry.

'He conned me.'

'Conned you?'

'He said, "You want periods, don't you? If you have sex, your periods will come." And they did. I wanted – I wanted boys to like me. He said they would, if I let him. But they don't.'

The defending counsel leaned forward. He had a full, fleshy face and his manner was mildly abrasive.

'But you say he conned you.'

'He did.'

'But if you knew you were being conned, why did you let him continue?'

There was a pause. The girl looked down. Perhaps she was twisting her hands but they were hidden below the bottom frame of the television screen.

'Carly,' the barrister said, 'did you hear my question?'

She nodded.

'I will repeat it. If you knew you were being conned, why did you let your stepfather continue?'

She whispered something.

'Carly, the court cannot hear you.'

She took a breath and said tiredly but with a simultaneous small pride as if she was quoting something authoritative, 'He was like a god to me.'

A god. A forty-five-year-old man playing god to a

besotted woman and her equally spellbound child. The terraced house, with its neat front garden and rather less neat back garden where the girls were allowed to keep pet rabbits in hutches, was, it seemed, less a family home than a cage for playing games in, improper, dangerous, degraded games, power games, cruel, harmful games. The jury had looked drained. Several of them looked as if, for all their worldly knowledge already gleaned from television and the press, they'd heard more than they'd bargained for, been faced with a raw reality they couldn't just switch off when they'd had enough. And this was only the first day.

But a god! That was what she had said, this fifteen-year-old child who had lived with her stepfather from the age of eight until a year ago, when she had finally told her mother what was happening. A god. You could, it seemed, go on about equality between the sexes until you were blue in the face, you could legislate, you could try to educate, but then along comes this child, this late-twentieth-century child, with her boldness and her unquestioned prospects, talking quite simply and unselfconsciously about a man being like a god to her.

Guy wondered, detachedly, if he had ever seemed like a god to Laura, even in that first glory of love when the love object is truly something quite extraordinary. They had met at university, he reading law, she reading French and Spanish. They had both worked diligently – she because she was conscientious, he because he was ambitious – and had emerged with similar degrees. He had gone immediately to Bar School and she had applied to join the Foreign Office, failed, and taken a translating job with a firm of small manufacturers who were developing their business in Europe. It was a dull job. Guy urged Laura not to take it.

'Try the BBC,' he said. 'Try the World Service. Try publishing. Try teaching.'

'I can't,' she said. 'If one of us doesn't make some money, we can't get married.'

'We *can*. We don't need money to get *married*. And if we do, I'll borrow it. I don't mind borrowing until I'm earning. But you can't do something your heart's not in.'

'I can,' she said. 'I don't mind.'

But she did. He remembered, now, how much she did. She didn't say anything because she had been brought up to endure in silence, but her attitude, her moods, even her walk indicated that she felt she was drudging, that she wasn't allowing her brain to race ahead of her, as his was doing.

'Are you resentful?' he said, every so often.

And she'd look at him, with that clear hazel gaze that appeared to display such transparency of mind and heart.

'No,' she said.

He used to take her shoulders, give her a little shake.

'Can I believe you?'

'Yes,' she said.

So he did. Or, at least, he lived as if he did. He read as assiduously for the Bar as he had read for his law degree, and every so often, he asked Laura to change her job. She refused. Once, he went to their bank manager and secured a loan for six months, to enable Laura to leave her job and take time to find a more congenial one. A week later, she too went to the bank manager and cancelled the loan.

'I hate it. I can't do it. You *know* Mum and Dad were always in debt and how much I dread it.'

'But we aren't like your parents. We don't have their problem with money. And I'm going to be earning. In two years' time, all being well, I'm going to be earning reasonably and I'll go on to earn well.'

'I can't believe anything,' Laura said, 'until it happens.'

That was not, he thought now, the sort of thing you said to a god. Laura's anxious practicality was not likely, ever, to find itself swept away by the presence of superhuman possibilities. Not as a young woman: certainly not now. Now! Well, how to think about that without a clutch of dread, of panic? Impossible. Laura was sixty-one. Not a particularly young or old sixty-one, but a nice-looking, well-kept, largely unassuming woman of sixty-one with the same clear hazel eyes but set, somehow, in a different context. Indeed, the way Laura's still young eyes looked out of her much older face was a metaphor for the way things had changed place, moved round in the last seven years: since meeting Merrion, the whole landscape in which Laura lived in relation to Guy seemed different. It was like walking very, very slowly away from something you knew very well, something you could visualise minutely when you were parted from it, and as you moved away, that something shrank against its background and lost solidity, lost significance.

Guy cleared the last of Stanborough's raw, newish suburbs and turned down a minor road towards open country. The street lights petered out into darkness and the tyres of the car began to click stickily through mud. Five miles now. Five miles, and then, across a curve in the road and before he got to the village, he would see the lights glowing along the façade of his house and the twisted bare black outlines of the apple trees in the little orchard in front of it.

They'd bought the house thirty years ago, when Simon was eight, and Alan was five. It had been three cottages, run-down and discouraging, sitting in a muddy welter of disused sheds and pig-sties. But there was the orchard, and a modest hill behind it, and a village with a church and a pub, and there were good rail connections to London from Stanborough, ten miles away. And, in any case, Laura wanted it. She had finally given up her job when she became pregnant with Simon, and presumably because Guy was now earning, she didn't mention getting another one after he was born. She became a conscientious mother just as she had been a conscientious student. From the tiny terraced house in Battersea which they could scarcely afford, Laura took him out to Battersea Park every day, and played with him. She cut out letters and taught him to read when he was four. She fed him bread she had baked herself and rationed his hours of television – he saw enough to enable him to fit in at school, but not enough to prevent him using his own imagination.

When Alan came along, three years later, he joined in this earnest and busy enterprise.

'Is this what you like?' Guy said to Laura, intending to be supportive whatever her reply. 'Is motherhood enough for you?'

'For now,' she said, not looking at him. She was pulling a soft tangle of coloured clothes out of the tumble-drier. 'There's nothing else we can do for now.'

'What do you mean?'

'I mean, with you working so hard.'

He crouched down on the little kitchen floor beside her. He was still in his dark suit from court, his black shoes, his sober tie.

'Laura, I have to work hard. I'm self-employed. Barristers *are*. You know that. The harder I work, the better I'll do.'

She sat back on her heels, holding the plastic laundry basket of clothes on one hip.

'Will it always be like this?'

'Like what?'

'You working all the hours there are, most weekends, lever-arch files even in bed –'

'Not if I become a judge.'

'A judge!'

'I can't even think about it for fifteen or twenty years. But if that's what you'd like –'

She got to her feet.

'It's not my choice.'

'Laura, it is. It's as much your choice as it's mine.'

She'd looked down at him, holding the laundry basket, biting slightly at her lower lip.

'I didn't quite visualise this.'

He stood, too.

'What?'

'Well, when I was working and you were still a student, I didn't think we'd – well, we'd get so *uneven*.'

'But we needn't be. You could go back to work. Alan's four, for heaven's sake.'

She rumpled some of the clothes in the basket with her free hand.

'Could we move to the country?' she said.

'Would that help?'

She gave him her clear, open look.

'Yes,' she said.

Even then, even temporarily relieved by a seeming solution, he hadn't been quite convinced. If she wanted to do it, if she was sure that a change of scene and society would, as it were, round her out once more, then they would do it. But he was haunted by feeling that it was possibly the worst thing they could do, that the hours he would have to travel would be added to the hours he would have to work, that a separateness would happen, that their priorities would cease to be united.

'Are you sure?' he said over and over.

'Yes,' she said, 'I want to be somewhere where I can make my own life. I'm – I'm confined here. I want the boys to have a garden.'

'You won't be lonely?'

She took a little breath, as if she was about to speak but she didn't say anything. He had an uneasy feeling that she'd been about to say, 'I'm lonely now,' and in her self-disciplined way had decided against it. Sometimes he wished she had less discipline, less reticence, that that elusiveness which had so captivated him when they first met – coming as he did from a family of loudly outspoken, opinionated people – was less opaque. Mystery was one thing, so was understatement and obliqueness and self-containment – but quiet stubbornness was quite another.

'Look,' he'd said, with some energy, 'I can't give up the Bar because it's all I'm trained to do and I'm good at it, but I'll do anything else you want, anything. Move house, move to the country, have another baby, anything.'

She put her arms around his neck.

'I'd like to go to the country. I'd like to be somewhere where I'm visible. To myself as well as everyone else.'

'But if you wanted to work again –?'

'I won't,' she said.

But she had. Two years into the restoration of Hill Cottage, and she had. Guy changed gear to negotiate the curve of the road before his drive, and saw the familiar pattern of lit house lights; sitting room and hallway, landing and main bedroom, front door and – glow only visible – back door. It was twenty years ago – twenty years! – that he had begun to see that Laura was feeling, however much she battled against it, that she had paid too high a personal price in marrying him.

And now. Now what was he about to do? He turned the car into the drive and felt the tyres crunch into the stones of the gravel.

'I feel like a slapper now,' the girl on the video link had said that day. 'I'm not a virgin any more. I feel dirty. I feel naive and stupid.'

Guy let the car coast quietly to a halt in the gravelled yard outside the back door. Inside the house, the dogs began barking, rapturously welcoming however long or short his absence. He turned off the engine. That's how I feel, he thought. Dirty. Naive and stupid and dirty. He opened the driver's door and climbed out, a little stiffly, on to the gravel.

CHAPTER TWO

Merrion Palmer's father had died when she was three. He was an engineer, working for a construction company in South Wales, and had come home one ordinary weekday evening complaining of a violent headache and a curiously stiff neck. Within six days he was dead, of meningitis. Merrion was never sure whether she could really remember him, or whether she had absorbed all the photographs of him, and all the things her mother told her about him until they had combined to make something so close to memory she could hardly tell the difference.

She looked like him, that was for sure. He'd been tall, square-shouldered and long-legged with thick dark hair and a face that relied upon personality rather than regularity for its charm. He was very straightforward, her mother said, you always knew where you were with him, and he had enough energy to fuel a rocket. And he was funny, she said, he'd had a keen sense of the ridiculous. By her bed, when she was a child, Merrion kept a photograph of herself and her father. She was about two, dressed in a dress she could remember more clearly than the occasion, a red sundress spotted in white, and she was sitting on his knee, very solemn, looking at the camera. Her father was looking at the camera solemnly too and he was wearing the tiny sunhat that matched Merrion's dress. It looked like a coin balanced on a grapefruit.

After he died, Merrion's mother married again, very quickly. She married her husband's best friend, who left his wife for the purpose, and took Merrion and her mother to live in France. He was a property dealer, in a small way, and he planned to broke deals between French farmers wanting to sell off cottages and barns, and English people wanting to buy them as second homes. Merrion remembered moving a lot, a succession of flats and small hotels and rooms in farmhouses where, more often than not, she slept in a bed in the same room as her mother and stepfather. She remembered the smell of French bathrooms and churches, black cherry jam and old men in caps playing *boules* on a sandy triangle under some pine trees in one of the little towns they ended up in. She also remembered the muttering. Her mother and stepfather muttered at each other all the time, in the car, in bed, across tables at meals while Merrion made patterns and small mountain ranges out of crumbled bread. It grew louder, the muttering, as time went on, and then Merrion's mother announced that it was time for Merrion to go to school, and took her back to South Wales.

She only saw her stepfather once, after that. He came to the little house her mother was renting in Cowbridge and gave her a monster bar of Toblerone chocolate. Her mother took the chocolate away and sent Merrion out into the garden. When, after what seemed an eternity, she came out to find Merrion, she looked dazed, as if she'd been smacked in the face. She picked Merrion up. Merrion was almost six and much disliked being picked up. She kicked vigorously, and wriggled.

'I should never have done it,' her mother said, and burst into tears.

It was quieter after that, but duller. Merrion's mother became a secretary at a solicitor's office in Cardiff, and Merrion's grandmother sold her house in Llanelli to come and live with them and help look after Merrion. For a few years, Merrion's mother talked non-stop about Merrion's father, as if by so doing, she could somehow obliterate the episode in France, but then everything settled and Merrion allowed the memory of her stepfather – an eager, angular man – to be assimilated into the myth-memory of her father. Men were there, it seemed, and then they weren't, and when they weren't, you got on without them.

It wasn't until she was about twelve that she began to notice the men in her schoolfriends' lives. There were fathers and stepfathers and brothers – the latter mostly discountable on grounds of age, lack of hygiene, and gormlessness. They lent, Merrion noticed, a different flavour to home atmospheres; there was more energy and noise, more adventurousness, more food, more danger. A house with men in it had a definite excitement to it. It was also more tiring. But Merrion liked it. She watched girls at school who had men at home, and wondered if anyone could tell, by just looking at them, that they had something she didn't have. She put the sundress photograph away and found others of her father and herself, less goofy ones, and one taken of her father alone on his graduation day from college, with tidy hair and polished shoes. She spent a long time looking intently at this picture, as if something might emerge from it and influence her, affect her, change the feminine round of the way she and her mother and her grandmother lived.

When her mother went out on infrequent dates, she grew hopeful.

'Did you like him? Are you going out with him again?'

'Yes, but nothing'll come of it. Don't worry. I've learned my lesson.'

'Will she get married again?' Merrion asked her grandmother.

'Unlikely,' her grandmother said. She was doing the crossword. She'd done the crossword in the same newspaper for forty years, at roughly the same time in the morning, and grew restive if something prevented her.

'Doesn't she want to?'

'No, I don't think she does. The last episode wasn't very encouraging.'

'You mean with Ray in France?'

'Yes.'

'She could do better than Ray,' Merrion said. 'Ray was creepy.'

'Creeps put you off, though,' her grandmother said.

Merrion twiddled the ladybird clips that held her hair off her face.

'I'm the only one in the class with a dead father.'

'But not in the school.'

'There are twelve hundred people in the school. I don't know them. I know my class.'

Her grandmother concentrated for a moment and wrote something down in her newspaper.

'You'll feel better,' she said unhelpfully, 'when you're married.'

By fourteen, Merrion's father-preoccupation had become a marriage-preoccupation. She always looked at people's left hands, particularly women's, and if the gold band was absent would scan their faces to see if something else was missing, too, if singleness showed visibly, as she had once wondered if fatherlessness did. She looked at couples together – middle-aged couples, not boys and girls – and tried to see if anything emanated from them, if they looked, somehow, more *right*, more natural than people by themselves. Just after her fifteenth birthday, Merrion's mother became engaged, to a local cabinet maker who had also lost his wife, and then disengaged herself almost immediately.

'But *why*?' Merrion said.

'I daren't risk it –'

'But you wouldn't have been risking anything! He's *OK*.'

'It wasn't him that was the risk,' Merrion's mother said. 'It was me.'

Merrion said, 'But you've got to just dare things sometimes –'

'Not,' her mother said, 'unless you really, really want to do it.'

When Merrion was sixteen, her grandmother died, very trimly in her sleep, of a heart attack. She had not been a big or troublesome personality in any way, but her death left a surprising gap and made Merrion and her mother feel suddenly a small and draughty unit. She had left them everything she possessed, including the modest proceeds from the sale of the house in Llanelli, ten years previously, and Merrion had the idea, quite suddenly, that they should move from Cowbridge into Cardiff and buy a flat.

'But you'd have to change schools!'

'I'd like to.'

'In the middle of your A levels –'

'I'll catch up.'

'And all your friends. And my friends –'

'We'll make new ones. You'll be nearer work. I can go wild.'

'Will you?'

'Probably not. But I'd like to have the opportunity. Mum, I can't just stay here always. I can't. I'm like a hamster on a wheel.'

They bought a flat – most reluctantly on Merrion's mother's part – in a seventies block with a view of a narrow public garden on one side and the back of an old industrial building on the other. It had two bedrooms, an L-shaped sitting room and a kitchen with a balcony big enough for a cat litter tray, so that Merrion could have a kitten. Merrion discovered clothes shops, bookshops, music shops, boys, clubs, libraries and ice skating. Her mother crept to and from her office and wished herself hourly back in Cowbridge where the postman knew her by name and Saturday-night drunks didn't career under her window howling obscene rugger songs in Welsh. They began to bicker. Merrion did better and better academically, grew her hair and had a butterfly tattooed on her ankle. Her mother could only see the wild hair and the butterfly. When Merrion's A level results were published, and she was discovered to have gained three A grades, she went out to celebrate with schoolfriends and didn't come home until six in the morning.

They had the first violent row of their lives. They stood in the narrow kitchen, while the half-grown cat watched interestedly from a forbidden perch beside the kettle, and screamed abuse at each other, about loyalty and disloyalty, about courage and cowardice, about love and possessiveness, about Merrion's father and Ray and France, about lack of proper priorities. Merrion was exhausted from a night of revelling: her mother equally so from a night of anxiety. After an hour or so, Merrion flung herself out of the kitchen and into her chaotic bedroom, stuffed a few clothes into the purple nylon rucksack she used as a school bag, and slammed out of the flat.

She had ninety-seven pounds in a Post Office savings account. She bought a train ticket to Bristol, and from Templemeads Railway Station, she called the brother of a schoolfriend who was at the university in Bristol, studying English and drama. He was unsurprised to hear her – unspecified young nomads seemed forever to be drifting through on some aimless journey that involved a lot of talking and rather less doing – and offered her the use of a sofa in the student flat he shared with four others. For five nights, she slept in a chaos of old newspapers, wadded pillows, unemptied ashtrays and smeared mugs and glasses, fighting off both the advances of two of the flat's inmates and the impulse to call home.

On the sixth day, she walked into a hairdresser on a

whim and had all her hair cut off, and then she returned to the flat, emptied the ashtrays, washed up the glasses and mugs, stacked the newspapers and left two bottles of Chilean chardonnay in the kitchen with a note reading, 'Thanks a million. All the best. M.' Then she went back to Templemeads Station and – not without a longing glance at the London rail timetable – bought a ticket to Cardiff. When her mother came in from work, Merrion was sitting at the table in the sitting room with the cat on her knee, filling in a university acceptance form.

'I'm going to study law,' she said. 'I've got the right grades and they've said they'll have me.'

She waited for her mother to start screaming again. It was a long wait, minutes at least, and then her mother went past her into the kitchen, saying as she went, 'You are just *exactly* like your father,' and then, seconds later, 'Pity about your hair.'

When Merrion went to university, her mother sold the Cardiff flat and went back to Cowbridge, buying a house in the street that ran parallel to the one Merrion had grown up in. From its garden, if you stood on a chair, you could see over the fences and hedges of the adjoining gardens to the one Merrion had tried to play in the day her stepfather bought her the Toblerone. It was like, Merrion thought, being in a picture you knew very well, which had been turned back to front. Her mother re-created the interior of the first house in Cowbridge as precisely as she could, and Merrion, standing in her bedroom doorway, saw that it was the room of someone who didn't exist any more and that it was therefore no longer hers.

During her three years at university, a courteous gulf grew between the two of them. Her mother was proud of her academic prowess and resolute in her refusal to know anything of her wayward social life. Love affairs, bursts of intimacy with other girls, expeditions, adventures and experiments of one kind or another all had, Merrion discovered, to be compressed and edited into phrases incapable of causing anxiety or upset. Sometimes, after a telephone call in which she had given an untruthful catalogue of essays delivered on time, regular meals eaten and early nights taken (alone), she would try and remember those various shadowy bedrooms in France, with their thin curtains and cold waxed floors and her mother – only in her early thirties then – in bed six feet away, muttering at Ray. Where had that woman gone, the woman prepared to defy the respectability of her upbringing and the outrage consequent upon taking another woman's husband, and skip to France with her four-year-old child? Or had that woman taken a whole lifetime's supply of daring and enterprise and left no energy behind her, nothing but a husk of apprehensiveness and profound conformity? Whatever it was, and however much sympathy – and exasperation – she might feel for it, Merrion knew that was not the way for her.

She obtained a good second-class degree at the end of her time at university, and moved to London, to enrol herself at Bar School. She shared a flat in Stockwell, financed by a loan from the bank – borrowing from her mother would have produced sleepless nights in Cowbridge – and at the age of twenty-three, was called to the Bar and pronounced to be Miss Palmer of counsel, in an august ceremony presided over by a judge who had no obvious trappings of the bench about him, Merrion thought, no wig or gown or spectacles, except for the authority and precision of his manner. Her mother came up from Cowbridge for the occasion and seemed only anxious that she would somehow disgrace Merrion by saying or doing the wrong thing or by wearing or not wearing a hat.

Only when Merrion was saying goodbye to her at the station did she suddenly relax and manage to say with real warmth. 'Oh, your father would have been so proud of you!'

And Merrion, standing looking at her mother, had found herself consumed with a fierce longing, a longing she had not felt for years and years, to have had him there.

She found herself a place as a pupil in a set of barrister's chambers specialising in family law. Her pupil master, a breezy, vain, quick-witted man in his early forties, was permanently friendly, occasionally flirtatious and intermittently instructive. He invited her home every so often, to supper with his doctor wife and two school-age children, and she was never quite sure what her role was, child or adult, upstairs or downstairs. She worked extremely hard, started a relationship with another pupil in an adjoining set of chambers – he too had a widowed mother who only liked to count the sunny hours – and once every four or six weeks, took the Friday-night train westwards to Wales, to see her mother.

It was on one of those journeys, a return journey to London, that she had met Guy. She had been rummaging, during the visit, in her mother's attic, and had come across a box of her father's possessions, a box of sports-team photographs, small silver-plated athletics cups and medals, a cap badge from his brief time in the Territorial Army, a Swiss Army knife and some books. Her father hadn't been a great reader, her mother said, he'd been too impatient a man for reading, but there were a few books that had plainly taken his fancy, stowed in this box, with his name – Ed Palmer – written on the flyleaf. Ed Palmer, 1964. Ed Palmer, 1966. There were a couple of Raymond Chandler novels, and a motorbike manual, and a book by Len Deighton. Then there was a small, slender book in a stiff mauve paper cover, illustrated with line drawings. It was called *Esprit de Corps*, by Lawrence Durrell. It had a different look to the other books, and Merrion took it downstairs.

'Oh that,' her mother said, glancing at it. 'It always made him laugh. I could never see why. You take it. See if it makes you laugh, like it did him.'

Merrion threw it in her bag and forgot it until she was on the train. When she remembered it, and retrieved it from under her sponge bag and the man-sized T-shirt she liked, to her mother's distress, to sleep in, she spent a long time looking at the flyleaf and the name written on it, and imagining her father's hand moving over the page, writing it. If he'd been alive, he'd have been fifty-four now. She looked round the carriage to see how many men of about fifty-four she could see. There were none. They were all young, either plugged into computer magazines or personal-stereo systems, or very old and asleep with the absorption that only babies and very old people seem to manage.

She opened the book. It was stories, she discovered, absurd stories of imaginary diplomatic missions and epi-sodes in the fifties. It was written in a stately and dignified manner and the accounts were ludicrous, farcical. The effect on Merrion was exactly as it had been on her father. She reached the description of two spinster sisters editing a newspaper in Cairo, and being compelled, owing to faulty typesetting machines, to write their copy on the Suez crisis of 1956 omitting all 'c's including in the often-used phrase 'Canal Zone', and collapsed laughing.

Despite collapsing, she was very aware, at Stanborough Station, of Guy entering her compartment. The rest of the passengers were fairly nondescript and dressed with great attention to comfort. Guy was not only tall and personable, with a thick head of greying tawny hair, but he held himself well and was dressed in a dark-blue, faintly chalk-striped suit that looked, in present company, as startling a contrast as a moonsuit. Merrion, who had put her booted feet on the seat opposite, quietly removed them to the floor.

Guy did not sit opposite her. He sat diagonally to her, across the aisle, and took out a newspaper. He read the newspaper with the sort of concentration Merrion had learned to associate with men who want to detach themselves from their surroundings. Round the cover of her book, held up close to her face, she examined his hair and his skin and his clothes and his hands and his shoes. It looked, as far as she could see, as if he had good ankles. It also looked as if he might be in his fifties. Mid-fifties maybe. The age, perhaps, that Ed Palmer might have been if he hadn't caught meningitis. Then, with a huge effort, Merrion went back to her book.

When she glanced up again, he was watching her. He was watching her with interest and amusement. He still held his newspaper up but he had turned his head sideways, quite openly, and was steadily, frankly, watching. She returned to her book. She couldn't read it. She began to feel giggles surging up inside her, caused partly by the mood the book had induced and partly by excitement. When she glanced his way again, their eyes met. He seemed perfectly comfortable, just looking at her in smiling silence, but she wasn't.

She felt obliged to say something. So she said, by way of explanation and gesturing at the book on her knee, 'I can't *help* it.'

'I know,' he said, 'I can see. That's what I like.'

He had what she would have called at school a posh voice. Hers was Welsh. It wasn't as Welsh as it had been when she was small, but she could hear that the rhythms were still Welsh, particularly if she got agitated, when her voice rose dramatically at the end of sentences.

'Have you read his other books?' Guy said.

'Lord no,' she said, 'I've never even heard of him. I just found this in my mum's attic.'

When they reached Paddington, he stood up before she did, and lifted her bag down from the luggage rack above her head. He said, still holding it, 'Would you have a drink with me?'

She stared up at him, much surprised.

'Will you? Just fifteen minutes?'

She struggled to her feet, not very gracefully.

'Do you do this often?'

'No,' he said, 'I've never done it in my life before. In fact, I shouldn't think I've had a drink alone with a woman who wasn't a colleague for over thirty years.'

He bought her a glass of red wine in the station hotel. He wouldn't let her eat the peanuts on the bar, pushing the glass dish of them out of her reach.

'They're filthy in these places. Endlessly recycled. And whose fingers have been in there before yours?'

She looked at his suit.

'Why weren't you in first class?'

'I'm not on business. Anyway, I prefer the company in standard class. Look at you.'

He drank whisky and water. She looked at the way his shirt collar sat, at the knot of his tie. She thought: I don't just want fifteen minutes.

He said, 'My name is Guy Stockdale.'

'Mine's Merrion,' she said. She sounded very Welsh to herself when she said it. 'Are you married?'

'Yes.'

'Silly question.'

'No. Necessary one. But you aren't.'

'No.'

He turned to look at her. He said with emphasis, 'I'm thankful for that.'

He insisted on getting her a taxi, and on giving the driver a ten-pound note.

'I don't want you to pay for me!'

'Give it back to me when we meet.'

He was standing stooped in the doorway of the taxi cab so that he could see her.

'Are we going to?'

'Yes. Very soon. If that's what you would like, too.'

She crossed the fingers of both hands and shoved them in her jacket pockets.

'OK,' she said.

It was almost two months before she went back to Wales. When she did she felt that she was, compared to the last visit, a completely different person, a person transformed, a person who had become – or was becoming – what she had always believed she could become, but had never known how. She wondered if her mother would notice. Her mother noticed hair and skin and weight change and signs of unconventionality, but would she notice anything subtler?

'You look well,' her mother said. 'I like your hair tied back.'

'I have to do that,' Merrion said, 'in court. Sometimes I put it in a pigtail, one of those French plait things. You know.'

'When I was a teenager,' her mother said, 'I had a ponytail. We all did. We wanted to look like the Americans. Or Brigitte Bardot. We had big gingham skirts with net petticoats underneath and waspie belts.' She plugged the kettle in. 'You didn't have it half so good in all those dreary jeans and T-shirts.'

Merrion sat down at the kitchen table. It was covered with a plastic cloth patterned with neat bunches of flowers confined inside arithmetical squares.

'Coffee?' her mother said.

'Please.'

'How's work going?'

'It's good,' Merrion said. 'I've got a chance of a tenancy in a set of chambers I really want to be in. They want a girl. They can't say so, of course, but they've given me very plainly to understand that they want a girl. For abduction work, people taking their children across international frontiers against the wishes of another parent, that sort of thing.'

Her mother put a mug of coffee down in front of her, and a bowl of white sugar.

'So sad. All those poor children.'

'Yes. But better to have someone like me trying to help sort out their lives than not.'

Merrion's mother sighed.

'Don't say things used to be easier, Mum,' Merrion said, 'because they weren't.'

'There were rules –'

'Largely unfair rules. Rules that mostly only applied to women.'

Merrion's mother sat down opposite her.

'Would you like a biscuit?'

'No thanks.'

'You look so well –'

'I am.'

Her mother took a spoonful of sugar and stirred it into her own mug.

'Can I guess?'

'I expect so.'

'A boyfriend?'

'A man,' Merrion said.

Her mother looked up.

'Why do you say that?'

'Mum, you're not going to like this –'

'He's married,' her mother said.

'Yes. And he's about your age, and he has sons a bit older than me, and three grandchildren, and he's a judge.'

Merrion's mother laid the spoon down on the plastic tablecloth with great precision.

'What are you *doing*, Merrion?'

'I'm in love,' she said.

'Where will it lead?' her mother said. She gestured wildly. 'What can possibly come of it?'

'I don't know,' Merrion said. 'I've only known him two months. I haven't seen him more than six times.'

'Oh,' her mother said. She brought her hands down flat and hard on the table. 'It's so *unsuitable*. Why are you throwing yourself away like this?'

'It's happened,' Merrion said. 'And I wouldn't stop it for the world.'

'But think of the pain you'll cause! His poor wife. His sons. What'll his sons say?'

Merrion took a swallow of her coffee.

'I don't know.'

'And grandchildren! What are you doing with a man with *grandchildren*?'

'You know, Mum. You know as well as I do.'

'When I've wished things for you,' her mother said, 'and I've wished for a lot of things for you, I'd have wished for *anything* but this.'

'I didn't wish it. It happened. I wasn't looking for it. It happened. And now it's happened, it really scares me to think it might not have happened. I might have caught the next train.'

'What train?'

'The train to London from here. The last time I came. I met him on the train.'

'A *judge*? On a train? On a Sunday night?'

'He was going to see his son. His son Simon.'

Merrion's mother got up. She went over to the sink and held on to the edge of it and stared out of the window at the bird feeder where three blue tits were hanging upside down and helping themselves to peanuts.

'I don't want you to make a mess of things. Like I did.'

'Dad dying wasn't a mess. That wasn't your fault.'

'But after. After Dad died. That was a mess. I never could seem to get the hang of things again. I want you to have a future. I don't want you to get to my age and not have a *future*.'

Merrion got up, too, and went to stand by her mother.

'What's a future, Mum?'

Her mother said, almost angrily, staring at the tits jostling each other for the best position, 'A good relationship. A good companionship. Children. Grandchildren. Knowing you're leaving something behind you, knowing you've done what we're here to do.' She looked at Merrion. There were tears in her eyes. 'All the things in fact that this man of yours has got, this judge. He's got it all, and now he wants more. He wants extra. But you're the one who's got to pay for that extra. You haven't got any of the things he's got. You're only just starting.'

'I want him, Mum,' Merrion said.

'He's your father's age –'

'Yes. I expect that has everything to do with it. I'm not hiding from anything. It's very complicated and it'll get worse. But I've never felt like this about anybody, not remotely, not ever, in my whole life. He's called –'

'Don't tell me.'

'Don't you want to know his name?'

'No. No, I don't. I don't want to know any more about him.'

Merrion said, on a rising note of anger, 'How will that help, Mum?'

Merrion's mother put her hands over her eyes.

'If I don't believe, maybe in time you'll see that you can't believe either.'

'And if you're wrong? If it turns out to be the real thing?'

'I'll cross that bridge when I come to it,' her mother said. 'Like I always have.'

CHAPTER THREE

'Turn that *down*!' Carrie Stockdale screamed up the stairs.

For several seconds nothing happened, and then a door opened on to the landing, releasing a yet more deafening blast of music, and a girl of about fourteen peered down.

'What?' she said sweetly.

'Turn that music *down*!'

Rachel shook her head. She smiled at her mother. She mouthed, 'Can't hear you.'

Carrie started up the stairs. Rachel straightened up and removed the smile.

'OK, OK –'

'I have told you and *told* you. No music until you have finished your homework and no music *ever* that is anti-social in either type or volume for the rest of us to live with.'

Rachel leaned back against the landing banisters. She said plaintively, 'Jack doesn't mind. And Emma *likes* it.'

Carrie pushed past her daughter into her bedroom. It was quite dark apart from the greenish glow from the CD player and a single small spotlight lamp on Rachel's desk. Her books were open, neatly arranged and looked entirely unattended to. Her bed was rumpled.

'Mum,' Rachel said, suddenly loud, 'don't you touch anything. You touch *one thing* –'

Carrie stooped behind the CD player and pulled the electric plug out of the socket in the wall.

'How *dare* you,' Rachel hissed.

Carrie stood up. The silence seemed almost as loud as the music had been.

'Very easily,' she said.

Rachel wailed, 'I can't work if it's quiet!'

'You'll have to learn.'

'You don't make Emma –'

'I would if she had her music up this loud.'

'I'll get headphones,' Rachel said. 'Jack has head-phones. Then I can have it as loud as I like.'

'Rachel,' Carrie said, going over to her desk and peering at the open books, 'try not to be so infantile. Is this your maths?'

'I hate it –'

'I'm sure you do. I used to hate it, too. You won't have to do it after the exams except if you fail. And you'll fail if you don't work hard enough and then you'll have to re-take it until you *do* pass.'

'Sadist,' Rachel said. She kicked a cushion lying on the floor. 'You're really enjoying this.'

'What?'

'Giving me a hard time.'

'Oh I'm loving it,' Carrie said. She looked at the open drawers out of which T-shirt arms and tights legs drooped dispiritedly, and fought back the urge to tuck them in and close the drawers. 'I'd no idea what fun being the mother of three adolescents was going to be. I'd no conception of how I was going to enjoy myself living with three perfectly intelligent people who choose to behave as if they were entirely subhuman. I'm having a *ball*.'

'OK, OK,' Rachel said again. She sidled past her mother and sat down in front of her maths books. 'Keep your hair on.'

Downstairs, the front door slammed and someone threw a rattling bunch of keys on to a hard surface.

'There's Dad,' Rachel said. She sounded relieved. 'You can go and take a pop at him now, can't you?'

Simon Stockdale, still in his crumpled mackintosh over a dark business suit, was standing at the kitchen table riffling irritably through his mail.

'Hi,' Carrie said.

She went across the room and kissed his cheek. He made a simultaneous kissing sound, but didn't turn towards her.

She said, 'I was upstairs, yelling at Rachel.'

'Music?'

'If you can call it that.'

'Oh God,' Simon said, throwing down a white envelope printed in scarlet. 'Telephone. Final demand.'

'I *paid* it.'

'You can't have –'

'I did. I paid it last week. If you remember, I took a half-day off work to pay all the bills and generally get household stuff up to date.'

'Then why this?'

'It's their computer,' Carrie said. 'It's *always* computers. It's programmed to send out a series of demands but not programmed to realise that a demand has been met.'

Simon took off his raincoat and dropped it over a chairback.

'When the kids were little,' he said, 'they'd come rushing downstairs to meet me when I came home. Remember?'

Carrie pulled a chair out from the table and sat down.

'That wouldn't be cool, now.'

He looked at her for the first time.

'Did we have them too early?'

She yawned.

'Yes.'

'You got pregnant though.'

'Hardly by myself. Are you suggesting we wouldn't be married if I hadn't been pregnant with Jack?'

'No,' Simon said. He rubbed his hands over his face. 'I was just thinking, here we are, not yet forty, and all we've done is work and have the kids.'

'That's life, babe.'

'Is it?'

'Simon,' Carrie said, 'what is the *matter*?'

'Would you like a drink?'

'Not really.'

'Sure? I've got something to tell you.'

She sighed. She spread her hands out on the kitchen table and noticed that her nails and cuticles definitely needed attention.

'OK then. You're leaving me.'

Simon went over to a cupboard on the far side of the room and took out two wineglasses. Carrie looked at him. His shirt had come untucked from his trousers and a tail of blue cotton hung below his suit jacket. He had a good figure, like his father's, and his mother's dark hair.

'Nope,' Simon said, 'but close.'

Carrie sat up.

'Close!'

Simon put the glasses down on the table and retrieved a half-empty bottle of wine from the refrigerator.

'Mum called me in the office,' he said. He poured the wine. His hand, Carrie noticed, was not at all steady. 'Dad's leaving her.'

'Oh my *God*,' Carrie said. She put her hands over her face. From behind them she said, 'Say that again. Slowly.'

Simon pushed one glass of wine across the table towards her and sat down in a chair opposite. He said flatly, 'My father is leaving my mother. He told her three days ago. He has been having an affair with someone for seven years and has decided he wants out.'

35

'Simon,' Carrie said from behind her hands, 'this isn't happening.'

'It is.'

'How did she sound –'

'Wiped out,' Simon said. 'Just – just kind of flattened. Hopeless.'

'Did she know? I mean, had she known about this woman?'

Simon took a swallow of wine and made a face.

'She'd suspected. She'd always thought he would, one day –'

'What,' Carrie said, taking her hands away from her face, 'leave her?'

'No. Have an affair. She said she sort of dreaded it. All the time.'

'This sounds more than an affair –'

'Yes,' Simon said. 'He wants to marry her.'

Carrie picked up her wineglass and put it down again.

'Wow.'

'I know.'

'Who is she?'

'Some girl, some barrister –'

'A *girl*!'

'She's thirty-one,' Simon said. He bent his head suddenly, his tie flopping on to the table. 'Oh, Carrie, oh God, help me, help –'

She got up and went round the table. She put an arm round his shoulders and held him awkwardly against her.

'I can't *stand* this,' Simon said, 'I want to *kill* him.'

Carrie stroked his hair with her free hand.

'We'll have to look after your mother.'

'It's not that,' Simon said. He drummed his clenched fists on the table. 'It's him. It's bloody *him*. It's always been him.'

'Hey,' someone said from the doorway. 'Hey, what's going on?'

Carrie looked up. Jack, who was sixteen, stood easily there dressed in a T-shirt, sweatpants and thick white sports socks with his heavy, bobbed, centrally parted hair hanging over his face.

She said, 'We've had a bit of a shock.'

Jack came into the room, lunged across the table and picked up Carrie's wineglass. He took a swallow.

'Someone died?'

'No,' Carrie said. 'Nothing as simple as that.'

Jack took another swallow. He looked at his slumped father, his mother stooped protectively over him.

'Is Dad ill?'

Simon raised his head.

'No,' he said crossly.

Jack flicked his hair back. He grinned.

'That's OK then.'

'No,' Simon said, 'it isn't OK. What has happened is extremely upsetting and will cause appalling complication as well as pain.'

Jack looked interested. He slid into the chair his mother had been occupying. He gestured at his father.

'Shoot,' he said.

'Jack,' Simon said, 'there's no point not telling you. You have to know. The girls have to know. Your Uncle Alan has to know. Shortly the whole bloody world will have to know. Your grandfather is proposing to leave your grandmother to whom he has been married for forty years and marry a woman with whom he has been having an affair for seven years.'

Jack was quite still. He stared at his father.

'Grando?' he said. 'Grando wants out and to start again?'

'Yes,' Simon said.

'This woman, how old's she?'

'Thirty-one,' Simon said with emphasis.

Jack grinned.

'Thirty-one! And Grando's over sixty, isn't he? Old, anyway.'

'Too old,' Simon said with venom, 'for *this*.'

Jack picked up Carrie's wineglass again and threw the remainder of the contents down his throat. Then he gave the tabletop a kind of delighted slap, a gesture of approval, of abandon.

'Hey!' he said, 'thirty-one! That's cool.'

Simon lay looking at the familiar night-time blocks of shadow in the bedroom: window, table piled with books and clutter, door, wardrobe, mantelpiece over defunct fireplace, chair, chest of drawers, old sofa piled with clothes, long looking glass glimmering like water. He supposed Carrie was asleep. She was turned away from him, anyhow, her bony shoulder protruding from the duvet, and she was very still. Even if she wasn't asleep, there really wasn't much more to say at the moment, no new version of the shock and amazement and – in his case anyway – anger that had preoccupied the evening and half the night already. There would be more to come of course, more details, more reactions, more plans, but right now Simon felt he was staring at a wall. It was a wall that hadn't been there the previous morning and which would now be there for ever: a wall he couldn't move and couldn't scale. Its presence made him feel weak with impotent fury.

He turned his head. Carrie's fair hair lay tousled on the pillow close to his face. He liked it loose, always had. She had to pin it up or tie it back for her job as manager of a local medical practice, but at home she wore it down or scooped up roughly with a clip if she was cooking or sitting at the computer. He remembered that long ago he used to brush it. He liked brushing it. He hadn't brushed it in years. Mind you, he reflected, Carrie wasn't a great one for brushing it herself.

He wanted her to be awake. He put a hand on her hip, as bony as her shoulder. She gave a small grunt, and didn't move. He had wanted her to be as angry with his father as he was but she said she couldn't be.

'It's this blood thing. If it was my dad I'd probably be incoherent with rage, but I feel more impersonal about yours. I mean, I like him and all that, but I don't feel betrayed by him.'

'I do,' Simon said.

'Yes,' she said. She was putting supper plates in the dishwasher. 'And you always have.'

He took his hand off her hip and moved himself gingerly to the edge of the bed, trying to stay flat so as not to let a draught of cold air in, down her back. Then he slid out on to the floor and padded out of the room.

A light still burned on the landing. Emma, at twelve, said she couldn't sleep without the light on. She had her bedroom door shut but insisted that, if the line of light showing under it from the landing was extinguished, she'd have nightmares about drowning. There were all kinds of things scattered about the landing; a lone trainer, two CD tapes, a belt, a copy of the *Big Issue*, a sweatshirt of Jack's with the Chicago Bulls' name and logo printed on it. Simon bent and picked up the sweatshirt and pulled it on over his pyjamas. The children thought his pyjamas were too sad for words, but he felt he could no longer sleep naked with three teenagers in the house, and nor could he wear a nightshirt because that was what his father wore. So he wore pyjamas and endured the gibes.

He went downstairs warily in his bare feet. Young parenthood had engrained in him the apprehension that all stairs were littered with lethal pieces of Lego, agony to bare adult feet stumbling down to dawn toddler break-fasts. There was, in fact, nothing on these stairs except a single black sock and an apple core. He picked the apple core up with distaste and carried it into the kitchen and dropped it in the rubbish bin.

He switched on the low lights that illuminated the counter tops and plugged in the kettle. Above the kettle hung a small mirror, framed in pine, which Carrie used for putting in her pierced earrings – 'I can never remember where the holes are' – and the girls, with much shrieking and shoving, for squeezing their spots. He peered into it now. He saw a tired man with bags under his eyes and sleep-rumpled hair and his pyjama collar caught up all anyhow under the neck of a red sweatshirt. Do I look thirty-eight, Simon thought, or forty-eight? Or seventy-eight? Anyway, what does thirty-eight look like? And does thirty-eight with three children and a mortgage inevitably look quite different from thirty-eight with no commitments and a Porsche? He put his tongue out at himself. It did not look pink and gleaming. He put it away again.

He made himself a mug of tea and carried it through to the little room they optimistically called the office. The house, like most of its identical Edwardian neighbours in this South London road, had an extension built out at the back, into the garden that was exactly the width of the house itself. Some people had made kitchens out of their extensions, or sitting rooms with doors to the garden. Others had just left them as the warren of sculleries and store rooms that they had originally been. Simon and Carrie had started out with the former intention and then, running out of money and enthusiasm, had allowed the extension to lapse into the latter category. The office, small and damp, with a window almost obscured by the winter jasmine growing against the wall outside, had the feel of an Edwardian back kitchen. It housed the computer, the household files – approximately kept by Carrie – Simon's law books and the overflowing heavy-duty grey plastic bags of outgrown clothing, intended for donation to charity shops, which never seemed to move and only to expand.

Simon sat down in front of the computer. There was an empty Coca-Cola can beside it, a sure sign that the last occupant of the chair had been Jack, no doubt playing war games or cruising the Internet in search of sport and pornography. Simon had spent hours in this room, hours in front of this computer, setting up the free legal-advice clinics which he seemed to feel driven to do, working out strategies for people who couldn't cope, couldn't understand how they had gone wrong, how to get redress, how to survive an apparent injustice. He knew his father felt he had always spent too much time and energy this way, too much of his own resources in trying to help people whose cases – lives often – seemed futile, incapable of advancement, of enlightenment.

'I need to,' Simon said, 'I have to. You live in an articulate world, where people have to explain themselves. But I don't. I can't, not while there are people who don't have a hope, ever, of explaining themselves to anybody.'

There had always been the assumption that Simon would follow Guy into the law. It wasn't Simon's assumption: it was Guy's. Laura, Simon knew, had begged Guy not to assume anything, but the law was what Guy knew, what Guy understood, what Guy was good at, and when Guy produced a clever son, the future of that son seemed to him a given, obvious. And it wasn't that Simon was averse to the idea of the law, it was only that he wanted his own approach, his own version, his own perception of it.

There weren't rows. You didn't have rows with Guy. You had heated, forceful discussions but there was no shouting or slamming of doors. That's what Simon grew to hate, the lack of release, the *appearance* of civilisation, the words, the torrents and torrents of clever, articulate, educated words which seemed to him, in the end, a mere substitute for real feeling, real sympathies.

'I don't want to be a barrister,' he'd said to his father when he was sixteen. 'I don't want to be all mentally ingenious and clever clever, leaving people tied up in knots. I don't want to confuse people, I want to help them, I want them to know that I'm on their *side*.'

Rather later, when Simon was twenty-eight and Guy became a judge, and explained to Simon, with what he believed to be both courage and honesty, that he thought Simon's teenage accusations had had some truth in them, Simon wouldn't listen.

'Now he's on the Bench,' he said to Carrie, 'he thinks all advocates are just there to prove their own points, score their own bull's-eyes, and only he, up there in all his red and black, can save the day. I can't *believe* it.'

Carrie was bent over Emma's high chair. Emma was two, then, and had discovered, a year before, the delicious tyranny of either eating at her own pace – interminable – or not eating at all. She had picked all the peas out of her dish, pushed the remainder of the food as far away from her as she could get it, and was eating a single pea in her fingers alternately with dropping every second pea on the floor.

'Give him a break,' Carrie said. 'He can't get anything right, ever, can he? He's wrong for being a barrister, now he's wrong for being a judge. Emma, I am going to leave you to starve.'

Emma closed her eyes.

'He only wanted the Bench,' Simon said, 'for the status.'

Carrie picked up a cube of carrot and inserted it into Emma's mouth. Emma held it there for a few seconds and then ejected it forcefully, like a cork out of a bottle.

'He didn't,' Carrie said. She turned her back on Emma. 'He did it because your mother wanted it.'

'He has never done anything my mother wanted in his *life* –'

'Simon,' Carrie said, 'don't be so bloody unfair. She's endured him working all the hours there are, all these years, and now she wants a *normal* husband, with regular working hours and a pension and health insurance.'

'Look at me!' Emma shouted imperiously. Carrie took no notice. Simon stood up.

'Why are you on his side?'

'I'm not. I'm not on anyone's side. Your father may not be an angel but he's not the exclusively selfish monster you insist on making him out to be.'

'You didn't grow up with him,' Simon said. 'You didn't see what he did to my mother –'

'*Look* at me!' Emma yelled. She picked her dish up and flung it to the floor, scattering carrot and potato and slices of sausage.

'Go away,' Carrie said to Simon, 'just go away. I've got enough children to deal with, as it is.'

She had always been good for him, Simon reflected now, always balancing, always refusing to let him get too worked up about things, too emotional. He appreciated that, he really did. But what she couldn't see, what she would never be able to see because she hadn't been there, was the pain his mother suffered, had always suffered, on account of her quiet, unhappy realisation that she had taken a wrong turning, made a choice she couldn't – or wouldn't – escape from. Simon remembered watching her when he was little, watching and watching her, waiting to see the cloud lift from her face, from her spirit, seeing the apprehension that joined the cloud when his father came home. Carrie had asked, more than once, and with some impatience, why Laura didn't go, just leave, if things were really that bad, and Simon said she couldn't, she was of the wrong generation, the wrong temperament, the wrong upbringing, she was held by a sense of obligation – call it old-fashioned if you like – to lie on a bed she had chosen and then made.

'Well, don't let her exploit *you*,' Carrie said. 'It's not *your* fault she's in a twitch about your father.'

Sitting in front of the computer now, cradling his mug of tea, Simon thought about that. He *did* feel responsible for his mother somehow, always had, always had known that he gave her a strength she didn't seem able to find anywhere else, even from his brother Alan. He remembered playing cricket with her in Battersea Park when he was tiny, watched by Alan from his pushchair. She would bowl to him for hours, patiently and encouragingly. He remembered some red jeans she'd had, a red hair band, too, and watching her red-jeaned legs running away from him across the worn grass to retrieve the cricket ball, time after time.

'Now watch it,' she'd call to him, preparing to bowl again. 'Watch it all the way on to your bat.'

He'd adored her. He could recall the feeling still of a room being incomplete if she wasn't in it. He used to hurtle out of school to find her waiting for him at the end of the day and every day was a reunion, a thankful, relieved reunion. Carrie had once asked him if he had been jealous when Alan came, resentful of this new and needy person in their lives, but he hadn't been, not for a moment. He'd always known he was safe, exclusive.

But it had been a relief to get away from his mother, later. He thought he'd probably been pretty unpleasant as a teenager, chilly and distanced, to punish her for having made her his whole universe when he was little. In any case, there was a certain perverse satisfaction in being tough with both parents when he was adolescent; it gave him a sense, however illusory, of his own separate stature. Sometimes he looked at Jack and wondered if that was precisely what Jack was now doing himself – removing himself crudely and visibly from the intimacy of the family circle to reassure himself of a separate and distinct identity. Simon picked up Jack's Coca-Cola can. Once, when Jack was three, he had taken him to the zoo. He had told him beforehand of the exciting and enormous beasts he

44

would see, the lions and tigers, the elephants and giraffes and camels. Jack had gazed at him with eyes like lamps, and had then said, in a voice acute with anxiety, 'Will Jack be safe?'

Simon got up. What tea remained in his mug was cold, and his feet were, too. He went back into the kitchen and put his mug down in the sink and ran water into it. It occurred to him suddenly and with guilty force that one of the strongest elements in his anger at this new situation was apprehension that his mother alone now, abandoned, might want him back, might somehow feel she could retrieve that little boy in Battersea Park and ask him to give her – silently; Laura always requested things silently – the unconditional love he had been so eager, so willing, so *anxious* to give her then.

He gazed down at the cloudy water in his tea mug. I couldn't do it, he thought, I simply couldn't. It had been such a relief to fall in love with Carrie, such a heady release to find he had made a choice with his own heart, a choice that had nothing to do with duty or pity and everything to do with enthusiasm and independence and change. It had taken Laura a long time to accept Carrie; she had always been kind and civil, but a spark was missing, the spark of true warmth and sympathy. Carrie had noticed, but hadn't minded. At least, not much, not angrily.

'Mothers-in-law are like that, aren't they?' she'd said. 'Especially the mothers of sons.'

Perhaps that was why Carrie and Alan got on so well, perhaps they shared the freedom – and exclusion – of not being Laura's chosen one, the apple of her eye. Alan! Simon banged the flat of his hand against his forehead. He'd forgotten Alan, quite forgotten in the turmoil of his own feelings, to call Alan as he had promised his mother that he would. He glanced up at the kitchen clock. It read twenty-past four. He couldn't ring Alan for three hours at least. He couldn't ring anybody, he couldn't do anything, except go back to bed and derive what comfort he could from Carrie's presence, her body there, warm and still and not always wholly sympathetic, but real.

He went slowly up the stairs, pausing on the landing to take off the Chicago Bulls sweatshirt and hang it over the banister. Then he opened the bedroom door and went quietly across the carpet and slid gratefully in under the duvet. Carrie stirred, but didn't turn over.

'Ow,' she said. 'You're *cold.*'

CHAPTER FOUR

The garden at Hill Cottage was Laura's creation. The house was, too, but Guy, who had an aptitude for seeing where walls should be taken out or put in, or furniture placed, had had a considerable part in the house. Also, significantly, he had paid the bills. He was earning well, as a barrister, those first twenty years at Hill Cottage, and he had paid – without demur, she always had to admit – the bills that gave the place a new roof, new heating, new bathrooms, a level gravelled drive, paved terraces, garages and garden store rooms made from old cow byres, old pigsties. But the garden was Laura's. She'd thought about it, planned it, worked on it. Out of a couple of acres of derelict farmyard and rundown paddock, she'd made a garden and an orchard.

As the boys grew up, the garden sidled quietly into that part of her psyche and personality that had nurtured her young children. She told herself that it was entirely typical, that Englishwomen of her age and type did succumb to gardening, at a certain stage, and allowed it to dominate their lives as little children had once done, with an accompanying and irritating preoccupation with weather forecasts. When Guy offered to take her to law conferences in Europe, or even the Far East, her first reaction – even above that of a small pleased excitement at the prospect of Paris or Tokyo – was whether the garden could manage without her for five or ten days. Suppose there was a late hard frost? Suppose the weather was unseasonably warm and dry and extra watering was required? Suppose she missed the apricots on the south wall being just at the perfect moment to pick? Once, Guy had insisted she come, to Stockholm, and there had been a freak hailstorm in their absence and all the early roses collapsed into sodden brown lumps of blighted petals. She'd been distraught.

'But even if you'd *been* here,' Guy said, in exasperation, 'what could you possibly have done to save anything?'

Nothing, she knew. She pictured the hailstorm, whipping round the cottage, battering the rose heads with icy pellets. Of course she couldn't have done anything. She'd have been out there, miserable and impotent in the storm, but at least she'd have been there. It seemed impossible to explain to Guy that she had a sense of having let the garden down, failed it by not being there when it needed her. She could visualise how he'd look at her. He'd look at her as he'd looked at her so often over the years, trying and trying to see if she meant what she was saying, and – even more difficult – to see if he could understand.

'I don't,' he said, 'quite *get* it, about the garden. I see it's a pleasure, a satisfaction. But I can't see the hold it has on you. Is it –' He paused.

'Is it what?'

'*Animate*, to you?'

She'd felt shy, suddenly. She felt she couldn't admit to someone who spent his days up to his armpits in demanding, messy, human things, that the garden was alive to her in a way; that it did have, if not a personality, then at least a spirit. And that that spirit was fragile, but vital, and in her care, because she had made it, she had somehow summoned it out of the muddy broken-brick-littered dereliction that had been there when they came. She was afraid Guy would think – as she had always been

48

afraid of him thinking – that she had abandoned reality and all its demands for something more insubstantial, more fantastical, which didn't, in the end, have a comparable validity. Of course, it was ridiculous, *pitiful*, to say, 'I can't come to Tokyo because nobody waters the pots on the terrace quite like I do,' but the awful thing was that that's what she believed, what she felt, with great, instinctive strength. It was a matter of belonging, of feeling at home, at peace and necessary. Heavens, it was so important to feel necessary! She thought Simon understood that a little, always had. But Guy didn't, Guy had never been in doubt about his own indispensability. And Alan – well, Alan didn't think like that. Alan never arranged things, in his mind or his life, in relative order. He just took people, events, job opportunities as they came, on their own merits. If his mother wanted to spend her life in the garden and got ecstatic when her camellia flowered, well, fine, that's what turned her on.

The trouble – the acute trouble just now – was that it wasn't turning her on. It was where she had fled when Guy had told her he wanted a divorce so that he could marry someone called Merrion Palmer, and instead of receiving and consoling her, the garden had lain around her quite inert, almost indifferent. She'd begun to dig – a vegetable bed, ready for her precise rows of carrot and parsnip and beetroot – in the hope that strenuous physical activity would not only distract her but restore to her a feeling that the world was still, after all, recognisable, and all she'd felt after half an hour was that it was utterly pointless, that the cold spring earth certainly didn't care, and that there was something deliberately masochistic about planting food for someone who had neither desire nor intention of being there to eat it. She flung the spade away from her and it clattered across a brick path and skidded into a leaning pile of glass panes she used for cloches over early lettuce, sending out a shower of green-white splinters. She sank to her knees, where she was, in the vegetable bed, and let herself howl like a toddler having a tantrum in a supermarket, rubbing at her wet face every so often with her earthy hands. When it began to rain, she didn't move: it was almost a comfort to have something, however slight, happening.

The dogs, she could see, were watching her from the dining room, their paws up on the low windowsill. They were eager for walks but considered gardening an incomprehensibly dull activity, best regarded as a spectator sport unless the sun was out. They were also anxious about her at the moment, anxious about Guy, about the atmosphere, about the suitcases on the landing ready for Guy to collect and take to his rented rooms in Stanborough, about the disruption of routine. Their anxiety took the form of following her about, even to the lavatory, lying down outside and breathing heavily at her under the door. When the telephone rang, they raised their heads and watched her. When she wept, they came and camped on her feet, leaning against her legs. When she gardened, habit kept them inside, but worry drove them from their baskets to watch her through the window, straining to be reassured that everything was all right, in order again, normal.

'Get down!' she shouted at them. 'You're worse than *children*.'

They gazed at her, not moving. She could picture their tails, poised to wag but not daring to while she presented so distraught and disconcerting a picture. They would be relieved when the boys came, when Simon and Alan arrived, and they could release themselves into habit, dashing about the kitchen bringing welcome presents of tea towels and stray shoes. Poor dogs. They should have been a comfort just now, she should be grateful for their loyal, loving agitation, but instead all she could feel was that she hadn't a scrap of comfort to give them because she had less than a scrap to give herself.

She got up out of the muddy spring earth and banged at the clotted patches on the knees of her trousers. She would have to change; change her clothes and brush her hair and find her pearl earrings and put the kettle on and do her best, however poor that was, to present herself to her sons as someone who had not, overnight, turned from being their support into being their burden. She went across to the brick path and with the side of her boot, pushed the glass splinters into a neat pile. Then she turned and went slowly into the house.

'Do we need to go at this speed?' Alan said.

Simon glanced in the driving mirror, moved the gear shift into fifth and pulled out into the outside lane to overtake an immense curtain-sided truck, with French number plates.

'Yes.'

'Mum isn't expecting us till four.'

'I need to get there,' Simon said. He glanced in his driving mirror again. 'And then I need to get away again.'

Alan looked out of the car window at the cold, empty-seeming landscape, not yet free of the deadness of winter. It made him feel slightly hopeless, looking at it, or at least compounded the hopelessness he'd felt last night when the prospective owner of the bar in Fulham that Alan had been going to redesign, redecorate, had rung to say that the whole project was off: he couldn't get the financing. He sighed now, remembering, staring at the dead fields.

'I might stay the night,' he said. 'I'll see how she is.'

Simon said, 'We know how she is.'

'Yes, but I expect she varies. I mean there's probably even a bit of *relief*, but being Mum, she'll be managing to feel guilty about that, not thankful.'

'*Relief*?'

Alan yawned.

'It hasn't exactly been wonderful, has it? This marriage –'

'But she's stuck to it,' Simon said. 'She's made it her life, she's shaped everything round it –'

Alan shrugged.

'Her choice, boy.'

Simon beat lightly on the steering wheel with his free hand.

'No, it isn't. That's the point. She hasn't had a choice.'

'We all have choices. That's what Dad's doing now, choosing.'

'It drives me mad,' Simon said, 'to hear you saying things like that, as if you didn't disapprove of Dad, as if it was perfectly OK just to duck out on four decades of a relationship because you're bored –'

'He's not bored.'

'Isn't he? Well, if he isn't bored, what the hell is he?'

Alan opened the glove pocket in front of him and began rummaging in the muddle inside.

'He's worn out with never knowing what she wants, what makes her happy, what he's doing wrong. Have you got any mints?'

'There's nothing edible left in this car, ever. The kids are like a plague of locusts except locusts don't leave litter. Dad has done exactly what he wants always. He doesn't know what Mum wants because he's never *asked* her.'

'D'you ask Carrie?'

'She tells me,' Simon said. 'Mum isn't like that. Mum's never insisted upon anything for herself, ever.'

'Then she's colluded with being made a victim.'

'Alan,' Simon said furiously. 'What's got *into* you? Where's your sense of justice? Where's your loyalty to Mum?'

'I just see both sides,' Alan said. 'I'm sorry for Mum but I'm sorry for Dad, too. I can see what's happened. Well, a bit anyway.'

'And if he marries this girl and she has a baby and he

alters his will in her favour, cutting us out, you'll feel just as calm and objective and bloody superior?'

'I expect so,' Alan said.

Simon changed gear at the wrong speed and the gears grated loudly.

'Hell,' he said. 'You and your moral high ground. You and your bloody smug refusal to be judgemental, as you put it. You and your fucking Buddhist elevation above all human dilemma. It must,' Simon said savagely, 'be such a comfort to know better than the rest of us. It must be such a *solace* to be gay.'

There was a small silence. Alan looked out of the window. He said, his head averted from his brother, 'Actually, it's the precise opposite,' then he took a breath and added, shrugging his chin down into the upturned collar of his leather jacket, 'but at least it stops you expecting the impossible from anyone else.'

Simon swallowed.

'Sorry.'

'That's OK.'

'I shouldn't have –'

'That's *OK*. I *said*.'

'I'm just a bit apprehensive –'

'I know. That she'll want you to take Dad's place. Well, you don't have to collude with that either.'

A huge blue-and-white junction sign loomed at the edge of the motorway. Simon flicked his eyes briefly up at it.

'There we go. Stanborough.'

'I wouldn't mind,' Alan said, 'if I never saw Stanborough again.'

Laura was waiting for them at the back door. She looked as she always did, composed inside conventional, controllable clothes – a shirt collar sitting neatly at the neck of a good sweater above well-tailored trousers and brushed suede loafers. She had brushed her hair, too, and found her earrings. She smelled of L'Air du Temps, which she had been wearing since she was eighteen. She said, kissing them both in turn as if the meeting was profoundly unexceptional, 'There's no etiquette for this, is there? I really don't know what to say to either of you.'

They followed her inside. The dogs raced madly about the kitchen collecting tributes, towels and cushions and a wooden bootjack Alan had made in a long-ago school woodwork class. He bent to retrieve it.

'I'd forgotten that. Woodwork Job Two. Job One was a key-rack shaped like a key. With hooks in.'

Laura said, 'I've still got it. It's by the garden door. I don't think you ever progressed to Job Three.'

Alan crouched so that the dogs could wag and lick ecstatically all over his shoulders and face.

Laura said apologetically, 'I'm afraid they're hysterical with worry –'

'I don't mind.'

'And you, Mum?' Simon said. 'Are you hysterical with worry?'

'On and off,' she said. She began collecting a teapot and mugs and a bottle of milk.

'Could I have coffee?' Alan said.

His mother held up a jar of instant-coffee granules. She said, 'I so don't want to be a burden, a problem –'

Simon put his hands in his pockets and rattled his keys and his change. Carrie was always asking him not to. She said it encouraged Jack, that it was the male equivalent of the girls' endless fiddling with and tossing of their hair, and equally exasperating. Simon had a sudden longing for Carrie, to have her there in this well-ordered kitchen where nobody was behaving like themselves except the dogs. Carrie would help them to be practical, not emotional. Carrie would remind Simon, by her very presence, that his first obligation was to her and the children, and not to his mother. She would take away his guilt. Wouldn't she?

'Just because you can see someone's problems,' she often said to Simon, 'it doesn't follow that it's up to you to fix it.'

Simon said, 'Mum, you need help, though. Your future needs sorting.'

Laura turned her back on them to unplug the kettle. Her back was eloquent of someone who doesn't believe they have a future. She said, 'I'll manage.'

Alan rose to his feet. 'Shhh,' he mouthed at Simon.

Simon said, 'We have to do nuts and bolts, Mum. Money, housing, that sort of stuff.'

'Oh, I know.' She turned and poured water into the teapot and into Alan's coffee mug. 'But do we have to do that today?'

'Why not?' Alan said gently.

She bent over the teapot. She was biting her lip. Simon was afraid she was about to cry.

'Isn't it a bit soon?'

'Soon –'

'Should we not talk about what's happened? How I feel? How – how I'm to cope?'

Simon moved across the kitchen and put an arm around her shoulders.

'Oh Mum –'

She turned and put her face into the shoulder of his jacket. He put his arms around her. Her own shoulders were shaking.

'Suppose I can't cope –'

'Hey, you can. You're shocked now. It *is* a shock, an awful one.'

Alan came round the table. He stood close to his mother and brother. He said, 'In a way, you've been coping for years. If you think about it.'

Laura felt in her trouser pocket for a handkerchief. It was white cotton, nicely laundered. The anachronism of laundered handkerchiefs was an abiding fascination for Simon's children.

'What's she think tissues are for?' Rachel had demanded.

'Ignoring,' Simon said.

Laura wiped her eyes and blew her nose.

'Sorry,' she said.

'Mum, you are *not* to say sorry. About anything.'

She blew her nose again. She said, not looking at either of them, 'Have you seen your father?'

Simon snorted.

'Not bloody likely.'

Alan said, 'I'm seeing him on Sunday.'

'With – with –'

'I don't know. I don't think so. But she exists, Mum. She's part of the pattern now.'

'Of the *problem*,' Simon said.

Laura moved out of Simon's arms and began to put the mugs and teapot on the tray.

Simon said, 'Can't we drink it in here?'

'I lit the fire,' she said. 'In the sitting room.'

'Better here,' Alan said.

'All right,' she said. She sounded offended.

Alan put a hand on her back between her shoulder blades.

'Sit down,' he said.

She sat, head bent. Simon and Alan sat, too, Alan beside her, Simon opposite.

'I always thought,' Laura said to the tabletop, 'that I'd turn out not to be good enough, not exciting enough. I always thought he'd have an affair with one of his pupils. There was one particularly, called Fenella, with red hair. I was always very suspicious. But he said he never did, not with Fenella, not with any of them. He said there'd never been anyone – until, well, this one.'

Alan picked up the teapot and poured tea into mugs for his mother and brother. He put one mug in front of Laura.

'You don't need to analyse, Mum. There's no point.

56

You don't need to tell yourself you're not this or not enough that –'

'I *do*,' Laura said, raising her face. 'Why else would he go?'

Simon said tensely, 'Because he is who he is. And always has been.'

'Si –' Alan said warningly.

'I'm not having Mum sitting here,' Simon said, too loudly, 'thinking it's her fault.'

Laura turned to look at him. She gave him a faint smile.

'What I can't get used to,' she said, 'is finding that something I've been afraid of happening for forty years actually is happening.'

Alan poured milk into his coffee. He felt in his pocket for his cigarettes, remembered he was in his mother's house, and took his hand out of his pocket again.

'All I wanted,' Laura said, 'was to be what *he* wanted.'

Simon shut his eyes and wrapped his hands hard round his tea mug.

'Oh Mum –'

'He wanted me to be like him, to be sure of who I was and where I was going and what my aims were. He wanted me to *know*. And I couldn't. I never have.'

Simon and Alan said nothing.

'You don't want to hear this,' Laura said. 'Do you?'

Alan made a face.

'It's not that –'

'Isn't it?'

'Mum,' Alan said. He put his forearms on the table and loosely clasped his hands together. 'Mum, it's not that we aren't sympathetic. It's not that we don't feel this is very hard for you. But there's no *point*, Mum, in talking like this.'

Laura said tensely, 'What do you mean?'

Alan avoided Simon's eye. He said, 'What I mean is, Mum, that we have to deal with what *is*, not what might have been.'

'And?'

'And nothing. What *is*, is that you are going to be on your own because Dad wants to marry someone else. *That's* what we have to deal with.'

Laura half rose, shoving her chair back with a clatter on the tiled floor. She said, her voice rising, 'Are you taking your father's side? Are you *condoning* what your father has done?'

'No,' Alan said. He didn't look up and his voice was deliberately steady. 'No. That's not what I said. I said –'

'If you can't at least understand how I feel,' Laura shrieked, 'then I really, really don't want to hear *what* you said!'

Simon stood up. Laura glared at him.

'Are you going to tell me just to get on with the wreck of my life, too?'

'Mum, he didn't say that, he didn't –'

'He did!' Laura screamed. Her face was flushed. 'He did!' And then she turned and fled from the room, slamming the door behind her. The dogs, back in their baskets for a temporary cessation of tension, looked as if they had been kicked.

'Oh my *God*,' Simon said. 'What the hell did you have to do *that* for?'

'She has to hear it –'

'Maybe, but not *now*. Not while she's so stunned she can't think straight. Not while all she can think of is that she's been rejected because she didn't make the grade.'

'The sooner she stops blaming Dad for every bloody thing, the better for her, for her recovery –'

Simon started round the table.

'I'd better go and find her.'

'Leave her,' Alan said.

'Al –'

'Simon,' Alan said, 'leave her. Just *leave* her. For your own sake as well as hers.'

Simon paused. He put his hands in his pockets and shook up his change. He looked at Alan. 'I can't,' he said unhappily, and went out of the room.

Jack Stockdale lay on the floor of his top-floor London bedroom, with his ear pressed to the carpet. He had turned his music off, and switched off all the lamps, too, in order to be able to concentrate better. Immediately below Jack's room was his parents' room. On his parents' bed, right now, lay his sister Rachel. She had made herself very comfortable. Jack could picture her lying among the piled-up pillows – pulled out of the bed for the purpose – with the telephone receiver tucked in against her cheek, leaving her hands free to pick off the purple glitter nail varnish she had applied the night before and was probably already bored with. On the other end of the telephone was Rachel's best friend, Trudy, and they were discussing someone else, called Moll. Moll was the reason Jack was lying on the floor with his ear pressed to the carpet.

Moll was in the year below Jack at school, and therefore a year above Rachel and Trudy. Moll was very athletic, with a strong, supple dancer's body and extremely straight brown hair which she wore either wound up on top of her head in a complicated knot or falling plumb down her back like a curtain. It was her hair that Jack had first noticed, walking by chance behind her down the main school corridor between physics and social studies, and seeing this long, calm, smooth sheet of brown hair. She didn't fiddle with it. She must have been the only girl in the whole school who didn't touch her hair except to brush it or pile it out of the way. She seemed to take it for granted, like she took her body for granted, the body that was so effortlessly proficient at gym and dancing and track sports. She'd only been in the school a term and already there was a buzz about her capabilities. In Jack's year, among Jack's mates, there was also a buzz about her sex appeal.

Usually, Jack joined in. He liked sex talk. He liked the jovial buddy stuff of boys talking dirty together; it gave him a feeling that he didn't have to go on this rather alarming journey alone, reassured him that there'd be an element of team work, that when – if – he ventured anything, there'd be somewhere to come back to. But he found he didn't want to talk about Moll in the comfortably abusive language of *Loaded* magazine. And even beyond that, he didn't want to hear Rich and Marco and Adam and Ed talking that way about her either. His disapproval had taken the admittedly pretty feeble form of merely not joining in so far, but they'd notice he wasn't joshing along with them soon and he'd have to say then, somehow, that he didn't want to. And then he'd really be in for it, he'd never, ever, hear the end of it and the news would spill out and eventually it would trickle round the school and reach Moll Saunders who'd hear in crude terms that Jack Stockdale had the hots for her whereupon she'd say – she'd be bound to say – in tones of utter contempt, 'Jack Stockdale? Jack *Stockdale*? Puh – *lease*. Gimme a *break*.'

But would she? That day, she'd caught him looking at her outside the school secretary's office where the notice-boards hung, and she'd said, 'Hi.' She hadn't smiled, she'd looked straight at him and just said, 'Hi.' He'd nodded. He couldn't think what else to do on the spur of the moment, but give her this cheesy nod. She hadn't seemed to mind. She'd gone on looking at him for several seconds after he'd nodded, and then she'd turned, quite naturally, to look at the gym-club notice. She left him feeling stunned, breathless, thrilled. He couldn't believe it, how thrilled he'd been. Like he wanted to turn cartwheels or do a backflip. And all for a 'Hi'.

At home, later, when he and Rachel and Emma were

tussling in front of the fridge for drinks and yoghurts and a saucer of cold sausages, Rachel had said, 'You know Moll? In fifth year?'

'Uh-huh,' Jack said. He put a sausage between his teeth and tore off the ring-pull on a can of Coca-Cola.

'She liked your painting.'

Jack ducked his head.

'What painting?' he said, round the sausage.

'That black one. The head thing. The one Mr Finlay put up. Moll said it was cool.'

Jack said carelessly, removing the sausage, 'What would she know?'

'Nothing,' Emma said, slurping strawberry yoghurt straight from the pot, 'because it's crap anyway.'

'Trudy heard her,' Rachel said. 'Trudy was trying to get Mr Finlay to let her do extra art instead of home economics. Moll was in there.'

Emma put the plastic pot on the table. She had a smear of yoghurt across the bridge of her nose.

'Mr Finlay's crap too.'

'Only because he told you you couldn't paint until you'd learned to draw.'

'I don't want to paint,' Emma said.

'OK,' Jack said, regarding his Coca-Cola can with great intensity. 'So this girl I don't know liked my painting?'

Rachel looked at him. She let a tiny pause fall.

'You know her,' she said. She bent into the fridge and retrieved the last sausage, a carton of apple juice and a mini Mars Bar.

'You're not allowed chocolate till after supper,' Emma said.

Rachel put her bounty into the crook of one arm and added a bag of crisps.

'I'm going to talk to Trudy. Before Mum gets back. I'll probably ask her to tell me what Moll really said about your painting.'

Jack shrugged.

'Suit yourself.'

Emma darted a hand into the fridge and snatched a couple of Mars Bars.

'Nobody's going to look at *you*, Jack,' she said. 'Not in a million years.'

The trouble was, Jack could now hear Rachel's voice, but not what she was actually saying. There was a lot of laughing and every so often, Rachel said, 'Wow!' and, 'Wow-*ee*!' but he couldn't tell if the subject of Moll and her admiration of Jack's painting was on-going or over. What, he wondered, had she actually *said* anyway? 'Cool,' or, 'Great,' or, 'Who painted that?' or, 'Who painted that, I'd really like to meet them?' Downstairs, the front door slammed. Carrie always slammed it in order to give her children fair warning to stop doing the forbidden things they were doing and revert to the things they were sup-posed to be doing. Jack sat up and banged with his fist on the floor to warn Rachel. He heard her scream, 'Bye-eee!' and then silence, and knew she'd be scrambling round the bed trying to get the crisp and chocolate crumbs out, and the pillows back in, before Carrie came upstairs.

He stood up. In view of the day's developments, he decided he'd give Rachel a break. He opened his bedroom door and shouted, 'Hi, Mum!'

From two floors below Carrie called, 'Hi,' and then, 'Can you give me a hand with the shopping?'

Jack loped downstairs. The hall floor was covered with supermarket bags, bulging with depressing things like giant bottles of clothes-washing liquid and jumbo packs of dustbin liners.

'This is what every girl should see,' Carrie said, gesturing at the floor, 'before she orders that white dress and books a beach in Bali. Can you put it all on the kitchen table?'

Jack looped his fingers through three bags for each hand.

'You love it, Ma.'

'Do I?'

'Yeah. You love being in charge. What'll you do when you've only got Dad to make life hell for?'

Carrie began unpacking a bag of vegetables.

'Poor Dad.'

'Why?'

'He went to see Gran today. With Alan.'

'Oh.'

'Yes. Oh.' She looked at the pack in her hand. 'Why did I get more sprouts? I am sick of sprouts and they're horrible at this time of year. All rank.'

'Is Gran OK?'

'No.'

Jack dumped four more bags on the table.

'Are you pissed off with Grando?'

Carrie gave him a quick glance.

'Not particularly.'

'Dad is.'

'It's different for Dad.'

'Why?'

'He feels – well, he feels it's tough on Gran.'

'Yeah,' Jack said, 'tough all round.'

The telephone rang.

'Oh,' Carrie said, her arms full of vegetables, 'you get it –'

Jack picked up the receiver.

'Hi,' he said. Then his expression changed. He made an embarrassed face at Carrie. 'Hi, Gran,' he said. He motioned to Carrie to come over, jabbing at the air urgently with his free hand. 'No,' he said. 'No, he's not. Yeah, well – well, I'll get Mum –'

Carrie stooped over the table and let all the vegetables she had just picked up roll out of her arms again. She crossed the room and took the receiver from Jack who pantomimed exaggerated relief and slithered to the floor.

'Laura?'

Jack, beside his mother's booted feet on the floor, heard his grandmother's voice faintly from three feet above his head.

'Carrie? Oh Carrie, is Simon back?'

'No, he isn't. I thought he was with you –'

'Not now. He left. Isn't he home yet?'

'No.'

'He should be,' Laura said. 'He should be by now.'

'I expect,' Carrie said, shifting her weight a little, 'he's got caught up in rush-hour traffic.'

'Will you ask him to ring me? As soon as he gets in?'

'Laura, has something happened, something –'

'No,' Laura said. 'No. But I need to speak to him. I need to speak to Simon.'

'OK –'

'Tell him,' Laura said. 'Tell him, won't you? As soon as he gets in?'

CHAPTER FIVE

'I can't come,' Merrion said. 'I simply can't.'

She was sitting on the edge of the sofa in her flat, nursing a gone-cold mug of herbal tea.

'He's a gentle soul,' Guy said. 'Very tolerant, very – well, whatever the opposite of volatile is. He isn't, perhaps, quite as clever as Simon but he's much less difficult.'

Merrion looked into her mug. The herbal tea was pale brownish yellow and smelled faintly and disagreeably of compost. She had decided she was drinking too much coffee and was trying to drink herbal tea instead. It was, she thought, like telling yourself that a dry, unadorned diet crispbread was a perfectly satisfactory substitute for a thick cheese sandwich.

'But he's still your son –'

'Who knows about you and what you mean to me and what you're going to mean. He knows your name. He knows the *score*, my darling.'

Merrion put the mug down on the floor by her feet. She leaned forward until she was bent double and her chin was on her knees.

'What I hate is that the prospect of meeting a son of yours makes me feel *guilty*. I don't know why, but it does. I feel as if I'd have to say sorry for upsetting his mother –'

'Not much logic in that. His mother is the same person

as my wife, and you very properly haven't been consumed by guilt there.'

'She's a different generation. Alan's my generation –'

'Merrion, what on earth has that got to do with anything?'

'I can't explain,' Merrion said, 'but it has.'

'Look,' Guy said. He came across the small sitting room and sat down beside her. 'Look, come and say hello very quickly, maybe even have a drink with us, and then go.'

She sat up straight and pushed her hair behind her shoulders.

'Would I be doing this,' she said, 'for you, or for me?'

'For us both. Even for Alan probably. He's going to love you.'

'Don't *say* this stuff –'

'Loving his mother doesn't preclude his loving other people that I love. Especially when they're lovable.'

'My mother doesn't think I'm lovable –'

'She does. She merely thinks your behaviour is unconventional and inconvenient. That's different.'

Merrion looked at Guy.

'Are you trying to show me off?'

'Of course.'

'And give us credibility?'

'That, too.'

'I tell you,' Merrion said, 'I do not like this stage at all.'

'I seem to remember –'

'Oh, I did,' Merrion said, standing up, 'I did want you to leave Laura and all that. I do want it. But you never know how the dynamics will change when you get what you want, do you?'

She stooped and picked up the mug from the floor. He caught her free hand.

'Are you losing your nerve?'

'No,' she said. 'But I just feel socially inadequate at the prospect of meeting your son.'

'We're all inadequate for that,' Guy said. 'None of us has ever done it before.' He gave her hand a little shake. 'Five minutes and it'll be over and that's another dragon slayed.'

She sighed.

'Give me a wet Monday morning,' she said, 'in court with the most useless, truculent client to defend and a judge who can't stand women advocates, rather than this.'

'That's easy. That's professional. This is personal.'

'Too right,' she said. She took her hand out of his. 'OK. I'll come. For five minutes.'

Alan leaned against the pub bar and ordered a mineral water. He rather wanted something stronger, but thought he would wait for that until his father came and they could use the ritual of deciding and ordering and paying to get them over the first few minutes. It wasn't, exactly, that Alan felt nervous about meeting his father, it was more that he felt anxious about conveying satisfactorily the important fact that he was going to stand by both his parents without getting heavy about any of it.

He didn't know this pub. He didn't actually know Bayswater at all, it wasn't his bit of London, but his father had suggested it because it was close to Merrion's flat and he was spending the weekend with Merrion. Guy had said they'd meet for a drink in the pub and then go round the corner to a good Italian, a plan which made Alan think his father intended to include Merrion in the pub part, but not the Italian. Alan felt, in advance, a little sorry for Merrion. It would be an ordeal for her, however they played it. When he thought of Merrion, he thought of himself saying – through tears – a year ago when Callum left, 'I didn't *ask* to fall in love with you.' It had been a pretty stupid thing to say, no doubt, but it had been true. Carrie had agreed with him.

'We can kind of make ourselves available to falling

in love,' she'd said, 'but that's all the control we do have.'

Alan took a mouthful of his mineral water. It was too salty and the bubbles were aggressively bubbly. He'd tried, during the long and distressing evening with his mother, to explain that neither Guy nor Merrion had planned the pain they were causing – to themselves as well as to anyone else – and that things happened in life, some good, more bad, and you had to just accept them without screwing yourself up apportioning blame and finding reasons. She'd got very angry with him, angry enough to ring Simon at home, twice, in order, Alan supposed, to get the kind of furiously sympathetic response she felt she was entitled to. Alan had tried to prevent her, but he couldn't. She felt he was no substitute for Simon, never had been, and she blamed him for, as she put it, making Simon go home and not stay the night as she'd wanted him to. Simon had needed a bit of urging, admittedly, but Alan could see that both Simon and Laura would be in pieces if Simon stayed. He'd have convinced her she was utterly wronged and she'd have convinced him that only he could save her. So Alan had put Simon's car keys into his hand and told him to go, almost pushed him out of the house. Then he'd poured Laura a gin and tonic and she said she never drank gin and tipped it down the sink.

Alan hadn't minded. In his world, in his life, people got awkward when they got upset, it was part of the situation, part of the result of losing control. Alan had learned very early on, when he realised that there was something deep in him that made him an outsider to his upbringing, that there weren't patterns. There were consequences, sure, often as random as the behaviour that caused them, but there wasn't order, there wasn't symmetry and tidy se-quence. There hadn't been much future in trying to ex-plain this to his mother, who interpreted his efforts as a peculiarly unkind form of detachment from her suffering, and in the end he'd had to give up and simply sit there, holding her hand, and hoping that his silence and his touch conveyed at least something of what she wanted from him.

The double doors from the pavement swung inwards and two men in leather jackets came in, then an older man in a flat cap, and then Alan's father, holding one door open for a tall girl with a mane of hair, wearing a dark overcoat that came almost to the floor. Alan straightened up a little and turned towards them, but didn't move. His father looked – well, how did he look? Familiar, Alan thought, handsome, friendly. And tense. Distinctly tense. He took a couple of steps forward and put his arms round his father.

'Hi, Dad.'

'Alan,' Guy said. He held Alan hard for a second. 'I don't know whether to say thank you for coming.' He gave a brief laugh and turned away, curving an arm out to include the girl in the long overcoat. 'This is Merrion.'

'I had to be,' the girl said. 'Didn't I?'

She didn't hold her hand out. Alan smiled at her.

'Glass of wine?'

'No thanks.'

'A short? Mineral water?'

'No thanks,' she said. 'I couldn't swallow anything right now.'

'She nearly didn't come,' Guy said.

Alan said, 'A drink would give you something to do.'

She shook her head.

Guy said, 'She won't ever do anything that makes life easier for herself. She was born in a hair shirt.'

'What d'you want, Dad, beer, wine –?'

Guy moved towards the bar.

'I'll get it –'

'No,' Alan said. 'You can give me lunch. I'm doing this.' He looked at Merrion. 'I'm going to order you a glass of wine. You can ignore it if you want to.'

She gave a fleeting smile.

'I wouldn't be that churlish.'

Alan turned back to the bar. Guy put out a hand and took Merrion's nearest one and squeezed it. He wanted to tell her that she didn't have to do anything, say anything, that she didn't have to perform for him, prove to his son what a winner she was. He wanted to tell her that any way she wanted to be was fine by him.

She took her hand carefully out of his and opened her coat. She was wearing jeans underneath, and a pale-grey sweater with a polo collar. She ran a hand round the inside of the polo collar, as if to let some air in to cool her thoughts, calm her. Alan turned back from the bar and handed her a glass of white wine.

'Thanks,' she said.

He held out a half-pint beer tankard to his father. Then he picked up his mineral water.

'No toast,' he said. 'We wouldn't know what to drink to.'

'I do,' Merrion said. She lifted her glass.

'You do?'

'Peace of mind,' she said. She lowered her glass and took a sip. 'I've never not had it before.'

In the sitting room of the house in Tooting, Simon lay asleep in a drift of Sunday newspapers. Jack had extracted the sports sections earlier in the day, and Carrie had taken the arts and review supplements to read on the kitchen table, leaving Simon with news. He thought briefly, before he fell asleep, that these sorts of age and gender divisions about newsprint were probably happening along precisely these lines, all over the world. Women only wanted news if it concerned the humanity of human beings and men only wanted reviews of things they were going to see. Teen-agers didn't want either. Culture smacked of school and news couldn't hold a candle to the gloomy drama of their own lives. Jack was very gloomy just now. Carrie thought he was in love. Simon thought he'd been left out of the long-jump team and had also begun to realise, dimly, that public academic examinations of real consequence were only just over a year away. Whatever the reason, Jack was fighting his demons with silence and an expression like doom.

Carrie had wanted Simon to go to bed after lunch, properly to bed with outer clothes off and the curtains pulled across.

'You look exhausted –'

He yawned.

'I ate too much lunch –'

'You know it wasn't that,' Carrie said. 'You know what this week's been like.'

She'd answered the telephone to Laura several times in the last few days and on a couple of occasions had not only said Simon was out when he wasn't, but had also not told Simon of the calls.

'I want you to sleep *properly*.'

'Then I won't sleep tonight and that I can't stand. Nothing seems manageable at 3 a.m.'

They'd compromised in the end and Simon had settled down along the length of the sitting-room sofa. He declined a rug.

'Newspaper's perfectly warm –'

'I don't understand,' Carrie said, 'why men are so unbelievably ungracious about being thoughtfully looked after.'

He blew her a kiss, his eyes on a front-page photograph of the Foreign Secretary. She went out of the room, closing the door behind her with something perfectly adjusted between a slam and a click. When she had gone, he found he would rather have liked to have had her back again.

In the kitchen, Rachel and Emma had cleared up approximately, doing the simple stuff like putting plates in the dishwasher and leaving anything that required application and conscientiousness, such as scouring out the roasting tin that had held the chicken. Carrie thought of summoning them back to finish, decided against it on the grounds of avoiding friction and the consequent attrition of her own energies, and dug in the cupboard under the sink to find her rubber gloves. They were yellow, as yellow as sunflowers, and for some reason a source of infinite amusement to her children. If my mother were still alive, she told herself, I'd ring her now and tell her how I was feeling. I'd tell her that I had this sensation of dragging a whole lot of boulders uphill – nice boulders, boulders that I can't help loving despite their shortcomings – and that just as I get near a resting place, never mind the actual summit, one or two of the boulders roll out of my grasp and bump steadily back down to the bottom again.

Behind her, the back door that led to the garden, and to the path that ran along the side of the house from the road, opened.

'Hello,' Alan said.

Carrie turned, her yellow-gloved hands still deep in the sink.

'How very nice.'

He came in and closed the door behind him. He was holding a slender tube of florist's paper with a small bunch of creamy narcissi heads sticking out of the top. He laid them on the table among the scattered place mats and unused spoons and forks and came to give Carrie a kiss.

He said, almost conspiratorially, 'I met her.'

Carrie looked at him intently.

'And?'

'Tall. Very striking. Nervous as a kitten –'

'And?'

'Nice,' Alan said. 'Very. Not –' He paused.

'Not what?'

'Not after Dad for anything except Dad. As far as I could see.' He looked round the kitchen. 'Where's Si?'

'Passed out under the papers.'

'I bought you some flowers.'

'I saw. They're very pretty. You are the only man I've ever known who gives me flowers.'

Alan picked the kettle up and leaned across Carrie to fill it from the cold tap.

'What's the score here?'

'In a nutshell,' Carrie said, 'Simon is worn out with confusion and being pressured, Jack thinks it's really cool to fall for someone half your age, Rachel thinks it's weird and Emma is worrying about Gran's dogs.'

'And you?'

Carrie put the last saucepan upside down on the draining board, pulled the plug out of the sink and took her gloves off with a snap.

'Alan –'

'Yes?'

She looked straight at him.

'I don't blame him.'

Alan said thoughtfully, his hand on the kettle as if it needed steadying while it boiled, 'You've never liked her much, have you?'

'Let's put it another way,' Carrie said. 'Let's say that she's never liked me much.'

'Oh come –'

'Alan,' Carrie said, 'I don't even think it's personal. I don't think she'd have liked anyone who married Simon.'

'Does it get between you and Si?'

'Sometimes. Depends on how I'm feeling. He forgets sometimes, that I haven't a mother myself to counter her with. She forgets that, too. Don't use that coffee – it was on offer, and no wonder. The stuff in the black jar is much better.' She went over to the table and picked the narcissi up, inhaling their astonishingly strong scent. 'These are lovely.'

'Would you like coffee?'

'No thank you.'

'Dad is so happy,' Alan said. 'I do this laid-back stuff but I can't always carry it off to myself. I liked seeing him like that, I liked him being, well, appreciated.'

'Does she flirt with him?'

'No. Not the type. She's a professional woman, she's got a kind of detachment. And a Welsh accent.'

'Welsh!'

'Not very. Just a lilt. It's lovely.'

'Do you,' Carrie said, sitting down by the cluttered table, still holding the narcissi, 'feel disloyal?'

'No,' Alan said.

'Strict truth, please.'

'Yes,' Alan said.

'Because your mother couldn't really hold a candle to this girl –'

'Because,' Alan said, taking a swallow of coffee, 'my mother's got nothing left to fight with. All these years, and that's all she's got. Just all these years.'

'There's you two –'

'Not when we're our age. It doesn't count any more. You should see her, Carrie. She's sitting in that house with every cushion plumped and the bath shining and the garden all perfect and you know she's trying not to ask herself what it's all for. For years she could kid herself it was for Dad, or Dad and her, but now that veil's been torn away, too. She's made something Dad's told her he doesn't want.'

Carrie began to unwrap her flowers.

'She didn't do it for him. She did it to show him he hadn't left any space for her, in his life.'

'Come on –'

'True,' Carrie said. 'Don't confuse independence and defiance.' She got up and began to search in a cupboard for a vase. 'When did she last earn a penny piece?'

'It's different for that generation –'

'No, it isn't,' Carrie said. 'My mother worked, my aunts do. Your mother stopped. She chose to stop.' She ran water into a narrow glass vase and put the narcissi in, unarranged. Alan held his hand out for the vase.

'Oh, *Carrie*. Let me –'

She passed it to him. The door to the hall opened and Simon came in.

'I feel awful. I shouldn't have slept. Hi, Al.'

Alan said, concentrating on the narcissi, 'I saw Dad.'

'Did you?'

'You knew I was going to. I told you.'

'Do I want to know?'

'I don't know. Do you?'

'Yes,' Carrie said, 'you do.'

Simon sighed. He came forward a little and leaned on the back of the nearest chair.

'Well?'

'He's fine,' Alan said. 'He looks well and happy.'

Simon grunted.

'And she –'

Simon straightened.

'She!'

'She was there. Just briefly. And given briefly and first impressions and all of us jumpy, she's great.'

Simon closed his eyes.

'Give me strength.'

'It's no good, Simon,' Alan said. He put the broken-off pieces of narcissus stem into a neat pile. 'You can't write her off as a gold-digger or a marriage-wrecker or a legal groupie or a sex bomb. You can't write Dad off, either, as a classic male menopause victim wanting to reassure himself he could still double the world's population if he wanted to. She's the real thing. She's a proper person.'

'I think,' Simon said, taking his hands off the chairback, 'I've heard quite enough for the moment.'

75

'One more thing,' Carrie said.

'What?' Simon said. His voice was full of weary distaste.

'I want to meet her,' Carrie said.

In her parents' bedroom, Emma was experimenting with Carrie's make-up. Emma had make-up of her own, but that was for using, not for playing with. Carrie didn't have much make-up – not like Rachel's friend Trudy's mother, who had drawers and drawers of it, boxes of it in cupboards, baskets of it under beds – but she had enough to offer an intriguing alternative to the geography project (The Nature of Oceans) that she was supposed to be doing before Carrie would let her use the telephone. She sat on the old sofa, comfortably nested in random piles of her parents' sweaters and shirts, and picked her way interestedly through the plastic box which had once held ice-cream and now held a fairly battered collection of mascaras and eyeshadows and lipsticks. Carrie, Emma noticed, favoured sludge colours: Emma would have preferred lilac, something with a bit of sparkle in it, something a bit wicked.

The telephone beside the bed rang. In a single swift movement, Emma was off the sofa and had the receiver in her hand. Even if the call was not for her, it was imperative for her to know who the caller was, and whom they wished to speak to. She crouched on the floor.

'Hello?'

'Hello, dear,' Laura said. 'Is that Rachel?'

Emma made a face at the telephone.

'No, it's Emma.'

'Emma dear, it's Granny.'

'I know,' Emma said.

'How are you?'

'Bored,' Emma said. She adjusted her crouch so that she was sitting on the floor. 'How are the dogs?'

'Well,' Laura said, 'they're not very happy, of course.'

'Did they see Grando?' Emma said.

'No. I thought it would upset them. I put them in the garden room.'

'Did they bark?'

'Yes, I'm afraid they –'

'They wanted to see Grando,' Emma said. 'Poor them.'

'Emma,' Laura said, in a different voice, 'is your father there?'

'He's asleep.'

'Could you wake him for me?'

Emma thought about the dogs.

'No, I couldn't,' she said.

'Please, dear.'

'He's downstairs,' Emma said. 'I'm upstairs.'

'Could you go down,' Laura said, 'and tell him Granny's on the phone?'

Emma wished that there was someone else to give the telephone to.

'I'll tell him when he wakes up,' she said.

'Dear –'

'He was really grumpy at lunch,' Emma said. 'He needed to sleep. I'll tell him when he wakes up. Have the dogs had their walk yet?'

'Of course. Emma –'

'Do they still like those biscuits with fake marrowbone stuff in them?'

'I don't think I know which biscuits –'

'Give them my love,' Emma said. She held the receiver a little way from her ear. She remembered a phrase Carrie and her friends used to each other at the end of calls. 'Bye, Granny,' she said. 'Take care,' and then she put the receiver down.

From down the landing, Rachel shouted, 'Who was that?'

'No one,' Emma called.

'Was it –'

'No,' Emma said, 'it was Granny.'

Rachel said nothing. The volume of her music went up again. Emma got up from the floor and looked at Carrie's make-up box. It was really very dull. When she had dogs, when she was older, she'd never shut them up against their wills and she'd never do things to worry them. The telephone began to ring again. Emma turned her back and walked out of the room, leaving it to it.

CHAPTER SIX

Above the desk in Carrie's office, a notice-board hung. It had a huge at-a-glance year-long calendar pinned to it, which recorded the hours worked by part-time staff, the doctors' days off and everybody's holidays. Round the edge, Carrie had pinned other things: photographs of Simon and the children, cartoons cut out from newspapers, notes to herself that she forgot about the moment she had put them up there and a postcard from her Aunt Cath on which Cath had scribbled, 'Try not to be perfect.' Cath had come to stay a year ago and surveyed Carrie's life and work and home and family with an astonished and slightly sardonic eye, and had sent the postcard as her thank-you letter. Carrie had liked the postcard, but had also reflected that her mother – two years Cath's senior – would never have sent it. 'You're doing brilliantly,' her mother would have written. 'Just try not to do too much.' That would have been comforting, to be sure. But it wouldn't have been so bracing.

Work, Carrie often thought, was the only area of her life where something even a quarter way to perfection seemed attainable. She had hours within which she worked, regulations and timetables that were comfortingly inflexible, and if the human element remained arbitrary, it almost always had to come to heel in the end. Doctors could throw tantrums, she had discovered, about not having the weekends off that they wanted, but if there was no one else available to be on duty, on duty they had to be.

'Sorry,' she'd say, staring straight at the doctor in question just as if he wasn't shouting at her. 'It isn't my fault and there isn't any alternative.'

'You enjoy this!' the doctor would yell.

'That's exactly what my children say,' Carrie would say and then she'd go back to her office and pencil the doctor's name in the relevant weekend on her year planner and picture his wife saying, that evening, when she discovered they couldn't have a weekend break after all for their eleventh wedding anniversary, 'But you *promised*.' She was sorry for the wife, of course, but detachedly sorry. That was work for you. That was why work was such a pleasure. You took it on and off, like an overcoat, and you only took it home with you on very rare occasions. Above all, it allowed you to concentrate. At work, Carrie could give it her full attention, her capable, impersonal full attention. At home she usually felt as if someone had seized her attention, torn it into a hundred small pieces and tossed them into the air.

'I never finish anything,' she'd said to Simon, over and over. 'I'm never *allowed* to.'

Today, however, this Monday morning with all its demands built up from crises not being dealt with at the weekend felt not like the finishing of things, but more like their beginning. Or at least, their developing. Alan had stayed for supper the night before and when he was leaving, had said in Carrie's ear, 'Do you want her number?'

'Oops,' Carrie said.

'Do you? Do you want Merrion's number?'

She'd stepped a little away from him.

'Are you plotting?'

'The reverse. This girl exists. Dad loves her. Demonising her helps no one.'

'I know.'

'I'll ring you at work.'

'I do want to meet her,' Carrie said. 'It's just that there's Simon –'

Alan pulled up his jacket collar.

'Does it really help Simon if you side with Simon?'

Carrie made a face. Alan gave her nearest cheek a quick kiss.

'I'll ring you at work. You don't have to do anything after that if you don't want to.'

She looked down at her desk now. Alan had left a message. Maureen, one of the district nurses, had taken it down while in Carrie's office looking, she said, for the list of babies born at the weekend and due for their first post-natal visit before Wednesday. Maureen liked taking messages.

'Carrie,' she'd written on a yellow sticker note, 'Alan called 9.07 Monday. He said the number you want is as follows.' She'd signed the note 'Maureen', with a smiley face after her name and a small fish symbol. Maureen was a born-again Christian.

Carrie looked at the telephone number. It was Central London. If she rang it now, she would get an answering machine and would have to leave a composed message. If she rang this evening, not only would she have to do it in some secrecy, but also her father-in-law might answer. Carrie had never had any previous trouble in speaking to her father-in-law, but she had an aversion just now, for reasons she couldn't explain, to telling him she wished to speak to his mistress in order to set up a meeting. She couldn't, she decided, deal with his pleasure at hearing she had such a purpose. Nor could she deal with deceiving Simon at home about her telephone call, nor with fending off Rachel and Emma's intense, instinctive curiosity while she made it. She looked at her watch. Ten-twenty. Ten minutes before the weekly administrative practice meeting, which she chaired with tremendous briskness, having no tolerance whatsoever for people who adored meetings and who would go to any lengths to prolong them.

She put her hand on the telephone receiver and dialled rapidly. Then she shut her eyes. The telephone rang out four times and then a woman's voice said, rather distantly, 'If you wish to leave a message for Merrion Palmer, please do so, after the tone.'

'Hello,' Carrie said, and stopped. Merrion's answering machine waited, in faintly humming silence.

'Hello,' Carrie said again. She opened her eyes. 'This is Carrie Stockdale. I'm Guy's daughter-in-law. Could you ring me at work sometime? Between nine and four-thirty? Thank you.'

She put the phone down. She thought, suddenly and with unexpected guilt, of Simon.

The door opened, and one of the receptionists put her head in. 'Carrie,' she said, 'Dr Mason's had to go off to an emergency anaesthetic at the hospital. And he has seventeen people on his list this morning. What are we supposed to do with them?'

Jack Stockdale leaned against the blank wall at the back of the science block. It was the place he and Rich and Marco came for a smoke usually, but he didn't somehow feel like a smoke today, and certainly not with Rich and Marco. Marco, blazing with unconcealed triumph, had taken Moll to the cinema on Friday night and had hinted at a night of clubbing together on Saturday. Rich appeared to think that this was fine, brilliant even, cool. Jack had never breathed a word of his secret and intense interest in Moll to either Rich or Marco, but discovered that he felt brutally let down and betrayed all the same. He couldn't speak to either of them; he could hardly look at them. When Adam said to him, 'What've you got the hump

82

about, mate?' he'd shrugged and muttered and gone off to mooch about by himself, hands in his pockets, kicking things.

The trouble was, he might not have said anything, but Marco knew, all the same. Marco glowed with the knowledge that he had somehow succeeded where Jack had failed. Marco had his Italian father's colouring and his Italian father's physical assurance and beside him, Jack felt suddenly raw and hopeless, physically and emotionally, pitifully unfinished. He knew he was being pathetic, like a big, sad, clumsy puppy, but he couldn't see, right now, how to feel any other way. His father had put his finger on the problem, quite by chance, the other night. They'd all been hanging about the kitchen, wanting supper hours before it was ready, and Simon was chopping carrots on the table, very slowly and carefully, and Jack was watching him and waiting for Carrie to notice how thickly he was chopping them and say she wanted them cut much thinner than that.

'You know something?' Simon said.

Carrie was making a casserole. She had her back to them all, dipping a big spoon in and out of the pot while she added things out of bottles and jars.

'No,' she said. 'What?'

'You can handle anything in life,' Simon said. 'You can get anything sorted, can't you, as long as your emotions aren't involved. That's why work works and life mostly doesn't.'

Carrie turned round.

'Weird,' she said, 'I was thinking almost exactly that earlier today. Could you cut those a bit thinner?'

Jack had leaned across and picked up a piece of carrot. He'd rather wanted to ask his father more about what he'd said, more about this emotion stuff and how it made you suddenly want things you'd never wanted before. And, worse, how it seemed to take away the feeling that

83

you were in any way in control any more. But he felt shy. Rachel was sitting at the table, too, supposedly slicing cabbage and learning a poem for English, but actually doing neither, and she had ears like a lynx and a mind like an Exocet. Mention emotion in front of Rachel and she'd say, clear as a bell, 'You fancy Moll Saunders, don't you?'

He squared his shoulders against the science-block wall. He did fancy her, it was true. He was, in fact, spellbound by the way she looked and moved, by the way her hair fell. But there was more than that. He wanted to know her. He wanted to hear her say things to him. He wanted to do things for her. After his father's remark, he'd gone and looked up 'emotion' in the dictionary and it had talked about states of feeling, about sympathy and personal involvements and sensitivity and love. His mother had said Grando was in love. This was at once impossible and perfectly possible to imagine. Jack knew enough to sense that the life of the feelings didn't automatically stop at twenty, but it was very hard to visualise that anyone could feel as strongly as he did now, and be as confused and as uncertain as to what to do next, as he was now.

He put his hands flat against the wall and pushed himself away from it. He didn't want a cigarette and he didn't want two periods of physics followed by one of current affairs and he didn't want to go home after that and have Rachel watching him and knowing she knew what was the matter. He began to move slowly along the science block towards the asphalt path that connected the block to the main school building. He felt he could summon up no interest in anything because the one thing he was interested in wasn't interested back.

On the asphalt path, just out of sight of the back of the science block, a girl was waiting.

'Hi,' Moll Saunders said.

Jack stared at her, speechless.

'Did I scare you?'

'No. No, but I –'

'I've got a bit of a down on smoking,' Moll Saunders said. 'My aunt died of lung cancer.'

'Oh God,' Jack said. 'I wasn't smoking, in fact I–' His head was spinning. He put his hand into his trouser pocket and tugged out his cigarettes. He held them out to her. 'Here.'

'You don't have to do that –'

'I do,' Jack said.

'We'll put them in the bin.'

'OK.'

'Jack,' Moll said, 'I really like your painting.'

He looked down at his feet. His ears felt the size of dinner plates.

'Wow –'

'I do,' she said. 'It's cool.'

When Laura brought the dogs back from their afternoon walk, their bellies and legs and paws were dark with mud. She tied them up to a ring set into the wall of the potting shed, and went to unravel the hose. They began to leap about and squeal. The hose was a horror worse than the vacuum cleaner. They hated the hose.

Laura turned the outside tap on and put her finger partly over the hose nozzle to intensify the pressure. She held each dog's collar in turn and hosed it down methodically, despite the yelps and squirming; she did this in winter, she reflected, twice a day usually, twice a day seven days a week. When Guy was there, he'd walked the dogs perhaps once or twice at a weekend, but he never washed them properly. He never seemed to see the need, nor the need to walk them so regularly. He said being so regular with them made them a nuisance, encouraged them to badger for walks or their dinner with maddening persistence. Dogs, he said, ought to accommodate to people's lives: not the other way about. She'd talked about her obligation to the dogs, to the garden, to the house, to the servicing of their joint lives.

'Laura,' he'd said tiredly. 'Laura, don't mistake a tyranny for an obligation.'

She turned the tap off. The dogs shook themselves vigorously, springing about in a theatrical manner on the ends of their leads. She untied them, and they leaped away from her, chasing and tumbling over each other in their exaggerated relief that the ordeal was over. She watched them and felt like crying. They could, in their blithe doggy way, forget pain so easily, so cruelly easily.

There was a car in the back drive, an estate car with a jumble of flower-arranging paraphernalia in the back. In the driver's seat sat a middle-aged woman in spectacles writing absorbedly in a notebook. When she heard the sound of Laura's feet on the gravel, she wound the car window down.

'Thought that's what you'd be doing, walking the dogs –'

'Wendy,' Laura said.

'I was perfectly happy, sitting here. Gave me a chance to do the hospital-volunteer transport rota. How are you?'

'I don't know,' Laura said.

Wendy opened her car door, and got out.

'Time to make me a cup of tea?'

'Oh yes –'

Wendy looked at the dogs. They were positioned by the back door, poised to dash inside.

'It's probably good for you, having to cope with them. Domestic routine has its uses.'

Laura put a key into the back door and opened it. The dogs shot inside, leaving damp footprints along the passage floor, and vanished into the kitchen to find welcoming presents for Wendy.

'It's kind of you to come,' Laura said.

Wendy looked at her sharply through her spectacles. They had blue frames and gilt sidepieces.

'My dear Laura,' she said, 'there, but for the grace of God, go *any* of us. Forty years of marriage. *Forty*. Do you think any of us went up that aisle forty years ago and thought about where we'd be forty years later? I didn't, for one. I'd have died of fright.'

Laura went ahead into the kitchen. The dogs had found a tea towel and an oven glove and were wagging round the table with these, as offerings for Wendy.

'Bloody fools,' she said.

Laura ran water into the kettle.

'I was very nervous about marrying Guy,' she said. 'But I thought that was normal. Everyone said it's normal to be nervous when you marry.'

'Roger fainted,' Wendy said, 'in the vestry when we were supposed to be signing the register. Not a wonderful omen, if you think about it. He's never fainted since.'

'And you still have him –'

'I do,' Wendy said, 'but only after some pretty close shaves.'

Laura put tea bags in a teapot.

'Would you marry him again?'

'Given half a chance,' Wendy said, 'I wouldn't marry anybody. Except to have children.' She glanced at Laura. 'How are the children taking this?'

Laura took mugs out of the cupboard and put them on the table.

'As you would expect. Simon perfectly sweet and very sympathetic, and Alan making me feel that as this sort of thing happens all the time I shouldn't make a fuss but just get on with the consequences.'

'Oh Laura,' Wendy said, taking her spectacles off and buffing the lenses up against her cardigan, 'he doesn't mean that. Alan's a sweetie.'

Laura put the teapot on the table and sat down.

'He makes me feel he thinks Guy has a point.'

'Laura dear, Guy is his *father* –'

'Who has been betraying me for the last seven years and has now walked out.'

Wendy put her glasses back on.

'I have, since I heard, rather wondered what I'd do if Roger walked out.'

'And?'

'I think I'd go and live in Cornwall and run a b-and-b and grow prize fuchsias.'

'You only think that because you don't have to do it.'

'Laura,' Wendy said, 'are you very, very sure you weren't actually rather *tired* of being married to Guy?'

Laura stopped pouring tea.

'What do you mean?'

'That it's insulting and upsetting and frightening to be left like this, but that it just *might* be a chance to start again on your own terms?'

'At sixty-one?'

'At eighty-one, if needs be. No milk, thank you.'

'I don't think,' Laura said, bending over her mug, 'that you understand at all.'

'Ah,' Wendy said.

'I have never been able quite to live up to Guy, you see. I've never quite been able to be what he wanted me to be, what he made it very plain he wanted me to be. The things I'm good at are the things he can't see the point of. I am a private person. He is a public person. He made me feel that the privacy of my life was a kind of selfishness.'

'Ah,' Wendy said again. She sipped her tea.

'I feel cast aside,' Laura said. 'Thrown away. Not good enough. Rejected.'

Wendy put her mug down.

'I have to say, except for very superficially, that isn't how it *looks*.'

'Oh?' Laura said sharply.

'It looks,' Wendy said, 'as if you'd just grown miles and miles apart. Simple as that. Nothing left but the formalities.'

'And if he'd never met this girl?'

'He'd probably have met another one.'

'Because of me?'

Wendy made a face.

'Because of your marriage. There were two of you in that.'

Laura got up to refill the teapot.

'Simon doesn't think that. Simon thinks it's all part of Guy's need to be centre stage.'

'Guy and Simon,' Wendy said, 'are very different people. How's that nice wife of his?'

'I haven't heard from her,' Laura said. 'One brief word on the phone and that was it. Sympathy has never been Carrie's forte.'

'She probably doesn't know what to say –'

'Wendy,' Laura said, 'Carrie has never been lost for words in her life.'

She held the teapot up. Wendy shook her head. She said, 'Will you be all right for money?'

'Simon will see to that.'

'Will he? Should he?'

'Who else is there?' Laura said.

'You and your lawyer.'

'I hate all this. I hate all this exposure, this having to cope. I hate the loss of all I've known, the *status* of marriage –'

Wendy stood up. She looked down at Laura's smooth hair, at her face hidden in her two small, pale hands.

'My dear girl,' she said, 'do wake up. There really isn't much status *left* in marriage in this day and age.'

Because it was a Friday, Guy came up from Stanborough on the five o'clock train, and let himself into Merrion's flat. It was a relief to do that, not least because he felt it was one of the few things he could do openly, one of the few things he had, because of at last coming clean about Merrion, given himself proper permission to do. During the week, in Stanborough, he lived a life he knew was – in a quite different way to his previous life – duplicitous. He said nothing about his changed circumstances to anybody. If anyone knew, they hadn't confronted him with the knowledge and hadn't yet caught up with the fact that the town's Resident Judge had left his wife and was living, during the week, in rented rooms, above a small shopping parade. The parade consisted of a chemist, a Chinese takeaway, a newsagent, a children's clothes shop and an electrical shop. The owner, who lived with his mother-in-law because he couldn't afford the rent on the flat above the shop, was glad to have a tenant above him. He'd had to put metal grilles up across the shop window at night already and a tenant gave him a feeling of extra security. He told his wife Mr Stockdale was an accountant.

'Must be. Or one of those financial managers. Goes off every morning in a business suit. Drives a Volvo.'

Guy was grateful for his anonymity in the flat above the electrical shop. They were unwelcoming rooms, bleakly decorated and furnished, but they fitted his sense of what was due to him just now, and he had no need, really, to tell anyone even his name. He had taken them for three months and moved into them just a minimum of clothes and books. Merrion – whom he refused to allow to see them – said they sounded like *his* hair shirt.

To Guy, they felt more like his limbo, his no-man's-land. When he left them in the mornings, they left no mark on his mind all day beyond giving him, when in his colleagues' company, a weird sense of rooflessness. At lunch, in the judges' dining room, he would listen to the usual banter, over gooseberry crumble served with custard, and find himself furtively wondering about everyone else's home lives, about the situations the others were going home to and how many of them, for various reasons, would try and spin out their days beyond the closure of the courts at four-thirty, delaying the moment of climbing into their cars and heading back to resume whatever it was. Sometimes, Guy felt, a time warp had happened, and that he was back in those early days at the bar, staying in peculiar hotels on circuit, conscious that, however dismal his surroundings or his dinner, there was also a certain beguiling freedom. He'd even come to Stanborough once, back then. He'd stayed at the accepted Bar hotel, the Bell; the district judges kept a cellar in the Bell, in those days. The chief administrator of the whole circuit was still known as the Wine Treasurer.

What haunted him, these days, by contrast, was that his colleagues assumed something about him that was no longer the case. They assumed he'd be going home to Laura. Only a few of them had ever met Laura, and might not have retained any very strong impression of her, but she would be there, in the vague mental sketch they carried of Guy in their heads, along with the fact that he lived in the country, that he had sons, not daughters, that he wasn't much of a fishing man but had been a good cricketer in his day. It would have electrified them to have that sketch come sharply into focus and reveal the presence of Merrion in it, too, and not only in it, but right in the foreground. Some of them might remember Merrion, too, remember her brief and effective performance at Stanborough, remember her because she was a woman. Most of them liked women, but couldn't get used to having them about as colleagues, as equals. When a previous Lord Chancellor had promised he would find judges who could be relied upon not to make dubious comments in front of female counsel, there had been much muttering over the gooseberry crumble.

'Hah! An attempt to appease the feminists, I see!'

Guy could not quite visualise the moment when he could reveal how his life was now, what had happened, how he had broken with the custom of forty years and taken a radical step into emotional territory he was very, very certain he had never even glimpsed before; and how he lived now, in a quiet and suspended state during the week – bringing home meals to microwave, taking his shirts to the laundry, changing the sheets punctiliously on his bed – and then on Fridays, taking the train towards truth and enrichment.

He left court promptly on Fridays, going straight to the station and carefully avoiding carriages occupied by visiting advocates going back to London. At Paddington, he took a taxi to Bayswater, and used his own key, the key Merrion had had cut for him, to let himself into the tall white-painted house that had been converted into flats in the seventies. There was a lift and a staircase in the hallway, the staircase carpeted in dark red patterned with lighter red fleur-de-lis. Guy always took the staircase, counting the steps.

Merrion lived at the very top. The flat was small, but very light, with views between the buildings opposite, to the tops of trees in Hyde Park. Her taste was spare, a reaction to the flower-printed fabrics and profuse cushions of her childhood. The floors were wooden, there were blinds rather than curtains and her make-up lived in a black wire-mesh basket in the bathroom. Guy had been shy about putting his shaving things next to it.

'I don't understand you,' Merrion said, kissing him. 'We have sex, don't we?'

He looked at his sponge bag.

'But this is more intimate –'

She made space for him in the bathroom, space for him in her hanging cupboard. His shoes lay at the bottom, next to her shoes and boots. He would have liked to have put them somewhere else, somewhere out of her way, somewhere unobtrusive. He brought as little to London as possible, anxious not to burden her, not to make demands, not to – well, not to seem too *husbandly*.

On Fridays, he always bought flowers. He bought them at the station and put them in water when he got to the flat, throwing away the dead ones from the week before which she seemed never to have got round to. He turned some music on, checked the fridge for a bottle of wine, washed and changed out of his court suit, admired the Hyde Park trees from the window, scrupulously avoided looking at her letters, at the papers on her desk, at the number of messages on her answerphone. And then he waited. He didn't mind how long he waited. She might be coming back from court in the Midlands, even the northwest, and while she did, he waited, his heart quietly lifting and lifting, until he heard the small crunch of her key in the door, and stood up to greet her.

CHAPTER SEVEN

On the train back to London from Croydon Crown Court, Merrion managed to find a seat in a different carriage from the defending counsel she'd been against in court that day. She'd won – not really to her satisfaction, not well – and he hadn't liked it and had wanted his solicitor to complain to hers about inadequate instructions. Merrion's solicitor had refused, and the defending counsel – a heavy, competitive man in his early forties – had said loudly that he'd have to have it out with Miss Palmer.

'I'd hop it,' Merrion's solicitor said to her, 'if I were you.'

She'd run, literally, to the railway station. As she hurried out of the court building, she'd seen her client – a thin-faced divorced woman in her forties with three wayward children – in a sulky huddle with her boyfriend and her mother. Merrion had won financial support, backdated for two years, from her ex-husband – who had briefly worked for an oil company in the Gulf and, while there, had made a half-hearted attempt to take his children with him – but her client didn't think it was enough. She'd wanted two hundred pounds a week. Her ex-husband was earning three hundred and ten pounds a week. She didn't care, she said, she wanted what she wanted. What did it matter if the bugger starved? Merrion had won a payment of eighty pounds a week, and the backdate. Her client had glared. She wouldn't speak to Merrion, after the judgement.

'Bloody shower,' she'd said, audibly, to her boyfriend.

A train for Central London was just pulling out as Merrion ran on to the platform. It didn't matter. There were trains from Croydon every twenty minutes and in any case, the timing of her meeting with Guy's daughter-in-law in a wine bar near Victoria Station had been left deliberately vague.

'I don't know why I feel we shouldn't meet somewhere too obvious,' Carrie said, 'but I seem to. Do you mind?'

'No,' Merrion said. 'It suits me.' It had occurred to her to point out that, if the meeting took place somewhere anonymous, and turned out not to be a success, then they could somehow pretend it hadn't happened, erase it from the story. But she refrained. Something in Carrie's voice told her that she was thinking that anyway: that she didn't need to be told.

Merrion bought a copy of the evening newspaper and retreated to the back of the railway platform, half hidden by a chocolate vending machine. She saw the defending counsel come on to the platform and look about him. He was a solid man, confident-looking, with a black velvet collar to his overcoat, and he stood out, as lawyers she had often noticed seemed to, in ordinary crowds on public transport. If he was looking for Merrion, he wasn't looking very hard. She held the newspaper up, opened out, in front of her face, and waited until he had passed her on his way to the station bar. She visualised him getting back to his family house in Clapham or Tooting or Stockwell and his wife – streaked hair, urbanely casual clothes – saying, 'Marcus, the Fergusons can't come this weekend after all, Sophie's got nits – what do we pay that school? – and you stink of whisky.' Merrion lowered the paper, and turned furtively to her horoscope for the next day – 'If they worked,' Guy said to her, 'the word "future" would cease to exist' – and read that she was to expect no surprises and should make no major decisions. She tried to remember what last night's horoscope had said about today, and failed. If it had felt her meeting with Carrie had any significance, it plainly hadn't shown it.

When the train came in, she allowed Marcus Hunt to board it ahead of her, and chose a carriage well away from his. Even if a single pub whisky had mellowed him, he would still unquestionably want to patronise her and in some ways being patronised was even more unpalatable than being quarrelled with: a quarrel presupposed, at least, some small equality. She found a seat next to a man engrossed in his laptop, opposite a girl in a leather jacket and red lipstick asleep with her mouth open. Merrion often fell asleep on trains and worried about her mouth dropping open. This girl looked as if she hardly cared.

'I think,' Guy said at the weekend, 'that you will like Carrie. I certainly do.'

'Does it matter?'

'If you like her? I suppose – I suppose I'd rather you did.'

'It was nice of her to ring me,' Merrion said. She was lying along her sofa, her head in Guy's lap, and he was reading a Sunday newspaper above her, with his arms held high, to keep the newsprint off her face.

'She's slightly acerbic in manner, but don't let that put you off.'

'I can be acerbic too –'

'I know.'

'Three kids,' Merrion said. 'Think of it. How old is she?'

Guy rested the newspaper on Merrion's stomach.

'Forty-ish. Maybe less.'

'Wow. Three kids.'

'But not a promising career at the Bar.'

'Why did you say that?'

'To stop you making pointless comparisons.'

'It doesn't, however.'

'Carrie's father is a doctor. A GP in East Anglia. Her mother died quite a long time ago. That's hard. Carrie loved her.'

'Lucky her.'

Guy had bent over to look at her.

'Why do you insist on regarding your mother in this way?'

'Because it's how it is.'

'I think you've never grown out of thinking how glamorous it would be to be an orphan.'

'Wrong.'

'I would never have expected to be close to my mother,' Guy said. 'I didn't regard our relationship as confidential and nor, I think, did she.'

Merrion reared up from the sofa and kissed him.

'But that's because things were different in your day –'

'Long, *long* ago?'

'Right,' she said. She grinned.

He smiled back.

'And now I can't talk to my own children, either.'

Merrion swung her feet to the floor and felt about for her shoes.

'Can you talk to Carrie?'

He put a hand out and took hold of a handful of her thick hair.

'I've never tried. It hasn't seemed, well –'

'Proper?'

'Perhaps. She's Simon's –'

'But with a mind of her own?'

'Oh yes,' Guy said. 'You'll see that. At once.'

Merrion thought it must be Carrie, sitting at a corner table with a glass of red wine in front of her, scowling at the crossword in the newspaper. She was tapping her teeth with a pen. She had fair hair held up here and there with combs, and she wore a grey overcoat slung across her shoulders. Merrion made her way among the tables, holding her heavy briefcase up high out of people's way. She stopped in front of Carrie's table and rested her briefcase on the edge of it.

Carrie looked up.

'Merrion?'

'Yes –'

'You're taller than I thought.'

'Five eleven,' Merrion said.

Carrie gave a faint smile.

'Lucky you. All my children will be taller than me any minute and then the last possibility of discipline will vanish.'

Merrion pulled a chair out and sat down. She put her briefcase on the chair next to her and shrugged out of her coat.

'Wine?' Carrie said. 'I'm afraid you have to go and get it.'

Merrion stood up again. Carrie watched her weave her way to the bar. She wore a black suit, the jacket quite fitted, the skirt narrow. She looked good in it, Carrie decided, good figure, good carriage, interesting hair. She imagined Guy looking at Merrion. Very exciting. Very gratifying. Very – well, unexpected, fresh, energetic. She thought of Simon looking at her, too, confronting the fact that she was distinctive, almost dramatic, but not vampish, not obvious, not in any way easily dismissable. Simon would be in a terrible confusion. So would she, for that matter, watching him watching Merrion. She took a big swallow of her red wine. Thirty-one! When she, Carrie, was thirty-one, she'd had three young children and no money and no ambition much beyond getting to the end of each day without spinning off into a vortex. She glanced at

Merrion's briefcase. She certainly hadn't had a career. The word didn't exist in her vocabulary, not then. If it had, she'd have scorned it, anyway.

Merrion put a glass of white wine down beside her briefcase. Carrie looked at her hands. No ring.

'No ring,' Merrion said. She was smiling. 'Guy wants one. I don't. So, no ring.'

'Will you have a wedding ring?' Carrie said.

Merrion slid into her chair.

'Shouldn't think so.'

Carrie looked at her own hands.

'I wear mine to work because it makes me look more approachable. Married equals cosy. I work in a medical practice. I manage it, in so far as I manage anything much.'

Merrion took a sip of her wine. She said, 'Did you just want to have a look at me?'

'Yes,' Carrie said. She took a comb out of her hair, and stuck it back in again, in exactly the same place. 'I wanted to see the reality. When someone's just a name in a situation like this, they can become a sort of bogy.'

'I wouldn't know,' Merrion said, 'I've never been in anything remotely like this in my life before.'

'There's a lot of drama –'

'Plainly.'

'And things get distorted. People get angry.'

Merrion looked down into her wineglass.

'Like your husband.'

'Like Simon.'

Merrion said hesitantly, 'He has his mother to protect –'

'We'll talk about that,' Carrie said, 'when we're further down the line. If we get that far.'

Merrion picked her wineglass up and put it down again.

'Presumably you have an agenda.'

'No,' Carrie said, 'I told you. I just wanted to see the reality. It's odd when a crisis happens in your partner's family – you are at once absolutely involved and not

99

involved at all. You spend a lot of time grappling with emotions on someone else's behalf. I just felt I could cope with what Simon's coping with if I met you.'

Merrion gave her a quick glance.

'Guy likes you.'

'I like him,' Carrie said. 'People have awful times with their fathers-in-law, being pawed or ignored or bossed about. He hasn't done any of that. He leaves me alone.'

'He'd like to talk to – to your husband.'

'Yes.'

'I don't know much about how men in families work together,' Merrion said. 'My father died when I was three. I haven't any brothers or sisters.'

Carrie picked up her wineglass.

'They're different. They watch each other all the time. They interpret actions instead of talking.'

'Are they competitive?' Merrion said.

Carrie gave her a sharp look.

'Yes.'

Merrion drank some wine.

'I see.' She flicked a glance at Carrie. 'So you have your own position to defend?'

'Don't go so fast,' Carrie said.

'I'm learning,' Merrion said. 'I'm learning all the time.'

'You've had seven *years* –'

'A secret love affair,' Merrion said, 'is a piece of cake compared to this.'

'Preferable?'

'In a way. But you can't keep it that way, either.'

'My Aunt Cath,' Carrie said, 'says life is like trying to pack kittens in a basket. You get the last one in and the first one is already climbing out the other side.'

'I'm not particularly possessive,' Merrion said, rolling her glass between her hands, 'but I've been taken aback by the degree to which people belong to other people. Or believe they do. Not feeling free to act is one thing entirely. But not feeling free to even *decide* is quite another.'

'Perhaps you never gave much thought to Guy's life outside yours before.'

'Perhaps,' Merrion said. She looked at Carrie. 'And perhaps nobody in Guy's life outside mine gave much thought to *Guy*, before.'

'Whoops,' Carrie said. She emptied her glass and began to put her arms into her coat. 'I ought to go. I told a lie about where I'd gone so I'd better not make it a very long lie.'

'Why did you lie?'

'My daughters would be insatiably curious and Simon would be hurt.'

'He'd think you disloyal?'

Carrie said nothing. She stood up and stuffed her newspaper into her handbag. Merrion stood, too. She moved the table a little so that Carrie could get out.

'Can I ask you one more thing?'

Carrie paused, but she didn't look at her.

'What?'

'Did I pass the test?'

'What test?'

'You know,' Merrion said, 'the real reason we're here. Which am I? Friend or foe?'

Simon drove down to Stanborough alone. He had told Carrie he was going, but not Alan. Alan would have offered to come, too, and Carrie would have encouraged him to. Both of them, Simon knew, wanted to save him from Laura and, at the same time, neither of them understood the precise nature of his obligation to her. Carrie said, in fact, that the precise nature didn't trouble her much: it was the *strength* she found so hard to contend with.

'We'd never have married!' she'd screamed long ago

during one particular row (the children had been lined up along the landing, horrified and spellbound). 'If I hadn't been pregnant! Your mother would have seen to that!'

Laura had, admittedly, told Simon he was far too young to think of marrying. Twenty-one was absurdly young, especially for a man, especially for a man not yet qualified, one year out of university. And twenty-one was too young for Carrie, too, particularly as, having abandoned medicine for no good reason Laura could see, she hadn't decided what else to do. Of *course* she got pregnant! What else was there for her to do, in her self-inflicted dilemma, *but* get pregnant and have all subsequent decisions taken out of her hands? Vainly, Simon had tried to explain that Carrie didn't want to be pregnant, hadn't meant to be, was only going to go through with it because the baby was Simon's, Simon's and hers. Laura saw Simon as trapped. Simon saw Carrie as trapped. Carrie saw Simon as trapped, twice over.

'Her. And now me.'

'I *want* you.'

'I hope you do.'

He did. Seventeen years later, he still did. Carrie was the one decision – if, indeed, she'd ever been anything so crisp and deliberate – of Simon's life that he had never doubted. He took her on, hoping at some unexpressed level that she'd set him free. And she did. Or, almost, anyway: certainly, as much as she could, as much as he'd let her. If he really let her, he'd either be driving down to Stanborough now with Alan, or not be driving down at all.

Carrie had asked Laura to come and stay.

'I won't, thank you. It's sweet of you, but –'

'Just a few days,' Carrie said, her eyes shut, concentrating on making her voice sound as she wished her feeling felt. 'Change of scene, a diversion.'

'The dogs –'

'Can't they go into kennels?'

'I don't like to send them, at the moment. I don't like to leave them.'

'Bring them then –'

'Oh, I couldn't. I couldn't do that. They never go anywhere, you see. It really is good of you, but I'm better here, really I am. Perhaps Simon –'

'Bloody maddening,' Carrie said, after she put the phone down. 'All that pure obstinacy masquerading as the poor victim.'

Rachel was leaning against the wall by the telephone, waiting for Trudy's line not to be engaged.

'D'you mean Gran?'

'I do, as it happens. But you shouldn't have been listening.'

'You shouldn't shout then.'

'I'm afraid,' Carrie said, sweeping past Rachel with an armful of unironed laundry, 'that your grandmother is enough to make anybody shout.'

Rachel looked at her father.

'Wow!'

'Sometimes,' Simon said stiffly, 'it's a bit hard for one generation to understand the problems of another generation.'

Rachel grinned.

'Tell me about it.'

'Very funny.'

'C'mon, Dad. Gran's never been very nice to Mum. Has she?'

'Rachel,' Simon said, 'I don't really want to talk about it. Not now.'

Rachel turned her back and began dialling Trudy's number.

'Or ever,' she said.

She was right, of course. He didn't want to talk about it. He didn't want to have to say out loud that he agreed with Carrie's view and Rachel's view – even if he did – because of the implications and consequences of such a confession as far as Laura was concerned. In fact, this Thursday afternoon driving westward, he felt fairly irritated by Laura himself, not just because of her attitude and current conduct, but also because it was so fiendishly difficult to get time away from the office, and his partners were beginning to complain.

'C'mon, Simon,' Ted Freeman had said, 'your father hasn't *died*, has he?'

Sometimes recently, Simon thought it might have been a lot easier if he *had*. If Guy was dead, there'd be none of these recriminations and resentments and endless, hopeless, pointless conversations about what went wrong. He could see Laura, as a widow. She'd make a very decent widow, quiet, carrying her grief and solitude with a sort of small distinction. Simon felt he could have handled the widow in a way he seemed unable to handle the wronged wife. Mothers make widows quite naturally, he thought, it's a kind of tradition. But mothers as abandoned women? Simon saw the turning off the Stanborough ring road almost too late and wrenched the steering wheel round, without signalling, causing a furious blaring of horns from surrounding braking cars.

'Sorry,' he mouthed through the window glass. 'Sorry.'

Stupid to do that. *Stupid.* He knew the Stanborough roads as well as he knew any besides those in his own part of South London. He leaned forward a little in the driving seat, as if to concentrate better. Six miles now. Six miles down lanes he had cycled so endlessly as a boy, not looking where he was going so much as staring at the speedometer to see if he was covering this stretch a few seconds faster than he'd done it the day before. He thought of Carrie. '*Plus ça change*,' she'd say.

Laura was stooping in the garden, pulling the dead heads off daffodils. The dogs were lying six feet away, waiting for her to do something more interesting. Above them, the apple trees were in fat bud. When she saw the car come down the lane, Laura crossed the rough orchard grass to the drive, so that she was standing, waiting, when Simon pulled up.

'You are so sweet to come.'

He bent to be kissed.

'You look tired,' she said. She touched his forehead.

'Probably because I am.'

'Did you have any lunch?'

'Do you really want to know?'

'Yes –'

'I had a Twix bar,' Simon said. 'I bought it when I stopped for petrol.'

'Why didn't you buy a sandwich? Something sensible?'

'Because, Mum, I wanted a Twix bar.'

Laura put her hand inside his arm.

'I'm going to make you a sandwich now.'

'Thank you,' Simon said. He glanced down at her. She looked small and pale and neat. She had her pearl earrings on. When she took off her gardening gloves and put a hand out to calm the dogs bounding round them, he noticed that she was no longer wearing her wedding ring. She'd always worn it, along, usually, with her engagement ring which she used to twist backwards, if doing any rough jobs, to protect the stones in it.

'No ring,' he said.

She didn't look at him. She disengaged her arm and took a step ahead and opened the back door. She said, over her shoulder, 'Well, it's over, isn't it?'

Simon said, 'I haven't seen him –'

'Haven't you?'

'No.'

'Have you spoken to him?'

'Once.'

'And?'

'It lasted three minutes,' Simon said. 'My fault. I lost my temper.'

Laura said, her voice warmed with pleasure, 'I don't blame you.'

Simon moved across the kitchen towards the bread bin. It was square and made of white enamel, with BREAD stencilled on the side in black. He had known it all his life. He put a hand on it now, as if for reassurance.

'I'll make your sandwich,' Laura said.

'Mum, I really can –'

'No,' she said. 'I'll do it. I want to.' She pulled a chair out from the table. 'Sit down.'

He sat, awkwardly. She took a banana out of the fruit bowl and put it down in front of him. 'Eat that while you're waiting.'

He looked at the banana. He said, 'I'm not ill, Mum. I'm not a child, either. I'm just a father of three with rather more on his plate than is quite manageable just now who, as I do most of the time, missed lunch.'

Laura was slicing bread, and cheese. She said brightly, 'How's work?'

'There's an endless amount of it and seemingly no time to do it in.'

'But you have partners –'

'Yes, I do. But we have more work than we have people to do it.'

'Why don't you hire someone else?'

Simon pushed the banana away from him.

'Because the figures don't quite permit that yet.'

Laura put a plate down in front of him. It bore a thick brown-bread cheese sandwich. His mouth watered.

'Then we're going to have to come to some arrangement.'

He looked at her. She had turned away and was rummaging in the cupboard.

'What?'

'Well, I can't expect you to do everything for nothing. Not with Carrie and the children to support. Here we are. Apple and walnut chutney. I made it last September.'

'Mum,' Simon said, 'what are you going on about?'

Laura went past him, putting the chutney jar on the table as she went, and plugged in the kettle. Then she turned back to Simon. Her expression was bright and slightly detached, as if she'd been rehearsing what she was about to say.

'I told you,' she said, 'it's over.'

'I know that –'

'And I don't want to have anything more to do with it. Or him. I telephoned him this morning and told him so. I want – I want to *erase* him.'

Simon pushed the sandwich plate away, too.

'But, Mum, nothing's sorted. Not the house, nor money, nor Dad's will or pension, not the divorce, *nothing*. We haven't even started.'

'I'm not starting,' Laura said. She spooned tea into a teapot.

'You –'

'I'm not,' she said, 'you are.'

Simon put his head in his hands.

'I came down today,' he said with resolute steadiness, 'at immense personal and professional inconvenience, to start talking to you about finding the right person to represent you and to discuss what sort of deal you wanted. I came, Mum, to get the ball rolling. You agreed. Alan agreed. We all agreed.'

'Sorry,' Laura said. She didn't sound it.

'What do you mean, sorry?'

'Sorry, but I'm not doing any of that.'

She put a cork mat painted with flowers on the table and then the teapot on top of the cork mat.

'I didn't want you to come down here on false pretences,' she said, 'but it would be worse if you went away under them, too. I'm not having any more to do with this, Simon. I'm not instructing solicitors, I'm not planning strategies, I'm not – most emphatically not – having one more single thing to do with your father.'

He leaned across the table towards her. He said incredulously, 'But you want a settlement, don't you? You want a fair share of the assets, don't you?'

'Of course I do. I want that very much. It's the least I'm owed.'

'Then we have to discuss it. You have to have a lawyer. You have to tell professional people what you want them to do for you. You have to have *some* communication with Dad.'

Laura began to pour the tea into blue-and-white-flowered cups.

'No, I don't.'

'Mum!' Simon shouted.

She pushed a teacup towards him.

'I'm going to leave it to you,' she said. 'You're on my side, you know what's due to me. I don't have to do anything more, Simon, because you are going to do it for me.'

CHAPTER EIGHT

Alone in his chambers in Stanborough Crown Court, Guy dialled Simon's work number. A girl answered. Simon, and Ted Freeman and Philip Stott, employed an endless series of girls as receptionists who stayed just long enough to have some idea of the nature and customs of the firm before leaving for an identical job, to relieve the tedium.

'Is that Nicky?' Guy said.

'No,' the girl said, 'it's Miriam.'

'Miriam,' Guy said, 'this is Guy Stockdale. Simon's father. I wonder if I could have a quick word with him?'

Miriam said laconically, 'He's with a client.'

'And when do you think he will be free?'

'He didn't say. He's got appointments until six-thirty.'

'Perhaps,' Guy said, 'you could give him a message then?'

'OK,' Miriam said. He heard her rustling for something to write on.

'Just say that his father called and would very much like to speak to him urgently. I'll give you my number.'

'OK,' Miriam said again.

Guy put the phone down. He looked at the notepad beside it. He had written, 'Ring Simon' at the top of the sheet, and while he was telephoning, he had somehow drawn lines round Simon's name, giving it black emphasis.

Simon had been in Stanborough yesterday. He had been to see Laura. Guy knew this because Laura had telephoned him to tell him that she was having nothing further to do with him, ever, and that Simon was now going to take her cause up for her, entirely, completely.

'Have you asked him?' Guy said, as gently as he could.

'I don't need to,' Laura said. She sounded hard and deliberate, as if she was saying something she'd set herself to say.

'Do you think that's fair?' Guy said. 'Fair on Simon?'

There was a small pause and then Laura said, in the same intentional voice, 'It will be what he wants.' Then she'd said, 'Goodbye,' with a formal emphasis on the first syllable, and put the telephone down.

Guy had looked at his watch. Simon would have been in his car, alone, on the motorway. Guy could have called him, on his mobile, before he got to Hill Cottage, before Laura gave him her extraordinary instructions. He could have, and he didn't. He spent, instead, a small and intense amount of time praying that Simon might think to come and find him, in the court building, even if it was only to shout at him, and then he tried to turn his attention, energetically, to work in hand. 'Please,' he'd found himself saying at intervals to himself all afternoon. '*Please.*' Simon didn't come.

'Keep hoping,' Merrion said, from London that night. 'Keep trying.'

'The former is easier than the latter.'

'That's why the latter works more often.'

'You're such a Puritan –'

'Are you OK?' she said.

'No,' Guy said. 'Not tonight.'

Guy had found if difficult to concentrate in court, afterwards. Twice, he'd been virtually reprimanded.

'Your Honour,' the prosecuting counsel had said

loudly, pointedly loudly. 'Your Honour, I am referring to sheet *eight* of the transcript.'

And then, an hour later on, a harried witness, whom he should have rescued from the prosecuting counsel ten minutes before, turned to him in anguish from the witness box and almost shouted, 'Do you think I would have waited thirteen months for this court case to stand here and *lie*?'

He had apologised. He had apologised twice. He felt obliged to. The barrister had looked complacent; the witness startled. Guy had put his hand on the stout legal volume that lay always on the bench before him – *Blackstone's Criminal Practice* (dark-blue and gold) – to centre himself, steady his thoughts. When the usher finally made the court stand at four-thirty, for his departure, he felt oddly weak, almost giddy, as if he'd been fighting to acclimatise himself to something utterly unfamiliar.

'You all right, Judge?' the court manager said, stopping halfway across the public foyer.

'Yes, thank you, Martin, I'm fine –'

'You look a bit pale –'

'Not much air in Court Two. You know.'

'Weird, isn't it? People who can design security can't design ventilation.'

The two advocates went past at a pace, robes swinging.

'Night, Judge –'

'Good-night,' Guy said.

'Fearful hotel,' one said to the other. 'Fearful. Used to be a knocking shop.'

'Still is.'

Martin grinned at Guy.

'The Bell. They were staying at the Bell –'

'A knocking shop?'

'Not a very successful one, Judge. More the railway trade. Can I get you some water?'

'Thank you, Martin, I'll be fine. I'll open the window in my room.'

He moved on towards the half-glazed door that led to the judges' corridor. Martin watched him. The usher came out of the courtroom's side door and watched him, too.

'He looks his age today,' the usher said. 'He doesn't usually.'

'Something's up,' Martin said.

Guy opened the door, went through it and closed it carefully behind him. They could see his big shadow looming behind the frosted glass. His shadowy arm went up and removed his wig.

'What kind of thing?'

'I don't think he's going home at nights,' Martin said.

'Where's he going, then?'

'Out towards Pinns Green. And he's off like a rabbit, Fridays. To the station.'

'You been following him?'

'No,' Martin said, 'but I've been noticing. He looks like a man with something on his mind. Doesn't he? Does he look like a happy man to you?'

Gwen Palmer had brought her own sandwiches with her, to eat on the train. Merrion would have laughed at her, she knew, would have told her she was turning into an old thing on an awayday pensioner's excursion ten years before she needed to. But for Gwen, the journey to London was quite enough by itself without worrying about train buffet cars and being ignored by the bartender in favour of big men buying spirits. After all, she was having to come up during an evening, in order to have any hope of catching Merrion on her own, and evenings spelled automatic alarm for Gwen anyway, never mind long-distance train journeys and the prospect of almost unknown London. She would take taxis. She had resolved upon that. She wouldn't make things harder for herself than she simply had to, so she had brought sandwiches, and would take taxis.

It had dawned upon Gwen, during the last telephone call with Merrion, that their lives were now so far apart in thought, word and deed, that it was sometimes difficult to believe that Merrion's childhood and adolescence had actually happened the way they had. Of course Gwen was proud of Merrion. Who wouldn't be proud of a daughter with such professional accomplishment as Merrion's? And yet there lurked in Gwen's mind an apprehension that Merrion had, for all the glory and shine of her life in London, taken some kind of wrong turning, set off down some path that seemed, almost inevitably, to lead away from all the things that Gwen believed – had believed all her life – contributed to womanly fulfilment. If she tried to intimate this to Merrion, Merrion told her she didn't understand, even angrily once, that she didn't know anything.

'I do,' Gwen said. She was angry, too, clutching a tea towel. 'I do, so. I've been married twice and I'm a mother, which is more than you can say for yourself.'

'I'm joining you,' Merrion said, her voice suddenly quiet. 'I'm getting married. I'm going to get married, too.'

Gwen had burst into tears. She hadn't meant to, but they had rushed up her throat and out of her eyes before she could stop them.

'Oh Merrion –'

'Don't,' Merrion said.

'It's you that needs don't!' Gwen had shrieked. 'It's you that needs stopping, from throwing your life away!'

Merrion had said nothing. She had risen from where she had been sitting at the kitchen table, collected her coat and her bag and her briefcase, and had walked out of the house. She hadn't even looked at Gwen; she certainly didn't speak to her. She just opened the front door and stepped out of it and went down the street in the direction of the town centre and she didn't look back. Not once.

That had been three weeks ago. Gwen had done a great deal of thinking in those three weeks. She catalogued, in her mind, all the things that in her view Merrion was doing wrong, all the things that would ultimately lead to a feeling that her life – as a human being – had hardly been worth the candle. Everything that was wrong came back, of course, to this man, this dratted man with his voice and his education and his legal position and his wife and his children and his grandchildren. Gwen could sometimes hardly believe Merrion's stubbornness about Guy Stockdale. Seven years! Seven years out of a young woman's life already thrown away, and now she was blithely proposing to throw away the rest. *Marry* him! Sleeping with him had been hard enough for Gwen to contend with – but *marriage*. She had conducted long diatribes to Merrion on the walk to her – now part-time – job. She had found that, without Merrion there in the flesh, the words came very easily, flowing furiously out of her mind and into her mouth. On these walks, Gwen told Merrion, angrily and silently, about everything that had ever happened to her, about how she'd felt, how she'd coped and how all that gave her both a right and a duty to try and prevent Merrion just wasting herself. Sometimes, so keenly did she feel what she was mutely describing, she dissolved into tears, just like that, walking the pavements on her way to work. It was impossible to believe that Merrion couldn't see how much she *minded*.

But then she began to notice that Merrion had stopped ringing. She hadn't rung since she had walked out. There weren't many people who rang Gwen anyway, heaven knows, but Merrion's calls were significant. Whatever Gwen felt about her life in London, there was no doubt that, when she rang, Gwen caught a breath of another air, the note of a different tune. It occurred to her that, if she refused to acknowledge Merrion's private life, if she resolutely pretended that what was happening wasn't happening, then Merrion would simply withdraw. Rather than tell Gwen things and be criticised, she would cease to tell her anything. The rare visits would stop. So would the phone calls. And with them would go Gwen's passport to Merrion, to – as far as she saw it – her future. If Gwen lost touch with Merrion, she would be left staring at a wall.

She considered telephoning. She liked answering the telephone but had always dreaded initiating calls. She thought of Merrion's answering machine; she thought of the chance of Guy answering the telephone. She was suddenly struck, instead, by a bold plan. She would just go to London. She would choose a day when she wasn't working the day after, and she would catch a late-afternoon train from Cardiff and go and see Merrion. In her flat. Just like that. She would simply *do* it. If Merrion was out, she would write a note and put it through Merrion's door. That would be almost as effective as actually seeing her. Whatever, Gwen told herself, it was a journey worth making.

She found a taxi at Paddington with no trouble. It was dusk and a light rain was falling, blurring the air and the car headlights and the lights in houses and shops. Gwen took her umbrella out of her bag. If Merrion wasn't in she might have a long, damp wait. She could wait two hours, she had calculated, there'd be two hours before she had to find another taxi and go back to Paddington for the train.

The taxi stopped in a wide street of huge white terraced houses, flat-fronted except for pillared porches over broad flights of steps. There seemed to be, as far as Gwen could see in the dimness, a froth of trees at the end of the street. She got out on to the pavement with her bag and her holdall and her umbrella and gave the taxi driver too much money out of nervousness that she might give him too little.

'Silly,' she said to herself. '*Silly.*'

She went up the steps. There was a panel of entryphone buttons beside the door, each with a dimly illuminated name beside it.

'Palmer. M.', the top one said. 'Flat 6'.

Gwen took a deep breath and shut her eyes. Then she opened them again and pressed the bell. There was a crackle and a hum and then a further crackle and a man's voice said, 'Darling? Did you forget your keys?'

Gwen froze. She gazed in horror at the entryphone panel.

'Merrion?' the man's voice said. 'Merrion?'

Gwen took a step back.

'Who's there?' the man said. 'Who is it?'

Gwen said nothing. She retreated to the edge of the porch and stood gazing at the entryphone. Something like a small sigh came from it, and then there was a decided click, as if a telephone receiver had been put down, and then silence. Gwen leaned against one of the huge pillars that held up the porch. It had '43' painted on it in decided black numbers, just above her head. She looked across, again, at the entryphone. It had been *him*.

She felt, suddenly, rather peculiar, almost faint, as if she'd had a shock. She took some deep breaths, the kind they'd told her to take all those years ago when Merrion was being born. She took several, obediently, leaning against the pillar, her eyes closed. Then she opened her eyes again.

'He's up there,' she said to herself. 'He's up there, in her flat, and she isn't home yet. Gwen, you wouldn't *dare*. Would you?'

She stood upright for a moment. Then she put her umbrella away, adjusted her bag and holdall and transferred them to her left hand, stepped quickly across the porch and pressed the bell again. The crackle came once more, then the hum and then the man's voice said, 'Either tell me what you want, or go away.'

Gwen stood up straight. She put her mouth close to the entryphone grille.

'It's Mrs Palmer,' she said.

There was a silence, a small, intense, complicated silence and then a buzzer sounded and the man said, 'Push the door. Come in.'

Gwen pushed. The door swung open, still buzzing, and Gwen found herself in a long high hallway with a staircase at the far end and a lot of mail scattered about, some on the ledge that ran the length of the hallway at chair-rail height, some just all anyhow, on the floor. Gwen went cautiously forward, avoiding the letters. It seemed wrong to tread on letters, even circulars. She reached the foot of the staircase and put her hand on the rail. Someone was coming down the stairs, fast, running. She got six steps up, almost to the first half-turn, and he appeared, almost leaping down.

'Mrs Palmer –'

Gwen said nothing. She held the handrail, hard. He came down until he was on the same step as she was. He was in a dark suit, she noticed. His shoes were polished. He leaned to take her bags.

'Let me take those. I'm so sorry, but the lift is broken. It's a bit of a climb.'

Gwen opened her mouth to say it didn't matter, and nothing happened. He was good-looking. Merrion hadn't said he was good-looking, hadn't said that, if you hadn't known his age, you wouldn't have guessed it. But then, she, Gwen, hadn't let her say such things, had she? She hadn't let her tell her anything about Guy Stockdale, in case knowing about him turned him into a reality, instead of some kind of unpleasant, improbable notion that might never come to anything.

They began to climb the stairs together. He was half turned towards her as they climbed, her bags in his right hand and his left partly outstretched as if to steady her, help her. He wasn't going to get out of breath, she could see that. She was. She hoped she wouldn't have to stop before they got to the top; she didn't want to be at any kind of disadvantage.

'I expect,' he said, 'you were hoping to find Merrion. Not me.'

She nodded.

'I don't usually come up to London on Wednesdays, but I'd had rather a tough day, so I indulged myself.'

She nodded again, her eyes on the fleur-de-lis in the carpet ahead of her, step after red step.

'She should be home any minute. She was in Peterborough today. She will be so pleased to see you.'

Gwen said, 'I don't think so.' Her voice came out in little gasps. It was the first thing she'd said to him.

He took her elbow.

'One more flight. Think of getting furniture up here.'

Or a baby, Gwen thought, without wanting to. She tried to remove her arm from his grasp, but he was holding her firmly. A skylight swung slowly into view above them, and then, at last, they were on a small landing with a weeping fig tree in a terracotta pot and a cream-painted front door. Merrion's front door.

Guy put a key in the lock and turned it, then stood aside so that Gwen could go in ahead of him. She stepped in, slowly, turning her head this way and that, taking it in, telling herself that this was how Merrion liked things, that this was how Merrion lived. It was very light, very pale. It looked, to Gwen, like something in a magazine, a flat where everything has been carefully chosen to make a whole, instead of just evolving because this was just the stuff she already had.

Guy put her bags down beside a long, cream-coloured sofa.

'Can I make you a cup of tea? Or get you a glass of wine?'

'Tea, please,' Gwen said.

He indicated the sofa.

'Do sit down.' He hesitated, and then he said, 'The bathroom is over there. Through the bedroom.'

The bedroom! Gwen swallowed. She sat on the edge of one end of the cream sofa. There was a low table in front of her, foreign-looking, with carved legs, covered with books and magazines and the newspaper Guy had probably been reading when she rang the doorbell. There was a vase of flowers on it, those Peruvian lily things that lasted so well, deep rusty red. On the floor – polished wood – there were rugs. They looked foreign, too, strips and blocks of rough weaving. No flowers. Gwen looked round the room. Except for the actual flowers on the low table, there wasn't a flower in the room. Merrion never wore flowers either, never had. Gwen couldn't remember when she'd seen Merrion in a flower-patterned anything, not even in summer.

Guy came out of what Gwen supposed was a little kitchen and put a tray on the table in front of her. There was a small white teapot on it and a white cup and saucer and milk in a white jug and a square blue box of sugar cubes.

'Sorry about the sugar,' Guy said. 'Shall I leave you to pour out for yourself?'

She nodded. He went round the table to a low chair opposite and sat down. He said uncertainly, 'I am – pleased to meet you.'

Gwen poured her tea. She added milk and one sugar lump. He had forgotten a teaspoon. She gave the teacup a little shake, to help the sugar dissolve. She was here, she told herself. She had come to London and found Merrion's flat and rung the bell and got herself up here. With him. She mustn't waste it.

'I want to say something to you,' she said.

He waited. He had leaned forward a little, his elbows on his knees. He was watching her.

119

'You are ruining my daughter's life,' Gwen said.

He bowed his head. She picked up her teacup – her hand wasn't at all steady – and took a sip.

'It's not that I think you don't love her. I know she loves you. But what's a man your age doing with a girl of thirty-one?'

Guy looked up at her. His eyes were veiled. Sad-looking.

'It's greedy,' Gwen said. She put her teacup down. 'I didn't mean to say this. I didn't intend to see you, after all. But now we're here, I've got to. I couldn't forgive myself if I didn't. You've got everything she'll never have because you're too old to let her have it. Suppose she wants a baby?'

He put his hands briefly over his eyes.

'If she has a baby,' Gwen said, 'you'll be dead before it's grown-up. Have you thought of that?'

'Yes,' Guy said.

'And she'll be on her own for years and years. All that proper family life you've had, children and grandchildren, she'll never have that. Or not in the way you've had it.'

He said, steadily, 'I've said this to her.'

'Have you?'

'And her reply is that she knows and she would still prefer to have the unorthodoxy of her relationship with me than – than any alternative.'

Gwen took another sip of tea.

'But she's never known anything but you. There was that boy when she first came to London but he didn't count. There's never been anyone but you. You haven't given her a chance.'

'I haven't kept her against her will –'

'But you haven't taken yourself off, either, have you? You didn't say to her, sorry, Merrion, I have a wife and family responsibilities and they are my first priority, did you? You didn't take yourself back to where you belonged, did you?'

'No –'

'You might have broken her heart,' Gwen said, amazed at the words lining up in her head all ready to march out of her mouth just as they did during those silent, one-sided conversations with Merrion. 'At the beginning. You might have broken it then, for a while, if you'd walked away. Just for a while. But you'll break it anyway, now, won't you, sooner or later?'

Guy stood up. He looked very tall, in that small light room, tall and imposing.

'Don't think you're saying anything I haven't already thought or said. I know. I know all this. Anything I say –' He stopped.

'Well?'

'Anything I say to you about the human heart will sound so feeble, so self-indulgent, so unrealistic . . . But she is my ideal companion. And I am hers. There's a feeling of – of *belonging* together. No – no, not a feeling. A knowledge. A recognition. It was there from the beginning. I wasn't looking for it. Nor was she.'

Gwen said sharply, 'Anybody can do that.'

He gave a little sigh. She looked up at him.

'I know,' he said. He went across to a tray of bottles Gwen hadn't noticed before and poured himself some whisky. He said, his back still turned, 'We may be a living cliché, but that doesn't make us any less *true*.'

Gwen drained her teacup.

'You're a stubborn man.'

He said, his voice suddenly much louder, 'That's the *last* thing I am!'

Gwen looked at the floor.

'I am trying to be patient,' Guy said. He came back to his chair, holding his whisky glass. 'I acknowledge the justice, for you at least, of what you say. Don't forget, I have children of the sort of age Merrion is, children – sons – of whom I still feel extremely protective. I know why you're saying what you're saying. I've let you call me greedy and selfish and unfeeling. But I will *not* be labelled stubborn, too. I will *not* have it implied that I'm not changing my mind for reasons of simple, stupid obstinacy.'

Gwen began to tremble slightly. The feeling of strange exhilaration that had buoyed her up so far was beginning to leak away, leaving her feeling – as she had so often felt, all her life – that she had bitten off more than she could chew. Her mother had always warned her, 'Don't start something, Gwen, if you can't finish it.' Ed had been different. Ed had egged her on. It was one of the things that had made her fall in love with him – he'd seemed to see capacities in her she couldn't see in herself.

She said, with a tremulousness she much regretted, 'You shouldn't shout at me. I'm Merrion's mother.'

He put his whisky glass down.

'I hope I wasn't shouting –'

'You raised your voice –'

'I shouldn't have done,' Guy said. 'I'm sorry.'

She said, still looking at the floor, 'I ought to go.'

'Mrs Palmer –'

She waited.

'Mrs Palmer, we ought to be on the same side. We both love Merrion better than anyone else.'

'Better?'

'Yes,' he said, 'even me. I love her more than I love my children. I didn't know it was possible to love anyone this much.'

Gwen stood up. She was suddenly extremely tired and longing, childishly, for the train to take her westwards, back to everything that was unremarkable and familiar.

'If you love her –' She paused.

He stood, too. He looked enormous suddenly, formal, authoritative. Gwen took a breath.

'If you love her that much,' she said clearly, 'if you love her as much as you say, then you know what you ought to do for her. Don't you?'

When Merrion put her key in the door, she knew immediately that something was wrong. The smell of it came out of the flat like a vapour, cold and raw. Guy usually put all the lights on, pulled the curtains, had music playing, supper started, sometimes even a bath run for her full of bubbles with a glass of wine sitting on one of the broad corners beside the taps. But tonight it was silent. And almost dark. Merrion stepped into the gloom and anxiety in a single stride.

'Guy?'

'I'm here,' he said. His voice sounded strained, as if it was difficult to speak, as if he'd been crying.

She moved into the sitting room. It was almost in darkness, except for a single lamp glowing in a corner. Guy was lying along the sofa, his jacket off, his arm flung across his face.

'Darling,' Merrion said, rushing forward. 'Darling, are you OK?'

He took his arm away, and held it out to her.

'Physically, fine.'

She took his hand. It felt the same as ever, big and warm and certain. She glanced down at the table beside him. There was a tea tray on it, a proper tea tray laid for one with a pot and a milk jug and a cup and saucer.

'Guy?'

He let her hand go abruptly and swung himself upright.

'I made it for your mother –'

'My *mother*?'

'Yes,' he said. 'Your mother's been.'

CHAPTER NINE

Jack and Moll spent the afternoon locked in the bathroom. At least, Carrie had supposed that the door was
locked, but when she went up to shout that, whatever
they were doing, could they please stop because other
people might need the shower, Moll called – disconcert-
ingly pleasantly – 'Oh, come in!'

Jack was sitting in the middle of the room on a chair
taken from Carrie's bedroom, draped in one of the hideous fish-patterned swimming towels Carrie had bought
in a street market on the principle that they were so
unattractive that nobody would ever nick them. His hair
– or at least the front of it – was intersected with neat little
aluminium foil packets. Moll was wearing latex surgical
gloves and her hair was tied back smoothly behind her
head with a red bandanna. The bathroom smelled crudely
of bleach.

'Hi,' Moll said. She had a poise that made her at once
very easy and very discomposing to deal with. 'I'm putting
highlights in Jack's hair.'

'Highlights –'

'Greyish blond,' Moll said. 'Ashy.'

Jack, under his frill of little silver packets, looked smug.
He said, 'It'd cost forty quid at a hairdresser –'

'Perhaps you'd do mine,' Carrie said. Her tone of voice
was somehow not quite what she'd intended.

Moll flicked her a glance.

'Sure. Any time.'

Carrie looked at her deftly moving hands. She had a proper hairdressing colourist's comb, with fine teeth and a spiked metal handle.

'I was thinking of having a shower –'

'We can move,' Moll said. 'Any time.'

Jack looked briefly at his mother.

'Why now?'

'Because I've had a long day at work, I'm having a drink with your Uncle Alan and then I'm collecting Emma from drama club and I wish to do the latter activities showered.'

There was a tiny pause. Jack and Moll caught each other's eyes, for a fraction of a second, in the bathroom mirror. Jack said, 'Where's Rach?'

'Gone to the movies with Trudy. Then she's staying the night.'

'Uh-huh.' He sounded nonchalant.

'And Dad's working late,' Carrie said. 'What's new. So such supper as there is won't be until about nine. I may even pick up a pizza.'

'We'll get supper,' Moll said.

Carrie stared at her.

'*Will* you?'

'Of course. Tell us what and we'll have it ready by nine.'

Carrie leaned against the doorframe.

'Nobody in this house has ever, ever offered to get a meal –'

Moll smiled. She folded another foil packet neatly around a strand of Jack's hair with the tail of her comb.

'We'll finish this off in the kitchen,' she said. 'And then you can shower. Just tell us what you want us to cook before you go.'

'Yes,' Carrie said weakly. 'Thank you. Heavens.'

Jack stood up, his silver frill glittering, the fish towel swinging round him like a cloak. He looked entirely unselfconscious, in fact, almost the reverse; pleased and proud. He picked up the chair he had been sitting on and went out on to the landing with it. Moll gathered up her bowls and brushes and comb and followed him. She still wore her small, pleasant smile but she didn't look at Carrie. Carrie watched them, in something approaching a daze, as they went along the landing with their burdens and then down the stairs together. When they got to the bottom, Jack leaned sideways across his chair – why was he still carrying her bedroom chair for heaven's sake? – and gave Moll a quick kiss.

'Bingo,' he said.

Moll giggled. The kitchen door shut behind them. Carrie looked at the bathroom. It suddenly seemed too much effort to take a shower, too much effort to take all her clothes off and think what to put on instead. Alan wouldn't mind anyway. Alan never expected anyone to go the extra mile if they hadn't the energy. She tugged at the jacket of her work suit. What did the world look like before everybody, all the time, everywhere, wore black?

Alan had already ordered for her. He was sitting with a glass of white wine in front of him and another glass, untouched, sat in front of the chair beside him. He was wearing a collarless white linen shirt under a black leather waistcoat. Carrie sketched a little gesture of approval towards him as she sat down.

'Nice –'

He grinned.

'I've got a date.'

'You haven't!'

'A doctor. Nice car.'

'*Alan*,' Carrie said, sitting down, 'his car is the *last* thing that matters.'

Alan made a face. He looked very happy, almost mischievous.

Carrie said, 'There's a lot of love about at the moment, isn't there? Even Jack –'

'Jack?'

'At this precise moment Jack is sitting in my kitchen having highlights put in his hair by a very sleek little number called Moll.'

'Good for Jack.'

'I suppose so –'

'Carrie,' Alan said warningly.

'What?'

'Don't use that tone of voice about Jack's girlfriend.'

'What tone?'

'That nobody's-good-enough-for-my-boy tone.'

'Was I?'

'Yes,' Alan said, 'you were.' He raised his glass. 'Cheers.'

'You, too. I hope you have a lovely evening.'

'I'd rather have a wild one –'

'I don't want to know about that,' Carrie said.

He grinned again.

'I wouldn't tell you anyway.'

She looked at him.

'You *are* cheerful.'

'I know. Isn't it a relief?'

'Yes,' she said, 'it really is. I'm getting so used to gloom and doom I'm in danger of forgetting there's an alternative.' She took a mouthful of wine. She said, looking at the tabletop, 'I met Merrion.'

'And?'

'As you said.'

'Nice?'

'So far so good. And certainly determined to fight her corner.'

'Shouldn't she?'

'Of course she should,' Carrie said crossly. 'It's just that if she does I get torn in two.'

'No, you don't.'

'I –'

'Carrie,' Alan said, leaning forward, 'you have more sympathy for my father and Merrion than you do for my mother. You know you do.'

Carrie looked at him.

'That's why I wanted to see you.'

'What now?'

'Your mother,' Carrie said, her gaze back on the table-top, 'has decided that although she wants what she sees as her fair share of your parents' assets, she is not going to soil her hands securing them. She has decided she is going to have nothing further to do with your father. Nothing. Ever. So –'

'Don't tell me.'

'You can guess the rest.'

'Oh God,' Alan said. 'And Simon agreed?'

'He doesn't seem to think he has any option. You can't *force* a person of sixty-one in their right mind to go to a lawyer, can you?'

Alan took a gulp of wine.

'When did this happen?'

'This week. He didn't mean to tell me about it, but when he got back from Hill Cottage in such a state, I could *see* she'd asked for several pounds of flesh.'

Alan said, between his teeth, into his wineglass, 'I *told* him.'

'I know.'

'Has he spoken to Dad?'

'I don't know. I think Guy left a message. The thing is, Alan, that almost leaving Merrion aside I can't help feeling your father has a point. I'm now facing the prospect of having to fight *your* mother for *my* husband.'

'Nonsense.'

'It isn't nonsense,' Carrie said. 'It's a fact. It's always been there, sort of latent, but she's never taken the gloves off before, never quite had to. Shall I tell you something?'

He nodded, waiting.

'It's not Guy's fault that Laura's always felt – lost. I bet he really tried to give her what made her happy, what gave her a greater sense of security and purpose, and all she did in return was make him feel he'd wrong-footed her deliberately, that he'd somehow made a career out of carefully removing life from her grasp.' She paused and then she said, 'I'm probably absolutely out of order, as the children constantly say, in telling you this, but in my opinion Laura is one of the most self-absorbed, self-pitying women I have *ever* met.'

Alan gave a little shrug.

'I had to worm everything out of Simon the other night,' Carrie said. She was breathing fast. 'He didn't want to tell me anything, he didn't want me to have proof of how unfair and exploitative Laura is. He didn't want me, did he, to tell him how pathetic I think he's being –'

'Do you?'

Carrie looked up. She said nothing.

'Do you think he's being pathetic?' Alan said.

'Oh,' she said miserably, 'I don't. Not really. I just think he's stuck. She's got him cornered. She always has had him cornered. She was just biding her time.'

'So you bawled him out –'

Carrie's gaze dropped.

'Yes.'

'Carrie –'

'Don't tell me I'm jealous,' Carrie said, 'I *know* I am. But he is mine, you know. Mine *first*.'

'He knows that.'

'But you can't always have what you want if someone persuades you that you *owe* them first instead, can you?'

'I don't know,' Alan said. 'It's never happened to me.'

'But you can *see*, for God's sake!'

'Oh yes. I can see.'

She leaned forward.

'Can you help Simon?'

'How?'

'Help him deal with her. Share it.'

'I'm not a lawyer. She'll say –'

'Alan!' Carrie almost shouted.

'Sorry. Look, I *want* to help. I've tried to. But the two of them have been playing this game since before I was born.'

Carrie's shoulders slumped.

'I know.'

'What are you afraid of?'

She made a little face.

'I suppose – that we'll never be free of her. That whatever we do, she'll be a consideration and, over time, the first consideration. That Simon will begin to put his obligation to her first. That – well, that he'll never be able to see her for what she is.'

'Could you say that?'

'What?' Carrie demanded. 'To *Laura*?'

'Yes –'

Carrie brought her fist down on the table and a tongue of wine leaped out of her glass and splashed down the side.

'*Alan*. Oh Alan, can't you stop daydreaming about your bloody doctor for just one second and *think*. I don't want to say all this stuff to Laura. It ought to be said, but if I say it, she can stop listening before I even start. Can't you see? I want *Simon* to say it! I want Simon to open his eyes and see this whole situation for what it is and tell his mother that he is her loving and supportive son and that he is *not* a bloody substitute husband! That's what I want!'

Alan put out a hand and lightly touched her nearest one.

'Oh dear,' he said.

The whole office was quiet. The computers were shut down, Miriam had lowered the Venetian blinds – with their horizontal furrings of dust that no cleaning company ever seemed to tackle – and the office doors stood open revealing overflowing waste bins and swivel chairs left askew and a litter of takeaway coffee cups and plastic mineral-water bottles. Ted and Philip had gone off at six to play squash together, half an hour after Miriam, whose only conscientious bit of time keeping was her departure time.

Two days before, Miriam had left a yellow sticker note on Simon's desk. It read, 'Please ring your father.' When he first saw it, he'd had a little burst of temper because the message was so peremptory, because after his interview with his mother he felt so jangled-up, so out-manoeuvred, that he was longing, just longing to find a scapegoat and for that, his father would do nicely. But, upon reflection, he remembered that Miriam, perpetually bored by all lives other than her own, was an inaccurate and minimal message taker, and that a habitually courteous paragraph from his father could well have ended up, at Miriam's hands, as, 'Please ring your father.' On further reflection, he'd probably been lucky to get the 'please'.

He had peeled the sticker off his desk and attached it to the side of his computer screen. Of course he should ring his father. He should have been in steady touch with his father ever since he learned of Merrion's existence, even if he could hardly visualise what form that being in touch would have taken. It wasn't helping the situation to have shied away from contact with Guy: it wasn't helping his mother, it certainly wasn't helping himself. And the proof of that was the position he now found himself in, because he had persuaded himself that he was standing on principle by refusing to speak to his father. Carrie had called it cowardice. She had also called it several other things which made the charge of cowardice seem quite mild. His attitude had, she said, played right into his mother's manipulative hands.

'Those weak little women!' she'd shouted. 'They're

always the ones you have to watch out for! They're lethal!'

Simon didn't think Laura was lethal. He didn't think she was weak, either, but he did think she was vulnerable. He also thought she was in some kind of shock, dazed by the revelatory blow of Guy's secret past and overt future and that that was why she couldn't face acting for herself, couldn't face dealing with a man who had betrayed her trust so comprehensively. Simon knew it wasn't at all fair of Laura to ask him to act for her. He *knew* that, he told Carrie. He'd even *said* it, to Laura. But all the same, he couldn't get out of his mind and heart that he had to do something for Laura, something to heal or soothe or compensate, because, quite simply, he was the only person in her life who could. As he had always been. He had never confessed that, openly, to Carrie. He could, he thought, have written down her response right then and there. Word for sharp word.

But now, somehow, some time, he had to speak to his father. Alan had said, insufferably, that he should never have let the speaking lapse, never have got to the point in life where speaking to any parent – whatever your opinion of them – became such a huge and daunting deal.

'He's *gentle*,' Alan said. 'You'll see. He's happier than he's ever been but he's not at all defiant. He's not trying to justify anything, he's just trying to deal with what is.'

'Your personal bloody mantra, in short –'

'I don't know,' Alan said, 'how Carrie puts up with you.'

Simon sighed.

'Nor do I. I often wonder how I put up with myself. But how do you get to be different from what you are? If you're a worrier, you worry. If you aren't, you don't. I'm a worrier. I can't remember a time in my life when I wasn't aware of something to worry about.'

Alan looked at him.

'Why?'

Simon looked back.

'Because I can't stop feeling that I have to *do* something about those worries. That it's up to me.'

And now it really is, Simon thought. He peeled the yellow sticker off his computer and stuck it on the side of the half-empty mineral-water bottle he had bought at lunchtime. Now, because I've let Mum think I'm her knight in shining armour, I really am. I'm committed. And Dad . . . Well, Dad has become something that, whatever I felt about him, I never intended him to be. He's become the enemy. I've got to fight him, for Mum. I've got to see him as a lawyer would, not as a son. And it is my own stupid, bloody fault. *Mine*. I'll tell myself that over and over, before Carrie has a chance to.

He unscrewed the plastic cap on the water bottle and took a long pull. Then he reached out for his desk telephone and dialled Stanborough Crown Court. A recorded message – a girl sounding as indifferent and mechanical as Miriam – told him that the court was closed for business until the following morning but that urgent matters might be dealt with at the following number. Simon then dialled the second Stanborough number Guy had left.

'It's some dismal flat,' Laura had said. 'Above a kebab house or something. Not that I care.'

The telephone rang out and out. Nobody answered. There was no answerphone and Simon wondered briefly if his father was actually there, lying on a rented bed in a rented room above a hairdresser or a takeaway shop listening to the telephone and not doing anything about it, the toes of his black, polished shoes pointing at a stained ceiling. Then, stupid, he thought, *stupid*. Why ever wouldn't he answer the phone? It might be Merrion.

He looked at the third number Guy had left. It was a Central London number. It was of course Merrion's flat, the flat where his father spent weekends, where he had those times, that kind of life, that Simon had never had, could hardly visualise having, because he'd scarcely had a moment ever in which love life and parent life weren't inextricably mixed. Guy and Merrion had nights, presumably, not pole-axed by fatigue, and evenings, Sunday mornings, bath times in which conversation could happen, general conversation and jokes and the sort of silence so hard to achieve in family life because it was always assumed to have a significance, usually dangerous. And, of course, times for sex. Sex for its own strong sake. Simon swallowed. It was not possible, he discovered, to think about his father and Merrion and sex.

He dialled the London number slowly. It rang out twice and then a woman's voice on an answerphone asked him in an impersonal tone to leave a message. He took a breath.

'It's Simon Stockdale,' he said. 'I was hoping to speak to my father.'

He put the phone down. Damn. He'd meant to say 'trying' not 'hoping'. He'd meant to leave a message without a shred of emotion. He took the yellow sticker off the water bottle and stuck it back on his computer. He stood up and stretched. Then he looked at his watch. Seven-fifteen. Carrie had said she was seeing someone and then she was picking Emma up from something so she wouldn't be home until around nine. Rachel was out somewhere. And Jack – Carrie hadn't mentioned Jack. The thought of an empty house was oddly soothing. He would go back and let himself in and not look at the post nor the wine bottle until he'd had an immense bath, with some music playing, and pretended to himself, for half an hour only, that nothing was required of him that he couldn't handle with ease. Complete, untroubled ease.

He let himself in quietly. Usually, it was necessary to announce his return home by banging the door and flinging his keys on to the chest in the hall so that they would all know. They mightn't react, they certainly wouldn't all come skidding down the stairs to meet him, but at least they'd all *know*, and the human chemistry in the house could shift a little, to accommodate him, to acknowledge that he, Simon, husband, father, chief bread-winner, was home in the house that he would finally actually own when he was sixty-three and a half years old and probably past caring.

He put his keys softly on the hall chest beside a scatter of unopened mail. Everybody went through the mail in an anticipatory frenzy every day, even though there was seldom anything for anyone except Simon and Carrie, and left the discarded envelopes in disorder, like a carcass from which the best bits have been picked. Simon didn't look at the mail. He went into the kitchen and dropped his raincoat – 'The universe's saddest garment,' Rachel said – over the back of a kitchen chair. The kitchen looked strangely tidy and smelled of something slightly chemical, like bleach. By the cooker was a pile of vegetables, tomatoes and peppers and aubergines and onions heaped up like a still life, on a wooden board. There was also a supermarket pack of pathetic little pink chicken strips confined under plastic film and looking as if they had never had the smallest association with anything living and breathing. Carrie, in a fit of forward planning, was evidently going to make supper when she got back. Simon looked at the vegetables again. It would be pretty nearly two hours before there was any hope of them resting comfortably on a plate in front of him. He opened the refrigerator and took out a saucer holding the rind end of a piece of Brie, two radishes and a cold leftover roast potato from a blue pottery bowl. He ate these, standing up by the kitchen table, and then he put the saucer in the sink. He ran his tongue round his teeth. He should have washed the radishes. He could feel faint traces of their residual grit.

He went out of the kitchen, hanging his suit jacket on the newel post at the foot of the stairs, and climbed upwards, loosening his tie and unbuttoning his shirt as he went. He felt, in a way he couldn't in the least account for, happier than he had felt for ages, oddly released, in the empty house with the late spring light fading outside and the street noises at a comfortable, companionable distance, and the prospect of a long bath with Ella Fitzgerald playing or maybe some Gershwin, something glamorous anyway, American, sophisticated. He went lightly along the landing, sliding his tie out from under his shirt collar, and opened his bedroom door.

The curtains were half pulled across, so that the room was dim. There was a sudden and peculiar silence in it, the silence you get with tension, or a terrific social awkwardness. Simon looked around. Carrie was in the bed, humped up as she was when she got one of her migraines and lay cursing and enduring under her breath. Poor Carrie. And sweet Carrie, to get everything ready to make supper before she took the new migraine drugs she'd been given which worked, but which knocked her for six while they did it.

He went softly towards the bed. He couldn't see her hair, only something dark and unfamiliar on the pillow. He said, whispering in case she was fathoms deep in drug-induced slumber, 'Carrie? You OK?'

There was a slow movement in the bed. The hump of Carrie stirred and flattened out into two shapes. Looking down, his tie still in his hand and his shirt unbuttoned to the waist, Simon found himself regarding Jack and Moll, their faces side by side and close together, looking up.

'Were you cross?' Carrie said. She was sitting on the bathroom floor, wrapped in a towel, clipping her toenails.

'No,' Simon said. He gazed down the length of the bath

at his feet, arranged neatly and braced, either side of the taps.

'Why not?'

'Because I didn't feel it.'

'I think Jack expected you to be furious. He kept shooting you glances, like someone waiting for the big firework to go off.'

'It was very peculiar,' Simon said, almost dreamily, 'but I didn't want to shout. I thought I probably would, but I didn't. I kept waiting for myself to say, "How dare you and in our bed," and stuff, but I never did. I felt . . .'

'What?'

'Rather envious.'

'*Envious?*'

'Yes –'

'Of Jack? Having Moll?'

'No,' Simon said crossly. He sat up and began to rub soap into a face flannel. 'No. Of them. Of, well, their freedom.'

There was a pause and then Carrie said, very shortly, 'Yes.'

Simon began soaping his face and neck and chest.

'They weren't really very embarrassed. Jack was a bit, I suppose.'

'What'd he say?'

Simon grinned.

'He said, "Hi, Dad." I almost expected him to say, "Had a good day at the office?" '

Carrie said, 'D'you think it was his first time?'

'I haven't the first idea.'

'They got through supper, though, didn't they –'

'They cooked it, even.'

'That's what I thought they were doing. That's what I left them doing.'

Simon put a wet arm out of the bath and pulled at the back of Carrie's towel.

'Don't,' she said. 'You'll make me jerk and I'll cut my toes not my toenails.'

'I'll suck them for you.'

'Simon!' Carrie said. 'What has got into you?'

'I don't know,' he said. He leaned back and floated the soapy flannel in the water above a rising erection. 'I just feel better. I don't know why. I grasped a small nettle today. Maybe –' He paused.

'What nettle?'

'I rang Dad.'

'And?'

'I didn't speak to him, but I left a message.'

Carrie finished the last toenail and dropped her clippers into a plastic box of scissors and files and combs.

'Very brave.'

'Carrie.'

'What?'

'Come here.'

She got up and came to half crouch by the bath. Simon looked at her. He was smiling. She had her hair held up in a tangle with one of Rachel's silly pink plastic spring-clip things. He loved it like that. She looked about sixteen.

He said, 'Get in the bath with me.'

She looked down at him. The flannel had floated free.

'Simon –'

'Get in.'

He reached out and took her nearest hand.

'Come on.'

'Si,' Carrie said, 'you may have had a good day and think the Jack and Moll episode is just a jolly jape, but I haven't. And I don't.'

Simon twitched her towel off.

'Forget all that. Just for twenty minutes.'

She pulled her hand out of his grasp and bent for her towel. He saw her breasts swing briefly, little pale globes. 'A mouthful,' he used to say to her. 'Just right.'

She stepped back.

'Sorry,' she said.

He looked at her.

'Even if I said please?'

She shook her head.

He said, 'When did we last have sex?'

She was struggling into her old cotton kimono.

'Oh, sometime last century, I should think. And what happened to the phrase "making love"?'

Simon grasped the edge of the bath. He leaned towards her.

'Carrie,' he said, 'I really, really want to make love to you. Now. Please. *Please.*'

She put her hand on the bathroom door knob.

'It has to be for real.'

'It *is*. My God, it is!'

She opened the door. She had tied the kimono sash tightly round her waist. She looked as fragile as a porcelain doll.

'Nothing's real just now,' she said, and went out.

CHAPTER TEN

The valuer from the estate agent's in Stanborough turned out to be a woman. Laura had been expecting a man, one of those predictable estate-agent men in a dark suit and a white shirt and a slightly too loud tie with a silly motif all over it: cartoon pigs, or elephants, or camels under palm trees. Laura knew how to deal with those kind of men, knew how to answer their questions. The valuer woman looked rather different. She was almost Laura's age, for one thing, and she had a quiet, firm manner that made Laura feel she was only interested in figures, and not in the least in Laura and Laura's plight.

Laura had made coffee but she declined it, and asked for a glass of water instead. She took two sips and then she left the glass on the kitchen table, and took out a huge tape measure on a black spool and began to make notes. She opened and shut the kitchen cupboards as if she were testing the hinges, and gave the kick boards at the bottom a little nudge with her foot. One of them fell off.

'It's the only one that does,' Laura said.

'Perhaps you would show me round,' the valuer said. 'And then I'd be most grateful to be left alone to measure up. Usually I have an assistant, but he has an exam today.'

Laura said, without intending to, 'Would you like me to help?'

The valuer looked at her. She gave a very small smile.

'No thank you,' she said.

Laura walked ahead of her through the house. She had put flowers in the sitting room and the hall and polished the front windows where the prevailing wind always blew dust up from the gravel outside. She had told Simon she wasn't going to bother, she wasn't going to go on making an effort, that it was both heartbreaking and pointless to show off something you'd given so much time and thought and energy to and that you were now forced to lose.

Simon said, 'Just think of the money.'

'I wish it was that simple.'

'It is. It has to be.'

He had sounded exasperated, almost cross. Laura could easily imagine how little help Carrie was being to him, how unsympathetic she'd be about any part of Simon's life that didn't concern herself or their children.

When Simon had fallen in love with Carrie, Laura had said to Guy, 'Don't you think she's hard?'

'No,' he said. 'She's just very candid.'

'But does she see how sensitive he is?'

'Yes,' Guy said, 'and she's candid about that, too.'

'You've always wanted to toughen him up –'

'Not toughen. Teach to defend. Defend himself.'

'Toughen,' Laura had said again, very quietly.

After a few years, when Simon had actually married Carrie – his wedding day had been a hard day for Laura, hard in a way she saw nobody could perceive but herself – he used to say to her, when she called him in the office, 'Mum. Why don't you ring Carrie? Why don't you just ring her?'

She'd always let a little silence fall. In that silence she let Simon know – she had to let him know – that it wasn't Carrie she needed to speak to, it wasn't Carrie who knew her history, understood her predicament, spoke her quiet, understated, meaningful language. After the silence had gone on for a little while, she'd say, 'I will. Of course I will,' and they'd both know she wouldn't. Only once had Simon said, 'Please, Mum, for my sake –' and she had said in reply, wanting him to know he was breaking their private rules, 'Simon. That isn't fair.'

'OK,' he'd said. 'OK. Forget it.'

He sounded tired, weary tired. Next day, she rang to apologise.

'It's so difficult –'

'Don't,' he said. 'Don't explain. You don't have to.'

She'd smiled into the telephone.

'No, I don't, do I? I never have to, with you.'

Now, she pushed the sitting-room door wide. The sun was coming in through the south-east-facing windows and lying optimistically across the sofa and chairs whose covers she'd made herself, across the cushions she'd collected over the years – there were two still left from that first little house in Battersea – across the pale-green carpet and the rug with its Tree of Life pattern that Guy had bought at an auction along with a chicken coop – never used – and a pair of Versailles tubs she'd stripped of their flaking varnish and painted dark green and planted with bay trees.

'Pleasant room, Mrs Stockdale,' the valuer said. She advanced across the Tree of Life rug and surveyed the room with an assessing eye. 'Good dimensions.'

'It was three little rooms,' Laura said, 'when we came. One was full of potatoes, all sprouting. You can imagine the smell.'

The valuer looked at her properly for the first time.

'How long have you been here, Mrs Stockdale?'

Laura moved to hold the back of the nearest armchair. She leaned on it. She wished, as she had said only yesterday to Wendy who had come on one of her attempts-at-bracing visits, that she could just stay plain angry all the time. Angry was fine. When she was angry she had purpose and energy, she could even sometimes glimpse

142

a new self emerging from all this muddle and emotional squalor, a clean new self shorn of all the restrictions placed inevitably on a human being by the need to negotiate, day in, day out, with another human being at close quarters. It was the times when the anger died that she dreaded. Without anger, she fell prey to desolation, to a feeling of disorientation so deep she wondered if she actually had fallen right through the web of the life she had always – even in her darkest moments – taken for granted. Desolation meant grief; grief for the loss of so many huge and so many tiny things that it was quite beyond her to try and number them.

'Mrs Stockdale?'

Laura stared fixedly at the cushion in the chair below her, a tapestry cushion, embroidered with auriculas, in a terracotta pot, which she had made one long, unremarkable, contented summer while watching Alan captain his school cricket team for the under-fifteens.

'Are you all right, Mrs Stockdale?'

Laura nodded. She made an immense effort and looked up.

'We came here thirty years ago. My boys were eight and five. Younger than my grandchildren are now.'

In a different tone of voice to the one she'd used earlier, the valuer said, 'It's a wrench, isn't it –'

Laura put her hands over her face. From behind them she cried, 'I don't want this to happen! I don't want to leave!'

'I'm so sorry –'

Laura took her hands away from her face. She said, almost gasping, 'Sometimes I think this is all I've done, all I've achieved. When I think of myself, Hill Cottage and the garden is *how* I think of myself. It's – it's my sort of landscape, my background. If I go –'

The valuer waited. She had put down her measure and her notebook and was simply standing there, almost as if she was braced to catch Laura should she fall.

143

'I'll vanish,' Laura whispered. 'Won't I? I'll just vanish. There – there won't be any need for me, any more. Will there?'

The valuer bent and picked up her measure again. She held it out to Laura.

'I wonder, Mrs Stockdale, if you would be very kind and help me with this? After all?'

'Sorry,' Carrie said the next morning.

Simon, in shirt and tie and suit trousers, was balanced astride the sink trying to fix the kitchen blind which had unrolled itself quietly in the night and was now declining to roll itself up again, and stay rolled. He gave a little grunt.

'About last night,' she said.

'I know.'

'It isn't very easy to explain –'

'Nothing is,' Simon said. 'Nothing bloody is, right now. That's why, in the midst of all these problems, twenty minutes of happy, uncomplicated sex would have been so great.'

'I know,' Carrie said. She poured cereal into two bowls. She said, rather hesitantly, 'Your – your mother –'

'What the hell has my mother got to do with our sex life?'

The blind, having hung limply above the sink, suddenly became galvanised with activity and rushed up into a tight roll, taking the tips of Simon's fingers with it.

'*Shit*,' Simon said.

'Are you hurt?'

'No,' he said. He put his fingers in his mouth. 'At least, not physically.'

'Don't –'

Simon crouched down and jumped lightly to the floor. He shook his fingers.

'My cheque-signing hand.'

She held her own hand out.

'Let me look.'

He put his hand in hers. She bent and kissed his fingertips.

'Oh Carrie –'

'I'm jealous,' she whispered into his hand. 'I want you back.'

'I haven't gone anywhere –'

'But you might.'

Simon took his hand back.

'I *have* to help her.'

'I know.'

'There's no one else.'

'But you can't be held responsible for that. It isn't your fault that she's never made friends, that she hardly speaks to her sister, that she thinks Alan isn't a fully operational adult.'

Simon poured milk out of a quart plastic bottle on to one bowl of cereal and held it out to her.

He said, 'What do you want to do?'

'What do *I* want to do?'

'Yes.'

She looked down at the cereal. She seemed to be struggling either to say something or not to say it.

'It's not me –' she said finally.

Simon picked up the second cereal bowl, and a spoon.

'Let's not start on what Simon is doing wrong again. Please.'

Carrie took a breath. She put her cereal bowl down.

'OK,' she said.

He took a mouthful, and crunched it. Through it, he said, 'OK what?'

'I do want to do something.'

The kitchen door opened. Rachel, in her school uniform with the addition of a small blue glitter butterfly stuck to her cheek and a chalk-pink lipsticked mouth, came in, yawning cavernously.

'Morning, darling,' Carrie said.

Simon ignored his daughter. He said, his eyes on his cereal, 'What? What do you want to do?'

'I want to ask Merrion Palmer here. For supper. Or Sunday lunch.'

Rachel stopped yawning.

'Wow,' she said.

Simon looked up from his cereal and stared at Carrie.

'Merrion Palmer?'

'Yes,' Carrie said. 'Her.'

'With or without my father?'

Rachel leaned across the table and drew Carrie's cereal bowl towards her.

'Without,' she said.

Carrie glanced at her. Then she stood a little straighter and looked at Simon.

'Yes,' she said, 'Rachel's right. Without.'

Merrion lay on her sofa. She had taken off her work clothes and put on the dark-blue bathrobe she had bought for Guy. It was new but he had worn it enough to have left it faintly impregnated, besides the smell of newness, with the smell of him. She had made herself a mug of tea and a honey sandwich. Guy had always been charmed by her passion for honey. He said it was so unlike her. He bought her exotic honeys from specialist shops, lavender and acacia honeys, honeys from Greece and Provence and the Italian Alps.

She had the telephone balanced on her stomach. In five minutes, she would ring Guy. He would be back in his flat then, in this flat he wouldn't talk about and wouldn't let her see.

'It doesn't matter,' he said. 'It's just a space, a passing practicality. I'm going to rub it out of memory when it's gone.'

Because he wouldn't tell her about it, she pictured it. She

imagined it worse than it probably was. She saw a rickety shower and a dank little kitchen smelling of drains and his suits hanging in a plywood wardrobe with fancy plastic handles and doors that wouldn't shut. He told her he read in the evenings and she imagined him in a too-small armchair covered in cut moquette with a grease patch where countless other heads had rested previously. She couldn't imagine him in bed. She'd tried, and the picture that had swum into her mind, the bleakness and the loneliness of those nights, had been too much to bear. It was worse – weirdly worse – than all those months and years of knowing he was in bed at Hill Cottage with Laura. There'd been envy in that, but also a small thrill because of the private, certain – oh, so certain – knowledge of where he'd rather be, where he was thinking of being. But his nights in the nameless rented flat were different. There was no secrecy to them, no illicit, gorgeous longing. There was just desolation instead.

She put her mug down on the coffee table and sat up sufficiently to be able to see the dialling buttons. She pressed the relevant ones rapidly, and lay back on the sofa cushions, the receiver to her ear.

'Hello, darling,' Guy said.

She smiled into the telephone.

'Good, bad or indifferent?'

'Patchy,' he said. 'Word has got out that Hill Cottage is on the market. They seem to know Laura and I have parted. I don't know if they know about you.'

'Course they do.'

'Really?'

'You know what gossips people are.'

'Well,' Guy said, 'everyone is treating me as if I was an invalid. Martin opened two doors for me today. He'll be giving me his arm up steps next.'

Merrion shifted her position a little.

'I've got something to tell you.'

'Something I'll like?'

'Yes,' she said. 'Carrie and Simon have asked me to supper. At least, Carrie has.'

'Oh!' he said. She could hear his voice warming, imagine him smiling. 'Oh, I *am* glad. Oh my darling, I am so glad!'

'I am, too, in a slightly alarmed way.'

'Because of Simon –'

'Yes.'

'Merrion –'

'It's just very hard to be disapproved of for what you represent rather than what you are.'

There was a little pause and then Guy said, 'I know.'

'Guy. You're not still thinking about my mother, are you?'

'Dearest, it isn't something I can pretend didn't happen.'

She said earnestly, 'But you don't have to *heed* her. What she says and thinks is for *her* life, *her* personality, *her* circumstances. It's not for yours and it's certainly not for mine.'

He said, slightly heartily, 'You're very good for me.'

'Not good enough. I can hear the doubt in your voice.'

'What I couldn't bear,' Guy said, 'is to do anything to impede your progress, clip your wings –'

'You don't. I've told you. Over and over, I've told you.'

'In ten years –'

'Stop it. Guy, *stop* it.'

'Things are changing,' Guy said. 'You take a step forward and all the landscape round you changes, the perspective is different –'

Merrion sat up. She wound the coiled telephone cable round her fingers and pulled it tight.

'Guy,' she said, 'I'm not having any more of this conversation over the telephone. We shouldn't talk like this when we can't get at each other.'

She heard him catch his breath, and then he said, in a

stronger, more impersonal tone, 'When are you having supper with Carrie and Simon?'

'Tomorrow. I'm in chambers all day. Conferences and paperwork. So – well, that's good.'

'It is.'

'I'll ring you later. I'll ring you at bedtime.'

'Please.'

'What's on the menu tonight? Chicken Korma and *Little Dorrit*?'

He laughed.

'Pretty nearly.'

She blew a kiss into the telephone.

'Miss you,' she said. 'Miss you all the time.'

She untangled the cable from her fingers and set the telephone down on the coffee table. Her tea was cold and her sandwich looked as if it might be an effort and not a pleasure to eat. She rolled back on to the sofa and faced the cushions along the back of it, running her forefinger along the bumpy lines of weaving in the nearest one.

Guy had been very shaken by Gwen's visit. In all their years together, Merrion had never seen him thrown to this degree, so disconcerted.

He said, trying to make light of it, 'She made me feel my age.'

'She does that to me, too,' Merrion said.

He'd looked at her.

'What am I depriving you of? What am I keeping you from?'

'Nothing!' she'd shouted. She'd got angry then, furiously angry, wanted to ring Gwen late at night in Cowbridge and tell her to mind her own bloody, narrow-minded business.

'Don't,' Guy said.

'Why not?'

'Because she has a perfect right, as your mother –'

'She does *not*!' Merrion yelled. 'You don't know her!

You don't know she never does anything unless it's to stop adventure, stop progress, stop enterprise! She wants the world, and especially me, to live in her tiny life by her tiny rules and never even think of doing anything that might remotely upset her! She's a bully, in her respectable little way. That's what my mother is, a coward and a bully!'

'I didn't think that,' Guy said. 'I saw a perfectly decent woman my own sort of age explaining to me with some force what effect my marrying her daughter might have on that daughter's life.'

Merrion cast herself across his knees and held him hard around the neck.

'Nothing like the effect you'll have if you don't marry her.'

He put his arms around her.

'Oh God. I can't even contemplate that –'

'Well, then.'

'Maybe,' he said, his face in her neck, 'maybe it's just such a long time since I've been ticked off, I've forgotten how to handle it –'

'And my mother is an ace ticker-off. It's one of her specialities.'

He raised his head and kissed her.

'I love you,' he said, 'I *love* you.'

She smiled.

'That's all I need to know.'

She thought, that night, that the problem was over. She thought, because she had had thirty years of practice in dealing with Gwen, that Guy could shrug off the encounter with that enviable male capacity not to indulge in teasing and worrying at an emotional annoyance. But his face had been clouded the next day. So had his mood. He had made Merrion promise she wouldn't ring her mother.

'I must.'

'No. You absolutely must not. Promise me. Promise.'

'OK.'

She rolled over on the sofa now and looked at the telephone. It was perfectly plain that Guy was unable to shake the effect of Gwen's visit off, unable to get various ingenious little phrases out of his mind. Merrion knew that feeling, could probably even, after assiduous years of teaching herself to come to terms with the uneasiness of the relationship between her mother and herself, recall in precise detail various little barbs of Gwen's – and the extraordinary, enduring small stabs of pain that went with them. Protecting herself had, over time, become one thing: a thing she could, given enough space of her own and distance from Cowbridge, handle without confrontation. But protecting Guy was another matter altogether. Protecting Guy required something more pro-active and if it meant a broken promise and a stand-up screaming match – so familiar still, from her late adolescence – then so be it.

Merrion sat up, tightened the sash of Guy's bathrobe and pushed her hair firmly off her face and behind her shoulders. Then she picked up the telephone, put it on her knees, and dialled her mother's number.

'It's only pasta,' Carrie said.

Merrion was leaning against the kitchen cupboards on the opposite side of the room. Carrie had poured her a glass of wine. She hadn't drunk any yet but she was glad to have it to hold.

'I like pasta.'

'So do I. But sometimes I get tired of it being such a staple. We eat it all the time, *all* the time, because I don't have to think about it and I know everybody will eat it.'

'When I was doing my Bar finals,' Merrion said, 'I ate baked potatoes like that. Every day.'

Carrie put a pan of boiling water on the stove.

'Can I help?' Merrion said. 'Can I chop something?'

'It's all done really,' Carrie said. 'Rachel even made a sauce –'

'Rachel –'

'My fourteen year old.'

'Does she cook?'

'No. Never. But she made a carbonara sauce because you were coming.'

Merrion looked down.

'I don't know how to take that.'

'I wouldn't take it any way,' Carrie said. 'I'd just be prepared for it to taste a little strange.'

In the hall beyond the kitchen, the front door slammed and someone threw their keys on to a hard surface.

'Simon,' Carrie said.

Merrion put her wineglass down on the counter behind her. Carrie gave her a quick smile.

'Deep breath.'

Merrion nodded.

'Yes –'

A man appeared in the kitchen doorway. Merrion had the impression of quite a tall man, a dark man, a man in a rumpled business suit and a blue shirt.

'Hi,' the man said to Carrie, in Guy's voice. He bent a little and kissed her. 'OK?'

'Simon,' Carrie said, 'this is Merrion.'

He turned towards her. The light from the window was behind him so she couldn't see him very well, only enough to establish that the outline was Guy's and the face was not.

'Hello,' he said.

She tried to smile.

'Hello.'

He put a hand up to his collar, to loosen his tie.

'Has Carrie given you a drink?'

'Oh yes,' she said and then, as steadily as she could, 'I'm glad to be here.'

He nodded.

'Good,' he said.

'It was brave of Carrie –'

'No, it wasn't,' Carrie said.

'To invite me.'

'She is brave,' Simon said. 'Reckless sometimes.'

'I like that,' Merrion said.

He was looking at her. He was sliding his tie out from under his collar and undoing his collar button, and looking at her. She'd put on black jeans and a grey sweater with a slash neck. She could feel the soft straight line of the neck against her throat.

'You've met my brother Alan –'

'Yes.'

'And then Carrie –'

'Yes.'

'And now me.'

'Yes.'

'Well done,' Simon said.

Carrie looked across from the pasta pot.

'Enough,' she said.

He glanced at her. He was slightly smiling.

'Just testing.'

'Well, don't. Don't play games.'

'Or only,' Merrion said, 'if I can play them, too.'

There was the sound of feet on the stairs, running feet, and then the thud of a jumped landing in the hall. A girl stood in the kitchen doorway, a big child girl in cargo pants and a tiny black top that showed a strip of pale soft very young midriff. Her hair was pulled up on one side in a tuft like the top of a pineapple, secured by an elasticated band of fake leopard skin.

'Merrion,' Carrie said, 'this is Emma.'

'Hello, Emma,' Merrion said.

'When's supper?' Emma said to Carrie.

'Say hello to Merrion,' Carrie said.

Emma looked quickly at Merrion. Then she looked at the floor in front of Merrion's feet.

'Hi.'

'It's OK,' Merrion said, 'none of us knows what to do.'

'We will, though,' Carrie said. 'We'll get better. We'll get used to it.'

Simon took off his jacket and hung it on the back of the nearest chair.

'Come and sit down,' he said to Merrion. He pulled another chair out slightly from the kitchen table and patted the back of it.

'Thank you,' she said. She moved towards the chair.

'Bring your wine –'

'Oh –'

'I'll get it,' Emma said.

She put the wineglass down in front of Merrion, spilling a little. There was a phone number written on her hand.

'Sorry –'

'It doesn't matter.'

'Get a cloth,' Simon said.

'Really, it doesn't matter.'

Emma dabbed roughly at the spill with a disposable cloth.

'Thank you.'

Simon went over to the fridge and took out a wine bottle. He waved it at Carrie.

'Got some?'

She nodded.

'Ems. Lay the table, would you?'

'I can do that,' Merrion said.

Simon put the bottle and a glass on the table opposite Merrion.

'Next time.'

She looked at him. He wasn't smiling, but he was looking back, straight at her.

'Oh –'

He sat down and poured the wine. Then he raised his glass.

'Cheers.'

Emma dumped a handful of knives and forks on the table.

'Rach's door is shut.'

'Maybe,' Carrie said, 'she's doing her biology.'

Emma snorted.

'Where's Jack?'

'Out,' Carrie said.

Emma snorted again.

'Jack,' Simon said to Merrion, 'has a girlfriend.'

'It's pathetic,' Emma said. 'Pitiful.'

Merrion smiled at her.

'You wait.'

Emma tossed her tuft of hair.

'I won't be pathetic, like Jack.'

'Maybe,' Simon said, 'you won't be able to help it.'

Merrion began to pick individual forks out of the pile of cutlery.

'How many places?'

The telephone rang. Emma said immediately, 'I'll go.'

'It rings all the time,' Simon said. 'All the time.'

'And never for us,' Carrie said.

'Hello?' Emma said, her back to the room. 'Oh. Oh – hi, Granny.' She swivelled round, gesturing. 'Yes,' she said, 'OK. No, no, he's here, I'll get him, I'll – hang on, Granny –'

She put her free hand over the telephone mouthpiece. Simon was on his feet already.

'It's Gran, Dad –'

'Yes –'

'Quick, Dad, it's awful, she's crying.'

There was a tiny pause. Then Simon said to Carrie, 'I'll take it in the office.'

'OK –'

'Tell her I'm coming, Ems, tell her I've just gone to another phone.'

He ran from the room. Emma took her hand away from the mouthpiece. She exchanged a quick glance with her mother.

Then she said into the telephone, 'It's OK, Gran. Hold on. Dad's coming. He's just gone to another phone. He's coming, OK?'

CHAPTER ELEVEN

Simon was standing behind his desk when his father arrived. He'd been about to go round it and meet Guy in the doorway of his office, at least, but Guy was too quick for him. By mistake, Simon took a step backwards towards the wall, as Guy came in.

He shut Simon's office door carefully behind him.

'Hello,' he said.

Simon swallowed.

'Hello, Dad.'

Guy seemed to hesitate for a second, and then he came determinedly forward, around Simon's desk, and took Simon in his arms.

Simon just stood there. He felt the bulk of his father, the size of him; he smelled the smell of the old-fashioned citrus-based men's cologne he had always used, the smell that had pervaded the laundry basket at Hill Cottage, Guy's wardrobe, his shirt drawers.

'Relax,' Guy said.

'Please –'

'What?'

'Let go,' Simon said.

Guy stepped back a short pace. He held Simon still by his upper arms. Simon could feel the warmth of Guy's hands through the cotton of his shirt sleeves.

'Don't take it out on me,' Guy said.

'What –'

'The fact that you have been put in an impossible position.'

Simon said loudly, 'She's afraid. She can't face anything she doesn't know. She's terrified.'

Guy gave Simon's arms a little squeeze and dropped his hands. He went back around Simon's desk and pulled up a chair.

'It won't help her, then, only communicating through you; it won't help her see that she might manage, that there is a future –'

Simon said shortly. 'I can only do what she wants. What she's able to want.'

'But surely a lawyer you know, someone you introduced her to –'

'No.'

'Have you tried?'

'That's none of your business,' Simon said politely. He sat down opposite Guy.

'I haven't seen you for so long,' Guy said.

'No.'

'Nearly three months.'

'Dad –'

'I'm not blaming you,' Guy said. 'I'm not blaming anybody. Except myself, probably. I could have come to find you any time. I could have told you any time. But I didn't. I didn't tell anyone. I told myself, instead, that a way would be made plain to me.'

'And it was.'

A look of intense and happy privacy passed briefly across Guy's face.

'It was.'

Simon leaned forward. He picked up a yellow ballpoint pen and flicked his thumbnail with it.

'Have *you* got a lawyer?'

'Yes,' Guy said.

'A friend of – Merrion's?'

'Yes.'

'So I will be negotiating with a friend of Merrion's. To whom you will make full financial disclosure.'

'Yes.'

'Dad –'

Guy leaned forward, too. He said, 'Shall we make a pact?'

'What?'

'Nothing but the facts? Only the facts? No opinions –'

'If we can stick to it,' Simon said. 'But there are things I have to tell you.'

'Like?'

'Mum is completely shattered about the house going. I mean devastated. Unhinged.'

'If I could afford to let her stay there,' Guy said, 'I would.'

'Make you feel better?'

Guy looked at him.

He said shortly, 'Make *her* feel better?'

Simon uncapped the ballpoint and began to scribble on the margin of a printed paper in front of him.

'It's worth three hundred and twenty-five thousand.'

Guy let out a breath.

'I paid six for it. Six thousand one hundred. Thirty years ago.'

'Half Mum's life.'

'Half mine, too.'

'But you're going *on* to something,' Simon said. 'You're moving *on*.'

Guy said quietly, 'Maybe I'd have done that anyway.'

'And she never would?'

'I did not say that –'

'But you meant it.'

'Yes,' Guy said, 'I meant it.' He looked at Simon again. 'Can you cope?'

'Of course.'

'You look tired –'

'I always look tired. I've looked tired since I was twenty for the simple reason that I am.'

'And angry,' Guy said.

Simon said nothing.

'Simon,' Guy said, 'you're my son as well as your mother's. You're my child, too.'

Simon said, his head bent, 'So what do *you* feel entitled to, then?'

'It's not that. It's just that because I'm your father I can't be indifferent to you, to your opinions, your actions, your attitudes.'

Between gritted teeth Simon said, 'Works both ways –'

'I'm glad to hear it –'

'Glad?'

'Glad that you do have a heart.'

Simon pulled a blank piece of paper towards him.

He said, 'What is the name of your solicitor?'

'Susan Dewar.'

'I know Susan Dewar.'

'Good.'

'To whom you and I will both reveal statements of assets we both know already and then argue about them.'

'I won't argue,' Guy said.

Simon flung the ballpoint across the office, hitting a month-by-month calendar from a local garage, hanging slightly crookedly on the opposite wall.

'This is all such a bloody *farce*!'

'Yes.'

Simon glared at his father.

'Susan Dewar is tough.'

'No more than I'll let her be. I'm not *fighting* your mother, Simon.'

Simon said, without thinking, 'She's fighting *you*.'

Guy stood up.

'It doesn't follow that *you* have to fight me.'

Simon said unhappily, 'I don't know –'

'Don't you?' Guy said. His voice was sharper. 'Don't you even know your *own* mind?'

Simon got up and went slowly across his office to retrieve the ballpoint. He stooped to pick it up. From his bent position he said, slightly muffled, 'You'd better go.'

Guy moved towards the door. With his hand on the handle, he turned to look at Simon.

'If we were Americans, we could tell each other we loved each other at this point.'

'Would that help?'

'I think it might – bridge a gap.'

'Would we have to mean it?'

'Oh Simon,' Guy said. He turned the door handle. Simon was still facing the wall and the garage calendar, flicking his thumbnail again with the ballpoint pen.

'Bye,' Guy said briefly, and went out.

Rachel stood in front of the mirror on Carrie's wardrobe door. She was trying on clothes. She'd put on her new baggy jeans – they sat on her hips most satisfactorily – and then over that a black lace mini dress she'd found in a second-hand shop for two pounds and over that a grey wool V-knecked sweater of her father's. Emma was out – drama club was rehearsing *Joseph and the Technicolor Dreamcoat* and Emma, to Rachel's disgust, had been cast as Potiphar's wife – so Rachel had borrowed Emma's new dark-blue wedge-soled rubber mules. The effect was good. Rachel turned and looked at herself sideways. Her bosom – it was going to be really small, like Carrie's – hardly showed at all. Her tummy (her obsession) didn't show either, but she could see it all the same, pushing obscenely, roundly, at the denim and the black lace and the grey wool. She'd eaten nothing that day but two carrots, a bag of barbecue-flavour crisps and two handfuls of raspberry crunch cereal dry, straight out of the packet. She wouldn't eat any supper. Or at least, she'd pick out the low-calorie bits of supper and leave the rest. Carrie wouldn't notice just now. Carrie had been anorexic for three years after her mother died and she had an eye like a hawk for not-eaters. But Carrie was preoccupied at the moment and not as observant as usual. If she'd been observant, she'd have noticed that Emma had had her belly button pierced by a friend at school using a needle and a cork and some ice cubes, that Rachel was hardly eating and that Jack had enough condoms in his bedroom to kit out the British Army.

Jack had discovered sex. Rachel was half intrigued and half repelled. The word at school was that Moll Saunders knew what she was doing, and although not exactly promiscuous – she didn't go in for one-night-stands or two-timing – she was pretty experienced. And whatever experience she had, she was plainly imparting it to Jack, session by absorbing session, to the point where it was plain to Rachel – and probably to half the school, too – that it was absolutely all he could think about. When you looked at him – Rachel did this frequently but covertly, because her own reaction to his state was so disconcerting – you could see he was just dazed, by Moll and sex, by sex and Moll. When Rachel had had a good illicit snoop around Jack's bedroom, she had expected to find a lot of pornographic stuff about, magazines and videos, even some of those toys and aids which Trudy said her father kept under his side of the marital bed in an old super-market carrier bag. But, apart from the condoms, there was nothing, no sign of fantasy or solitary dreaming. Rachel had thought she felt disappointed; she expected, she knew, to find more; cruder evidence of Jack's una-voidable adolescent-boy preoccupation. But when she got back to her bedroom and lay on the bed in the dark listening to Brandy, she realised that she wasn't so much disappointed as jealous. She was jealous of Jack's intensity of feeling. She was jealous of Moll for having someone *that* interested in her, that obsessed. Rachel and Trudy scoffed at boys, scoffed together about them. But faced with Jack and Moll, Rachel knew she'd sell her soul to have someone – someone attractive, that is – so keen on her that he couldn't see straight. Lying on her bed, staring at the ceiling which still had the glow stars on it she'd stuck up there when she was seven, she made a slow mental review of the sixth-form boys at school. Nobody under sixteen would do, nobody shorter than her, nobody blond, nobody with such a big opinion of himself he'd laugh at her (that knocked out most of Jack's friends), nobody who wouldn't cause Trudy to sit up and take notice. Trudy's opinion would be crucial in this. It would be important for Trudy to feel just an edge of the jealous yearning that Rachel felt then, lying on her bed and thinking about Moll.

There was a movement outside Carrie's bedroom door.

'Rach?' Carrie said.

'Yeah –'

'I'm coming in.'

'Course,' Rachel said.

The door opened. Rachel held one foot up, shod in Emma's mule.

'Don't tell me, don't tell me, I'm going to put them back.'

Carrie looked at her.

'I like the dress and the sweater but why the jeans?'

'It's cool.'

'Is it?'

'It's the layered look.'

'But doesn't it matter what the layers are?'

'Jeans are OK, Mum.'

'If you say so.'

Carrie went past Rachel and opened her wardrobe door. She took off her suit jacket – rather tiredly, Rachel thought – and put it crookedly on a hanger. She lifted it to hang it inside the wardrobe, and it immediately fell off.

'Damn.'

Rachel bent and picked it up. It was still warm, from being on Carrie.

'Where's Dad?'

'Guess,' Carrie said. She took the jacket and hung it up again, her face averted so that Rachel couldn't really see it. Rachel hesitated, then she said, 'I forgot he'd gone. He – he asked me to go with him.'

Carrie stared at her.

'To Granny's?'

'Yes.'

'What did you say?'

'Well, I couldn't, could I? There's school.'

'It's half term,' Carrie said. She pushed the wardrobe door shut.

'I forgot.'

Carrie turned to look at her.

'He'd have had company,' she said. 'On the journey.'

Rachel squirmed faintly. She took one foot out of Emma's mules and rubbed it up and down the back of her other leg.

'I don't like going there.'

'Why not?'

'The ferret man,' Rachel mumbled.

'Rachel,' Carrie said, 'that was years ago. You were nine.'

'Eight,' Rachel said.

She'd been sent to stay with Laura, just her and Emma. Emma had loved it, had loved the meals on time and the big bed with fat pillows and the ritual of picking vegetables and the dogs. She'd begged and begged Laura to let her take the dogs out alone and at last Laura had relented

164

on condition that Rachel went, too. They were only to be twenty minutes, Laura said. She lent Rachel her watch, to be sure. After about seven minutes only, in the hilly field behind the cottage, they'd met a man with two lurchers. He had a flat cap on and a small wet mouth, and he was carrying a dead rabbit, swinging from one hand. Emma had screamed.

Rachel said, almost in a whisper, 'Did you shoot it?'

He grinned at her. He jerked his head towards his dogs. 'She got it.'

The girls had stepped back clutching Laura's dogs – quelled by the presence of the lurchers – by their leads.

The man grinned again. Rachel saw his tongue shoot out and lick his lower lip.

'It'll do to feed the ferrets,' he said.

They'd run. They'd dragged Laura's dogs down the field and run and run until they reached the garden. Rachel hadn't wanted to tell Laura, but of course Emma did, sobbing and snuffling, wanting to be comforted and given a piece of chocolate. Laura thought Emma was crying because of the poor dead rabbit. Rachel let her think it. She didn't really care what Laura thought. All she cared about was getting out of the hateful country and back to London, double quick.

Carrie unzipped her work skirt and let it fall to the floor. She was wearing black tights underneath, and one leg had a narrow white ladder in it, running up Carrie's thigh from the knee. She stepped out of her skirt and picked her jeans up from the muddle of clothes on the couch.

'Poor Dad,' Carrie said. She began to pull her jeans on, struggling unsteadily on one leg.

Rachel watched her. Something about her new-found discovery of jealousy made her think Carrie looked sad, really sad, putting her jeans on, and not stupid or inept or typical-Mum-ish as she would have expected herself to think. She said awkwardly, turning up the long, baggy sleeves of Simon's sweater, 'Poor you.'

Carrie stopped pulling her zip up and looked at Rachel. Her hair was falling everywhere. There was a comb on the carpet.

'Is that why you didn't go?'

Rachel shrugged.

Carrie said, a little unsteadily, 'I don't want you to have to take sides.'

Rachel muttered, her head bent, 'I'll decide that.'

'It isn't that I don't understand,' Carrie said. 'It isn't that I don't see how difficult it is for him.' She finished pulling up her zip and reached for a red sweatshirt. 'I wouldn't like you to think –'

'I don't,' Rachel said. She took both feet out of Emma's mules and bent to pick them up.

'I know, really,' Carrie said. She pulled the sweatshirt over her head. 'Do you know where Jack is?'

'No.'

'You mean you wouldn't tell me, even if you did.'

Rachel said, holding Emma's mules out, 'I'd better put these back –'

'Yes,' Carrie said. She ran a hand through her hair and took out the remaining comb. Then she came quickly over to Rachel and gave her a light kiss on her cheek. 'Thank you,' she said.

Rachel couldn't look at her. There was a sudden lump of misery in her throat, hard and tight, like a hazelnut.

'That's OK,' she said, and went out.

Merrion's room in chambers looked down on to a narrow walk that led into New Square. People went up and down the walk all day, lawyers and ordinary pedestrians, visible and weirdly inaudible because of the double glazing across the windows. Sometimes on the telephone to a solicitor or another barrister, Merrion let her gaze drift down through the window to watch these gesticulating, walking, talking people and wondered if they really felt as animated, as purposeful, as they looked.

Nobody in her personal life had ever seen her room; not even Guy, certainly not Gwen. Gwen would have thought it very impersonal, cold even, with its white-painted shelves of law books, its Hogarth-framed prints of the Law Courts, of Lincoln's Inn, its complete absence of photographs or flowers or even a carrier bag to indicate a little lunchtime shopping. It was how Merrion liked it, however: it was where she could think. It was the place where this person, Miss Palmer of Counsel, had a life where the rules were both known and adhered to, where whatever turbulence she had to deal with was manageable because it was at a slight distance and her relationship to it was, however sympathetic, defined by her paid professionalism.

'It's making you cold,' Gwen had said to Merrion on the telephone. 'The law is hardening your heart.'

'That's not the point.'

'What isn't the point?'

'What you are saying is not the point of this phone call.'

There'd been a small, sulky silence Gwen's end of the telephone line.

'You had no business to attack Guy like you did,' Merrion said. 'Me, well, OK if you simply have to, though I could probably write your speech for you. But it wasn't fair to go for him and you had absolutely no right to. You took advantage of his good manners. He should have thrown you out.'

Gwen said, with a small note of triumph, 'He didn't think it was none of my business. He said –'

'I don't want to know what he said. It's happened, it's caused great misery and complication, but it's over. I'm just ringing to tell you it won't happen again. Ever. You will mind your own business in future.'

'I won't be patronised,' Gwen said. 'I won't be told.'

Merrion gripped the receiver. 'Too right,' she said. 'You won't be told *anything*.'

Gwen had written to her, after that. She had written a letter ostentatiously addressed to Merrion in chambers. She had written 'Strictly private and personal' on the envelope and one of the junior clerks had handed it to Merrion with a wink. Sometimes, barristers got fan mail. Very occasionally, the fan mail was quite frisky. One young man, whose mother Merrion had successfully defended, had taken to coming to chambers with thin bouquets of mixed flowers – chrysanthemums and carnations on spindly stalks – and asking to be allowed to see Merrion to present them. He had caused a lot of mirth in the clerks' room, particularly because he was so awkward, and wore an anorak with a drawstring waist.

'This is from my mother,' Merrion said to the junior clerk, with emphasis.

It was a good letter, Merrion had to admit that. It was calm and dignified and made the point that Merrion's welfare could not possibly be a matter of indifference to Gwen, unless Gwen were a monster, and that Gwen's standards and opinions, even if very much less sophisticated than Merrion's, did not on that account lack their own validity. It was not Guy as a *person* she objected to, but the consequences of his age in relation to Merrion's and the strength of his emotional desires which, even if they coincided with Merrion's, were nevertheless forcing a pace whose long-term outcome nobody seemed to be prepared to face squarely and openly.

Merrion did not show the letter to Guy. She did not tell him, either, that she had telephoned Gwen because she had promised him not to, in the first place. She was aware that this was not like her, that her instinct and habit had always been to tell him everything, not least because he was so wonderfully able to restore her sense of proportion. But in the past, her feelings about him had not been particularly protective. He had never asked for her sympathy over his marriage, had never suggested that he believed himself due any kind of reparation, or compensation for the curious, chilly, diffuse nature of his and Laura's form of communication – if communication was in any way the word for it. Merrion was aware from the beginning – rapturously aware – of Guy's delight in being able to talk to her, being free, even encouraged, to talk to her, but she had never, until recently, felt the need to defend him, and, in the process of that defence, not only curb her own tongue but also refrain from asking too many questions. What had been so clear between them, what she had always felt she could easily, contentedly describe, had become less definable. A veil had appeared, a series of veils, which made the business of loving no less ardent, but much less simple.

It came down in the end, Merrion thought, marshalling the papers on her desk into the series of rectangles she needed them to be in before she could think straight, to all these *people*. These people who had been names and images before, but no more, people who had a reality for Guy but who hadn't needed, for years and years, to have much of a reality for her. For years Simon and Carrie and Alan and even Laura had been in Merrion's consciousness, at one remove, the wife and the sons and the daughter-in-law. They weren't enemies, they didn't even need winning over for the simple reason that they didn't know, and for so long neither Guy nor Merrion needed or wanted them to know. They belonged in a mental in-tray marked 'one day'. Merrion got very used to having that intray there, very used to thinking that the future was something like Christmas, undeniably there, not particularly threatening, which would quietly arrive in its own good time with an accompanying set of rituals and instructions.

But it hadn't been like that. It hadn't been like that, at all. One day, the future was where it had always been, comfortably upon some fairly remote horizon, and the next day, it had arrived. It arrived without warning and without any helpful information and within hours Merrion had gone from an acceptance of how things were to a real, profound and painful longing for something more.

'I can't bear this,' Guy had said. 'I can't bear living this part-life with you any more. I can't bear the waste of it, the fact that it is so wrongly unacknowledged.'

And almost before the words were out of his mouth, she had realised that she had been desperate for him to say them, that she had had enough of not minding – not minding Christmas, not minding weekends, not minding Laura's birthday – and that (most extraordinary of all) what had for seven years seemed thrilling and potent and truly essential had become, in moments, to feel contrived and furtive and distasteful. In the space of a day secrecy became something Merrion could hardly remember as alluring; its charms (upon which she had so relied) withered as she watched them. Her sheer pride in being Guy's *mistress* turned into something, at a stroke, whose glamour she could scarcely remember.

And then the people came in. The names were fleshed out, the personalities grew from little lists of adjectives into palpable beings, beings to be reckoned with, taken into account, negotiated with. Guy – no less loving, no less attentive – seemed all the same to retreat into the landscape of these people who had known him for three and four decades, and more. Whatever he did or didn't do, these people reclaimed him, recalled him, reminded him of what they felt he owed them, what he was most definitely not free to do without them. And, as a result, a kind of helplessness had descended upon Guy and Merrion; she saw the two of them sometimes, in her mind's eye, like figures in a German Romantic painting, clinging together on a plain or a clifftop while a huge, bruise-coloured storm rolled inexorably towards them in a whirl of wind.

She looked at her watch. It was two o'clock. She had a conference at three for which she had not done sufficient preparation. It would, with luck, be over by four-thirty, and then she would telephone Guy.

'Come up to London,' she'd say.

'What? How lovely. A not-Friday –'

He never said no. She didn't know what she would do, if he said no. He'd come up, on the five o'clock train, and be in the flat by six-thirty, where she'd already be, with supper bought and wine in the fridge and her black suit exchanged for trousers and a jersey, and her announcement. She would announce – and he would listen; he always did – that she was tired of taking what came, feeling her way, being paced and checked by other people. Whether he was divorced or not, whether Laura was dragging her heels or not, whether Simon and Susan Dewar were in agreement or not, she was going to announce a wedding day. Had he heard her? She wanted to decide a date to be married.

CHAPTER TWELVE

'Three offers!' Wendy said. 'That's wonderful. Aren't people odd, always fired up about living in the country when spring comes, just as if winter was never going to happen again.'

Laura said, 'One of them is quite a bit above the asking price –'

Wendy gave the garden table in front of her a little slap.

'Well, now, *that's* something to rejoice over!'

'I'd have to share it with Guy,' Laura said primly.

'You said Simon was making him give you the lion's share –'

'Oh yes.'

'Then if you get more money for this, *you'll* have more –'

Laura looked down the garden. The herbaceous border – such extraordinarily hard work, such equally extraordinary satisfaction – was full of bright clumps of new leaves, the first stirrings of lupins, aquilegia, delphiniums, foxgloves.

She said, 'It isn't about that.'

Wendy looked at her coffee mug. Then she looked at the almost empty coffee pot. Then she looked at the tubs of huge blue pansies beside her and at the aubretia and the iberis spilling over a nearby low wall and then she looked at Laura.

'You could do this garden again.'

'What for?'

'For exactly the same reason as you did this. Because you're good at it. Because you like it.'

'But there'd be no point to it –'

'Don't kid yourself.'

'About what?'

'That there was any point beyond your own pleasure in making *this* garden. Guy isn't a garden man. Never has been.'

Laura said to her lap, 'I wanted him to be.'

Wendy poured herself some cold coffee. She added milk and although she didn't usually take it, a spoonful of brown sugar. She stirred the mixture. It looked muddy and unattractive. She pushed the mug away from her.

'Laura –'

'Yes.'

'This business of Guy –'

Laura raised her head and looked at Wendy.

'What about Guy?'

'I just wonder –' She stopped.

Laura waited.

'Did you ever love Guy?' Wendy said. 'Or did you just want him to love you?'

Laura grasped the arms of her green plastic garden chair.

'How dare you –'

'You think about it,' Wendy said.

Laura said, half crying, 'Why would I want him to love me if I didn't love him in the first place?'

Wendy leaned back. She shaded her eyes despite her sunglasses and looked up at the sky. Three ducks were going overhead in neat triangular formation, like stunt-flying aeroplanes.

'You tell me.'

'He's been the centre of my life for forty years, he's been the pivot, the heart –'

Wendy said nothing. She stopped looking at the sky and looked at her hands instead. On her left hand she wore her wedding ring and the eternity ring Roger had given her when they'd survived ten years and three children and an escapade of his with the captain of the Stanborough tennis club's women's team. She'd lost her engagement ring years ago. It had probably gone out with the rubbish or down the drain with the laundry or the children's bath water. She didn't miss it. It was an amethyst, a biggish amethyst surrounded by diamonds, and it had belonged to Roger's Aunt Lilian. It was a gloomy ring, Wendy always thought, just like Aunt Lilian. She twisted the eternity ring. It could do with a clean, poor thing, a freshen up. She'd have a go at it later, she thought, with some washing-up liquid and an old toothbrush. She looked at Laura.

'You'll have to stop this.'

'Stop what?'

'All this pretending. All this being sorry for yourself. It's not fair on anyone, particularly not on your children.'

'Simon doesn't mind. Simon –'

'You aren't *allowing* Simon to mind,' Wendy said. She looked at her watch. 'I must go. You're treating Simon just like you treated Guy. Just taking the bits you want.'

'Oh!' Laura cried, and covered her face with her hands.

Wendy stood up.

'Tell you what –'

Laura waited, her hands over her face.

'I think you could do with a little therapy.'

Laura snatched her hands away.

'*Therapy?*'

'Yes.'

'I'm not mad!' Laura shrieked. 'I'm not out of my mind!'

Wendy picked up her bag, and adjusted her spotted-framed sunglasses on their black bead necklace.

'I didn't say that.'

'But *therapy* –'

'To reconcile yourself. What some therapy could do is help to reconcile you to what's happened, to the future.'

Laura glared at her. She stood up abruptly, knocking the table so that Wendy's cold coffee slopped out of her mug. She seemed to be simmering with things she wanted to say and somehow couldn't. Wendy slung her bag on to her shoulder.

'Unless, of course,' she said, 'you really have no intention of ever being reconciled to anything.'

The senior clerk looked at his watch. Then he looked at Alan. He said, 'I'm expecting Miss Palmer back from court in about fifteen minutes, sir.'

Alan said, 'Can I wait?'

'Certainly, sir. Do you have an appointment?'

'No,' Alan said, 'I'm family.' He paused. The senior clerk had gold-rimmed spectacles and the air of someone who expects to know, expects to be informed and, subsequently, to decide.

'I'll wait in her room,' Alan said. This was all an impulse, finding himself walking through New Square after a prolonged and happy lunch with Charlie, and deciding just to drop in on Merrion, see her on her own territory, in her chosen setting. It might be the Chianti – they'd shared a bottle and been hugely tempted by a second except Charlie had a four o'clock surgery – but Alan didn't feel inclined to be intimidated by Gold Spectacles. He put a hand on the counter that separated the clerks from the outside world. 'If you'll just tell me where it is?'

The senior clerk hesitated for a second. It was plain he was deciding whether to escort Alan to Merrion's room, or merely to instruct him as to how to find it.

'Your name, sir?'

'Alan Stockdale. My father –'

'Exactly, sir,' the clerk said. He leaned across the

counter and indicated to the right. 'If you take the stairs to the right, sir, to the first floor, and follow the corridor round to the left, you'll find Miss Palmer's room on your right, at the end.'

'Thank you.'

'I'll tell her you're here, Mr Stockdale.'

'Thank you,' Alan said again. He transferred his jacket from over his arm to over his shoulder. He was wearing a dark-green shirt and jeans. Gold Spectacles was in black and white. Alan gave him a grin and went across the reception to the staircase.

Merrion's room was oddly quiet with a sealed-in feeling. Her mackintosh hung behind the door, and her barrister's wig hung on the knob of an upright chairback. Alan peered at it. Weird thing, bizarre, all those neat little horsehair rolls and rows. He sniffed it. It smelt dusty and faintly of something that might have been scent. Presumably, if it was hanging here, Merrion wasn't actually appearing in court, whatever else she was doing there. Alan wondered what else she did do. Talk to people, clients and stuff? Get judges to agree to things outside the courtroom? He thought of her arguing very steadily with heated people who didn't want her to be sensible, didn't want to hear the reasonable, practical things she had to say. He picked the wig up and put it on his own head. It was a bit small. There was a little mirror hanging behind the door. He leaned forward to see himself, see the crisp grey-white wig perched on his own dark hair which even Charlie – who liked long hair – said needed a cut. He made a face at himself. The wig might be too small, but it was also strangely becoming, especially the straight line of it across his brow. It made him look slightly authoritative in a distinctly attractive way. He thought, briefly, delightedly, of wearing *only* the wig.

The door opened.

'You!' Merrion said.

Alan snatched the wig off.

'Sorry –'

'Feel free,' she said. 'It's a peculiar bit of kit, isn't it?'

She went past him, sliding her bag off her shoulder, and an armful of papers on to her desk. She was in a black suit and her hair was in a trim, fat pigtail which started almost at the crown of her head and ended below her collar, tied neatly with a black ribbon. She glanced at him.

'To what do I owe –'

'Nothing,' Alan said. 'Just an idea, a spur of the moment idea. I was walking back from lunch.'

Merrion said, smiling, 'Don't you work?'

He shrugged.

'In bursts.'

'Would you like some tea?'

'Is that –'

'A nuisance? No.' She gave him another quick glance. 'I'm glad to see you.'

He beamed.

'Oh good.'

'Sit down,' she said. 'The kettle lives outside in a cupboard. The sort of thing a designer would call a coffee point. I won't be a moment.'

She went out of the room. Alan sat in a green leather chair, opposite her desk. This was presumably where Merrion's clients sat, and looked at her across her desk top and thought: This is my lawyer who is going to save me, and who is going to cost me x pounds an hour at the same time. What did Merrion cost people? Eighty pounds an hour? A hundred and twenty pounds an hour? How were these things calculated anyway? He looked at Merrion's bag. It was black leather, big enough to hold a book or a file of documents. Alan wondered what private stuff it had in it, too, lipsticks and tampons and photographs. Probably, in that businesslike-looking bag, there were photographs of Guy, photographs Alan had never seen, taken on occasions he had never known about and never would. Merrion had seen aspects of Guy that nobody else had ever seen, maybe aspects that nobody else had ever noticed. That was what happened when you fell in love, that was what Charlie had been talking about over lunch, the way that falling in love enabled you to go to places in yourself you'd never been to before, places you didn't know about, places you wouldn't have dared to go to without this particular person to go with you. Being in love with Charlie made Alan feel a kind of sympathetic intensity towards Merrion. He looked at her bag again and hoped that it was stuffed with mementoes of Guy, photographs and letters and tiny portable presents, key rings and pens and things. The kind of little, often-used thing that kept the giver in your mind a dozen times a day.

Merrion came back into the room carrying a small tin tray with two mugs on it and a pint carton of milk.

'Do you have sugar?'

'No.'

'Just as well.'

He got up and took the tray from her. He said, 'I know you had supper with Simon and Carrie.'

She made a space on her desk for him to put the tray down.

'I can't get used to the way news travels round families. I don't have a family really, just my mother, so I expect things I do to stay private and of course they don't.'

'I talk to Carrie a lot,' Alan said.

'Yes.'

'We have a kind of unspoken pact. I don't know how it started.'

'I imagine,' Merrion said, pouring milk into their tea mugs, 'that once she's on your side, she stays there.'

'Just about,' Alan said. 'Though she wouldn't pull any punches.'

Merrion pushed a mug towards Alan.

'I like her.'

He said, smiling and looking at his tea, 'I expect she likes you.'

Merrion sat down in the high-backed chair behind her desk.

'Nobody can really come clean, though, can they?'

'What do you mean?'

'I mean,' Merrion said, 'that we can't, any of us, express our real, true opinions. We all have to behave beautifully, diplomatically. We have to edit what we say, all the time.'

He leaned back in his chair.

'What would you like to say?'

She looked at him.

'Ready?'

'Ready.'

'Right,' she said. 'Well, it seems to me that the person who is creating the most difficulties right now, the person who is setting people most successfully against one another, the person who is being supremely unreasonable – is your mother.'

Alan looked down again into his tea.

'Simon would say she is the most justified because she is the most injured.'

'Simon isn't here,' Merrion said. 'Anyway, from what I gather, she isn't exactly fair to Simon either.'

'Has Carrie said anything?'

Merrion drank some tea.

'She doesn't need to. While I was there for supper your mother rang in hysterics about the house sale. Nobody *said* anything, of course. Because they didn't need to.'

Alan said thoughtfully, 'My parents have been married longer than I've been alive.'

'And me.'

'Does longevity give a situation precedence?'

'Not legally –'

'Morally?'

'I don't know,' Merrion said. 'All I do know is that your father wouldn't have fallen in love with me and stayed in love all this time if he and your mother had everything it takes to keep a marriage going.'

'Why didn't he leave her before?'

She said calmly, 'I didn't ask him to.'

'Did you now?'

'Not really. It sort of coincided with his offering to. It got to a point.'

'Between you?' Alan said. 'Or between him and my mother?'

She drank more tea.

'Both, I should think. But we'll never know precisely –'

'It just happened –'

'Yes.'

'And now you're kind of fighting her for my father.'

'Am I?'

'I think so,' Alan said. 'And Carrie is fighting her for Simon.'

Merrion said nothing. She got up and leaned against the window. Two men were down on the paved walk below, both still wearing their court tabs, peering at the top sheet in a pile of papers one of them held. Merrion knew the one in spectacles. He'd asked her out for a drink once, years ago, when she was still a pupil, and then forgotten to turn up. When she saw him subsequently he either pretended not to remember he'd forgotten, or genuinely didn't.

'I've decided to take a bit of a stand,' Merrion said, to the window glass.

'Oh?'

'We're going to get married in October. Some time close to my birthday.'

'October –'

'Yes.'

There was a tiny pause and then Alan said, 'Six months.'

'Yes.'

'Suppose the divorce isn't through by then?'

'It will be.'

'How can you be sure?'

'I can't. But I can be confident.'

'Dad's being advised by a friend of yours.'

'Not a friend. Just a solicitor I know who I have confidence in. It's an incredibly tricky situation because of Simon representing your mother. It wouldn't stand up in court, a son representing his mother. We have to just hope it doesn't come to that.'

'You sound very crisp,' Alan said.

Merrion turned from the window. She said, in quite a different voice, almost a whisper, 'I want to rescue him –'

'Dad?'

'Yes,' Merrion said. She put the back of one hand up briefly against her eyes. 'I want him to see how it can be, how it's supposed to be. I want him to see that he's got it right, he's had it right, all the time, by just being who he is, the person he is –'

She stopped. She sat down in her chair again abruptly and put her elbows on the desk in front of her. Alan leaned forward and put his tea mug down on a pile of pamphlets and then he stretched an arm out and touched her very lightly.

'Good luck,' he said.

Guy was late, arriving at the court building. He wasn't very late – a mere ten minutes – but he disliked being anything other than early, always had. The morning train from London was slightly delayed at Reading – some typical, predictable signalling problem – and it was raining which always meant a dearth of taxis at Stanborough Station. When he did find one, it dropped him at the main court building entrance, and not the side entrance which he and the other judges always used, and when he complained, the taxi driver pointed out with satisfaction that the entrance to the court building's private car-park was blocked by an enormous truck, parked half on the pavement, and with no driver in the cab.

He went through the public lobby as rapidly as possible, and up the staircase to the courtroom floor. He was conscious of carrying an overnight bag in front of the court staff, as well as being in parts of the building they were not accustomed to seeing him in. Two security guards were standing by the public doors to Court Two, jingling their keys the way most men jingle their change.

'I've got three down there this morning,' one of them was saying. 'Straight off Planet Lager and it isn't even Friday. Morning, Judge.'

'Morning,' Guy said.

'Martin's looking for you,' the guard said. 'You might find him in your room.'

Guy pushed open the door to the judge's corridor. It was quiet there, as it always was, and slightly stuffy; the air smelled of dusty carpet. Outside the door to Guy's own chambers, Martin was standing. He was jacketless, as was his custom, and his shirt cuffs were rolled up above his wrists.

'Martin,' Guy said. 'Have I kept you waiting?'

'No,' Martin said. He opened the door to Guy's room and held it for Guy to pass through. 'I didn't have an appointment, did I?'

'I'm always in by eight-forty-five –'

'Except when the trains are late,' Martin said.

Guy hesitated. He put his briefcase down on his desk and heard Martin close the door behind him.

'Yes,' he said.

'I'm not prying, Judge –'

'No,' Guy said. 'Of course you're not.' He turned round. 'It's rather difficult to get the timing right.'

Martin put a hand up and adjusted the knot of his tie. 'That's why I thought I'd come and see you.'

Guy made a gesture towards a chair.

'Do sit down –'

Martin sat. He crossed his legs. He linked his fingers together in his lap.

Guy leaned against the edge of his desk. He said, with a shyness he didn't seem able to control, 'I imagine – you have a good idea –'

Martin waited.

'My wife and I are separated,' Guy said. He leaned his hands on the desk edge, either side of him, and stared at his shoes. 'We are to be divorced. When we are divorced, I shall be marrying again.'

Martin said, 'Miss Palmer?'

Guy nodded.

'When I am in London, I am staying at Miss Palmer's flat. When I am in Stanborough, I have a flat out at Pinns Green. Usually, I confine my visits to London to the weekends. If you need those contact numbers as well as my mobile-telephone number, of course you shall have them.

'Thank you, Judge.'

Guy transferred his gaze from his own feet to Martin's.

'Is that what you needed to see me for?'

'I just needed the fact,' Martin said. 'On account of the rumours.'

'Are – there many?'

Martin said steadily, 'You know how it is, Judge.'

'Well, I don't, you see,' Guy said. 'That's half the trouble. There's no rehearsal, is there, for something like this.'

Martin leaned forward. He put his elbows on his knees.

'I was divorced eight years ago.'

'I had no idea –'

'You wouldn't, Judge. It was before I took this job, I

was working in London then.' He glanced up at Guy. 'It's never easy.'

'Thank you, Martin. Has – has there been much talk?'

Martin stood up.

'Only when they haven't got the football to think about.'

'Do you have children?'

Martin moved towards the door.

'Three, Judge. Thank you for your time and for your confidence.'

'And do you see them?' Guy said.

Martin opened the door. As he went out he said, 'Like you, Judge, I spend my weekends in London,' and then he closed the door behind him.

Guy stood up. He went round his desk to the window and stood looking down at the car-park, at the familiar cars of all his colleagues with familiar things visible through the back windows, maps and rugs and plastic bottles of water, quiet evidence of lives lived a car journey away from this building and all its preoccupations. Poor Martin, poor man, probably living, as Guy lived now, in a strange homeless no-man's-land where the sense of be-longing that characterised so much family life was torn away, leaving a feeling of acute disorientation behind it.

'It's so odd,' Guy had said to Merrion not long ago, 'but sometimes, when I'm not with you, when I'm not in court, I have a feeling that I've become invisible. That I've vanished.'

She had been puzzled. To her, his status, his profes-sional achievement, was more than enough to give him an inescapable identity. He saw that she couldn't understand – because she had never really known them – those subtler, quieter measures of singularity, or specificity, those marks of self conferred by being tied by blood to other people. There were, after all, almost no relations in Merrion's life: she belonged to nobody beyond her mother and was in turn possessed by nobody beyond her mother. This state of affairs spelled liberty, certainly, but it also spelled a curious lack of human landscape, a landscape that Guy now knew he had simply taken for granted as the natural backdrop to everything and anything he might accomplish. All those years, all those taken-for-granted mornings, he had, as poor Martin must have done, stepped out of that human backdrop to go to work and returned to settle confidently into it again at night. It was accepted, a given, so much part of him that he had not really given it a thought except in a hurried, practical, often exasperated way. And now it wasn't there. It existed still, but not in the same relationship to him any more; the dynamics had changed. He thought of Hill Cottage; he thought of the steep field behind it and the well-known idiosyncrasies of both places – dark corners and sudden steps and uneven paths. It wasn't, he thought, staring unseeingly down on the dusty car roofs below him, so much that he longed for the place, that he missed Hill Cottage, but that he felt – had felt for some weeks now – a painful space where his simple sense of domestic and family belonging had once been.

The door of his room opened at the same time as somebody tapped lightly on it. Penny put her head round. She had taken to dragging her hair off her face with little metal clips so that she looked as if she was enduring some arcane kind of punishment.

'Five minutes, Judge,' she said. 'Court One.'

Laura was weeding. She was a meticulous weeder, on her knees hand-weeding with a small, light aluminium fork Guy had given her two Christmases ago. He nearly always gave her something for the garden. In the early days, he gave her books and jewellery, but the books were seldom to her taste and the jewellery was invariably too bold. There were boxes of it lying in the drawers of her dressing table, complete with the cards Guy had written to go with them. Laura had looked at some of those cards only the other night. 'To my darling Laura,' they said, year after year. 'All my love, Guy.' It was, now she came to think of it, seven or eight years since the jewellery stopped and the garden forks took over. About the length of time, in fact, that he had been having his affair with Merrion Palmer. Simon had told her he was sure it was just coincidence, that Guy had at last realised there was no point in giving gold gypsy hoops to a woman who only ever wore her twenty-first birthday pearls. Laura could not believe him. It was extra evidence to her that the garden forks never came with little cards expressing a completeness of love. They'd presumably had cards, of sorts, but Laura hadn't kept them. She'd certainly have kept them, she told Simon, if they'd been worth keeping.

A car was coming down the lane. The engine note was familiar. Laura sat back on her heels and looked across through the orchard to the hedge that divided Hill Cottage from the lane. A grey car was visible, coming down the lane. Guy had a grey car, an elderly grey Volvo he'd had for years, having bought it from a retiring judge when he was elected to the Bench himself.

'It's a bit silly,' he'd said to Laura. 'A bit of pseudo gravitas, really.'

The grey car slowed as it approached the gates to the drive and turned in. Laura stayed where she was, sitting on her heels, holding her aluminium fork. The car was Guy's, and Guy was driving. He went up the drive and stopped, just out of sight, where he had always stopped, by the back door. Laura heard the dogs barking and squealing. She heard Guy's car door slam. She looked down at the patch she had weeded, at the moist, crumbly, dark earth, so finely forked it resembled chocolate-cake crumbs. She waited.

'Laura!' Guy shouted.

'Here,' she said, in a whisper.

She heard his voice going shouting round the far side of the house, and then the dogs came racing round to find her and tell her the joyful news that Guy was home. They were extremely over-excited, and bounded around her, trampling across her lap, licking and wagging.

'Don't,' she said, shielding her face. 'Don't.'

'There you are,' Guy said, following the dogs.

Laura looked steadily at the earth. He came over the grass towards her and crouched down two feet away from her.

'Laura,' he said.

She didn't look at him.

'What are you doing here?'

'I came to see you,' he said. 'I came to see Hill Cottage.'

'Why?'

'For some simple reasons and some rather more obscure ones.'

'Typical,' Laura said. She leaned forward and stuck her fork into the earth, under a flourishing clump of groundsel.

'Laura,' Guy said, 'could we talk, do you think?'

'You know what I said about that. I *told* you.'

'Yes. You did. But it doesn't work. It just makes things harder.'

Laura shrugged. She shook the groundsel roots free of earth.

'And it is extremely unfair to Simon,' Guy said.

'Please leave Simon out of it.'

'I can't,' Guy said. 'Like it or not, he is my son as well as yours. You can't appropriate him like this and if you are going to instruct him as you have, then he is automatically involved.'

Laura said nothing. Guy knelt on the grass to get closer to her. She could see the creases on the knees of his dark suit. She could smell, very faintly, the scent of his cologne, the scent that lurked so unkindly in the linen cupboard, in the little room off their bathroom where Guy had kept his clothes.

'Look,' Guy said, 'I will let you have as much of everything as I can. I will just leave myself enough to manage on.'

'Will that make you feel better?'

'Simon said that to me,' Guy said. 'And my reply is the same to you as it was to him. I hope it will make *you* feel better.'

'*Things*,' Laura said bitterly.

'Perhaps.'

'Please go,' Laura said.

'I will, but I have to ask you first if you will please, *please* release Simon and let him find you a solicitor to represent you whom he recommends?'

Laura took her fork out of the earth, and rubbed the tines clean on the grass beside her.

'This isn't the right kind of control,' Guy said. 'The control you need is the power to lead your own life, not manipulate other people's.'

'Why did you come?' Laura said again.

'I told you. I wanted to see Hill Cottage. I wanted to see you and ask you to reconsider this course of action. I wanted – I wanted to see if you were OK.'

Laura put the fork into the pocket of her gardening apron. Then she stood up, awkwardly and stiffly. She'd been on her knees too long. Guy rose, too, and put a hand out to steady her. She ignored it.

'Go away,' she said.

'Laura,' he said. 'Oh Laura, for your own sake if not for anyone else's, *please*.'

She looked at him, for the first time. Then she looked away.

'If you're homesick,' she said, 'then you'll just have to bear it, like I shall have to. And don't mention Simon to me again. I'm not making Simon do anything he doesn't want to do, is *glad* to do. If you're lonely, then you know who you have to blame.'

And then she turned and began to step deliberately across the grass, slightly stooped, towards the house and away from him.

CHAPTER THIRTEEN

Carrie looked at the piece of lamb in the roasting tin. It didn't look big enough. It looked big enough for five people, perhaps, but not for seven, which is what they were going to be at lunchtime since she had invited Guy and Merrion. She'd done it on impulse, she hadn't even told Simon she was going to. Something about her funny little broken conversation with Rachel had made her feel more confident, less helpless. She had felt that she wasn't powerless, that she could strike some small blow for herself. So she had rung Merrion and left a message on her answerphone.

'Come to lunch,' she'd said. 'On Sunday. Just family. Just you and Guy and us.'

It was Guy who'd rung back to say they'd love to. He sounded pleased but tired.

'It's a lovely thought –'

'It won't be anything much. Just Sunday.'

When she told Simon, he had simply nodded.

'OK.'

'You're not going to bite my head off?'

'I haven't the energy.'

'Oh, *wonderful*,' Carrie said.

'No need to be sarcastic –'

'No need to be so self-pitying. Sometimes I –' She stopped.

He looked at her.

'Sometimes you think I am just like my mother?'

'Yes,' Carrie said.

He'd shrugged. She heard him go upstairs and then the sound of running water and then he'd come down again before going out to one of the free legal-advice clinics he ran with Ted.

'Do you have to?'

He kissed her.

'Yes,' he'd said.

Now, looking at the under-sized piece of lamb, she thought she'd better wake him. She'd let him sleep in – heavens, she'd let them all sleep in – but Guy and Merrion were due in an hour and a half and, in any case, her feelings of self-sacrifice for the family were running dry. Lay table and cook lunch, fine. Tidy up sitting room, find wine, clear hall of school clutter, check downstairs lavatory, too, not fine at all. She ground salt and pepper over the lamb and opened the oven door. It ought to have garlic as well, but Emma had taken the last clove to school, for some domestic-economy lesson, and of course had forgotten to say, or bothered to replace it. Carrie put the roasting tin into the oven and closed the door.

She climbed the stairs. Rachel's bedroom door was shut and music was coming from Emma's, although the curtains were still pulled. She glanced up the second-floor stairs towards Jack's room. There was a black T-shirt lying on them, and a single high-top trainer and a crumpled magazine. Carrie sighed. She'd tackle Jack later. She went on towards her own bedroom and opened the door. Simon was asleep on her side of the bed, clutching the pillow against him as if it were a person.

She went across the room and pulled the curtains back. Then she went to the bed and sat down on the edge, next to Simon.

'Si,' she said.

He detached a hand from the pillow and held it out to her. She took it.

'Getting up time.'

'Mm,' he said.

'Getting up and helping-good-patient-wife time.'

He smiled faintly without opening his eyes.

'You're wonderful,' he said.

'I know. And about to be wonderfully cross.'

He yawned.

'Where are the kids?'

'Guess.'

He flung back the covers with sudden energy, and opened his eyes.

'OK,' he said. 'Sprint to bathroom before they do.'

From the floor above, Jack heard the groan and shudder of the water pipes as the shower was turned on. He'd been thinking about a shower, on and off, for some time. It was a funny thing, but if you slept in the T-shirt you'd been wearing all day, you didn't feel quite the same in the morning. It wasn't so much that you felt dirtier, but rather more that you felt tireder. Jack rolled sideways and stared at the floor. His jeans were crumpled on it and one trainer lay a few feet away. His socks and his boxer shorts, he discovered, were still on him.

He'd been too tired, he remembered, to take them off. Then he'd been too tired to sleep, really. He hadn't been tired in ages, quite the reverse, he'd been full of an enormous, brilliant energy, a feeling of wanting to run everywhere and vault gates and fences and take stairs and steps three at a time. And then yesterday, out of nowhere as far as he could see, Moll had said she was busy on Saturday night.

'You mean I can't see you?' he said.

She smiled right at him.

'Yes.'

'What are you doing?'

'Something my mum wants me to do,' Moll said.

'Your mum –'

'We always do a lot together,' Moll said. She was still smiling. 'I just haven't lately. Because of you.'

'Oh.'

She gave him a quick kiss on the side of his neck, a Moll special which involved a flick of her tongue.

'One Saturday,' she said.

'But it's a *Saturday* –'

'That's why Mum wants to go out with me.'

Of course, he'd smiled. Of course, he'd said yes. She'd given him one of her long steady looks, right up close, her face only an inch or two from his, and then she'd gone swinging off and he sat where she'd left him watching her bottom and her hair and the way she carried her bag over her shoulder as if it weighed nothing at all. He was so used to seeing her every day, so used to the assumption of seeing her, that he felt quite displaced, as if his life had suddenly been swapped for somebody else's. He beat his fists lightly on the seat of the bench he was sitting on.

'Get a grip,' he told himself. It was something Carrie often said. 'Get a *grip*.'

He went out for a beer, instead, on Saturday, with Adam and Rich. Marco had a date somewhere. The three of them went to two pubs and then tried to get into a club and were turned away for being too young by a doorman so stupendously bored with having to deal with anyone so juvenile that it rather put a damper on the evening. Adam suggested going round to a friend of his who always had something interesting going, but Jack found his heart wasn't in it.

'You go,' he said.

The others exchanged glances.

'Come on, mate –'

He shook his head.

'I'm beat. I'm going home.'

He'd left them there, on the pavement outside the club with the bored bouncer, and loped home. It was a twenty-five-minute walk and in the course of it there were moments when he felt both solitary and vulnerable. He'd forgotten in these recent, heady weeks of seeing Moll, what it was like being the outsider, being the one without a social purpose, a place, a meaning. When he got home, he went straight to the telephone in case she'd rung. She hadn't promised, but she'd sort of indicated she might. There were three messages there, two for Simon and one from Emma's friend, Sonia, about drama club. Jack trailed out of the kitchen and up the stairs. It was almost midnight. His parents' bedroom door was shut and so were his sisters'. He sat on the bottom step of the staircase up to his floor and took off one shoe, leaving it where it fell. Then he took off his top T-shirt – the black one – and his copy of *Loaded* magazine fell out of his jeans pocket. He was almost too tired, he'd thought, to get as far as his bedroom.

The shower was turned off. He heard the pipes grumble into silence. Then he heard his mother call, 'No, now, Rachel, *now*.' He waited. He didn't want the day to begin, he didn't want to start feeling tired again.

'Jack!' Carrie shouted.

She was at the foot of his staircase. He could picture her, hand on the wall, face turned up towards the darkness of his floor.

'Jack!' she shouted again. She was louder this time. 'Jack, will you please get *up*?'

'What'll we talk about?' Simon said. He was pulling a cork out of a wine bottle. He'd put on a blue denim shirt and his hair was still damp from his shower. Carrie rather wanted to go over and lean against him, but she didn't. She stayed her side of the kitchen table and sliced apples into a pie dish.

'We could start with the sale of Hill Cottage and the consequences of extra-marital affairs.'

'Very funny.'

'Well, really,' Carrie said, 'what d'you think? We'll get by. The kids will be there. Emma and Rachel have been in the bathroom for hours.'

Simon pulled the cork out with a jerk.

'Because of *her*?'

'It didn't escape Rachel's notice,' Carrie said, 'that Merrion was wearing a sweater from agnès b. when she came to supper.'

Simon ran a piece of kitchen paper round the inside of the wine bottle's neck.

'Who is agnès b.?'

'Clothes,' Carrie said. 'Classic but cool.'

Simon shook his head.

'Just think if Mum finds out –'

'She won't. Unless *you* choose to tell her.'

'I feel awful –'

'Ill? Or disloyal?'

Simon threw the screw of kitchen paper roughly in the direction of the waste bin.

'Disloyal.'

'Oh *Simon* –'

He said, 'She's so vulnerable –'

'Is she?'

'You haven't seen her.'

'I've tried to,' Carrie said. 'I've asked her here. I've asked your father here. The difference is that he said yes and she said no.'

Simon went across the kitchen and picked up the screw of kitchen paper.

'It isn't at all comparable.'

'No,' Carrie said. 'It isn't.' She was slicing the apples very fast. 'The other difference is that your father has always been very nice to me and your mother never has.'

'Carrie –'

'I'm sick of it,' Carrie said. She put the paring knife down and held her hands over her face. 'I'm sick of you leaping to attention every time she so much as raises an eyebrow. I'm sick of her polite but determined refusal to acknowledge that I'm your *wife*. I'm sick of you refusing to see what your priorities are. I am sick, sick, *sick* of coming second.'

There was a small silence.

'I think –' Simon said, and stopped.

She waited. She took her hands away from her face and picked up the paring knife again.

'Aren't you exaggerating a bit?' Simon said.

She said nothing. Simon put the paper in the waste bin. He said, his back to her, 'Why be angry with me? Why aren't you angry with my father?'

'Increasingly,' Carrie said through clenched teeth, 'I have every sympathy with your father.'

'In that case –'

'Shut up!' Carrie shrieked.

He looked at her.

'Carrie –'

'I've had enough! I've had enough of your evasions and your cowardice and your self-absorption and your bloody, fucking *mother*!'

Simon looked pained.

'*Please* –'

She shook her head violently. Tears of fury and frustration were beginning to leak out of her eyes.

'You're so *obtuse*.'

'Yes,' he said, 'I expect I am. Along with all my other failings.' He picked up the wine bottle. 'It's a wonder you stay.'

She glared at him. She'd put her hair up quite carefully earlier and it was beginning to slip down. She could feel a lock or two sliding down her neck.

'Think about it,' she hissed.

'About what?'

'*Think* why I stay.'

He looked at the floor. Carrie jabbed the point of the paring knife into her chopping board.

'*Think* about it, Simon. Think why I'm still here, why I put up with your work commitments, your mother commitments, running this house, *everything*. I'm not the sort of person, am I, who'd stay just for the children. If I was going, I'd take them with me. But I don't. I stay. Why, stupid, stupid Simon Stockdale do you *think* I stay?'

He gave her a quick glance. Then he looked down at the wine bottle in his hand.

'I suppose –' he said, and stopped.

The doorbell rang. They looked at each other in horror.

'Oh my God,' Carrie said. 'It's them.'

During lunch, Jack watched his grandfather. His sisters, he noticed, were watching Merrion, albeit covertly. Her hair was all loose today – it had been in a kind of plait when she came to supper – and he could see Rachel looking at it and wondering how you got hair to do that. Rachel's hair was like Carrie's, slippery and straight, with a tendency to divide over her ears. Merrion's hair curved behind her ears and looked quite content to do so. It was very thick. Jack had never really looked at girls' hair before. Before Moll, that is.

When you first looked at Grando, Jack thought, he seemed fine; normal, ordinary. But after a while you could see he was a bit on edge, that he was holding himself in a deliberately relaxed way, rather than being truly relaxed. He was sitting next to Carrie and he was listening to her. When he wasn't eating, his hands and wrists rested on the table and you could see that his hands were the same as Simon's hands, the same shape, the same fingernails. Grando had a checked shirt on, open-necked, under a dark-green sweater. He smiled at Carrie a lot. She was telling him about her job. 'You're amazing,' he said, several times. 'I don't know how you stand it.' Sometimes, when he reached to pick up his water glass, he gave Merrion the quickest of glances across the table and Jack felt a little jerk when he did that, a little twist of recognition and pain. He'd expected to think Grando pathetic; he'd told himself he was probably just a sad old bloke who'd made a fool of himself. But that wasn't how he seemed, it wasn't how he seemed at all. He might be tense, but he wasn't apologetic, he wasn't pitiful, he was instead indicating – quietly but unmistakably – that the reason he was so happy to be in this room was because Merrion was in it, too. It filled Jack with awe and misery. It also quite took away his appetite so that when he looked down at his plate and found that it was empty he was astonished.

His father, he noticed, was talking law to Merrion. He wasn't looking at her, he was looking at the table just in front of her plate, at the dull patch where Jack had spilled some water while filling her glass and forgotten to blot it up. Jack thought his father looked rather sarcastic; there was a smile on his lips that didn't manage to look very smiling. For her part, Merrion seemed able to look at Simon. She looked at him quite steadily. Jack wondered what a girl would think of his father, someone who saw him as a bloke and not as a father. He wondered what Merrion was thinking, whether it was odd to look at a son and see something of the father you were really in love with. In love. Jack swallowed. He picked up his knife and traced patterns with it in the gravy left on his plate. Moll had said she'd call. 'Call you Sunday if I don't Saturday night, OK?' she'd said. The telephone had been quite silent, all morning, not even Trudy or Sonia or one of Dad's clients who always rang on Sundays because they thought they'd have a better chance of catching him in then. He pushed his chair back.

'Jack?' Carrie said.

He didn't look at her.

'I've got to do something –'

'Could you do it in a minute? After you've cleared the plates?'

Jack hesitated. He stood up. Grando was looking at him with an expression that oddly gave him courage.

'In a sec,' he said. 'I've just got to make a phone call.'

'Is Jack all right?' Guy said.

He and Simon were standing in the garden, their hands in their pockets. The garden was remarkably untidy. Neither he nor Simon had commented on it for the simple reason that neither of them had really noticed it and if they had, their noticing might have led rapidly and dangerously to the subject of Laura.

'Never better,' Simon said.

'Really?'

Simon looked up to watch a passing aeroplane.

'He's got a girlfriend. The first serious one. He's really star-struck.'

Guy looked at the grass. He jabbed at a dandelion with the toe of his shoe.

'He didn't look star-struck at lunch,' Guy said. 'He looked miserable. He hardly said a word.'

'He seldom does. Not in front of grown-ups anyway.'

'Everything else going all right? School and so on?'

'I think so,' Simon said. 'You'd better ask Carrie.'

'Why can't I ask you?' Guy said. 'You're the boy's parent, too, aren't you?'

'She's the one –'

'Well, she shouldn't be.'

'Look,' Simon said with some heat. 'Look, don't get at *me*. Anyway, who are you to talk? Who knew anything much about my schooldays but Mum?'

'Exactly,' Guy said. 'And I regret it.'

'So you'll salve your conscience by tearing me off a strip?'

Guy kicked at the dandelion again.

'Carrie's not happy,' he said. 'You're not happy. Jack's not happy. And don't tell me it's all my fault because that's neither fair nor accurate.'

'Did you come here to give me a lecture?'

'I'm not giving you a lecture.'

'Dad,' Simon said, 'it was Carrie's idea to ask you both here and up to now, we've got through it all right. Don't start on me now.'

Guy said, 'I tried to see your mother.'

'I know.'

'I am advised,' Guy said, 'by my own experience and instincts, *and* by Susan Dewar, to beg you both to find your mother an independent legal adviser.'

Simon looked at the sky again.

'We've been through all that.'

Guy put a hand on Simon's arm.

'But you're *suffering*, Simon. And you're making Carrie suffer.'

Simon lowered his arm so that Guy's hand slipped from it.

'I can only do what I think is right.'

'Oh Lord,' Guy said and briefly closed his eyes.

'We're talking conscience here,' Simon said. 'Not just emotion. It's dictates of conscience, a sense of what is *right* to do.'

'By everybody?'

'I can't possibly do right by everybody.'

'So you are choosing to do right by just one person at the expense of everybody else?'

'Dad,' Simon said. 'Dad. That's the whole point. I'm not choosing. I haven't *got* a choice.'

Guy was silent. He had dislodged the dandelion by now and bent to pull it and its long white root out of the lawn. The root broke off halfway.

'Damn.'

'I shouldn't be here with you,' Simon said. 'I shouldn't be talking to you. I should only be talking to you through Susan Dewar.'

Guy said crossly, 'Don't be so *idiotic*.'

Simon shrugged.

'I've got something to tell you,' Guy said.

Simon looked at him.

'Legally, I suppose Susan should tell you but I'm still your father, whatever you say, so I'd prefer to tell you this myself.'

'Merrion's pregnant,' Simon said.

'No. Merrion is not pregnant.'

'Well then?'

'We have fixed a date to be married.'

'You can't.'

'We have done it.'

'Dad,' Simon said, 'we haven't even got full statements of assets yet. It'll take weeks, months even. We have to get Mum's consent on *every*thing.'

'Your job,' Guy said.

'What?'

'I intend to marry Merrion on October the twentieth. I intend to be divorced and thus free to marry her well in advance of that date.'

'But you can't, it isn't practical, we haven't agreed completion on the house even –'

Guy took a step away.

'That's up to you.'

'Dad –'

'You insist that you have no choice,' Guy said. 'These are the consequences. We can all be amazingly unreasonable if pushed hard enough. I don't go back on anything I said about generosity to your mother, but I'm not waiting for ever while she plays games with me. It's your job, Simon, to get this divorce as fast as you can. You say you have no choice about your mother. In this instance you have no choice with me, either.' He looked at the broken dandelion in his hand and then hurled it into the bushes that fringed the lawn. 'And now I'm going to find the girls.'

Merrion lay in the dark, eyes wide open. Beside her, Guy was asleep, on his side in a characteristic pose with his left cheek resting on the back of his right hand. If she thought he looked uncomfortable, she had discovered, and gently took his hand away, he would murmur politely in his sleep and put it back again. He looked very contented. He had made love to her an hour ago and was sleeping in the comfortably completed way men seemed to, after sex. She put a hand out and ran a finger over his uppermost cheek, and then she turned her head and looked up at the ceiling.

She was happy, too, happier than she had been for weeks now. She had been so apprehensive about lunch at Simon and Carrie's house but when it happened, it was fine. Not easy exactly, except when she was alone with Carrie washing up, but fine. The children were a help of course, not saying much, but there, and definitely not hostile, not making her feel that her presence was unwanted, improper. She was an object of curiosity to them, plainly, but not a threat, not an intruder. When she took her shoes off, in the kitchen, so that Rachel could try them on, she'd had a sudden extraordinary sense of what family life might be like, had been like in fact all those years ago in Cowbridge, when schoolfriends took her home and she saw their brothers and the crammed contents of their store cupboards and the number of toothbrushes in their bathrooms.

'They suit you,' she'd said to Rachel.

Rachel hooked her hair behind her ears. She peered down at her feet below the black lace dress and the jeans.

'They're great,' she said.

On the way back to Bayswater, Guy told her he had informed Simon of their wedding date. Merrion had learned not to say, 'Was he angry?' Instead she said, 'Oh good.'

'I told him that it was his problem. He may be fool enough to tell his mother, but I can't help that.'

Privately, Merrion thought, Guy had been a slight fool to tell Simon, but then Guy felt so keenly his separation from Simon, was so pained by Laura's effective and relentless divisiveness between father and son that small lapses of self-indulgence were understandable. She sighed. She put her hands up in the dusky air and held the finger that would be the married one. Perhaps she'd have a ring, after all. Perhaps she'd want to show that she was married, show everyone. She thought of herself in Carrie's kitchen, showing her ring to Rachel and Emma, sliding it off so that they could try it on, like her shoes, and see what it looked like, how they felt wearing a wedding ring. She found she was smiling. It had been a good day, an unexpectedly good day. Even Simon hadn't been that difficult; poor Simon, with the ghost of his mother stalking him at every turn. He couldn't look at her, of course, but he talked to her; he'd even talked to her as if he'd quite liked it, as if she interested him. Perhaps, by the time she had a wedding ring, he'd be so used to the idea that he could look at her, too. She liked the idea of that. She liked Simon. Just tonight, just for the moment, she liked almost everything.

CHAPTER FOURTEEN

'OK, mate?' Adam said.

It was the third time he'd said it that morning. The first time he'd said it, he'd put an arm across Jack's shoulders. Jack had shrugged it off.

'Get off me –'

'Sorry,' Adam said. He didn't seem offended. He kept looking at Jack, as if he was waiting for something. Rich did, too, although he didn't say anything, but then Rich never did say anything much. He came from a family of seven, with a mother who talked all the time, like a tap left running, and a completely silent father. Rich took after his father.

'I'm fine,' Jack said. He broke off a piece of the hot dog he was eating and pulled a strand of limp fried onion out of it with his teeth. 'I'm *fine*.'

'Good weekend?' Adam said.

Jack stopped chewing and stared at him.

'You what?'

Adam grinned. He was eating corn chips out of a bag.

'I said did you have a good weekend –'

'I heard you.'

'Well?'

'What kind of a question is that?' Jack said. 'You suddenly turned into my mother or something?'

He looked at the rest of his hot dog. It suddenly seemed

gross; greasy and rubbery and fake. He wanted a cigarette, not a hot dog. He got up from the bench where they were sitting and dropped the remainder of his hot dog into a wire litter bin.

'Hey,' Rich said, 'I'd have had that.'

Jack didn't turn round.

'Too late,' he said.

He pulled his cigarettes out of his trouser pocket, the first cigarettes he'd bought since that incredible moment he and Moll had thrown his last packet away together and they'd been laughing and she'd kissed him for the first time, not a heavy kiss, not like the kisses they'd graduated to, but full on the mouth all the same, full on. He felt seized by a sudden yearning, thinking about that kiss, all three seconds of it, by the litter bin on the edge of the netball court where the little kids hung out at break times. He took a cigarette out of his new packet and lit it. Then he drew a deep mouthful of smoke. It tasted great, but not as great as he'd hoped it would. He turned back to the others.

'Ought to make a move.'

Adam was tipping the last crumbs out of the corn-chip bag down his throat.

'Hey! What's the hurry –'

'Double physics.'

'And when did you ever give a toss about double physics?'

Jack dropped his cigarette on the ground and screwed the heel of his shoe into it.

'It was your idea to come out,' Adam said.

'I wanted some fags –'

'And you got them. And we came with you –'

'You didn't have to.'

'We did,' Rich said.

Jack looked at him.

'Why?'

'Why what?'

'Why did you have to come with me?'

'See if you were OK,' Adam said.

'Why shouldn't I be OK?'

Adam screwed his chip bag into a ball and chucked it in the direction of the litter bin. It hit the rim and fell on the ground.

'You – just didn't seem OK,' Adam said.

'There was a lot of stuff at the weekend,' Jack said. 'Family stuff. I got tired.'

Adam said, 'The weekend's three days ago.'

Jack gave Adam's chip bag a flying kick.

'I know.'

Adam stood up.

'C'mon, then.'

Jack eyed him.

'What do you know that I don't know?'

'Nothing much –'

'I'm not asking for much,' Jack said. 'I'm just asking for anything.'

Rich stood, too.

'Race you,' he said.

'What?'

'I said I'll race you.'

'Why?' Jack said. 'Why'd I want to race you?'

Rich shrugged.

'Rich,' Jack said. 'Just tell me.'

Rich looked at Adam. He put his hands in his pockets and hunched his shoulders.

Adam said, 'It's probably not anything –'

'Rich, tell me,' Jack said. He took a step forward and put his hands on Rich's shoulders.

'Moll?' he said.

Rich nodded. Jack gave him a little shake.

'What? *What*?'

'Saturday,' Rich muttered.

'Saturday? What about Saturday?'

Rich ducked his head. He stared at the mid-point of Jack's school tie.

'Marco,' he said.

Jack took his hands off Rich's shoulders. He looked at Adam.

'Moll went out with Marco? On Saturday?'

Adam nodded.

'Sunday?' Jack said.

'Dunno –'

'Monday and Tuesday? Wednesday? Never there to answer the phone because she's out with fucking *Marco*? Not in school, faking a period so she doesn't have to *see* me?'

'Dunno,' Adam said.

'You knew.'

'Yeah.'

'You knew on Saturday?'

'Sort of,' Rich said.

Jack shook his head. He said dully, 'She said she was with her mum.'

'Yeah. Well –'

'She said she'd ring.'

Adam put a hand out and tried to take Jack's arm.

'C'mon, mate. Double physics.'

'Fuck off!' Jack shouted.

He pulled his arm free.

'Cool it, mate –'

He glared at them.

'Fuck off, I said.'

'OK, OK –'

They took a step away from him. Rich's eyes looked odd, as if he was squinting or something.

'You *knew* –'

They said nothing. Jack wanted to rush at them, hurl himself at them and shove them back against the wall behind the bench and really give their heads a banging, skull against brick, thud, thud, thud. He put his hands in his pockets. They weren't worth it. Nothing was worth it. Nothing.

'Fuck you,' Jack said. His voice was hoarse. 'Fuck you both,' and then he pushed past them and began to tear up the pavement among the Thursday-lunchtime shoppers.

Emma was in her bedroom. She had a headache. She'd had a headache for two days now but when she told Carrie about it, Carrie had given her a paracetamol tablet and told her to drink lots of water.

'I had a headache yesterday,' Emma said.

Carrie said, 'So did I.'

'*Since* yesterday,' Emma said. She looked at the paracetamol. 'I hate these.'

'Swallow it,' Carrie said. She had her work suit on. 'Swallow it and go to school. You'll be late.'

The paracetamol blunted Emma's headache but didn't take it away. She felt herself watching it come back, creeping back, until her whole skull seemed to be full of black tendrils, all pressing on something until they hurt it. Emma endured the black tendrils through maths and French and religious studies and then in break, she made Sonia come with her to find the school nurse.

'I've had a headache since yesterday.'

The school nurse was filling in forms. She hardly looked at Emma.

'Why are you in school then?'

'I thought it was better.'

The school nurse wrote something and underlined it.

'Are you having your period?'

Emma looked at Sonia. She'd only had two. Sonia had started when she was eleven. She was really regular now.

'No,' Sonia said.

'Have you had your eyes tested?'

'Yes,' Sonia said.

Emma wanted to giggle. She looked at the school nurse's hair which was stuffed into an elasticated band, in a crooked lump.

'Is your mother at home?'

Sonia nudged Emma.

'Yes,' Emma said.

The school nurse reached for a pad.

'I'll write a note for your form teacher,' she said, scribbling rapidly. 'Then you go home and tell your mother that if the headache isn't gone by tomorrow you should see your doctor.'

She tore the form off a small pad and handed it to Sonia.

'There you are.'

Sonia tried to walk Emma home.

'I better. Your mum's not there.'

'I'll be OK.'

'C'mon, Emma,' Sonia said. 'Then I can bunk off second English.'

'I don't want you to,' Emma said. 'I don't want to talk.' She gave Sonia's hand, still holding the sick note, a little slap. 'You hand that in for me.'

'OK,' Sonia said. She always gave in, Emma had discovered; she'd put up a little fight and then she'd give in. It was one of the things about her that Emma liked, that and the way her dad spoiled her. Sonia's dad had left Sonia's mum for Sonia's mum's cousin, so he had to give Sonia things, to make up for it. Sometimes Sonia didn't want the things her dad had given her and gave them to Emma. That was how Emma had acquired the dark-blue mules. Sonia wouldn't wear them because Sonia's mum's cousin – who was only twenty-seven – had some exactly the same.

'See you,' Emma said to Sonia.

'See you later,' Sonia said. She always said that, even if she wasn't going to see Emma again for days.

Emma let herself into the house. It felt weird; not quite empty but more as if it was waiting. She put her house keys in the zipped pocket of her school bag and went into the kitchen. Breakfast was still partly on the table, as it always was if Carrie wasn't the last to leave the house; smeary bowls and spoons and a cereal box with the inner packet still standing up so the air could get in and turn the contents soft. Emma hated soft cereal. She hated soft biscuits, too. She didn't like anything old.

She went across to the fridge and opened it. She wasn't exactly hungry but she felt she'd like to look and see what was in there all the same. She helped herself to a yoghurt and a cheese portion wrapped in plastic and two chocolates out of the box Merrion had brought Carrie when she came to lunch on Sunday. Emma rearranged the layers in the box a little so that it wasn't so easy to see where the missing chocolates had been. Then she opened the cupboard beside the fridge and found a bag of smoky bacon-flavour crisps and a tub of salted almonds that Carrie had bought for Sunday and forgotten about. Emma put everything on the table while she rummaged in the box under it for a can of Coca-Cola. She felt as she did when she and Rachel raided the fridge after Simon and Carrie had gone to bed, a slightly exciting mixture of being afraid of being caught, and all poised to be defiant.

'It's our home, isn't it?' Rachel would say. 'It's our fridge and food. Isn't it?'

Emma bunched up the hem of her school skirt until she had made a loose sort of pocket, and put the food and the Coca-Cola can into it. She added a banana; not one of the brown speckled ones that Carrie said needed to be eaten first, but a smooth yellow new one. Carrie said the new ones tasted of nothing, but to Emma, they tasted clean. She went slowly upstairs, holding her skirt pouch, and tipped the contents on to her bed.

She'd made her bed, that morning, headache or not. She

always made her bed, not because Carrie told her to, but because it felt dirty to get into, at night, if she hadn't made it. If you pulled the bottom sheet tight, Emma had discovered, it felt cleaner, newer. She kicked off her shoes and pulled her socks off. Her toenails had tiny pink stickers glued to them, shaped like flowers. She'd varnished over the top of them with clear varnish so the flowers looked as if they were under water. Emma hated her feet. They were too fat, even her toes were fat, like little sausages. It was a real affliction, Emma thought, to have fat feet.

She unzipped her skirt and dropped it on the floor, and then her school cardigan. Her cardigan had been Rachel's, and the elbows were thin and shiny and the cuffs had frilled out and had ragged edges where Rachel had chewed them. Emma had fought very hard for new school uniform, but had only won a skirt. Carrie was adamant about the rest, absolutely adamant. And it was no good going to Simon. Simon would be so bored by the topic of Emma having to wear Rachel's cast-off school uniform that he wouldn't even be able to hear her. He'd have looked at her as if she was both completely mad and also speaking an incomprehensible foreign language. He'd have made her feel a fool.

Emma got into bed in her knickers and her school shirt. She lay carefully down on her pillow, feeling all the items of food tumbling about on her duvet as she pushed her legs down the bed. Her headache, she decided, was still there, but it wasn't worse. If she lay very still and ate very slowly, it might go away. If she ate with her eyes closed, it might go away even sooner. She reached down the duvet, patting it in search of one of her trophies. She found the yoghurt. You couldn't, she thought, eat yoghurt out of the pot while lying down with your eyes closed. It would run into your ears. She put the yoghurt down and patted on. Her fingers found the small neat brick of cheese in its shiny plastic cover. She picked it up and put the corner of the cover between her teeth, to tear it open.

Below her, on the ground floor, the front door opened and shut with a slam. Emma froze. There was the thud of a bag being dropped and a clatter of keys. Then somebody went into the kitchen. Emma sat up. She put the cheese on her bedside table. Then she slid out of bed and went out on to the landing so that she could see down into the hall. It was Jack's bag in the hall and his keys were on the floor beside it. Emma went back into her room and found the mauve-and-white-striped pedal-pushers that Sonia had lent her – 'They're only a lend, mind,' Sonia had said. 'Just till Friday' – and pulled them on under her school shirt. Then she went down the stairs in her bare, pink-stickered feet and crossed the hall to the kitchen.

Jack was standing by the kitchen table eating sliced white bread out of its packet.

'What are you doing here?' Emma said.

He gave a little start. He said, round the bread in his mouth, 'You, too.'

'I've got a headache,' Emma said. 'I've got a sick note.'

Jack grunted.

'I didn't think there'd be anybody here –'

'Me either,' Emma said. She looked at him. He looked awful, sort of greyish and lifeless. 'Did you get sent home?'

'No.'

She advanced towards the table and snatched the bread bag away. Carrie hated them eating things straight out of packets and cartons. She'd hate it that Emma hadn't taken a spoon upstairs with her yoghurt.

'What're you doing here then?'

Jack lunged forward and whipped the bread bag back out of Emma's hand.

'Going somewhere –'

'Don't do that!' Emma said. 'Mum doesn't like it! Mum doesn't like you eating out of the packet!' She leaned on the table. 'Where're you going, anyway?'

'Doesn't matter.'

'It does. You've got to tell Mum. Tell me and I'll tell Mum.'

'No,' Jack said.

Emma sighed.

'Why you going, anyway?'

'Doesn't matter.'

'It's a school day,' Emma said. 'You can't go anywhere on a school day.'

'Look,' Jack said. He finished the slice of bread he was eating. 'Look. It's none of your business where I go and what I do.'

'It is,' Emma said. 'I'm your sister.'

'So?'

'So I need to know stuff.'

Jack went past her without replying. She heard him go across the hall and into the downstairs cloakroom, which she never used because it was dark and smelled of rubber boots and because Simon and Jack used it and left the lavatory seat up. She heard him pee, and then she heard the sound of water flushing. Jack came back across the hall.

'You didn't wash your hands!' Emma called.

He picked up his keys. She heard the brief scrape as they were lifted from the tiled floor. Then he appeared in the kitchen doorway. He'd taken his school tie off, but he was still in his school grey trousers and his school black blazer.

'See you,' he said.

She said, 'Aren't you going to change?'

He shook his head.

'No.'

'When will you be back?' Emma said.

'Dunno –'

She reached across the table and picked the bread up, holding it out to him in its plastic wrapper.

'Want to take this?'

He shook his head again.

'No.'

'OK,' Emma said. 'What'll I say to Mum?'

'Tell her I'll be back.'

'When?'

'Sometime,' Jack said. He looked down, jingling his keys, and then he turned without another word and went back across the hall to the front door. Emma heard the door slam again. He'd looked, she thought, like someone who'd been really told off, like people did when the exam results were put up and they discovered, despite saying they didn't care what their marks were, that they'd done really badly, not cool badly, but moronic badly. Emma went round the kitchen table and put the bread back in the big plastic bread box that got soft greenish crumbs in the bottom if Carrie forgot to clean it out. Her headache, she discovered, had quite gone.

'All stand!' the court usher said.

Guy rose from his seat on the small dais of Court One, and went out. It had been a long, trivial afternoon, full of applications by bailiffs for this and that.

'Your Honour, as you are aware, Mr Simmons has failed to oblige –'

'I respectfully submit, Your Honour, that without an order this could run and run –'

'The plaintiffs, Your Honour, have decided to withdraw for the moment. Their reasons, Your Honour will find, are not, in the circumstances, allowable.'

Mrs Weaverbrook had been back, more exhausted than ever with the effort of finding excuses for Mr Weaverbrook's persistent non-attendance in court, and simultaneous steady acquisition of farm machinery whose provenance he could not account for.

'My problem,' Mrs Weaverbrook said desperately, gazing at Guy, 'is the legal aid board.'

Guy had leaned towards her. He said gently, 'I don't

think, Mrs Weaverbrook, that legal aid really has anything to do with it.'

Outside Court One, Martin was waiting.

'Could I have a word, Judge?'

Guy paused.

'Of course –'

Martin reached up a little so that his face was close to
Guy's.

'Your grandson's here,' Martin said.

'My grandson!'

'Yes, Judge. I've put him in your chambers. Penny found
him in the lobby about half an hour ago.'

'Is he all right?'

'I think so. Penny's taken him some tea. He's a bit
subdued, I'd say. Sometimes playing truant takes them
that way –'

'Heavens,' Guy said. 'Heavens.' He glanced at Martin.
'Thank you. Thank you very much indeed.'

Jack sat at Guy's desk and wondered whether he could
turn on his computer. It was an old computer, an old Dell,
the sort of ancient computer that would need someone
very clever indeed to get anything much out of it. Jack
wondered if Grando could do that. He'd never thought of
Grando and computers before, he'd never thought of what
his office would look like either, what his place of work
would be like, what people in it would think of him.

'Your grandad's in court,' the girl called Penny with the
hairclips had said. 'He'll be in there till four-thirty. It's
booked solid this afternoon.'

She'd asked Jack if he wanted some tea. He'd said no
thank you, but she'd brought it anyway, in a mug on a
plastic tray with a cellophane packet beside it containing
two shortbread biscuits. He'd eaten the biscuits and left
the tea. Tea seemed to him an extraordinarily sad drink,
like cocoa or Horlicks, a drink for people who were ill or

old or both and could only swallow squashed-up baby stuff.

When he'd eaten the biscuits, he wandered round Guy's room a bit. It was a dull room. It had beige walls and a brown carpet and grey plastic furniture. There were shelves of files and shelves of law books and a few photographs on top of a cabinet, photographs of Simon and Carrie, and Alan, photographs of him and Rachel and Emma – all taken long ago, all pretty embarrassing – and a photograph of Granny with the dogs and one of Merrion taken with a lot of sky behind her and her hair blowing. Jack only gave the one of Merrion the briefest of glances. It made him miserable to look at, acutely miserable, for reasons that had nothing to do with Merrion herself. He sat in Guy's swivel chair and swivelled a bit. He looked at Guy's robe hanging on the back of the door. He peered at his wig, perched on a weird object like a big wooden lollipop. He poked it, gingerly. It felt stiff, almost hard, and you could see the stitches in it plainly. It felt a bit strange, looking at Grando's wig, like looking at a bit of someone dead, a bit that didn't work any more, or have any life in it. He straightened up. He felt, abruptly, rather nervous, a bit shaky. He went across the room and sat in the chair behind Guy's desk, an armchair upholstered in grey tweed. There was a blotter on the desk, with scribbles on the blotting paper, and on one side, a stack of files in thin cardboard folders and on the other, the computer.

The door opened. Jack sat up.

'Jack,' Guy said. He was wearing a dark suit and a blue tie and carrying a big file under one arm. 'Dear fellow –'

Jack felt suddenly shy. He got up and shuffled sideways, away from Guy's desk.

'You haven't got your wig on –'

'I didn't need it this afternoon. It was just a string of little civil cases.' He put the file down on the nearest grey plastic desk. 'Are you all right?'

Jack nodded. He kept his eyes down. He heard Guy's feet move quietly on the carpet and then Guy's arm went firmly round his shoulder.

'Are you in trouble?'

Jack shook his head. He felt he shouldn't be leaning against Grando but he couldn't help it.

Guy said, 'Something has happened, though.'

'I wanted to go somewhere –'

'Yes.'

'Sorry,' Jack said.

'A row?' Guy said. 'Something at school? Something with your parents?'

'No.'

'I see Penny brought you some tea.'

'Sorry, I didn't –'

'No. It doesn't matter. Are you thirsty? Would you like something else?'

'No,' Jack whispered.

'Look,' Guy said, 'I think you'd better sit down.'

He pulled Jack gently sideways.

'Sit here.'

'It's your chair –'

'It doesn't matter. Sit here.'

Jack sat. He couldn't look up. He felt worse than ever. He'd thought, when he got here, when he got to Grando, something would happen, something would get easier. But it hadn't. Nothing had changed. He'd just left the house and crossed London and got on a train and asked a woman with a baby in a buggy where the court was and got here and that was it.

He said, to his knees, 'I don't know why I came. I don't – I'm sorry.'

Guy had pulled another chair up, opposite to him, the other side of the desk. He said, 'I'm pleased you did. Though I'm sorry you needed to.'

'It was after Sunday –'

'What was?'

'When I saw you, when you came, when –'

'Jack,' Guy said, leaning forward towards him across the desk. 'Jack, is it your girlfriend?'

Jack said nothing. He stared at his knees.

'Has she left you?'

Jack shrugged.

'Is that it, Jack? Did she tell you she didn't want to see you any more?'

Jack raised his head a fraction.

'She didn't *tell* me –'

'Oh,' Guy said, 'I see. She just did it.'

Jack stared at the desk top.

'She said she was going out with her mother on Saturday. But she didn't. She went out with Marco. She said she'd ring.'

'But she didn't.'

'She didn't even come to school this week –'

'And left you to find out?'

'Yes,' Jack said.

Guy sighed. Jack glanced at him. He looked really sad, really unhappy.

'Poor boy,' he said. 'My poor boy. I could tell you the first time is always the worst, but it wouldn't be true. It's dreadful, every time. There's no pain like betrayal.'

Jack said, without thinking, 'Dad says –' He stopped.

'Your father says that that is what I've inflicted on Granny?'

'I didn't mean –'

'I know you didn't. But you're right. Your father's right. Jack –'

'Yes?'

'Why didn't you go to your parents? Why didn't you tell them?'

Jack made a face.

'Couldn't.'

'Because of the teasing, because of your sisters?'

'No,' Jack said, and then added uncertainly, 'It doesn't matter to them.'

'Your happiness does.'

'They didn't think this was a big deal, they thought this was just – well, kids' stuff. Anyway –'

'Anyway what?'

'You couldn't talk to them now. You can't tell them anything.'

Guy was silent. He looked down at his hands lying in front of him on the desk. He seemed to be thinking. After a while he said, 'We must tell them where you are.'

'Emma will tell them I'll be back –'

'Does Emma know where you are?'

'No,' Jack said.

'Then you must ring them.'

'Are you sending me back –'

'In the morning,' Guy said. He stood up. 'I must just make a call, and then you must ring home.'

Jack stood, too. He said awkwardly, 'Do you want me to go out?'

'No,' Guy said. 'No. I won't be long. You can stay.'

Jack moved away from Guy's desk and leaned against the shelves where the law books were. A green paperback had fallen forward. It was called *The County Court Practice Supplement*. Jack picked it up and riffled the pages. It seemed, well, polite not to do nothing, not to watch.

Guy dialled a number on the telephone on his desk. He sat balanced against the edge of his desk, his back to Jack, his shoulders square against the light from the window.

'Hello?' he said. 'Hello, my love, it's me.'

Jack fixed his eyes on a page and read a lot of words without seeing them.

'Look,' Guy said, 'I won't be coming up tonight. Yes, I know I did, but something's happened. No, no, not Laura.

It's Jack. He's had a bit of a crisis and turned up here an hour ago. Yes. Yes, I will, but in the morning. I'm going to give him some supper and take him back to the flat with me. He can get an early train in the morning.' There was a pause. Jack glanced at Guy's back. His head was bent, as if he were listening very hard. 'Darling,' Guy said, 'I wouldn't be upsetting our plans if it *wasn't* important. It *is* important. The very fact that he has come to find me is important.' There was another pause. Guy lifted his head and looked out of the window. Very quietly Jack closed the green paperback and slid it back on to the shelf among the other books. 'I'll ring you later,' Guy said, 'I'll tell you more then. No, not now. Later. I'll ring you from the flat,' and then there was a tiny break and he said, 'Goodbye, darling,' and put the phone down. He sat there, quite still, his back to Jack.

Jack cleared his throat.

'Sorry,' he said.

'Don't be,' Guy said. 'You've done nothing to be sorry for.' He turned to look at Jack, swivelling one thigh on the desk top.

'You're supposed to be in London –'

'I can go tomorrow,' Guy said. 'And then I can go on Friday. I always go on Fridays anyway, for the weekend.'

'Thanks,' Jack said. Somewhere, obscurely, a small light was breaking, a tiny beacon of relief. He took a step away from the bookcase. 'Thanks, Grando.'

Guy looked at him. 'There's nothing to thank me for. Now. Ring your parents. With luck, you'll get them before they even start to worry.'

CHAPTER FIFTEEN

Miriam had, as usual, spilt Simon's coffee. It had been one of their office's footling New Year economies, to stop sending her out for coffee to the excellent tiny Italian coffee shop fifty yards away every morning, and to get her to make it instead. She seemed incapable of using even the simplest filter machine so had, after only two days of half-hearted trying, resorted to making mugs of instant coffee which she often put synthetic whitener into, having forgotten to buy milk. It irritated all of them, every morning, and they had frequent exasperatingly inconclusive conversations about it. The trouble was that reverting to the Italian coffee shop might mean much better coffee, but it would also entail Miriam inevitably extending her time out of the office while she fetched it, to do her own errands. The dreariness of the instant coffee was also compounded by the fact the Miriam carried all three mugs round the office to distribute them, in a single handful, with the result that she spilled coffee as she went along, and even more as she put the mug down on each desk. Ted said he was not only driven round the bend when it happened, but also by waiting for it to happen, regular as clockwork, every single morning.

Simon picked up his coffee mug and blotted the wet ring under it with a piece of junk mail that had come in that morning's post. It was proving difficult to concentrate this morning, so difficult that he'd even found himself reading the junk mail in an idle, unseeing sort of way before he put it under his coffee mug. He hadn't slept very well, of course. Nor had Carrie. They'd lain side by side in bed and had silent and separate mental tussles about why Jack, upset by Moll's defection, should have gone to find his grandfather rather than one of them.

Carrie, Simon knew, blamed him. After Jack had rung from Stanborough and said he was staying the night and would be back in the morning, Carrie had looked at Simon for a long time. She hadn't said anything, she'd just looked.

After several minutes, Simon said, 'Will he be back in time for school?'

'Yes,' Carrie said. She was still staring at Simon. 'Guy's putting him on the seven-fifteen.'

'Will you meet him?'

Carrie said, 'I rather thought you would.'

He made a face. He said, 'I've got an eight o'clock meeting –'

'I see.'

'He can surely get himself across London –'

'It isn't really about that,' Carrie said. 'Is it?'

Simon made one hand into a fist and folded the other round it. He said, 'I can't quite see why this little episode is my fault, too.'

'Can't you?'

'No,' Simon said.

'Ah.'

'Jack gets upset because Moll starts dating someone else so he does a bunk. It isn't dramatic enough just to go home, so he goes to Stanborough. Really original thinking.'

'Doesn't it strike you as significant that he might have chosen Stanborough because he thought he had a chance of a sympathetic reception there?'

'Oh come *on*,' Simon said. 'When did Jack and my father ever have much to say to one another?'

'Things have changed,' Carrie said. Her expression, he observed, was one of unmistakable anger. 'When something like this whole family crisis happens, everything changes, all the dynamics. It's only you that won't see that.'

She went out of the room then. She was hurt, he could see, badly hurt that Jack, in pain, had chosen a confidant other than her. But what Simon couldn't work out was why she was still angry with him, and not with his father. He would have understood, he thought, if Carrie had resented Guy for comforting Jack instead of her. But she didn't seem to feel resentment, she only seemed to feel that Simon had somehow made home impossible as a refuge for Jack when he needed one. Twice, in the night, Simon had reached out a tentative hand to touch Carrie, to see if he could convey something sympathetic, apologetic even, by action rather than words. The first time, she ignored his hand; the second time, she pushed it away.

After his eight o'clock meeting, Simon had rung Jack's school to see if he had arrived. He had, and was about to go into a double period of business studies. Simon said, 'Give him my –' to the school secretary, and then stopped. What could he possibly send Jack in these circumstances, via Mrs Pritchard in the school office, whose son he was advising legally about a turbulent neighbour? 'Tell him I'll see him later,' Simon said. 'Tell him – I'm glad he's OK.'

He took a mouthful of coffee. It was lukewarm and thin-tasting and speckles of artificial whitener floated on the surface like tiny clots of sour milk. He put the mug back down on the damp junk-mail mat and pushed the whole thing away from him. A steady misery was settling on him and with it, a definite and rather tremulous desire to see Jack. He looked at the telephone. Perhaps he would ring Carrie: perhaps he would ring her before she went into her ten o'clock meeting and tell her he'd go round to the school in the afternoon and meet Jack coming out. He put a hand out towards the telephone and it immediately rang. He picked it up.

'Simon Stockdale.'

'Simon,' Laura said.

He shut his eyes.

'Hello, Mum.'

'Simon,' Laura said. 'What on earth do you mean by this?'

He took a breath and opened his eyes.

'What –'

'This letter,' she said. Her voice was high and strained. 'This horrible, formal letter advising me to accept the offer on the house.'

'It has to be formal, Mother. I am your lawyer –'

She said nothing. He could feel the tension of her saying nothing like a hum down the line. He said, as forbearingly as he could, 'Mother, you have asked me to act for you legally. I have to deal with your affairs in a proper, professional way because I am also dealing with another lawyer in this matter and there are certain rules of conduct to be observed.'

'I accept that,' Laura said, in a voice that belied her acceptance of any such thing, 'but why must you write to me in such language?'

'Because I have to demonstrate that I am acting for you properly –'

'But you *still* don't have to write to me as if you hardly *know* me! Simon, please don't treat me like a fool. I've lived with lawyers all my life. I understand legal language, of course I do. But there is a difference between clear legal language and cold indifference.

Simon took the telephone away from his ear and laid it on his desk. Faint cheeps could be heard from it. He counted to ten and then he picked it up again.

'Mother.'

She was crying.

'It just gets worse, every day gets worse, every day I think I've only got months left here, weeks maybe, it's the last thing I've got, it's all I am, it's –'

'*Please*,' Simon said.

There was a small, uneven silence at the other end of the telephone. Then Laura said, with difficulty, 'I am so *afraid*.'

'I know.'

'I can't imagine how I'll live, how I'll be.'

'I know.'

'I just feel I haven't an identity any more.'

'You *do* have,' Simon said. 'We all have. We have them just by being ourselves. We aren't identified by where we live, how we live –' He stopped.

Laura said, 'Then perhaps I'm different.'

Simon wound a pencil into the coil of the telephone wire.

'Mum, look. I'm sorry about the tone of the letter but I *have* to write to you like that. I *have* to demonstrate that I have given you the best legal advice I can. And the best advice I can give you, as your lawyer and as your son, is to accept this offer on the house. It's an excellent offer.'

There was a pause. Then Laura said, 'I see,' almost in a whisper.

'It'll mean you can buy another house. A nice house, with a garden.'

'Simon –' Laura said.

'What?'

'Can you come?'

'What, now?'

'Yes,' Laura said.

'Mum –'

'Please,' Laura said. 'Please. I know I'll be able to cope if you just come and talk to me about it. I'll feel differently if you're here. I know I will.'

'Mum,' Simon said, 'it's a working day, a weekday.'

'This afternoon, come this afternoon. Just for an hour.'

'I can't,' Simon said.

'Why can't you? Surely someone else can cover for you?'

'It isn't work,' Simon said. 'It's Jack.'

'What's happened to Jack?'

'He's been very upset by something.'

'What thing?'

'It doesn't matter –'

'It does,' Laura said. Her voice was rising again. 'What is it? *Drugs*?'

'No,' Simon said, too loudly. 'No, it's nothing like that. But his first – well, he's just been jilted. He's very cut up.'

'Jilted?'

'Yes. His first girlfriend –'

'Do you mean to tell me,' Laura said, almost shouting, 'that you won't come and see me because Jack has had some – some little romantic *tiff*?'

'It isn't like that. It's more than that –'

'Like what?'

'I mean it's more complicated than that, more emotional –'

'More *important*!' Laura shrieked. Simon took a huge breath.

'Yes,' he said, and put the telephone down.

Merrion's case had been cancelled. The clerks had failed to reach her before she left home for chambers, and she had forgotten to turn her mobile phone on, so she arrived to find a blank diary.

'My apologies, Miss Palmer,' the senior clerk said.

She looked at him with irritation. Why couldn't he just say, 'I'm sorry,' like anybody else?

'It doesn't matter, Michael,' she said, enunciating every word. 'I have plenty to do, preparing for Monday.'

He said, 'There is something that's just come in, a threatened abduction matter, in Reading –'

'Give it to someone else,' Merrion said, and went past him through the double doors.

Her room was inevitably just as she had left it, the file for the cancelled case lying ready on her desk, her wig on its chair knob, yesterday's newspaper thrown into the waste-paper bin. She dropped her briefcase and bag on the floor and went over to the window. It was a sunny day, a bright, heartless, all-seeing sunny day and the light was coming down clearly between her own building and the one opposite and showing up the thick pale layer of dust on the windowsill outside. Merrion sighed and drummed a little rhythm on the double glazing with her fingers. It would have suited her mood better if it had been raining.

She turned and went across to her desk. There were no telephone messages. Guy had rung her that morning in the flat, as he always did, to say he would be on the usual train and that he would like to take her out to dinner to compensate for the night before. She had nearly said, 'Don't bother.' Only in the nick of time had she checked herself and said, 'Lovely.' She hadn't said it in quite the voice she would have wished, but at least she had said it.

'Darling,' Guy said. His voice was slightly teasing. 'Darling, don't have a sense-of-humour failure. It *was* only dinner.'

'Yes,' she said. She wanted to say, 'No, it wasn't *only* anything.' Nothing, it seemed, was only anything now, everything had come to matter, to have significance and echoes and implications. She felt – and she had chastised herself over and over for feeling this – that she was suddenly having to fight for something that had, for seven years, been effortlessly and superbly hers. She found herself wanting to go *out* with Guy, to be *seen* with Guy, to be included in things with Guy. That was what last night's dinner had been about, an expedition to a restaurant where not only did it not matter if they were seen together, but where she secretly hoped they *would* be seen, and the slow process of their real public acknowledgement as a couple could begin.

She sat down at her desk and pushed the file aside. She was ashamed of herself for feeling as she did, for behaving as she was, for being unable to feel genuine pity for poor, gawky, heartbroken Jack. She liked Jack. She found him appealing almost *because* he was so unfinished and because he couldn't help a certain softness in his nature showing through the cultivated nonchalance of his manner. But last night, she had been jealous of him. Plain, angry jealous. When Guy rang the second time – Jack was in the shower – she had wanted him to sound sorry, really remorseful, really disappointed at not seeing her, not having the chance to be with her in a public place. He'd sounded regretful, certainly, but only gently so. His main preoccupation had been with Jack and their evening together and the extraordinary and unexpected success their conversation had been. It was really easy, Guy said, talking to Jack, talking to a sixteen year old whose outlook must, by virtue alone of a forty-five-year age difference, be completely poles apart from his own. But it wasn't. It had been a revelation.

'Oh good,' Merrion said.

'He doesn't seem to disapprove of me, either,' Guy said. 'You can imagine the relief *that* is?'

'Oh yes.'

'He's thought about more than you'd think. I suppose that's boys, really. Girls seem to do their thinking while talking. Boys do one and then some of them do the other, later. He isn't, oddly enough, very like Simon.'

'Oh.'

'I must get him out of that shower and into bed. The flat looks as if a bomb has hit it. How can one boy with no possessions but what he stands up in do that?'

Merrion looked down at her blotter. It was covered with doodles, the peculiar, asymmetric angular shapes she'd always idly drawn on scraps and in margins since she was little. And there were the letters. She liked forming and illuminating letters. 'M,' she'd written, over and over, in different scripts and sizes. At the bottom of the blotter there was a row of letters in pairs, linked together by a scribbled chain: 'MS, MS, MS. Merrion Stockdale.' She looked at it. Guy was Stockdale. So was Jack. So was Alan and Simon and Carrie. And Laura. They were all Stockdale. And she had envied them, wanted to be part of this Stockdale thing, wanted to wear that badge that was Guy's, that would make her his. But did she? Did she want, now, to give Guy every reason to make her part of – even lump her in with – this Stockdale family of his? Might it be surrendering, rather than joining? Might she lose, it suddenly occurred to her, the right to assume she took precedence with Guy, precedence before Jack, before Simon, before Laura even, if Laura were to fall ill? If she became Stockdale, what might happen to Merrion Palmer? Might she become just a lawyer, an earner, an expert in the abrupt procedures of abduction and its legal consequences, and might the woman who had been Guy's lover for seven years, his cherished and particular lover, just blur and blend into Merrion Stockdale until she was as if she had never been? Merrion sat very still. She put her feet together under her desk and her hands in her lap. Think, she said to herself, think about it. Think it through. *Think.*

When Charlie had asked Alan if he could cook, Alan had thought he'd meant just that, 'Can you cook?'

'Course I can.'

'Oh good,' Charlie said, 'because I can't.'

He'd been grinning at Alan, as if he could see a joke Alan couldn't see.

He said, 'And operate a washing machine?'

'Yes –'

'And iron?'

'So-so. What *is* this?'

'I just wanted to be sure –'

'Sure of what?'

'Sure of your domestic skills before you move in with me.'

Alan had gaped.

'Charlie –'

'Will you? Will you move in with me?'

He remembered a little ecstasy. He'd known Charlie was in love with him, known he wanted to spend time with him, but there was something so carefree about Charlie, something so unpossessed, that he, Alan, had never quite dared to hope that Charlie would suggest what he was longing for him to suggest. He could only nod, he remembered, nod and nod like some daft mechanical toy.

And now here he was, early evening in Charlie's kitchen, throwing out all the rubbish in Charlie's cupboards, all the packets and tins and tubes and bottles long past their sell-by dates. It was hugely pleasurable. It felt, Alan thought, dumping a broken box of elderly poppadoms in the bin, as if he was throwing away Charlie's past, all the people he'd loved before Alan, all the people he'd known before Alan even knew he was on the same planet. He was getting rid of all the stuff that didn't count any more, all the stuff that was over, in order to make way for something not just new, but lasting. It was this sense of its being lasting that filled Alan with a kind of awe; a sense that he had stumbled upon exactly what he had been looking for, for years, exactly the person who could give a point to everything.

He'd said to Charlie, a bit drunkenly the other night, that he wondered if they'd been making their way towards each other for years, constantly being diverted or encountering difficulties, but keeping on because – because, well, it was sort of *meant*. And Charlie, so given to teasing, so given to making light of the most serious things, had simply said, 'I know.'

Charlie had hoarded the most extraordinary food. There were jars of peculiar East European vegetables and tins of nursery puddings and crumbling packets of obscure pulses and spices. It looked as if he had bought them on impulse and immediately forgotten he'd done it, since Alan knew for a fact that, up to the moment that they met, Charlie had lived on a truly appalling diet of random takeaways and indifferent hamburgers.

'I'll eat vegetables,' Charlie had said. 'Of course I will. I *like* vegetables. It's just that they don't ever exactly *occur* to me.'

Alan was looking forward to correcting that, looking forward to making Charlie eat breakfast and vegetables and olive oil and organic bread. He picked up a jar of grey-green pickled cabbage and dropped it, with a satisfactory thud, into the bin.

From the sitting room, his mobile phone began its shrill squeal. He hurried through, smiling, his face and voice ready for Charlie, ready to be tough and teasing about Charlie saying his surgery had overrun again and he'd got two emergencies at the hospital.

'Hel*lo*,' he said, with the special emphasis he reserved for Charlie.

'Alan,' Laura said.

His face changed.

'Hi, Mum –'

'Are you busy?'

'Not especially –'

'Where are you?'

Alan looked at Charlie's swaybacked sofa piled with newspapers and discarded sweatshirts. Laura did not know about Charlie.

'At home.'

'Oh,' Laura said.

'What's the matter, Mum?'

Laura said tightly, 'Simon put the telephone down on me.'

'What –'

'Earlier today. I rang to ask him why he had taken to writing to me with such hideous formality and he said he was too busy with some family crisis and put the telephone down.'

Alan moved across the sitting room and sat down on the sofa. He pulled one of Charlie's sweatshirts across his knees and patted it, as if it were a cat.

'What crisis?'

'Oh,' Laura said irritably, 'some storm in a teacup between Jack and a girl.'

'Moll?' Alan said.

'I don't know. Why should I know? Jack is sixteen and will probably think he's in love another dozen times before next Christmas.'

Alan smoothed a sleeve of the sweatshirt and folded it up neatly.

'I think it was quite serious, Mum. For Jack at any rate. The first time he'd –'

'But not comparable,' Laura said.

'Not –'

'Not comparable in any way to what I am faced with!'

Alan said nothing. He retrieved the second sleeve and folded it on top of the first one.

'Are you there?' Laura said.

'Yes –'

'Simon wants me to accept this offer on the house. He has *instructed* me to accept the offer. He has sent me an absolutely dreadful formal letter virtually commanding me to do it.'

'It's a good price, Mum. And he is your lawyer.'

'I know. Of course I know.'

'You *asked* him to be your lawyer.'

'Because I believed he understood. I couldn't go to a lawyer who didn't know our history, didn't understand how things were between your father and me. I couldn't just be a statistic, a set of figures, a typical example. I asked Simon because he knew. Because he *cared*. I needed a supporter, Alan, someone to turn to, someone who would feel what I was feeling, someone to take my part. Can you really not see?'

Alan moved the sweatshirt to one side and lay down along the sofa so that he could pillow his cheek on it. He said into the phone, with his eyes shut, 'You've asked for his advice, Mum. He gives you the best advice he can. Then you refuse to take it.'

'Yes, I do,' Laura said.

Alan opened his eyes.

'What?'

'I am not accepting this offer. I am not selling Hill Cottage.'

Alan sat up abruptly.

'Mum, you *have* to.'

'Why do I?'

'Because it represents the largest chunk of equity you and Dad have, and it has to be divided.'

'That,' Laura said, 'is your father's problem.'

Alan said patiently, 'It doesn't work like that.'

'What do you mean?'

'I mean that you can't stop things, ultimately. You can delay them, but you can't prevent them.'

There was a small scrape of a key in the lock. The front door opened and then slammed.

'Home!' Charlie shouted.

'Who is that?' Laura said.

Charlie appeared in the sitting-room doorway. His hair was tousled and his tie was at half mast. Alan's heart rose like a bird.

'A friend –'

'I want you to do something,' Laura said.

Charlie tiptoed over to the sofa and sat down beside Alan. He pointed to the phone, raising his eyebrows.

'My mother,' Alan mouthed.

Charlie grinned and picked up Alan's free hand. He put his fingers in his mouth.

'What?' Alan said.

'I want you to tell Simon that I'm refusing the offer on Hill Cottage. I am not going to be treated like this. By *any* of you.'

Charlie bit gently on Alan's fingers.

'OK –'

'Are you listening?'

'Yes,' Alan said faintly, his eyes on Charlie's face.

'Then ring Simon,' Laura said. 'Ring him and then ring me back.'

'OK. Mum, I've got to –'

'What?'

'I've got to go,' Alan said. He took the phone away from his ear. Charlie took it out of his hand and switched it off. He winked at Alan.

'Unless she'd like to join in?'

When Jack saw Simon on the pavement outside the school gates, he had an immediate panic. Simon had never come to meet him from school, not since his nursery-school days, and the sight of him hanging about rather apprehensively on the edge of the pavement, his hands in the pockets of his inevitably crumpled suit, made Jack think immediately that there'd been a disaster. He forgot Adam and Rich, dawdling along beside him as they seemed to at the moment, like a couple of spaniels, and sprinted forward.

'What's happened?'

'Nothing,' Simon said. He was trying to smile.

'Where's Mum?'

'At work,' Simon said. He put a hand out to touch Jack and it hovered, uncertain where to land. 'Where did you think she'd be?'

'Is she OK?'

'Yes, of course –'

'And Rach and Ems?'

Simon's hand brushed Jack's shoulder and slid off.

'Everyone's OK, Jack. Everyone's fine. I'm not here with bad news. Nothing's happened, promise.'

Jack peered at his father.

'Why're you here then?'

Simon shrugged a little. He said with difficulty, 'I felt bad. I felt – well, I felt I'd let you down –'

Jack glanced over his shoulder. Adam and Rich were standing eight feet away, pretending they weren't anything to do with anything. Jack jerked his head in their direction.

'See you,' he said to them.

Adam glanced up.

'Later?' he said.

'Nah,' Jack said. 'Tomorrow.'

He willed Adam not to say, 'You OK?'

'You OK?' Adam said.

Jack nodded. Rich pulled at Adam's sleeve.

'See you,' he said. Jack nodded again. They went wandering off, their school bags bashing into one another.

'Your friends?' Simon said.

'Yes. Some of them –'

'Looking after you?'

Jack shrugged.

'Seems like it –'

'Sorry,' Simon said.

'Sorry what?'

'Sorry it wasn't me. Or Mum.'

Jack said, 'Could we get a move on?'

He stepped past Simon into the gutter and began to walk along the road. Simon ran to catch up with him.

'I didn't mean to embarrass you in front of your friends –'

'You didn't.'

'I just wanted to see you, to tell you I was sorry.'

Jack put his head down. He began to walk faster.

'You did. It's OK. I *said*.'

'Can I ask you,' Simon said, dodging other people on the road edge to keep up with Jack. 'Can I ask you something?'

Jack nodded.

'When – when it happened, when you found out –' He stopped.

Jack stopped walking.

'What?'

'When you found out,' Simon said, stopping, too, and facing him, 'why didn't you come and tell me or Mum?'

Jack sighed. He shifted his school bag from one shoulder to the other.

'I couldn't.'

'Why not? We'd met Moll, we'd seen what she meant to you –'

'Dad,' Jack said, interrupting.

'What.'

'You weren't listening,' Jack said.

Simon said earnestly, 'But you didn't *try* us.'

'I couldn't.'

'You couldn't? Why couldn't you?'

'There wasn't any point,' Jack said, and began to walk again.

'Can you tell me –'

'There hasn't been any point for ages. Ever since this Grando thing. You're always too tired or too busy or out or something.'

Simon said, 'And Mum?'

'Same,' Jack said briefly.

They stopped to cross the road by some traffic lights. Simon put a hand on Jack's arm.

'Probably,' Jack said, 'I cross twenty roads a day all by myself.'

'I don't,' Simon said. He waited for Jack to shrug his hand off. Jack didn't. The lights changed and they went across together, Simon's hand under Jack's arm.

'So you went to Grando.'

'Yes.'

'Can you tell me why?'

Jack screwed his face up.

'He's OK.'

'Could you try a bit harder?'

Jack stopped walking again. He said, staring past Simon rather than at him, 'He talked to me.'

'Just that?'

'He listened,' Jack said, 'he made time for me.' He looked quickly at Simon. He said, quite slowly, 'He didn't make me feel I was just a bloody messy teenage pest.'

Simon's face twitched.

'I see.'

'He's in this grotty flat,' Jack said. 'He's only got his clothes and some books. But he never –'

'He never what?'

'He never asked me to be sorry for him. He was just sorry for me.'

'Yes.'

'Because he knew,' Jack said loudly. 'He *knows*.'

Simon said tentatively, 'And I don't?'

Jack's gaze dropped. He kicked at the uneven edge of a pavement slab.

'I don't know what you know,' he said. 'How can I? You never say.'

CHAPTER SIXTEEN

Rachel had left her bedroom door slightly open. The landing light was on as usual so that Rachel could see across the stairwell and notice that Emma's door was shut. Emma had gone to bed halfway through supper, saying she had a headache.

'The same headache?' Carrie said. Carrie looked as if she had a headache herself.

'I don't know,' Emma said.

'Is it in the same place?'

Emma had twiddled some spaghetti into a nest shape and then taken her fork out of the nest and laid the fork aside on her plate.

'I can't remember.'

Carrie had found a packet of paracetamol in a kitchen drawer and made Emma swallow one. Then she'd taken Emma upstairs and put her to bed as if she was six.

When she came down, she said to Rachel, 'I wonder if it's her eyesight –'

'You'll never get her to wear glasses. She'd freak.'

'Why should she keep having headaches?'

Rachel was reading the weekly colour supplement of the evening newspaper. There was an article in it on how stress made some girls into sticks and some into balloons.

'Stress,' she said.

'Why should Emma be stressed?' Carrie said.

Rachel shrugged. If Carrie didn't think the whole evening hadn't been stressed, with Simon first playing superdad all over Jack and then insisting on taking him out for a drink, then she wasn't going to point it out. Jack looked as if he didn't know what to do, as if he hadn't a clue as to what was expected of him. He hadn't eaten his spaghetti either, he'd just picked some bits of ham out of the sauce and left the rest in a tomato-y mess, like Emma had. Rachel had eaten hers. She wished she hadn't, but she had. She tried not to think of how her tummy would look in the shower. She pushed the colour supplement away from her.

'I'll clear up,' she said to Carrie.

Carrie was nursing a mug of herbal tea. Her hair was all over her shoulders. It needed a wash, Rachel thought, or a brush at least.

'Will you?'

Rachel got up.

'Yes.'

'Actually,' Carrie said, 'don't bother. It's very kind of you, but I'll do it. I need something mindless to do while I wait for Dad and Jack to get back.'

'OK.'

'Have you got homework –'

'Don't ask,' Rachel said. 'Just don't *always* ask.'

'Sorry. Reflex.'

Rachel looked at the table. It was appalling to realise that she could easily have eaten what Jack and Emma had left on their plates. She jerked her tummy muscles in, and held them.

'See you later,' Rachel said.

Carrie lifted her face.

'Give me a kiss.'

'You never want a kiss –'

'I do now.'

Rachel bent and kissed Carrie's cheek. It felt dry and a

little rough. Trudy thought Carrie was pretty but didn't make the best of herself.

'What d'you mean, the best?' Rachel said. 'She doesn't make *anything*.'

Once upstairs, Rachel lay on her bed. She raised her legs into the air, first left, then right, then both together, and felt the satisfactory pull in her abdomen. You ought really, she knew, to do these exercises on the floor, but it was too much to do at night, too much to ask of somebody with all the preoccupations Rachel had. She turned on her side and looked out through her open door at Emma's closed one. She thought of going in and sitting on Emma's bed and trying on the butterfly hair clips Sonia had given her. But it would be a hassle. Emma wouldn't want her to, out of sheer perversity, and she'd shriek if Rachel so much as put a hand on the butterfly clips and then Carrie would come up and there'd be a scene and Emma would say her headache was worse.

Downstairs, the telephone rang. Rachel became alert.

'Hello?' she heard Carrie say. 'Hello?' and then, in a different voice, 'Oh, hello, Laura.'

Rachel rolled quietly off her bed and on to the floor. Then she crawled out on to the landing and lay against the banisters, peering down towards the hall and the open kitchen door.

'No,' Carrie said. 'No, he isn't.'

Rachel heard the scrape of furniture on the kitchen floor as if Carrie was pulling a stool over towards the counter where the telephone was.

'He's out, Laura,' Carrie said. Her voice was quite loud, louder, Rachel thought, than it needed to be for an ordinary conversation. 'He's out with Jack. They have gone out together. No. No, I don't know when they'll be back, I didn't ask, Laura. I did not *ask*.'

There was a pause. Rachel pictured Carrie perched on a stool, her elbows on the counter, and her hair swinging forward over the hand that held the receiver.

'I'm not sure,' Carrie said, 'that that is any of your business, is it, Laura? If Simon and his son choose to go out together, they aren't really obliged, are they, to account to you for their reasons? Yes, Jack has been upset this week, but that's a family matter, a family affair –'

She stopped. Rachel raised her head a little. Emma's bedroom door opened a few inches and revealed Emma, in her pink trackpant pyjama bottoms and a white T-shirt with a *diamanté* heart on the front.

'Granny?' Emma mouthed.

Rachel nodded.

'No!' Carrie said with vehemence from the kitchen.

Emma opened her door a little wider and sat down in the doorway. She had the headphones from her personal stereo slung round her neck.

'Is she –?' Emma whispered.

'Shhh!' Rachel said.

'Yes, you did hear me,' Carrie said. 'You heard me perfectly clearly. I said no. I said – or I meant – no, I will not get Simon to ring you when he comes in. I may not even tell him you rang.'

The stool scraped on the kitchen floor. Carrie must be gesturing.

'Because he has had enough!' Carrie shouted. 'Because I have had enough! We have all had enough of your demands and your complaints and your absolute refusal to blame yourself for anything! You are making our life intolerable, you are putting so much pressure on Simon and then he takes it out on us and we *all* suffer!'

She stopped again, abruptly. Emma crept forward until she was leaning against the opposite banister to Rachel.

'I don't care!' Carrie yelled. 'I don't bloody *care* any more! You can cry your eyes out but I've utterly run out of any sympathy I've ever had for you. And I'll tell you something else. I'll tell you something else, Laura, something I should have told you months ago, years probably.

242

If you fight me for Simon, Laura, I'll not only fight you back, tooth and nail, but I'll win. Do you hear me? I'll *win*!'

Then the telephone was crashed down. Rachel and Emma sat up.

'Wow,' Emma whispered. Rachel didn't answer. She crawled to the top of the staircase and crouched there, as if she was wondering whether to go down. They heard Carrie get off the stool and pad across the kitchen and then they heard the soft rip of paper being torn off the roll of kitchen towel that hung by the cooker on a wooden bracket. Then they heard something else, a small, jerky, piteous sound, like a little animal in pain.

'Oh God,' Emma whispered. 'Rach, she's crying.'

Guy was possessed by a huge restlessness. He'd tried to sleep; he'd even thought he would be able to sleep, but the illuminated green numbers on Merrion's clock radio said it was ten-past two and then five to three and then a quarter to four. Guy got up, gingerly, and went out to the kitchen, not turning any lights on in case Merrion woke up and asked him if he was all right. 'Absolutely fine,' he'd say, and she'd say, 'No you're not,' and it would all start again.

He slid the kitchen door shut and turned on the lamp that stood in the angle of the tiny kitchen counter and threw such interesting angles of light and shadow. Guy had never considered light as an aesthetic form in a house before: he'd only, at Hill Cottage, regarded light as being sufficiently dim to watch television properly or sufficiently bright to see to read or shave. But Merrion thought about light. Her blinds and lamps and spotlights let light fall in certain pools and patterns and degrees so that moods and atmospheres were altered. Like so much about Merrion, her way of looking at things had made such a difference to him, such an intriguing, illuminating difference.

He filled the kettle and plugged it in. He wasn't sure he really wanted anything to drink but he had a feeling that to go through the ritual of making a drink would be reassuring. His mother had been a habitual insomniac and had constructed a series of rituals around the problem, as if to assert that she was in no way defeated, re-making her bed a dozen times a night, opening and closing the curtains, walking briskly up and down the stairs. Guy pictured her still at it, in her eighties, dressed in his father's old pyjamas, going up and down the stairs at Hill Cottage whenever she came to stay, counting as she went.

'It has to be fifty. Fifty steps. Forty-nine doesn't work and nor does fifty-one.'

She had been possessed, right to the end, with formidable energy, helping Laura barrow loads of manure for the vegetable garden only two months before her death. The garden was the one thing that united Laura and his mother, the one space of territory where Laura didn't feel inadequate and Guy's mother understood at least something of her daughter-in-law's nature.

'Glad she's got the garden,' Guy's mother had said, and then after a pause, almost reflectively, 'Bloodless girl, your Laura.'

If only, Guy thought, opening cupboards in search of a tea bag, his mother could see Laura now. Or Merrion, for that matter. What on earth would she make of it all? Whatever would she think of a son who had found love – true love – in his fifties when already a grandfather? What would she think of Laura's reaction and her insistence upon Simon's succour? She had been a teacher, Guy's mother, a biologist, but for her the heart had been chiefly a vital and ingenious organ and not the seat of all joy and all anguish. Guy and his brothers had assumed, without ever looking at it too closely, that their parents' marriage had not only been one of the meeting of two extremely competent professional minds, but also one of mutual

244

devotion. But then, of course, they never really knew, did they? It was the custom of their parents' generation neither to explain nor to complain and if the steady beat of that marriage had faltered – which it surely must have done, sometimes, mustn't it? – nobody would ever know. Poor old Mum, Guy thought, pouring boiling water on to the tea bag in one of Merrion's white mugs, but then lucky old Mum, too. Rules made a cage but they also made a structure.

Guy turned off the lamp and slid the door to the sitting room back again. It was a clear night and the glow from the sky and the street filled the room with itself, and with big, soft shadows. Guy sat down on the sofa – the cushions were still crushed from where they'd both been earlier, half sitting, half lying – and put his mug down on the table. He leaned back and looked at the ceiling, at the narrow track of minute, brilliant spotlights that ran across it and which, when switched on, created such extraordinary effects. It was, he thought, like being with Merrion or being without her, like bumbling along in the half-light or suddenly seeing things with freshness and novelty. If only – he shut his eyes and grimaced to himself in the dimness – if only it were possible to keep that novelty from turning itself into strangeness, to prevent it from colliding with other things, refusing to co-exist.

'I could not bear,' he'd said at dinner, 'to feel I was in any way limiting you.'

She was eating a complicated salad with a fork. She didn't look up at him, instead endeavouring to fold a long leaf of rocket in two.

'We've had this conversation.'

'That doesn't deal with it,' Guy said. 'Looking at Jack the other night brought home to me how *young* you are. You're far closer in age to him than to me. *Far.*'

She put the rocket into her mouth, pushing the stalk in after the leaf, with her fork.

'Are we talking about babies again?'

'I suppose it's part of it –'

'Maybe I don't want a baby.'

Guy said gently, 'Don't be childish.'

'I'm so tired,' Merrion said, 'of you bringing up difficulties. You never used to.'

'And you always said they'd be there.'

'They *are*. But they don't need talking up a storm all the time.'

'Or ignoring.'

She speared a piece of red pepper, inspected it, and put it on the side of her plate.

'I'm not ignoring anything,' she said. 'I'm just finding it very difficult to cope with your preoccupations. It's very hard, Guy, to see you mentally miles away from me. I know you're having a hard time, I know Laura is being impossible and the flat is horrible and dealing with your children is at best difficult but it seems to me – I have to say this – that you are *drawn* towards all that, almost that you're returning to something you knew long before me, that you've gone somewhere I can't follow you.'

He turned his wineglass round and round, twisting it by the stem.

'I have never loved anyone as I love you.'

'I know,' she said. She put her fork down. 'But that isn't really the point, is it?'

He stared at his plate.

'You've found something,' Merrion said, 'haven't you? You've found your family again.'

Guy said, 'But I want you to be part of that family –'

She said sharply, more sharply than she meant to, 'And is that a good thing?'

He raised his head.

'A good thing?'

'For me,' Merrion said. 'Is it a good thing for me to be sort of *subsumed* into your family? Is that what you and I are about? Is that what we've been aiming at, all these years?'

He shook his head. He said, almost inaudibly, 'No.' And then he said, 'We didn't know, did we, we didn't know what was coming –'

'No,' she said. She pushed her plate away. 'I don't want to talk any more. I don't want to have to say things. I'm not ready for saying things yet. Not some things, anyhow.'

He opened his eyes now and reached for his tea. It didn't taste of anything much: he hadn't let the tea bag soak long enough. What he had wanted to say at dinner and been unable to bring himself to say had been that he couldn't, for reasons he couldn't explain, visualise how their life together was going to be in the future. In the past, he'd always seen it: it hung in his mind, a clear picture in equally clear contrast to the half-life he lived with Laura. He'd seen an urban flat, a big flat, full of his books and her objects. He'd seen a house somewhere, maybe even a townhouse, with doors opening to a small summer garden and music playing. Sometimes, they'd even talked about these pictures, playing the luxurious game of how things could be if they were free to make them so. And now that freedom was, round extraordinary obstacles, slowly coming, and as it advanced towards him, it seemed to be blurring his vision of the future. What was even more disconcerting was that he suspected it was blurring Merrion's vision, too, that vision that had always been so unclouded, that had always sustained him, reassured him.

He looked round the sitting room. They couldn't stay there, that was for certain. It was too small, too feminine, too emphatically the flat of a single life. He tried, as he had tried so often recently, to visualise somewhere else that would be right for them; to conjure up that fantasy flat, that fantasy house where they could amplify that sense of complete belonging that they felt together. He could think of nothing. When he tried to imagine, all he saw was what he already knew; this flat, Hill Cottage, the dreary rooms at Pinns Green.

He stood up. The light was getting stronger, dawn triumphing over street lamps. He went quietly across the sitting room and opened the door to the bedroom.

'You've been ages,' Merrion said.

'Have I? I thought you were asleep.'

She turned towards him. He could see the dark mass of her hair on the pillow.

'At least an hour. Are you all right?'

He sat on the edge of the bed, his back to her. She put a hand out and laid it flat on his back, on his spine below the shoulder blades.

'I don't know,' he said.

'Get in,' she said.

He swung round and pushed his legs back in under the bedclothes.

'Guy,' she said. 'What is it?'

He looked at the ceiling. He said, 'I can't seem to see the way ahead. I always could, but at the moment, I can't.'

She felt for his hand, under the covers, and held it in both hers.

'Keep saying "at the moment",' she said. 'Just keep saying that.'

Her voice was apprehensive, almost frightened. He put his second hand over hers and they held on to each other, under the covers, hard.

'Just keep on,' Merrion said.

The pub Alan had chosen had tables on the pavement. When Guy approached, Alan was already there with all the accessories on the table before him that Guy had come to recognise as urban essentials – a mobile telephone, a newspaper and a drink. Alan was wearing sunglasses and a blue linen shirt. He got up as Guy came towards him and held his arms out.

'Hi, Dad.'

Guy held him.

'That's nice –'

'You OK?' Alan said. He shifted his arms in order to put his hands on his father's shoulders.

'A bit tired –'

'I'm not surprised,' Alan said.

Guy smiled. He looked at Alan's glass.

'What are you drinking?'

'Campari.'

Guy made a face.

'I think I'll get myself a beer.'

Alan pushed down lightly on Guy's shoulders.

'You sit down. I'll get it.'

Guy sat down on a white plastic chair with his back to the wall of the pub. He felt tired indeed, tired in body and spirit.

'Do I look my age?' he'd said to Merrion that morning.

She'd been in the shower and was making coffee, wrapped in a bath towel.

'I've no idea,' she said, and kissed him.

Alan came back with a tall glass of lager.

'This sort of beer?'

'Excellent,' Guy said.

'Dad –'

'Yes?'

'I've got something to tell you.'

Guy looked at him. He was back in his chair and resting his elbows on the table.

'I've moved in with someone,' Alan said.

'Someone –'

'He's called Charlie Driver. He's a doctor.'

Guy raised his beer glass.

'*Good.*'

'That sounded a bit hearty –'

'It wasn't meant to.'

'It's such a relief,' Alan said. 'Being in love again.'

Guy smiled at him.

'Of course.'

'I want to tell the world –'

Guy looked down at his beer.

'I remember.'

'Dad. I'm not telling Mum.'

'No –'

'In fact, I'm not sure I'm even speaking to Mum for the moment.'

Guy said unhappily, 'Nobody seems to be able to –'

'That was the other thing I wanted to see you about.'

'Besides Charlie.'

'Yes.'

Guy put a hand out and held Alan's nearest wrist.

'I am really pleased about Charlie. As long as he's good to you.'

'None better,' Alan said. He took a swallow of Campari. 'But Mum –'

'Yes.'

'She's now refusing to take Simon's advice.'

'I know.'

'I think,' Alan said, 'that I have to have another go at Simon.'

Guy said with sudden vehemence, 'Alan, I've suddenly got no skins left about it any more. I can hardly think about it, let alone do anything about it. I just seem to dread it all, dread the difficulties and refusals and complications. Dread the decisions. It was such a relief to see Jack the other night. Someone else's problems, someone else's life –' He stopped.

Alan waited.

'Sorry,' Guy said.

'Why sorry?'

'I've created these complications,' Guy said, staring past Alan along the pavement, 'and I feel the least I can do is shoulder the consequences, and not complain.'

'But you didn't know what the consequences would be –'

'I thought I did. I thought I could guess. And that I could deal with them.'

'But you can't –'

'No,' Guy said. He pushed his glass away. 'Once, I seemed to know what I was doing so clearly that I didn't even have a choice to make. And now it's all choices.'

'Is it?' Alan said. He picked up his cigarettes.

'No,' Guy said. He glanced at Alan. 'No, it isn't choice now. It's dilemma.'

It was almost nine-thirty before Rachel heard Carrie go downstairs. On Sunday mornings, it used to be Simon who went down first, and he'd put a tracksuit on and go out for the newspapers and then he'd bring them upstairs, with a cup of tea, for Carrie. When they were all little, Rachel remembered, Simon would get cross with them if they tried to get into bed with Carrie on a Sunday. Saturday was OK, but Sunday was forbidden. But the last few months, Sundays had been the other way about. It was Carrie who went downstairs first, and made tea. She didn't go and get the newspapers until she was properly dressed, and she made the tea wearing the old kimono with blue cranes and flowers printed on it which Rachel could remember all her life. Simon had once bought Carrie a new dressing gown, a white one made of thick waffle woven cotton, but Rachel knew it was still in its plastic bag on top of Carrie's cupboard, and Carrie was still wearing her kimono.

Rachel got slowly out of bed. Simon's grey sweater was on the floor where she had dropped it the previous night, and she picked it up and pulled it over the outsize T-shirt she'd slept in. Then she pulled her hair back, unbrushed, and pushed it through an elasticated towelling band.

It was silent on the landing. Emma's door was shut and

so was Simon and Carrie's and there was no sound from the little staircase up to Jack's room. Rachel padded downstairs. Carrie was standing in the kitchen, dressed in jeans and a checked shirt and a fleece jacket, with her hand on the kettle as if that would help it to boil faster.

'Hi,' Rachel said.

Carrie turned round.

'Morning, darling.'

Rachel went to lean against the counter near the kettle.

'You going to get the papers?'

'Yes,' Carrie said. 'Why d'you ask?'

'No reason.'

Rachel yawned. She put a hand up and scratched her collar bone through her T-shirt. She said, 'Is that for Dad's tea?'

'Yes,' Carrie said.

'I'll do it.'

'Will you?'

'Yes.'

'He's still asleep –'

Rachel looked at the clock.

'It's twenty to ten.'

'Thank you,' Carrie said. She took her hand off the kettle. 'I'll go and get the papers then.'

She picked her handbag up and went out of the kitchen. Rachel heard the front door shut, not slam. She looked at the kettle. Still trying not to wake Dad, still trying not . . . Rachel went across the kitchen and took a mug out of the cupboard. She banged the door shut, loudly. If that didn't wake Simon, she would, in two minutes.

She carried the mug of tea upstairs and along the landing. Emma's door was still closed. Rachel paused by her parents' bedroom door, transferred the mug from her right hand to her left, and turned the door handle. The room was half dark with the curtains still pulled across. Simon was just a long hump in the bed.

Rachel put the mug down on the chest of drawers and went across the room. She pulled all the curtains back with great energy.

'I know, I know,' Simon said from the pillows, his voice muffled.

'It's me,' Rachel said.

She went back to the chest of drawers and picked up the tea mug. Simon lifted his head from the pillow and stared at her.

'How very kind –'

'Yes,' Rachel said.

She went round the bed until she was facing the way he was lying, and held the mug out.

'Here.'

Simon sat up slowly. He was wearing his pitiful dark-blue pyjamas and his hair was tousled. A lot of Rachel's friends had fathers who were going bald. At least Simon wasn't doing that. He held a hand out and she put the mug into it.

'What have I done now?' Simon said.

Rachel thought of sitting on the edge of the bed and decided against it. She pulled at the hem of her T-shirt so that it came well below the hem of Simon's sweater.

She said, 'You need a shave.'

Simon took a swallow of tea.

'I need one every morning. And sometimes in the evening, too. Dark men do.'

'Jack shaves sometimes. Round his spots.'

'Rachel,' Simon said, 'can you say what you've come to say?'

Rachel inspected the cuticles of her right hand carefully.

'It's Mum.'

'What's Mum?'

'She's upset,' Rachel said.

Simon took another mouthful of tea and leaned away

from Rachel to put the mug down on the cluttered table beside the bed.

'Of course she is. We all are. And Jack being so unhappy upsets everyone.'

'It isn't that,' Rachel said. She peered at a hangnail and put her finger between her teeth.

'What isn't what?'

'Mum isn't upset about Jack,' Rachel said, chewing at her hangnail. 'I mean she is, but it isn't the worst thing. It's you.'

Simon flung himself across the bed, tossing the duvet aside, and put his feet on the floor.

'Oh, I *know* it's me –'

'Not like that,' Rachel said.

'What d'you mean?'

'She's not upset because you're such a pain. She's upset because of Granny.'

Simon said steadily, 'I have to help Granny.'

Rachel started on her other hand.

'She was crying the other day.'

Simon turned to look at Rachel.

'Crying?'

'She said if Granny made her fight for you, she'd win. Then she was crying.'

Simon stood up.

'She said this to you?'

'No,' Rachel said. 'She was on the phone. I was listening. She's been upset for ages.'

'Did she know you'd heard her?'

Rachel put both hands by her sides and held them there. If she chewed any more, she'd make herself bleed.

'No.'

'Why didn't you say?'

'There was no point,' Rachel said. 'I know what she thinks. I know what she's feeling. It's *you* that needs to know.'

Simon swallowed. He looked down and gave a hitch to his pyjama bottoms.

'I see,' he said.

'You don't,' Rachel said rudely.

Simon looked at her. Rachel could suddenly, for a fleeting moment, see what he had once looked like, what he had looked like at Jack's age. He said uncertainly, 'What don't I see?'

Rachel put her hands on her hips. She said, almost contemptuously, 'That she likes you.'

CHAPTER SEVENTEEN

Laura had bought two dozen new delphinium plants. They were excellent specimens, leafy and robust. She was going to make a new border along the wall where the old cowshed had been, a blue border edged with French lavender which could spill over on to the brick path she had laid herself seven years ago with the help of a boy from the village. He had been looking for a summer job, any job, because he was saving up to buy a motorbike. For three weeks, one August – Guy was at a legal conference in Kuala Lumpur, she remembered – the boy helped Laura carry and then lay the bricks on a membrane of black plastic to stop the weeds coming through. She couldn't now remember his name, which was rather awful. Steve or Gareth or something. He was very thin and hardly spoke but he didn't seem to mind being told what to do. When she looked at the path now – a careful, pretty herringbone pattern – she felt a surge of envy for the mood in which she must have laid it, the unworried, carefree absorption in something simple and creative. When she had planted her blue border, she thought she might change the dining-room curtains to echo it, since the dining-room windows faced across a small lawn to the old cowshed wall. In fact, she could go round the whole house and look out of every window as if it were a picture, and see how she could, as it were, frame it.

She placed the delphiniums carefully on the dug – and fed – border and stood back to see if they would be in the right relation to one another for size and colour. She was good at that. Everybody said so. Just as everybody said that she had a particular knack with pruning, so that her garden flowered longer and stronger than anyone else's. Even Wendy conceded that, and Wendy had a distinct pride in her own garden and was, in any case, like many people with multiple competences, not very good, in Laura's opinion, at dishing out the praise. You had to confront her to get any; stand up for yourself, point out that, although you might not do things Wendy's way, your own way was pretty good in its own right. It had happened the other day when Wendy had arrived with a bottle of wine and banged it down on the kitchen table.

'We're drinking *that*. I'm not having any more cups of tea and accompanying fiddle faddle.'

Laura had decided to be dignified. She put the bottle and two glasses on a tray with the corkscrew and a little dish of enamelled-looking Japanese rice crackers, and carried it into the sitting room. She said, with her back to Wendy, 'I suppose you have come to tick me off again.'

'Of course I have,' Wendy said. She flung herself back into an armchair and took off her spectacles. 'What on earth else do you expect? You get offered twenty thousand pounds over the asking price for this house and you turn it down!'

Laura put the corkscrew very precisely into the neck of the wine bottle.

'How do you know?'

'For God's sake, Laura, *everybody* knows! Everybody thinks you are completely insane! It's only me that knows you practically *invented* obstinacy.'

Laura poured neat half-glasses of wine. She arranged a tiny smile on her face and carried the glass over to Wendy's armchair. There was a little polished table beside it bearing a coaster with a camellia printed on it. Laura put the wineglass down carefully on the centre of the camellia.

'Suppose we don't talk about that?'

Wendy was breathing heavily on her spectacle lenses before polishing them. She stopped, mid-breath.

'What?'

'Suppose,' Laura said, putting the dish of Japanese crackers beside Wendy's wineglass, 'suppose we don't start again, all over again, on all the things you think I'm not doing right.'

'And?' Wendy said.

'Concentrate on the things you think I *am* doing right.'

'Heavens,' Wendy said. She took a gulp of wine.

Laura sat down in the opposite armchair. She put her knees and feet together. She smiled at Wendy, more broadly.

'What am I doing right?'

Wendy gestured wildly with her hand holding her spectacles.

'Well, you haven't gone to pieces –'

'No.'

'You look, well, neat as a pin as you always have, so does the garden and the house –'

'Yes.'

'And you haven't slagged Guy off in public, I suppose. You may have to me, in private, but in public –'

'Yes,' Laura said.

Wendy put her spectacles back on.

'So, well done. Well done for that.'

'Thank you,' Laura said.

Wendy heaved herself forward in the armchair.

'But that doesn't mean you get good marks for everything.'

Laura stiffened.

'Here we go again –'

'Yes,' Wendy said, 'we do.'

'I am not talking about this house any more,' Laura said. 'I've decided.'

'You can't decide. You can't take a unilateral decision. Half belongs to Guy. Legally. It belongs to him.'

Laura looked straight ahead. She held her chin up, higher than was normal, high enough for defiance.

'I've made my position quite plain,' Laura said. 'And I'm not discussing it any further. They can all come to me when they have everything sorted, but I'm not involving myself any more. I am going to get on with my new life instead.'

'Your new life?'

'Living here,' Laura said. 'Living here alone and making something of it.' She took a minute sip of wine. 'I may take in bed-and-breakfast guests. I read that you can charge guests up to twenty-five pounds a night each. I *may* do. I haven't decided.'

Wendy had left soon after that. She had left in a slightly clumsy, flurried way, not even finishing her wine, which was irritating because it was a waste, really, of having opened the bottle in the first place. Laura put the cork back in and stored the bottle in the refrigerator. Perhaps Simon would like it, when he next came. *When* he next came.

Now, regarding the delphiniums and wondering whether to grade the blues from dark to light, or to mix them, Laura reflected that her conversation with Wendy had been something of a small triumph. It was extraordinary how, when you could take charge of your life again after a profound shock, you found you had the power to choose again, to decide, to arrange things in a way both satisfactory and suitable to yourself. There had been that terrible time when she thought she would *have* to leave Hill Cottage, when she saw her whole identity being somehow melted out of her and poured away by people who simply could not see where the core, the mainspring, of her being lay. She had been terrified then, almost desperate. There had been moments when, despite her fear of driving in London, she had almost got into her car and found Simon's office in that awful part of South London where he insisted on working and just flung herself at him. She'd seen herself, in her mind's eye, clinging to him, sobbing, *making* him see that he was literally the only person who could save her from being just rubbed out, obliterated. But then something amazing had happened, some weird new strength had come to her, and it had come to her most inexplicably after Simon had written her that dreadful letter which really ordered her to sell Hill Cottage. It was as if a voice had said inside her head, 'Don't.' She had felt relief surge up in her, an unspeakable comfort after pain. 'Don't agree. Don't give in. Don't move.'

'I needn't,' she said aloud to the dogs, almost in wonder. 'I *needn't*! I don't have to move!'

After that, nothing seemed to hurt so much, nothing seemed to touch her with quite the exquisite painfulness that everything had touched her with previously. Simon's exasperation, Alan's offhandedness, even Guy's betrayal seemed all much more bearable, much more possible to reconcile herself to. Instead of running pitifully behind them all, begging for sympathy and understanding, she had somehow gone to the head of the line and they were all having to run after her. And she would make them run. She would see that that is what they did, until she had got what she wanted.

From inside the house, the telephone began to ring. Seconds later, the dogs began barking, a maddening habit they had developed lately in order to tell her that the telephone – which she could hear perfectly well anyway; she had even installed an extra-loud bell for the garden – was ringing. She pulled off her gardening gloves, dropped them beside the tools on the path, and ran in.

'Hello?' she said. 'Hello?'

'Mum,' Simon said.

She smiled broadly into the receiver.

'Darling!'

'You sound out of breath.'

'I was in the garden.'

'Oh –'

'Planting a new border.'

'A new –'

'It'll be lovely. All blues and greys. By the old cowshed wall.'

There was a silence and then Simon said, 'I was wondering. Could I come and see you?'

'Of course!' Laura said delightedly. She thought of the bottle of wine in the fridge. She wondered if he would like cold ham or something roast, lamb perhaps, a half-leg. 'I'd love it. When?'

'Tomorrow?' he said.

'Perfect. Lovely. For lunch?'

'I really don't need lunch,' Simon said. 'I just need to see you for half an hour –'

'Lunch,' Laura said firmly. 'Twelve-thirty.' She smiled into the receiver and put up a hand to touch her hair to smooth it back into place. 'Drive carefully.'

'This is the last time,' Ted said to Simon.

Simon nodded.

'It isn't that I'm not sympathetic, but we can't just go on with you so preoccupied with your family troubles you're only half with us.'

Simon nodded again. Ted was eight years older than Simon and when he wanted to make a point, behaved as if the age difference was almost a generation, as if he were a father reprimanding a son. Mostly, Simon bore it. In the first place, he liked Ted and in the second Ted did all the personal-injury work in this office. If you did personal-injury work, you got paid by the insurance companies at about a hundred and twenty pounds an hour. If, however, like Simon and Philip, you did mostly employment and immigration and housing, you got paid at the legal-aid rate which was only about a quarter of that. Ted never said, overtly, that he was the one who paid most of the bills, but the implication was there, all the time, in his attitude. Simon picked up his jacket.

'I'll be back at four.'

'Four!'

'It's an hour and a half's journey, minimum, each way.'

Ted blew air out between his teeth. He shook his head.

'It's only half-ten now –'

'I can't concentrate,' Simon said. He picked his car keys up and dropped them into his trouser pocket. 'I'm no use here this morning.'

'I'm fond of my mother,' Ted said. 'But basically she does what I tell her.'

Simon went past him to the door.

'Lucky you.'

His car was parked in the derelict yard behind the office building. The yard also contained Ted and Phil's cars, and the overflowing industrial-sized waste bins from the kebab house on the ground floor. Simon had often seen rats around these bins. It had occurred to him to telephone the local health and safety inspectorate, but the brothers who ran the kebab house were both well over six foot and already extremely suspicious of having a bunch of lawyers working in the offices above their premises. He'd had visions of opening his front door at home and finding a posse of vengeful Greeks standing outside, and had decided to let the rats alone. Dealing with trouble was a very different matter from provoking it.

He drove the car out of the yard and headed west. It was a warm day, humid, and the car's fan system blew tired, gritty air into the car. At least only Ted knew where he was going. Carrie didn't; nor did Rachel. He had seen them both briefly that morning before work, but neither had really looked at him. It was better, perhaps, that they should not know he was going to see Laura; better that they should know nothing until the deed was done.

Laura looked better. It was remarkable how much better she looked. She had on a pale-yellow shirt and dark-blue cotton trousers and her pearl earrings. She looked almost happy; almost girlish. She greeted him without any of the heavy, needy dependency she had greeted him with for months, and took his arm, and led him around the house to the place where she was making her new border. There were delphiniums planted all along the back, in the painstakingly turned earth, and a neat regiment of lavender plants sat on the path in pots, ready to go in.

'Lovely,' Simon said. He put his sunglasses on.

'I knew you'd like it,' Laura said. 'You've always been interested in my garden.'

Simon squinted at the sky. He wasn't sure he'd ever been very interested in any garden. His own garden was a shambles. Ask Carrie.

Laura led Simon round to the terrace and sat him in a garden chair under a dark-green canvas umbrella. Simon didn't remember the umbrella.

'Is this new?'

'Yes,' Laura said. 'Isn't it nice?'

Simon looked up at it. It was solidly made, with wooden struts and brass fittings.

'Expensive?'

'A bit. But it will last. I'm going to get you a glass of wine.'

Simon gave her a quick smile.

'No thanks, Mum.'

'But to celebrate, to celebrate your being here –'

'I'm driving.'

'Just one glass –'

'Mum, no thank you. And anyway, I haven't come to celebrate anything.'

Laura sat down in the chair next to Simon's.

'What do you mean?'

Simon took his glasses off. He said awkwardly, 'I'm glad – really glad – to see you looking so much better.'

'I am!' Laura said. She smiled at him. 'Of course I am! I just couldn't bear not knowing what was going to happen to me. But once I knew I was staying, everything fell into place.'

Simon leaned forward. He put his elbows on his knees. He said, staring out across the grass and the borders and the greenhouse to the field that rose steeply behind the house, 'I'm not sure you can assume that.'

Laura said sharply, 'Simon I hope this nonsense isn't going to start all over again.'

Simon glanced at her, over his shoulder.

'Nonsense?'

'You ordering me about as if I had no mind of my own, as if I had no say in the matter.'

Simon said slowly, 'I am not advising you about one more single thing.'

'Excellent,' Laura said. 'Now let me get you something to drink.'

'No,' Simon said. 'No. I'm not staying.'

'But you came for lunch! You said you were coming for lunch!'

'I didn't,' Simon said. '*You* did.' He sat up straight and turned towards her. 'I've got something to say to you.'

Laura put her head slightly on one side. She smiled, the small, dignified smile she had used on Wendy.

'Pleasant, I hope, darling.'

'I'm not acting for you any more,' Simon said.

'Acting?'

'I can't be your lawyer any more,' Simon said.

'What?'

Simon looked straight at her.

'I can't cope with you any longer. I can't handle being your lawyer in this matter. I shouldn't ever have agreed in the first place, but I did and now I have to get out before any more damage is done.'

Laura put her hands to her face. Her eyes were wide.

'I'm not quite sure –'

'I mean it,' he said. 'I was sorry for you, I *am* sorry for you but you've exploited me and played games with me and set me against my own family, and I'm afraid I've come to the end. I'll help you find a new lawyer, but it won't, most definitely, be me.'

Laura said, with rigorous control, 'I'm not quite sure I understand what you are saying –'

'That I'm still Simon,' Simon said. 'But I'm not your lawyer any more and I can't compensate you for anything Dad has or hasn't done.'

'I see,' Laura said. She moved her hands a little. 'This doesn't sound like very typical Simon talk to me. I imagine that Carrie –'

'She doesn't even know I'm here. No one does, except the office. And they don't know what I'm here *for*.'

Laura said unsteadily, 'I can't quite believe this.'

Simon said nothing. He crossed his legs. He observed that the sole of his left shoe was beginning to part company from the upper.

'It's very hard,' Laura said, 'to believe that I am hearing this from you, of all people. Perhaps I was silly; I'm sure I am in many ways silly, but I really thought you understood, that – well, that you minded for me.'

Simon stared at his shoe.

'I do.'

'Do you?' Laura said. Her voice rose a little. 'You tell me you are abandoning me but you still care?'

'Yes,' Simon said.

'Oh Simon,' Laura said, 'who has made you so heart-less?'

'You have.'

'I –'

'You've pushed me to the limits, and beyond.'

'Don't speak like this to me, don't –'

'Mother,' Simon said, 'I love you. As my mother. I always will. I'll stand by you as much as I can, as much as you make it possible. But you are not first with me. You were, I'm sure, when I was little. All mothers are like that, to their little children. But you aren't now. You haven't been, since I married.'

'I *knew* Carrie came into it!'

'Not because of anything she's said,' Simon said. 'Not because of any pressure she's brought to bear on me. But because –'

'Don't say it!'

He shrugged. He took a step away, out from the shade of the new umbrella.

'OK. If that's what you want.'

Laura moved towards him.

'What am I supposed to do? What do I do now?'

Simon put his sunglasses on again.

'Find a new lawyer.'

'How do I do that? How can I know who to choose? Who will I be able to trust?'

'I'll send you a list,' Simon said. He took another couple of steps away.

'Don't go,' Laura cried. 'Simon, don't go! I'll do any-thing, I'll –'

'Sorry,' Simon said. He turned and blew a sketchy little kiss towards her with his right hand. Then he took his car keys out of his pocket. 'Got to go.'

Laura cried, 'You can't leave me like this!'

He didn't look at her again. He said, 'Bye, Mum,'

almost with his back to her, and then he went quickly across the terrace and out of her sight round the corner of the house towards his car.

Rachel was standing by the kitchen table, eating crispbreads out of the packet. There were scattered crumbs all across the table. She glanced up when Simon came in.

'What are you doing here?'

He dropped his jacket over the nearest chairback and tugged his tie loose.

'Thanks, darling, for the welcome –'

'It's ten-past four,' Rachel said. She put a forefinger in her mouth to dislodge a piece of crispbread. 'Why aren't you in the office?'

'I have been in the office.'

'Why're you home now?'

'I wanted to be,' Simon said. He went over to the sink and turned the tap on. Then he stooped and drank from the tap, his face sideways on to the water, holding his tie out of the spray.

'You never come home early,' Rachel said.

Simon stood up and wiped his mouth on his shirt sleeve.

'Then today's different, isn't it? Can I have one of those? I'm starving.'

'They're pretty boring.'

He bit into it and crunched. She watched him.

'Where've you been?'

'None of your business,' Simon said.

'Why won't you tell me?'

'I will. In due course. Where's Mum?'

'She isn't back yet.'

Simon reached across the table for the crispbread packet.

'When will she be back?'

Rachel looked at the clock.

'Soon.'

Simon took two crispbreads out of the packet.

'I'm going to have a shower. Before she gets back.'

'Lucky her.'

'Rachel,' Simon said, 'when Mum gets in, will you tell her I'm here?'

'OK.'

'Thank you,' he said.

She watched him go out of the room and heard his feet go up the stairs, quite fast, as if he was running. Then she heard various doors open and shut and the thud of his feet across the floor above and then the unmistakable groan and shudder of the shower being turned on. Rachel never used the shower. She preferred baths. She liked lying in the bath with the door locked and her music on, very loudly, so that, if anyone banged on the door and told her to hurry up, she genuinely wasn't able to hear them.

She folded the torn edges of the crispbread packet over and put the packet in a cupboard. Then she took out a small cardboard drum of raisins and tipped some into her hand. Then she took a tired apple out of the fruit bowl – Carrie would never buy new fruit until the old fruit was eaten – and sat at the table, chewing at the apple with one hand, and picking at the wood grain on the tabletop with the other. Simon had looked, well, sort of OK. Not exactly happy, but not tired and grumpy either. She heard the shower being turned off. He'd wind a towel round himself and pad into his bedroom before drying, leaving blotches of wet on the carpet. Jack did that, too. Perhaps it was men. Rachel looked at Simon's jacket, hanging on the chairback. It looked male, too, even without Simon inside it. Rachel sighed. Thinking about men made her think about women, too, and she didn't want to do that at the moment. She'd thought about love for years, it seemed, years and years. It was really all that she and Trudy had ever talked about. But now – or for now – she discovered she didn't want to think about it. It didn't seem an adventure, if her family were anything to go by, it just seemed to be a mess.

A key turned in the front-door lock and the door opened.

'Hi!' Carrie called.

'Hi,' Rachel said, nibbling tiny last pieces out of her apple core.

Carrie appeared in the kitchen doorway. She was carrying her bag and her briefcase and her jacket.

'Hi, Rach. Whew, it's hot.'

Rachel put the apple core down on the table.

'Dad's back.'

'What, home?'

'Yes.'

'Is he ill?'

'No,' Rachel said. 'He's having a shower. He said to tell you.'

Carrie leaned forward and dumped all her things on the table.

'Heavens.'

'I heard the shower turn off –'

Carrie straightened up. She put her hands to her hair and let them fall again.

'He'll be down in a minute.'

'He wants you to go up,' Rachel said.

'What's going on?'

'I don't know,' Rachel said. She got up and picked up her apple core. 'Why don't you go and see?'

Simon was standing in their bedroom, dressed only in his boxer shorts, towelling his hair. Carrie stood in the doorway, leaning against the frame. She took one shoe off and flexed her toes.

'Hello,' Simon said.

Carrie stepped out of her other shoe.

'You're early.'

'I couldn't concentrate. I went back to the office, but I was just too restless.'

'Back?'

'Yes,' Simon said. 'After I got back from Stanborough. I went to see Mum.'

'Oh,' Carrie said. She bent and picked up her shoes. In a careful voice she said, 'And how was she?'

'Devastated,' Simon said.

Carrie didn't look at him. She went past him slowly in her stockinged feet and dropped her shoes by the sofa.

'What about this time?'

'Me,' Simon said.

Carrie turned to look at him. He stopped drying his hair and threw the towel on to the bed.

'I went to tell her something.'

Carrie sat down on the sofa and bent forward to massage one foot.

'I went to tell her,' Simon said, 'that I'm not acting as her lawyer any more.'

Carrie stopped massaging. She stared at the piece of carpet immediately beyond her foot. It had a stain on it, a small greyish stain about the size of a fifty-pence piece. It could be anything, tea, coffee, mascara, ink, mud. If she was a proper housewife, a true homemaker, she would have dealt with it long ago, long before it had settled itself so firmly into the carpet that nothing would shift it.

'I told her that she was on her own now,' Simon said. 'That I'd always be her son but I couldn't be anything more than that. And that I'd had enough of being manipulated. I had quite a lot of things planned to say about the nature of love, too, about generosity in love, but there wasn't a chance really. Rather a waste. I'd done a lot of rehearsing in the car.'

Carrie stared at the stain. There seemed to be two or three of them. The harder she stared, the more they seemed to multiply. She felt Simon come and sit down next to her. He was damp and warm. She could see his thigh and calf out of the corner of the eye nearest to him.

'Carrie,' Simon said.

She turned her head and put her face down on her knee, sideways on, so that she was looking away from him.

'I'm sorry,' Simon said, 'I am so, so sorry.'

She felt his hand on her back through the cotton of her shirt. She imagined how her back would feel under his hand, bony and unhelpful.

'Could you sit up?' he said. His hand moved to her arm. He helped her to sit up. She felt she couldn't do it, on her own.

'I went to tell her that you come first,' Simon said.

She looked at his chest. It was very familiar, the way the hair grew, the moles and the shallow grooves of flesh and bone. He put his arms round her. She laid her face against his shoulder. He lifted one hand and pressed her head into his shoulder.

'I should have done it years ago,' Simon said. 'When I first met you.'

He kissed the back of her head. She lifted her hands and put them tentatively on his sides. Then she slid them round his back and held him.

'I don't know if I couldn't see or I wouldn't see,' Simon said. 'But the thing is, I do now.'

Carrie nodded. She thought: I'm going to cry. I don't want to cry, I *hate* crying. Simon loosened his hold on her, disengaging her arms, and then put one arm under her thighs and one around her back and lifted her across his lap. He said, right into her face, 'All yours now. All yours. If you'll still have me.'

She shut her eyes. She felt him lick along under them, where the tears were. She nodded again. 'OK,' she said. Her voice sounded tiny, as if it came from far away. 'OK.'

CHAPTER EIGHTEEN

Penny had left the customary pile of folders in Guy's chambers. He had asked her not to leave them without at least forewarning him of the court order of any day, but as she was incapable of ever doing exactly as she was asked, she left them stickered with yellow adhesive notes instead, covered with her small, sloping, unformed script. It was the handwriting of a twelve year old and it would probably never change. When Penny was a narrow old woman of eighty, she'd still be writing with the writing of somebody of twelve.

He sat down at his desk. He had risen at six that morning, in order to catch a train to Stanborough that would have him in his chambers by eight-thirty. Because he had woken, Merrion had woken, too, and they had showered and dressed around each other, silent with the faint oppression of another Monday morning, and with the knowledge that it was better to say nothing much than to court even the smallest danger of saying too much when there was neither time nor atmosphere to say it in. He had left the flat before her. She'd kissed him. Neither had said anything significant, even then, just, 'Speak later.' He had gone down those long flights of red-carpeted stairs very slowly, a weight upon him, silent and muffling.

He shuffled the folders. Mr Weaverbrook was again among them. Guy did not feel like Mr Weaverbrook. He did not feel like anything that reminded him of the intractability and persistence of human things. He put his fingers into his waistcoat pocket and took out his father's watch. Ten-past nine. It was unlikely, Guy thought, that his father had ever looked at that watch and confessed to himself that he did not feel like dealing with the working day ahead. He would have regarded such thinking as unprofessional and self-indulgent. 'I don't mind if you don't want to do it,' Guy's father would say, only half-humorously, to his sons, 'I only mind if you don't do it.'

The telephone rang. It might be Merrion. She had a conference at nine-thirty. He picked the receiver up and waited, half smiling.

'Dad?'

'Simon!'

'Hello,' Simon said. He sounded shy.

'Hello to you, too. This is a very nice surprise.'

'Is it?'

'I was just looking at the day ahead and wondering –' He stopped and said, slightly heartily, 'Monday morning. You know.'

'Yes –'

'How is Jack?'

'A bit better. I think. At least he ate something over the weekend.'

'No sign of the girl?'

'No,' Simon said. 'I rather think even Jack doesn't want to see her.'

'I wonder.'

'Dad –' Simon said.

Guy looked at the ceiling. There was a plume of discarded cobweb hanging from the light fitting. It swayed slightly in the faint draught. There were two, now he came to look at them.

'Has Mum spoken to you?' Simon said.

'Silly question.'

'It's just – well, I went to see her at the end of last week.'

'Yes,' Guy said levelly.

'No,' Simon said. 'Not like that.'

'Like how, then?'

'I went to tell her that I can't act for her any more. Legally, I mean. It's caused so much trouble, it's –' He stopped, and then he said, 'I should never have agreed in the first place.'

Guy looked down at his blotter. With his free hand, he picked up a pen and wrote 'Simon' on his blotter. Then he drew a box round the name.

'Good for you,' he said.

'I thought,' Simon said, slightly hesitantly, 'that you ought to know. I ought to tell you.'

'Thank you. That was brave of you, telling your mother.'

'She –' Simon said, and stopped again.

'I can guess. But you've survived.'

'Yes!' Simon said. His voice rose a little. 'Yes, I have. In fact, I – well, it seems to have sorted out quite a lot of things.'

'I'm so glad. What will Mum do now, for a lawyer?'

'I don't know. I'll suggest some names, of course –'

'So it's back to the drawing board.'

'Dad, it couldn't actually be any further back than it is at the moment, anyway.'

'I suppose not.'

'Look,' Simon said, 'are you busy at the weekend?'

'I don't know,' Guy said. He was conscious that his voice sounded surprised. 'I don't know yet. Why –'

'Would – well, would you like to come over? Sunday supper, or something?'

'That's very sweet of Carrie –'

'It wasn't Carrie,' Simon said. 'I mean, I know she'd like to see you, but it's me asking. Me asking you.'

Guy suddenly felt rather unsteady. He held the receiver, hard, gripping it.

'Thank you –'

'Think about it –'

'I will.'

'And Merrion, too, of course.'

'Thank you.'

'Give me a call,' Simon said. 'A bit later in the week?'

Guy nodded.

'I will. Thank you. Thank you for ringing. And telling me –'

'That's OK,' Simon said. There was a small pause, and then he said awkwardly, 'Take care, Dad,' and put the telephone down.

Jack could see her, all the way down the main corridor. She was standing by the notice-board, with a group of other girls, reading the end-of-term arrangements. She had pulled the long side-pieces of her hair back tightly and secured them with a band at the back of her head. Jack had never seen her hair like that before. He didn't like it. It made her look hard.

Adam thought Jack should just ignore her.

'Make like you can't see her. Like you've never heard of her.'

'That won't finish it,' Jack said.

'But it *is* finished,' Adam said. 'She's even going to Italy this summer with Marco's family –'

'It isn't finished for *me*,' Jack said. 'I never said anything. I just got dumped.'

'Well, you don't want it to happen twice –'

'It can't happen twice. It's happened.'

He looked now down the length of the corridor, considering. She had her back to him now. Her school-uniform skirt fitted sleekly over her bottom and her legs looked as he remembered them, smooth and pale brown.

She shook her head a little every so often, and the curtain of her hair shivered with the movement. Jack took a breath. He shifted his bag to his right shoulder and set off down the corridor.

The girls round her saw him coming before she did. He saw their eyes widen. One of them, a heavy girl with thick black curls who had always hung round Moll, put a hand out and touched Moll's arm. Jack saw her say something, too. Moll turned and saw him coming. He wondered if she would just toss her hair and walk away. She had done that already, three times, when Marco was around. But Marco wasn't here now, only the group of girls.

Jack stopped in front of her.

'Hi,' he said.

She gave the heavy girl a sideways glance, then Jack an even more fleeting one.

'Hi.'

'Got a minute?' Jack said.

She put her chin up.

'I've got nothing to say –'

'I have,' Jack said.

'I don't want to hear anything you've got to say.'

The girls giggled faintly.

'I'll tell everyone else then,' Jack said. 'I'm not fussy.'

Moll gave a small, private smile. She glanced down at herself and brushed an imaginary piece of lint off her skirt.

'It wasn't being dumped I minded,' Jack said.

The girls stared at him. He hitched his bag a bit higher.

'I mean,' Jack said, 'nobody wants to be dumped, but it happens. You go off people like you go on them. It happens.'

Moll shrugged. She looked at Jack's feet.

'What got me,' Jack said, 'was not being told. You couldn't even *tell* me, could you? You just did it.'

'Nothing to tell,' Moll said. She looked for support at the heavy girl. The heavy girl was looking at Jack.

'Oh really?'

She shook her head. Jack leaned forward a little.

'Well,' he said, 'when you dump Marco, try and re-member to tell him, will you? Try just to have enough guts for that, OK?'

'Fuck off,' Moll said.

Jack took a step back.

'Oh, I'm going,' he said. 'I've said what I came to say.'

They watched him go. He went down the corridor, the way he had come, with long, loping strides.

'He looks like Steve,' one of the girls said. 'Doesn't he?'

'Steve who?'

'Steve from Boyzone,' the girl said. '*You* know.'

Moll turned back to the notice-board. She lifted her hair with both hands and dropped it smoothly down her back again.

'Dream on,' she said.

Alan had made a curry, a careful, hot, Bengali curry. He'd read an article in one of the Sunday papers which said that the British had become so used to eating Indian food in Indian restaurants that they didn't bother to cook it at home any more. Alan had bought a copy of one of Madhur Jaffrey's Indian cookery books, and decided to do it properly; shop at an Indian grocer, grind his own spices, everything. It looked wonderful when he'd done it, shining and exotic. It had taken all afternoon to make, what with trying to do everything absolutely authenti-cally, but that was a good thing because it had taken his mind off Laura. She had left four messages on his mobile, and now she had written. She had written a letter to his old address and he'd picked it up there and brought it to read in Charlie's flat out of an instinct that it would be better to read it in supportive surroundings.

It lay where he had left it, on the couch in Charlie's sitting room. Every so often, as he moved across the kitchen in the course of his chopping and pounding and grinding, he lifted his eyes from all the red and brown and yellow in the bowls and saw the white square of letter lying there, on the squashed cushions. In the letter, she said that Alan was the only ally she had left in the world. Alan didn't want her to say things like that. He wouldn't, if he was honest, even want Charlie to say things like that. In Alan's book, human beings shouldn't put that kind of pressure on one another, shouldn't try and hand the burden of themselves to someone else to carry. It distorted things, ruined things. You couldn't make progress with someone who tried to surrender themselves completely to you.

The letter had made Alan think a good deal about Simon. Splitting the stiff little grey-green pods of cardamom seed with a sharp knife, Alan had wondered if this was the kind of thing Simon had had, one way or another, all his life, with Laura. When he was little, maybe the surrender had naturally been his, and then there'd been a tricky time as he grew up and found Carrie and gradually tried to withdraw his submission, and then, bit by bit over the years, Laura had taken the dependency over, as if she were calling in the dues of the past, the dues of Simon's childhood. Was that how it worked? Was that how the pattern was? Alan could see how, in any relationship, each day brought negotiation of some kind, but could these unspoken bargains also be struck, insidiously, over the years? And could they be struck unilaterally, so that even if you didn't think you'd agreed to anything, you found you were involved and compromised by what had been done *to* you? The thought made Alan shiver. He'd had moments over the years, admittedly, of feeling jealous of Simon and Laura, but jealousy was quite eclipsed, and in a flash, by the apprehension of an imposed obligation, a duty which resulted from something other than choice. And that apprehension was followed by a sudden and blinding sympathy for Simon, a pang of knowing, in his guts, of the emotional marsh Simon had waded through all his life, a marsh of obligations owed and demanded and expected, rather than of anything given out of the sheer desire to give.

And then there was Carrie. Alan didn't feel very comfortable about Carrie, either. They'd always talked about Laura, sure, they'd talked about most things, but it had been easier – for Alan anyway – to keep Carrie and Laura's relationship as a joke: a tired joke, a typical, conventional, clichéd joke, but a joke all the same and therefore manageable. But perhaps it had all gone deeper for Carrie, really deep, to a level where an irritant became a threat, a menace, and you couldn't think how to fight it, you seemed to have no weapons. Of course he'd listened to Carrie, he'd listened to her recently when she got quite vehement about Laura, quite specific, but he seemed to remember that his reaction had been along the noncommittal lines of, 'There, there.' It was patronising, he thought now, unsympathetic. He was ashamed of himself. But it was only now, only today, with this new situation of being exposed to Laura without the shield of Simon, that he could see for himself. He could see what that letter lying on the sofa might lead to. He could see where Laura might try to take him from here, and if she succeeded – she wouldn't, he told himself, he wouldn't let her – where would that leave Charlie? It was thinking of what a clamorous commitment to Laura might do to Charlie, to himself and Charlie, that made him think of Carrie. And when he thought of Carrie, he told himself that he'd been no support to her at all.

'Hey there!' Charlie shouted from the front door.

'Kitchen,' Alan called.

'I can smell,' Charlie said. 'Boy, can I *smell*. What have you been doing?'

'Curry,' Alan said. He didn't look up.

279

Charlie put an arm round Alan's neck. He still held his car keys. He put his face into Alan's neck and bit him gently.

'What's the matter?'

'I had a letter,' Alan said. 'It just got to me a bit –'

Charlie looked at him.

'What's the yellow on your face?'

Alan put a hand up and brushed at his cheek.

'Turmeric –'

'Where's the letter?'

'Over there,' Alan said. 'On the sofa.'

Charlie let go of Alan's neck. He went through into the sitting room, dropping his keys on the coffee table, and picked up the letter. He stood reading it, his back to Alan, legs apart. Alan watched him.

'Well,' Charlie said, finishing the letter. 'Who's a poor wee me then?'

'My brother's had it for years,' Alan said. 'All his life.'

'The favourite?'

'Always.'

'I was never anyone's favourite,' Charlie said, coming back to the kitchen, still holding the letter. He gave Alan a quick kiss. 'Until now.'

'You're too awkward,' Alan said. 'And criminally untidy.'

'I *know*.' Charlie looked at him. He said, 'Do I gather your brother has thrown her over?'

'Yes.'

'Oops. So you're next in line.'

'Yes,' Alan said. 'But I can't. I can't do it.'

'You don't have to,' Charlie said. He dipped a forefinger into a bowl and licked it. 'What's that?'

'Lassi.'

'As in dog?'

'As in yoghurt. I just don't want to be pursued. I don't even want to be *asked*.'

'She's on her own,' Charlie said. 'She doesn't know how

280

to cope, she doesn't know how to run life. Lots of women her age don't. Men, too.'

'Whose side are you on? You can't want me to take her on, can you?'

'No,' Charlie said. He peered into another bowl. 'We'll take her on together.'

'You can't mean it –'

'I do,' Charlie said. 'I'm good at mothers. Ask mine.'

'But you don't know her –'

'All the better.'

'And,' Alan said, 'she doesn't know about you.'

Charlie came round the kitchen table. He put his arms around Alan.

'She soon will.'

'Charlie,' Alan said into Charlie's shoulder, 'I don't want you dragged into this. I don't want you mixed up in it.'

'If it gets nasty, I'll get out. Taking you with me.'

'Are you sure?'

'Course I am.'

'You haven't got time –'

'If it helps you, I have,' Charlie said.

'Oh God –'

'We do everything together. No exploitation permissable or indeed possible.' He gave Alan's back a thump and shifted his arms to hold him by the shoulders. 'Right?'

Alan grinned.

'Right.'

'Now then,' Charlie said, 'why don't you make a phone call?'

'Shall I?' Alan said.

'Sure you shall. You ring your mother and tell her that you'll see her on Sunday. And that you're bringing a friend.'

'I think we should go for a walk,' Guy said.

Merrion moved slightly under the crackling mound of Sunday newspapers.

'I thought,' she said, 'that you were going to see Simon and co.'

'That's later.'

'Oh.'

'I do wish,' Guy said, 'that you'd come with me.'

She shut her eyes. She said, 'I'm not being unfriendly, I like them all, I really do, but I sort of can't.'

'What sort of can't?'

'I can't get my head round it,' Merrion said.

He reached for the nearest section of newspaper and folded it up.

'It isn't a big deal, dearest. It's just supper.'

'It's a big deal for you,' Merrion said. 'Simon asked you.'

'Yes –'

'So you go. I'll come another time.'

Guy stood up.

'Come on. Walk.'

She stretched.

'Can't.'

He bent and took her hands and pulled her up.

'Got to.'

'Bully,' she said. She took her hands out of his and moved towards the bedroom. 'I'll just get some shoes.'

Guy bent and picked the newspapers up, section by section, smoothing them and folding them. He made a pile of them on the table. Then he shook the cushions out.

Merrion appeared in the bedroom doorway. She had put trainers on.

'Ready,' she said.

He smiled and held his hand out to her.

'Got the key?' she said.

They went down the long flights of stairs in silence. In the entrance hall, someone had left a double baby buggy chained to the bottom of the banisters with a plastic-covered cycle chain. There was a green plush frog in one seat of the buggy. Merrion glanced at it when she went past. It had huge yellow plastic eyes and a wide red felt mouth. Why give a child anything so gratuitously ugly to play with?

'Hideous,' Guy said, glancing at it, too.

She nodded. He went past her and opened the huge front door to the street and held it.

'Thank you,' she said.

They went down the pavement together, towards the park. He took her hand, as he always did, and held it with their fingers interlaced. It was warm and clear and there were bright soft leaves on the trees and drifts of spent blossom in the gutters and up against the railings. People were out, everywhere, couples and families, and people with dogs and people lying on the grass and sitting on the benches. All through the park, along the paths and across the grassy spaces and in and out of the shadows cast by the trees, you could see these little figures, running and cycling and walking and sitting and lying. The sight made Merrion feel intensely lonely. She thought of her hand lying in Guy's hand and it felt as if it didn't belong to her.

They took a meandering route through the park, past the Reformer's Tree and round the Tea House and back towards the Serpentine, where the crowds were, moving along the paths with weekend aimlessness. There were ducks on the Serpentine, and three huge swans and little gabbling dark groups of moorhen. Guy led Merrion away from the water and the people and the darting children, towards the nearest trees.

'Sit down,' he said.

She looked at the grass.

'Here?'

'I think here will do.'

She released her hand and sat down on the grass, holding her knees. He sat beside her, turned towards her. Even without looking, she could see how he looked, how he had arranged himself.

He said, 'I didn't plan to have this conversation this afternoon. I didn't plan to say what I'm going to say. I just knew I had to say it sometime.' He put a hand out and laid it on her clasped ones. 'I think – oh, my dearest, I *know*, that I shouldn't marry you.'

She stared straight ahead. She said softly, 'Here it comes.'

'It's not your age,' Guy said. 'It's mine.'

'And suppose I not only don't mind your age, but I like it?'

'Now,' he said, 'now you do. But not later. In eight years I shall be seventy and you won't even be forty still.'

She unclasped her hands and swung her knees to the grass so that she was facing him. Her hands were shaking terribly. She tucked them under her thighs.

'Are you –' She stopped.

'Am I what?'

'Are you going back to Laura?'

'Absolutely not.'

'Have you thought about it?'

'Only in the sense of knowing I never could.'

She said, her eyes on the grass beside her bent knees, 'I always knew it would be hard. I always knew it would get complicated and painful, but – but I never knew it would get like *this*.'

'How could you?' he said. 'How could you? You'd never done anything like this before. Nor had I.'

She inched forward and laid her head against him.

'I'm not – sure if I can bear it.'

He put a hand round her head, round her thick, strong hair.

'Nor me.'

'Guy –'

'Yes?'

284

'Please –'

He said desperately, 'My darling, if there *was* a way to do our future, don't you think we'd have thought of it by now?'

She nodded.

'Imagine it,' he said, 'you going deservedly up the scale, me retiring soon, all those impossible checks and balances, all those things you might not say or do because of me, all the things I might feel but could not say because of you. We've seen what it's like confronting all the elements we couldn't allow for, already. There'll be more. It will get harder. You'll still love me, I've no doubt of that, but that love will change as time goes on. It's bound to. It'll change with being secure, being socially accepted. It'll change because we'll become orthodox, not forbidden.' He moved his hand so that it lay lightly over her eyes and mouth. 'I could not bear it if your love for me turned *motherly*.'

She said faintly, from behind his hand, 'I'm not sure I've got much mother love in me –'

'You haven't tried it. And I can't be the one that stops you from trying it. Not me, above all people.'

She lifted both her hands and took his away from her face and held them.

'I'd still risk it.'

He looked away for a moment.

'I can't,' he said, 'I can't risk *you*.'

'But all this love –'

'Not wasted,' he said. He looked down at the grass. He said, round incipient tears, 'Never wasted. Nothing lovely ever is, not people, not feelings –'

She said wildly, 'I just think I'm going to break up!'

'I know.'

'I can't bear it, I can't stand it, I can't –'

He twisted and put his arms round her and held her tightly against him.

'You can. You will.'

'You're everything,' Merrion said, her face in his shoulder. 'You're where I came home to –'

'It's all homes,' he said. 'Home after home. All our lives. It's just that now, maybe, you know where you're setting out from.'

'I've been so vile,' she whispered, 'these last few months. Awful to live with.'

'No, you haven't.'

'I was frightened –'

'Rightly so,' he said sadly.

She pulled away a little.

'Where will you go?'

'I don't know. Do you?'

She said, 'I've never felt so lost –'

'No,' he said, 'not in this way. Neither of us have.'

She got on to her knees and began tearing at little tufts of grass. She said childishly, 'I don't *want* to live life without you.'

'No.'

'I'll be walking wounded, I'll be half alive –'

'Not for ever.'

'And you?'

'I don't know,' he said. 'I really don't know anything at the moment except what I've got to do. I don't know how I'll do it, any more than you do.'

He got to his feet, slowly and stiffly. Then he bent and held a hand out to her.

'Come on,' he said. 'Up you get.'

She took his hand and let him pull her up. He held her for a moment and then he took her left hand as usual, interlacing the fingers with his, and began to lead her back across the park towards the flat.

286

CHAPTER NINETEEN

It had been, Gwen calculated, two months since she had spoken to Merrion; two months and three days. It was exactly two months and one day since she had posted her letter. Merrion hadn't replied to the letter, but Gwen hadn't really expected it. She wasn't sorry she had sent the letter and she wouldn't have expressed herself any differently if she'd delayed writing it, until her feelings were cooler. She had said things that needed to be said, that she had needed to say, and she had tried to say them in a way that Merrion couldn't take exception to because of being unable to avoid seeing that Gwen loved her and was anxious for her welfare.

It had been a long two months. There had been times when Gwen had had her hand literally on the telephone, ready to dial Merrion's number, never mind who she got the other end. There had been moments when she thought she might send a postcard – a local scene, perhaps, a picture of somewhere Merrion would remember from her childhood – and just write simply on the back that she was thinking of her. 'Thinking of you. Love, Mum.' But she hadn't done it. She hadn't done either. She had, instead, like a girl waiting for a boy to make the first move, felt that the right thing to do was to wait for Merrion. She had to let Merrion feel she was making the moves, dictating the pace. She had to allow Merrion to feel that she had stepped out of the childhood space where any kind of confrontation might result in a ticking off.

She had tried to keep herself busy. She had filled in at work with extra hours, while people went on holiday, and had permitted a serious boy who had just been taken on as junior clerk to give her rudimentary computer lessons. He was learning computer skills at day-release classes at the local technical college, and each week he attempted to pass on to Gwen everything he had learned.

'Why's it called a mouse?' she'd say. 'Why is that an icon?'

'It's its name,' the boy would say. 'That's what it's called.'

His name was Ivor. He read long, incomprehensible passages to her out of his computer manual and she typed away at the keyboard, marvelling at its lightness.

'Isn't it quick?' she'd say. 'Isn't it clever?'

At home she washed all the curtains and starched the nets and planted her hanging baskets with petunias and trailing lobelia. She went up into the attic and sorted boxes and suitcases and found a whole lot of photographs, taken in France all those years ago, with Ray and Merrion. Merrion was scowling in a lot of the pictures, scowling into the sun or into the camera lens.

How could I? Gwen thought, looking at Merrion's scowl. How could I ever have put her through all that?

She brought the box down to the kitchen. Left to herself, she'd have thrown them away, lit a little bonfire of painful memories in the bottom of the old galvanised dustbin. But she felt she ought to show them to Merrion before she did that, show them, and suggest, by showing them, that she, Gwen, didn't think she'd got life right, either. Not by miles. Not by a million miles. But of course, she couldn't show anything to Merrion until she saw Merrion again; she couldn't do more than make plans of what she'd do when the lines of communication were open again. When Merrion chose to open them.

She put the box on the kitchen table. Perhaps she would at least sort them, throw out all the views she had taken, all the hills and valleys and little town squares she had photographed as if they'd had significance. Perhaps they had, then: or perhaps she'd just hoped that, if she took their pictures, they'd acquire some. She took the lid off the box – an old shoe box, it was, brown Start-Rite sandals of Merrion's, size eight with a daisy pattern, she remembered, stamped out of the toe – and tipped the photographs out on to the plastic tablecloth.

The telephone rang. Gwen jumped. She dropped the photograph box and hurried round the table to the telephone.

'Hello?'

'Mrs Palmer?'

'Yes –'

'Mrs Palmer,' Guy said. 'This is Guy Stockdale.'

'Oh,' Gwen said. It came out as a little gasp.

'Am I interrupting you?'

'No, no, I was just –'

'Mrs Palmer,' Guy said, 'I wonder if I could come and see you?'

Gwen took a breath. She gripped the telephone receiver and stared at the wall, at the wallpaper she had chosen when she moved into the house, a washable kitchen wallpaper printed with grapevines growing through trellises, black grapes and greeny yellow grapes with tightly curling tendrils, like springs.

'Why?' she said sharply.

'There's something I'd like to tell you –'

'Tell me now,' she said. 'Tell me over the telephone.'

'I'd rather see you. I'd rather see you face to face.'

'Is it Merrion? Is Merrion ill?'

'No,' he said, 'Merrion isn't ill. Merrion is fine.'

'Why isn't *she* ringing me?'

'Because I said I would. Because I asked her if I could.'

Gwen put her free hand out and traced a vine tendril.

'Very well,' she said. She'd heard that at the office. 'Very well,' her boss said, several times a day, on the telephone, 'Very well.' It sounded dignified, a slight put-down. It was far better, Gwen decided, than 'All right'.

'Thank you,' Guy said.

Gwen looked round her kitchen. She tried to imagine Guy, in his suit, sitting at her plastic-covered table, staring out of her kitchen window at her bird feeders, at the bright, cheerful things she grew in her garden, the marigolds and nasturtiums and geraniums.

'I'll meet you in Cardiff,' she said.

'Of course –'

'I'll meet you on Friday. At the Angel Hotel.'

'Thank you.'

She took the receiver away from her ear and looked at it. There didn't seem to be a way of saying goodbye, of ending this conversation. After a moment or two, Gwen put the receiver quietly back into its cradle and went back towards the kitchen table. The photographs lay there where she had spilled them, the views and scenes of provincial France, Ray in the Hawaiian print shirts she'd so detested, Merrion in her sundresses and sandals with her hair in fat bunches and her scowl. Gwen bent over and began to scoop the photographs together, into a rough pile that she could put back into the shoe box. The sight of them suddenly made her want to cry.

Laura had all the sitting-room windows open. She had opened them the minute Alan and Charlie had gone, to try and get rid of the smell of cigarette smoke. Alan had smoked quite openly, quite, well, comfortably, in front of her. Of course she'd always known he smoked, but she had made it very plain that knowing and condoning were two very different things. When he came to Hill Cottage in the past, he had never smoked in her presence. She'd sometimes found butts ground into the gravel outside, after he'd gone, but she had felt indulgent about those, conscious of Alan's thoughtfulness. Now, however, he didn't seem to wish to be so thoughtful. He seemed to have a new confidence, almost an assertiveness. He came into the house with something like a swagger, laughing, a lit cigarette in his hand. With Charlie.

Laura had in no way been prepared for Charlie. Like the smoking she knew, without admitting she knew, that there was a reason for Alan's not being married, for Alan's never having had a girlfriend. But she'd never been confronted with it before. She'd never had to have evidence of Alan's sexual orientation standing in her kitchen before, perfectly at ease, swinging his car keys.

'Hello,' Charlie had said. He had his hand out. He was smiling. He seemed, like Alan, almost indecently at ease.

Laura had put her hand in his, hesitantly. His hands were huge, huge hands on this tall, gangling red-haired man with jug ears and a wide smile. She wondered if he was laughing at her, teasing her hesitation.

'I'm Charlie,' he said. 'I'm a doctor. I expect Alan told you.'

She looked at Alan. He was perched on the edge of the table.

'Nope,' he said cheerfully, 'I haven't told her anything.'

Laura tried to extract her hand. Charlie held it.

'Plenty to say then,' Charlie said.

He'd brought her a bottle of wine and a book. Not flowers, or chocolates, or something conventional, but a *book*.

'It's about a woman restoring a house in Tuscany,' Charlie said. 'An American woman. My mother loved it.'

'Thank you,' Laura said faintly.

They uncorked the wine and poured out huge glasses. Laura watched them. Alan didn't take her pretty modest-sized cut-glass wineglasses out of the cupboard but the big rough green Spanish ones that Guy had bought once, on holiday. Then he almost filled them. When he had poured the wine, there were only a few inches left in the bottle.

'I couldn't drink all that,' Laura said.

Charlie smiled at her again.

'Yes, you could,' he said. 'Good for you. Trust me.'

They went out into the garden with their glasses. The dogs thought Charlie was wonderful and he threw sticks for them and rubbed them under their chins and they lay panting on his feet and slavered worshipfully. He told Laura about growing up in Devon, and how he missed the sea and sailing and walking on Exmoor. His father built boats, he said, and his mother ran art courses for people wanting to make pottery and jewellery.

'You ought to go,' Charlie said to Laura. His wineglass was almost empty already. 'You ought to go and do one of her pottery courses. They're very successful. People love them. They come back year after year.'

Alan held out his wrist. There was a thin black bangle on it, threaded with a single red bead.

'She sent me that.'

Laura stared.

'His – his mother?'

'Yes.'

'Have you – have you met her?'

'No,' Alan said. 'But when Charlie told her about me, she made me that.'

Charlie leaned forward.

'Drink up,' he said to Laura.

She felt slightly dizzy when she went into the kitchen to dish up lunch, dizzy and disorientated. She could hear them laughing, all the way from the terrace, laughing and sort of *shouting*. She looked at the chicken she had roasted. It looked small and tame. Charlie's potter mother wouldn't have roasted a chicken, she was sure: she'd have served up something far more bold and artistic, something colourful and Mexican full of chillies and garlic. Laura thought of Alan's black bracelet. It was a present, an apparently approving present, from a person he had never met, a person who appeared to be welcoming him into a family he hadn't met either. Except for Charlie. Laura drained the chicken fat out of the roasting tin. She had better put some wine in the gravy. Hadn't she?

The men ate lunch with relish. Feeding Charlie was like feeding an enormous adolescent. He ate everything: two, three, four of everything. Alan watched him with pride. After lunch, they put Laura in a chair in the garden and brought her coffee, in a mug. It seemed churlish to say she would have preferred her coffee in a cup, but she said it, all the same.

'Too late,' Charlie said cheerfully. He winked at her and went back inside to help Alan wash up, leaving her with the mug. She lay back in the chair and looked at the garden and tried not to notice that Alan had dropped two cigarette butts on the lawn.

She must have gone to sleep. When she was conscious again, the coffee was cold and the dogs had gone and there were no more sounds of washing up. She got up and went into the house. They'd washed up, certainly, and the kitchen table was strewn with the results, haphazard piles and clumps of plates and spoons and damp tea towels draped across chair-backs and worktops. Laura looked into the sink. The waste was blocked with carrot peel and a dirty ashtray sat under a dripping tap. She looked about her, for her rubber gloves.

'Good, but not good enough?' Alan said from the doorway.

She turned from the sink.

'I was just –'

'We took the dogs out,' Alan said. 'Up the hill.'

Charlie appeared behind him, in the doorway.

'Lovely place,' he said. He had his hand on Alan's

shoulder, not just resting it there, but holding, holding on. 'Lovely view of it, from above like that.'

They moved forward into the kitchen. Laura held her gloves.

'So glad,' Charlie said, 'that you've had such a good offer for it.'

Laura opened her mouth. They were standing on the other side of the kitchen table, looking across at her, and smiling.

'I –'

'It's awful to have to leave somewhere like this,' Charlie said. 'Somewhere you've made. But it must be amazingly satisfying to know what you've made it *worth*, over the years.'

Laura said, 'I don't think you quite understand –'

'He does,' Alan said. He glanced at Charlie. 'He understands completely.'

Charlie leaned forward. He put his huge hands down on the kitchen table among the piles of cutlery and plates. He said comfortably, 'We're here to help you, you know.'

'We?'

'Oh yes,' Charlie said. 'We.'

Alan took his cigarette packet out of his pocket.

'We'll help you find something else, Mum,' he said. 'Help you move.'

'I'm not sure –'

'We are,' Charlie said.

Laura looked at Alan. He was lighting a cigarette.

'Alan –'

He took a breath of smoke and blew it out. Through the faint blue cloud he looked at her.

'We're quite sure, Mum,' he said.

Guy reached the Angel Hotel twenty minutes before his appointed time for meeting Gwen. He chose a corner sofa in the lounge, a sofa with an armchair opposite to it and a low table between them bearing a glass ashtray and a triangular cardboard menu for afternoon tea and cocktails. Guy positioned himself on the sofa so that he could see the doorway through which Gwen would come and ordered tea for two, Indian tea, with a selection of something called finger sandwiches. What on earth else, he wondered, would sandwiches resemble? Feet?

He took out his new, and disliked, reading spectacles and a legal journal that he felt obliged to take each month and seldom read. He crossed his legs and balanced the journal on his knee. A boy in dark trousers and a white shirt and a maroon tie arrived with a huge metal tea tray and began to unload its burden of cups and plates and pots and jugs with immense laboriousness, tucking paper napkins around potentially hot handles, arranging knives and teaspoons at precise angles.

'Will that be all, sir?'

'Yes,' Guy said. 'Yes. Thank you, it will.'

He took his reading glasses off. The boy went back across the lounge, holding the metal tray in front of him like a shield. In the doorway he paused, then retreated a step and turned sideways with an elaborate movement to allow a woman to come in. Gwen entered very falteringly, and paused, looking about her. She was wearing a printed summer dress with a pale jacket over it and she was holding her handbag in both hands. Guy got up from his sofa and went across the lounge towards her.

'Mrs Palmer –'

She looked up at him. She said in a small voice, 'Oh yes.'

He gestured towards the corner where he had been sitting.

'I ordered us some tea.'

'Oh yes,' Gwen said again.

He put a hand out, as if to take her arm, but felt that perhaps he shouldn't touch her; so he guided her across the room with his arm out behind her, as a gesture.

'Would you like the armchair?'

'Thank you,' she said.

He went round the low table burdened with tea things and sat down again on the sofa. Gwen put her handbag on the floor beside her chair. She didn't lean back into it, but sat up straight, as if she were in a dining chair, looking towards him, but not at him. Guy reached out and poured tea into the nearest cup.

'Is that too strong?'

Gwen peered.

'No. No, that will be fine.'

'I'm very grateful to you for coming.'

He passed her the cup. It rattled in its saucer as she took it.

'That's all right,' Gwen said.

Guy poured his own tea. He said, watching the steam, 'I want to reassure you that Merrion is fine. I'm not here because there is anything –' He paused and then he said, 'Anything the matter with Merrion. Physically, I mean. Nothing for you to worry about.'

He put the teapot down.

'I wouldn't have come,' Gwen said. 'I wouldn't have agreed to meet you, if I wasn't worried. Would I?'

He looked down at his cup. She was such a disconcerting mixture of sharpness and shyness.

'No,' he said. He leaned his elbows on his knees and linked his fingers. 'Mrs Palmer –'

'Yes?' Gwen said.

'You remember when we last met –'

'Oh yes,' she said. Her voice had a little edge of triumph to it. 'I remember *that*.'

'And you remember what you said to me?'

He watched her add two lumps of sugar to her cup, and a generous amount of milk.

'I do,' she said. She was nodding.

He flexed his fingers. He said slowly, 'You told me I was

greedy and selfish. You told me that by persisting in my relationship with your daughter, I was depriving her of all the natural human joys of a traditional family life because, at my age, I already had all those things and would not want more of them.'

Gwen stirred her tea vigorously. She said with emphasis, 'I'm sure I didn't put it like *that*.'

'No,' Guy said. 'No, you didn't. But I think that is what you meant.'

Gwen gave her head a tiny toss.

'I may have done –'

Guy leaned forward. He said, looking straight at her, 'Mrs Palmer, you were probably right. You probably *are* right. There are other factors of course, but I never forgot what you said, I never wanted, never meant –' He stopped, and bent his head. It was suddenly, physically, impossible to go on. He looked hard at his linked hands and fought with the obstruction in his throat. He could feel Gwen watching him, watching him intently.

'What are you trying to say?' she said.

He shook his head. He could not trust himself either to look up or to speak.

'Mr Stockdale,' Gwen said, in a voice sharp now with anxiety rather than reproof, 'what are you trying to tell me?'

Guy swallowed hard. He made himself look up. She was gazing at him with the wide eyes of someone dreading to hear the worst.

'I am not going to marry her,' Guy said indistinctly.

'What?'

'I am not going to marry Merrion,' Guy said. 'It isn't fair, I shouldn't – I can't ask her to –'

Gwen gave a little scream.

'Oh no,' she said. 'Oh *no!*'

Guy put out a hand towards her, almost involuntarily.

'Mrs Palmer, I thought –'

'Oh!' she said. 'Oh!' She put her hands up to her face, holding her cheeks, staring at him now with eyes like saucers. 'Oh!' she cried in anguish. 'What *have* you gone and done now?'

'Just Mrs Akimbi left,' Miriam said. She stood in the doorway of Simon's office, holding a cardboard file by the very edges, as if it was distasteful to her. She had painted her fingernails ice blue. Ted said he couldn't look at them: they turned his stomach, somehow.

'Thanks,' Simon said. He stood up and reached across his desk for the file. 'Is she here?'

'Yes,' Miriam said. 'She's been here for ten minutes.'

Simon sat down again. He said, his head bent over the file, 'Just give me a moment before you bring her in, will you?'

'OK,' Miriam said. She was perfectly used to people waiting. Sometimes there were three or four people waiting, on the shabby polyester-tweed-covered chairs in the reception area, staring at the weeping fig tree she seldom watered, or the pamphlets and out-of-date magazines she seldom tidied, and she took no more notice of them than if they were the chairs themselves, rather than people sitting on them. 'I'll give you a couple of minutes.'

Simon opened Mrs Akimbi's folder. Mrs Akimbi was forty-four. She had worked for fifteen years for the local council, through all the problems of being abandoned by her husband and bringing up their three children alone, and it had suddenly dawned upon her that, in all those fifteen years, she had never been promoted.

'I'm conscientious,' she said to Simon. 'I'm a good worker. I'm never late, I never take days off sick. I've gone into those offices, regular as clockwork, since 1985.'

He looked at her. She wore metal-rimmed spectacles on her broad black face and earrings like tiny gold crucifixes.

'Have you applied for promotion?'

'Oh yes,' she said. She nodded emphatically and her

earrings shook. 'Oh yes. Every year. Every year I apply for promotion and I never get it. And I tell you what, I tell you something, Mr Stockdale, I've noticed something, I've noticed every year.'

'Which is?'

'It's a man who gets it,' Mrs Akimbi said. 'Every time, it's a man who gets the promotion I've asked for. It's a man. And it's always a white man. It's white men who get my job.'

Simon looked up now. Mrs Akimbi stood in his office doorway. She wore a cream tunic and matching trousers and she had exchanged the gold crucifixes for silver ones. Simon rose and held his hand out.

'Mrs Akimbi.'

She took his hand gravely.

He said, 'I think I have a plan of action for you.'

'Good,' she said. She didn't smile.

'I've decided,' Simon said, 'that I can take your case to the London South Employment Tribunal in Croydon. I'm afraid you won't get legal aid.'

'I can't pay,' Mrs Akimbi said. 'Out of the question.'

'I know,' Simon said, 'I understand. I suggest a contingency fee.'

'A what?'

'No win, no fee. But if we do win, you pay me a third of what you get.'

Mrs Akimbi looked at him levelly.

'Like what?'

'Like if I win you ten thousand pounds compensation, you pay me one third of that.'

'Ten thousand!'

'I'm not promising,' Simon said. 'I can't promise. All I can do is my best for you. I know your union people, I'll have a word with them.'

'OK,' Mrs Akimbi said. She turned her head a little and looked at him sideways. 'So what do we go for?'

Simon looked at her folder again.

'I'm going to apply to the tribunal on two grounds, Mrs Akimbi. Racial and sexual discrimination.'

She nodded.

'That's right.'

'I'll do the case myself, I won't instruct counsel. It'll be me representing you.'

'That's right,' she said again. 'Sex and race.'

'I'll prepare the application and then we'll go through it together.'

'Yes.'

'Don't get stressed out about it,' Simon said. 'It'll only take a day.'

'Stressed!' Mrs Akimbi said. 'Stressed! You have no idea. I am altogether stressed out already.'

Simon held his hand out again.

'I'll do my best for you.'

'Yes,' she said. She took his hand. 'Sex and race. Discrimination.'

'That's it.'

She turned towards the door.

'Ten thousand pounds!'

'At best. If we win.' He went round his desk in order to open the door for her. As he opened it, he saw that someone else was standing there, waiting, someone in a black suit with long hair tied back behind her head.

'Merrion!' Simon said.

She said, 'I don't want to interrupt.'

'You aren't,' Simon said. 'My client was just going.'

'We are finished,' Mrs Akimbi said. She hardly looked at Merrion. 'For now.'

'Goodbye,' Simon said.

Mrs Akimbi moved her head but said nothing. She went past them down the short corridor to the reception area.

'I should have rung,' Merrion said.

'It doesn't matter.' He held the door. 'Come in.'

She went past him and sat in the chair Mrs Akimbi had occupied.

'Are you all right?' Simon said.

She looked at her lap.

'Not very.'

He propped himself on the desk edge, close to her. He said, 'I'm quite surprised to see you, I have to say.'

She glanced up at him. She said, with a faint smile, 'Lion's den and all that?'

'Sort of, I suppose –'

'I just felt I ought to come. In person, I mean. There are some things you have to say face to face.'

'Oh God,' Simon said, trying to sound facetious. 'What's coming now?'

'It would have been easier to go and see Carrie, I suppose,' Merrion said, looking away from him. 'Which is probably why I didn't do it. As Guy would say, typical hair shirt. He thinks I was born in one.' She stopped.

Simon looked at her partly averted profile. She didn't look very well, very happy. He said gently, 'What's going on?'

She turned her head. She said, looking up at him, 'We aren't going to get married.'

He said nothing. He felt an extraordinary stillness settle on his mind, freezing it.

'It's sort of mutual,' she said. 'I mean, it wasn't a great scene with one of us begging and pleading for a change of heart. We sort of knew. I suppose we'd known for ages.'

'What had you known?' Simon said, almost in a whisper.

'That – that what we had, what we felt, might not survive being married. That – that the change would kill it. That we couldn't bear what that – might do to us.'

'Oh my God,' Simon said.

'We couldn't,' Merrion said, 'bear to hurt each other. We couldn't risk it. Not hurt like that.' She looked down again and said in a voice so low he could hardly hear her, 'Though at the moment I can't imagine hurt worse than this. He's been my whole life, my –' She stopped again.

Simon moved a little against the desk. He looked down at her bent head, at her bowed shoulders.

'So it's over?' he said.

She nodded.

'Are you sure?'

'Yes,' she said, 'it has to be. You can't go back ever, can you?'

'No.'

'Only on,' Merrion said hardly audibly. Her shoulders shook a little.

'Come here,' Simon said.

She lifted her head.

'What?'

'Come here.'

She stood, uncertainly. He held his arms out.

'Here,' Simon said. He stood upright and pulled her towards him and then held her in his arms, his face against hers.

'Poor girl,' he said. 'Poor, poor girl.'

He felt her lean against him; he felt her beginning to shake slightly, her body loosening. He gave her cheek a brief kiss.

'You cry,' Simon said. His own voice was far from steady. 'If you want to, you cry.' He moved his head so that his cheek was against her hair. 'This is the place to do it, Merrion. This is the place. If you want to.'

CHAPTER TWENTY

The shadows, Jack noticed, were getting longer. The most extensive one, belonging to the chimney pots on the roof, had now reached three-quarters of the way across the lawn, pulling the dark bulk of the house's own shadow after it. When it reached right across the grass, Jack decided, he would get out of his deckchair and go in and find someone. Anyone, really.

He looked at his hands. They were earthy, especially his fingernails. He wasn't sure he'd ever had earthy hands before: oily hands, grimy hands, paint-covered hands, yes, but not earthy ones. He ran the nail of the second finger of his right hand along under all the nails of his left hand and extracted satisfactory half moons of dried earth which then broke up dustily down the front of his T-shirt. He brushed at them, idly. His back hurt a bit, and his shoulders, but he quite liked that. He liked it in the same weird way he liked looking at the border he had weeded, the whole border that ran the length of the wooden fence that separated their garden from the one belonging to the house that backed on to theirs.

When Jack had said, that Saturday lunchtime, that he'd tidy up the garden a bit, Simon had stopped doing what he was doing (putting a new fuse in the vacuum-cleaner plug) and said, incredulously, 'What?'

Jack shifted from one foot to the other.

'I don't mind. I'll do a bit out there if you want.'

'In the *garden*?' Simon said.

'It's a right mess –'

'I know,' Simon said. He put down the plug and the screwdriver. He said, a little awkwardly, 'Do you mean do some gardening as – as a *job*?'

'No,' Jack said. He kicked at the nearest skirting board. 'No. I'll just do it. If you want.'

'Thanks,' Simon said. He sounded startled.

'No big deal –'

'No. Thank you. Thank you, Jack.'

They'd gone out into the garden together and looked at the border. It was, to Jack's eye, just a huge green tangle.

'Which are weeds?'

Simon scratched the back of his neck.

'Not sure.'

'That is,' Jack said, nudging a clump with his toe. 'That's groundsel. I remember that, from primary school.'

'Start with that, then,' Simon said. 'And just go on to things you don't like the look of. Make a pile.'

'OK.'

'Grando's coming later,' Simon said.

'Is he?'

'He's at a bit of a loose end –'

Jack ducked his head.

'Yeah.'

'I asked him round. Might take him out for a drink.'

Jack looked at a huge lilac bush still bearing the rusty bunches of its spent blossoms.

'Can I cut stuff?'

'I don't see why not.'

'Will Mum mind?'

'Mum will be ecstatic.'

'OK,' Jack said.

He went across the grass to the shed where the tools were kept and where he'd once kept his bike, too, before he'd decided it was juvenile to ride a bike and sold it, for far too little, to Rich's kid brother. He wished, rather, that he hadn't sold it now, that he hadn't been so impulsive. Rachel and Emma's little bikes were still in there, baby bikes with transfer pictures on the mudguards and little girly baskets on the front. Emma's had bells on. Jack remembered the hideous embarrassment of having to ride with Emma and her basket and her bells, and look after her. He couldn't: of course he couldn't. Nobody could look after Emma; she'd been born impossible.

Above the bikes was a crooked shelf laden with cobwebby tins of paint and mower oil and beside them was a heap of garden tools, thrown down against the shed wall. There were rusty nails banged into the wall, to hang the tools on, but nobody took any notice of them, and the tools just lay where they had been thrown, tangled up with stray lengths of wire and wood. Jack didn't know much about garden tools. He turned the pile over gingerly and selected a spade and a fork and various blades and large scissor-like things and carried them out on to the grass. It was difficult to know where to begin. He stood back and looked at the green tangle. Front to back? Or left to right? He picked up a pair of secateurs and released the safety catch. Maybe he'd start with a bit of cutting; he had a feeling cutting would be satisfactory.

He wasn't at all sure why he'd made this offer of gardening. He hadn't really planned to, he had just found himself saying it, offering, and then, after he'd offered, being sort of glad he had. Maybe it was something to do with the way things felt around the house now, the way the girls didn't have their bedroom doors shut all the time and Carrie didn't bang meals down on the table as if she was so fed up with getting them that she didn't really care if anyone ate them or not. She'd had her hair streaked, too. Not much, just a few highlights in front, but it made a big difference. They'd all noticed. Rachel wanted to know how much it had cost and when Carrie wouldn't tell her said, 'Well, too much then.' But you could see Rachel thought she looked OK, and that she knew it. There were a few new clothes, too, nothing major but definitely some new tops and a pair of sandals he'd seen Emma trying out, along the landing. Emma and Rachel never wore their own clothes if they could wear someone else's.

And then Simon had said that they were going on this holiday. They'd all been completely amazed, stunned.

'A *holiday*?' Rachel said, as if she hardly understood the word.

'Yes,' Simon said. He was grinning. 'I thought we'd go to Majorca.'

Jack wrenched off another branch of the lilac bush and threw it behind him on the lawn. They never had holidays. They never had had. They'd had school trips, sometimes, and once in a blue moon, Simon and Carrie went away for a night at a weekend, but Simon always said there wasn't any money for holidays, that there was hardly enough money for ordinary days, let alone holidays, and then he dropped this bombshell. It was such a bombshell that Jack wasn't even sure he wanted to go at first.

'Course you bloody do,' Adam said.

'With my kid sisters? With my parents?'

'Forget them,' Adam said. 'Think of the other things.'

'Like?'

'Sun,' Adam said. 'Booze.'

'Girls,' Rich said.

'Girls!'

'You can go out on the pull every night,' Adam said. Rich gave Jack a nudge.

'You've got the knowledge now –'

'You'll score,' Adam said. He closed his eyes. 'Think of it. Sun and booze and scoring. All day, all night. What are you bloody waiting for?'

Jack stood back and looked at the lilac. There was much

less of it, certainly, but rather unevenly less. It looked a bit naked and pathetic, like somebody caught half-dressed. Jack chucked the secateurs on to the grass and picked up the garden fork. He stuck it into the earth, trod it in and lifted. The earth was hard, baked solid. His forkful came up too suddenly, spraying grit and small stones and a long, uneven red worm. Jack peered at the worm. He thought of Majorca, and what Adam had said. He didn't want to score every night, indiscriminately, after a skinful. But he'd like to score once, maybe, with somebody nice, somebody he liked, somebody he'd remember as a person and not just as a body.

'Jack,' Guy said, from behind him.

Jack turned.

'Hi, Grando.'

Guy came close and put his hand on Jack's shoulder. He looked at the lilac bush.

'Do you know what you're doing?'

'Not a clue,' Jack said.

'Would you like some help?'

Jack pushed the red worm out of sight with his toe.

'Do you know about it?'

'Maybe,' Guy said. 'A bit more than you do.'

'OK.'

'We could level that up a bit.'

'OK,' Jack said. He stooped for the secateurs and handed them to Guy. Guy gave him a quick glance.

'How are you?'

Jack looked down.

'All right –'

'Better?'

'Yup,' Jack said. He picked up the fork again. 'I did what you said.'

'Did you?'

'I told her.'

'Good for you,' Guy said. He stepped into the border and

began to even up the lilac bush. Jack looked at his back. He was wearing one of his usual check shirts, with the sleeves rolled up. From the back, he looked just as usual, just as he always did, always had. It was from the front that he looked different. Jack couldn't quite define why, but it was as if something behind his face had fallen in, leaving hollows and lines and shadows. Perhaps it was that he looked old, now. Jack wasn't sure. He *was* old, of course he was, but Jack knew now that just because you were young – or old – you couldn't make assumptions about age, about looks or feelings or anything. Look at Carrie. Some days, just now, Rachel looked older than Carrie.

'Grando,' Jack said.

Guy turned and came out of the border with an armful of branches.

'Is that better?'

'What's happening?' Jack said.

Guy dropped the branches on the grass.

'I thought,' he said, 'that you were going to Majorca.'

'Yes, we are.'

'Simon asked me to come, too –'

'Come,' Jack said.

Guy looked at him.

'It's – it's lovely of you. Lovely of him. But no, I think. Not this year. Another year maybe.'

'There mayn't *be* another year.'

'Oh, I think there will be,' Guy said. 'I think there will be. Now.'

Jack said again, 'What's happening?'

Guy reached out and took the fork from Jack's hand.

'I'm moving to the north.'

'Why?'

'There's a judge up there, a Crown Court judge like me, who has cancer, poor fellow. So he has to retire early and I'm being transferred up there, to take over. Resident Judge. Just like Stanborough.'

He turned away and began to push the fork into the matted earth around the lilac tree. Jack watched him, watched the rhythmical treading, pausing, turning movements.

'Don't go,' Jack said. He hadn't meant to. He felt a fool the moment he had spoken.

Guy paused long enough to give him a quick look.

'I have to, old boy.'

Jack sat down on the grass. He felt, suddenly, like a little kid, like a little lost kid.

'Why d'you have to?'

Guy stopped digging. He turned round completely.

'Because I'm divorcing Granny so I shouldn't stay in Stanborough. Because I'm not marrying Merrion so I shouldn't stay in London.'

Jack swallowed hard. He began to rip at tufts of grass round his bent knees.

'I'll recover,' Guy said. 'Like you have. It'll take me a bit longer and I may never get over it completely, but I tell you one thing.'

'What –'

'I couldn't have borne it not to have happened. I couldn't have borne not to know Merrion. I couldn't have borne not to have loved her.'

Jack got up. He bent and picked up a hand fork.

'Sorry.'

'What are you saying sorry for?'

'Being such a bloody *juvenile*,' Jack said.

'There isn't any ideal way to behave,' Guy said. 'We just do the best we can.'

Jack knelt on the lawn edge and began to plunge his fork into the border.

'What'll she do?'

'Merrion?'

'Yes –'

'She'll go on to be an extremely successful family law

barrister and probably take silk in about ten years' time, become a Queen's Counsel. And I hope she will marry and have children, too.'

'Do you?'

'I'm training myself,' Guy said. 'Now look. Can I show you how to do that?'

Jack surrendered his fork. Guy knelt beside him.

'Doors close in your life,' Guy said, 'doors open. They don't always do it together and they don't always do it when you want them to. But they keep doing it. Now watch. You have to sift the earth through the fork as you dig to break up the lumps and let the air get in.'

'Air?'

'Yes, you chump. Air.'

Jack stretched now and felt the unyielding bars of the deckchair behind his head and his thighs. They'd done the whole border after that, foot after unyielding foot, and at the end, Guy had made him cut the grass at the edge of the border with the shears, to give it a finish. He'd done that with great care, really paid it attention, and then Simon had come out and admired what they'd done and taken Guy away to do something, Jack couldn't remember what, and have a drink somewhere, before supper. After that, Carrie had come out, bringing Jack a glass of lemonade, and said the kind of things Jack didn't associate with Carrie at all. He hadn't quite known how to react. He'd looked at the new stripes in her hair and the way they made her hair look thicker, somehow, and shinier, and it occurred to him that maybe she'd actually brushed it, too, because it looked smooth and almost curtain-like, the way he now knew he liked girls' hair to look. When she'd finished talking and he'd finished the lemonade, she took the empty glass back inside and Jack lay down in the old deckchair he'd found behind the girls' bikes in the shed, and looked at his handiwork. He felt it was pretty sad to want to look at a border, a garden border, but there was no one to see how sad it was, after all, no one to spoil this bizarre and perverse pleasure.

He looked up at the sky. It was clear and pale blue and the sunlight was getting lower and more golden. He thought of Carrie in the kitchen, probably opening and shutting cupboards with her striped hair swinging. He thought of Majorca and the sea and a girl in the sea with hair like that, only wet, plastered to her shoulders. He thought of Simon and Guy in a pub somewhere, maybe sitting on a pavement on metal chairs next to a little round metal table, with glasses of beer, sort of circling round each other like dogs who know they're going to play together in a minute but have getting-to-know-you-stuff to do first. He thought of Adam and Rich and Marco and Moll, of Moll reduced to saying, 'Fuck off,' pathetically, because she couldn't think what else to say, how to reply to him, how to concede that she hadn't, as she thought she had, called the last shot. He thought of what Guy had said about doors; doors closing and opening in a ceaseless, irregular movement all down those corridors of life, those long corridors that were sometimes terrifying to think about. He leaned forward and eased himself slowly and stiffly out of the deckchair. He liked those doors. He liked the idea of looking through them, seeing what was there. He put his arms above his head and stretched as high as he could, and then, giving the border one last glance, he sauntered across the grass towards the house to see what, if anything, was going on.

A NOTE ON THE AUTHOR

Author of eagerly awaited and sparklingly readable novels often centred around the domestic nuances and dilemmas of life in contemporary England, Joanna Trollope is also the author of a number of historical novels and of *Britannia's Daughters*, a study of women in the British Empire. In 1988 she wrote her first contemporary novel, *The Choir*, and this was followed by *A Village Affair, A Passionate Man, The Rector's Wife, The Men and The Girls, A Spanish Lover, The Best of Friends, Next of Kin* and, most recently, *Other People's Children*. She lives in Gloucestershire.

A NOTE ON THE TYPE

The text of this book is set in Linotype Sabon, named after the type founder, Jacques Sabon. It was designed by Jan Tschichold and jointly developed by Linotype, Monotype and Stempel, in response to a need for a typeface to be available in identical form for mechanical hot metal composition and hand composition using foundry type.

Tschichold based his design for Sabon roman on a fount engraved by Garamond, and Sabon italic on a fount by Granjon. It was first used in 1966 and has proved an enduring modern classic.